Christina Minaki's novel is so beautifully written that I found myself immediately absorbed into its world. In *Burning the Boats,* Minaki effortlessly weaves a compelling story about a teenaged girl and her complicated relationships. Diversity and difference are a seamless part of the story, and that's what's so important about this book. This is exactly the kind of novel that that is so vital to have available on bookshelves everywhere. Not only do all readers need to see themselves reflected in literature, but we also need to experience the diverse world outside ourselves. *Burning the Boats* gives us this opportunity in a very memorable way. Christina Minaki has written a wonderful, important, relatable book with a main character and supporting characters who stayed with me long after I finished reading.

Melanie Florence is the author of *Stolen Words,* and is the 2016 TD Children's Literature Award winner and the Forest of Reading Golden Oak Award winner for *Missing Nimama,* Florence has also authored *Righting Canada's Wrongs: Residential Schools,* as well as the teen novels *He Who Dreams, The Missing, One Night* and *Rez Runaway.*

Christina Minaki spins a complex coming-of-age story about a young woman with cerebral palsy who faces down judgment and her own preconceptions about family and friends. Pain, hope, romance, prejudice and reconciliation combine to make *Burning the Boats* a dynamic story and a great addition to the #OwnVoices canon.

Allan Stratton, award-winning author of *The Way Back Home*, *The Dogs*, *Borderline*, *Chanda's Secrets* and *Chanda's Wars*

Teen readers need more options and access to stories that represent the disability experience in authentic and life-affirming ways. Minaki's *Burning the Boats* explores multiple complex issues such as abuse, neglect, and mental health while developing themes of family, love, friendship and forgiveness, and deftly weaving in tenets of social justice. Minaki's poignant depiction of strong female friendships develops a theme often lacking in the media —especially involving teens. Starting with a literal punch and concluding with a ***message*** of hope, Minaki presents nuanced, multifaceted characters who mature through the challenges they face in this beautifully written, thought-provoking novel.

Janine J. Darragh, NBCT, Ph.D.
Assistant Professor of Literacy and ESL
Department of Curriculum and Instruction
University of Idaho

Powerfully written with sensitivity and deep knowledge, this book will touch and change everyone who reads it.

Sharon E. McKay, Canadian War Artist & award-winning author of *End of the Line*, *Prison Boy*, *Thunder Over Kandahar*, *Enemy Territory* and *War Brothers*

BURNING THE
BOATS

Christina Minaki

◆ FriesenPress

Suite 300 - 990 Fort St
Victoria, BC, V8V 3K2
Canada

www.friesenpress.com

ISBN
978-1-5255-1686-3 (Hardcover)
978-1-5255-1687-0 (Paperback)
978-1-5255-1688-7 (eBook)

1. FICTION

Distributed to the trade by The Ingram Book Company

This book is lovingly dedicated to:

Abigail and William, with love forever. I would burn every single boat for you.

My mother, and in memory of my late father. Together, you perfected the art of commitment, and taught by example.

And to Charlotte, whom I carry in my heart always, who left me with the gift of Mary.

PART ONE
A Family's Heart

Chapter One
Born this Day

Naomi

The day Mom left for good, she slapped me. It was hot and sharp against my ear, like the sting and burn of angry fire.

She had been leaving in a trickle for months, maybe even years. It felt to me like she had turned the temperature down between us, with her stiff hugs and the ugly clothes she would pick for me. The green dress with the bright watermelon print in sloppy, broad strokes was mine, but the clean, deep red one with the black sash—the one I really wanted—Mom bought it for my sister Jo.

All at once, there were no more bubble baths with my sister, with laughter and splashes floating along the warmth of a foggy bathroom. I got my baths alone, just Mom and me and lukewarm water, and one wind-up brown plastic turtle. And I didn't understand then why she was the one teaching me that people would leave me. Remembering now, eight years later, my nails dig into my palms, and I imagine the half-moon indents I'll see on my skin when I relax my fingers again. It hurts, but I don't care.

My riding coach here at 'A Gift Horse' stands in the sand that covers the floor of the ring, with one hand on her hip, the other relaxing at her side, as if she is only half annoyed. The other half must be bewildered. I can nearly feel her thinking 'Why would anyone be so tense on her birthday?' If she only knew.

"Naomi, you're stiff again. Take a deep breath and relax a bit please. Remember, Lancelot can feel that tension right through his body. Sit up straight, loosen your knees, and give me a birthday smile. I wanna see teeth!"

A birthday smile? Lovely.

My poor horse. I know I'm taking my anger out on him. I can imagine the current of my stiffness flowing down through me to him—a live wire running as my muscles clench. Lancelot is probably plenty annoyed and I don't blame him. It's been eight years since Mom took off on us, but sometimes, when I'm this mad, it feels like yesterday. I'm angry at her all over again, because I know this heat spreading through me now is her fault. She's screwed me up, and now she's reaching through me to piss off my horse.

Typical.

It's on my fourth lap around the ring that I see her, and I jolt in the saddle, Lancelot nickering in protest. It's as if all my angry thoughts have summoned my mother here. The riding ring has one glass wall, and anybody watching the sessions can sit on chairs in the adjoining room and look inside.

There she is, crossing, uncrossing and re-crossing her legs, rubbing the side of her neck over and over, without even realizing she's doing it. And she keeps hitting her knee with that pen, almost like she's flogging herself. If it weren't pathetic, it would be funny. She catches me looking at her and gives me a sad little smile and wave.

I gather Lancelot's reins in one hand and use the other to wave back, but by the time I've performed this manoeuvre, she's not looking anymore. Textbook us, that is: always a few (sometimes more than a few) beats off each other's rhythm. This is actually symbolic of our whole lives with each other. Her on the outside dropping in and out of my life, showing up and then disappearing. On the outside looking in at my life going on without her. It sucks, but that wasn't my idea.

For my ninth birthday, I was invited to my best friend's cottage for the first time ever. I wanted to go so badly, I ached. A whole weekend away, with ice cream and the beach, marshmallows and board games, and hide-and-seek and ghost stories.

"My mom makes a wicked strawberry pie," Lynne reminded me on the phone. She didn't need to. I could already taste it—summer on my tongue.

I can still see the note, produced in my mom's careful writing. She slid it across the table to me, so that it landed uninvited under my nose with only a whisper of movement.

You can't go. Remember Mary.

I told Lynne I had to go to the bathroom, and hung up the phone. It wasn't really a lie. Not if wanting to hide in there forever counted for anything.

I was thinking of a million things to say, words to fling at my mother, reasons to use like a shield, but only this came out: "But Ma, you said."

"I said what?"

"You said I could have a real birthday this time."

"What do you mean, a real birthday? All your birthdays are real."

She didn't have a clue.

"I mean a normal one, without Mary. I don't want a picnic at the stupid grave. I wanna have fun with Lynne. It's my birthday."

The slap came from the middle of nowhere, like the hand of God, etching doom onto the wall.

That night, I tossed and sweated for hours. I didn't remember falling asleep. When I woke, though, it was still night outside my window, and there were lights and our parents' raised voices in their bedroom. Other sounds, too. Sounds I couldn't place for a minute.

"You can't, Irene." My dad.

"Watch me." Her.

"Where will you go?"

"I'll figure it out." *Screech.*

"Shit!"

"Don't look at me, Charlie. It's her I can't take anymore." *Scrape.* "Her and that attitude. She should be grateful, after everything I've done." *Plunk.*

I lay propped on my elbow, trying to concentrate on the sounds and not the words. The closet door opening. Clothes hangers dragging across metal. A suitcase thrown on the bed.

"Everything *you've* done? We've all done our best. And we've done everything any decent parents would do for her, nothing more or less. She should have a say in—"

"You're taking her side."

"You would never treat Joanna like this, Irene. Why doesn't Naomi get freedom? You've always given it to Jo. We're talking basic freedom here. You're not even letting Naomi choose things in her own life. What the hell's the matter with you? Would you make Jo spend her birthday at the grave?"

I couldn't breathe.

"That's different!"

"How in heaven's name is it different?"

"Jo's the best thing I ever did!"

"And what's Naomi?"

Silence. Horrible, bottomless, black silence. Then:

"I want my life, Charlie. If you love her so much, you stay."

In the morning, she and Jo were both gone, but Dad was there. Solid.

Thinking of him, there in the morning—there every morning—brings me back to now, and I ride. Today is my seventeenth birthday, my twilight year. This is the year before I cross the line. Next year, I'll be an adult on paper. I'll be able to vote, and speak up so people'll listen. That sends chills down my spine and dissolves all the knots in my stomach at the same time. Fine by me. I'm used to this, perfectly at home with contradictions.

As if my horse is my marionette, he relaxes as I do. Lancelot's head drops and he exhales. I can feel his rocking motion under me, like waves that carry me. We make our way around the ring, his hooves creating a wake of sandy clouds coming up from the arena floor as we cover ground. Out of the corner of my eye, I catch sight of my wheelchair, empty and waiting for me on the platform beside the lift.

I lift my finger from the reins and offer my wheelchair a brief salute. It has more in common with Lancelot than people might think. My horse and my wheelchair; both vehicles of freedom. I click my tongue and press my heels against him, and on cue, Lancelot picks up speed. We pass the wheelchair as I focus on his rhythm, feel it rock through me in the pattern of a steady, fast swing toward a clear sky. This is Lancelot's gift.

Riding's like flying, even on the birthday I share with my dead twin Mary.

Which says a lot, because I don't do birthdays.

I've just dismounted, and I'm thinking about how getting off Lancelot is quite a production: flying in reverse. We've just wrapped up the whole routine. My arms around the necks of two volunteers as a therapist eases my knees from around the horse, another to support me as I drop to the floor standing. I push my weight through my feet and feel the shiver of muscles reconnecting to the ground.

Zing.

Most people would say the walk to my wheelchair— more hands, more support—is a long walk back from freedom. But I don't think of it that way. I get reminded more often than some people that we all need each other. Who can function alone in the world anyway? And what kind of world would that be?

I'm back in my wheelchair when my cell jumps.

"Hi Lynne. You've got timing," I say.

"Happy birthday, horse whisperer."

"Cute. Where are you?"

"At the bakery, picking up your favourites. Are you free?"

"You know I'm not. I'll see you Saturday. We'll party then."

"I'm holding you to that, lady."

"Got it."

"Good. And Ny?"

"Yeah?"

"Quit beating yourself up. You deserve to celebrate your birthday."

"I'm not beating myself up. And I am gonna celebrate. I'll see you Saturday, and I'm going out tonight."

"Dinner with your mom is not a party, babe. It's a guilty verdict."

I don't know why the urge to defend my mother surges through me at all. I mean, when did she ever defend or protect me? But there it is.

"Lynne—"

"Sorry, but it's true. I was around when your mom left and took your sister. She's a selfish flake, Ny…"

"I'm going out with her because I wanna see Jo."

"So Jo can't come to dinner by herself? She's attached at the hip to Our Lady of Graveyards?"

I don't mention that as we speak "Our Lady of Graveyards" is no more than ten feet away. "Bye, Lynne."

"Happy birthday, Naomi."

I almost say "That sounds funny, coming from you," but I stop myself. I have to have dinner with this woman later today. And I should be glad that she came to watch me ride on my birthday. "Thank you, Irene."

She flinches slightly, but that's the only indication I've hurt her. She keeps her voice steady and sunny. "Are you still up for dinner later?"

"Yup. I'll see you and Jo at Red Lobster at seven." I begin to wheel away, mildly pleased with myself. She hates it when I abbreviate my older sister's—my surviving sister's—name. "Gotta go home and get changed." I offer the last detail of what I'll be doing next—a tidbit I choose to share, like a tiny morsel of candy—as penance for the idiot I know I'm being.

She jumps at this, like a puppy. "I'll give you a lift if you want."

It's strange how I ricochet between hating myself and hating her, usually in reverse order. "No, thanks. I've got WheelTrans coming. Besides, you probably don't even remember how to put my wheelchair in the trunk."

Oh, well. She was an idiot first. Maybe I won't go to dinner. But then there's always Joanna, the only living sister I've got...

Okay, so here's the bottom line.

I'm supposed to be a twin, and it's supposed to come easy. Twins are meant to be real allies. We have each other's backs, move through the world with the built-in security of each other. The story goes that we're designed to be best friends, an instant twosome with a bond so strong, we can feel its tug and find each other, even if continents or oceans are the expanses we have to cross to make it work. We're meant to be survivors. There's always meant to be room for two. But I didn't even do that right. Mary and I were born together, both of us a month-and-a-half early; I came out two minutes before her and haven't forgiven myself yet. Two more minutes of air and light, and maybe that's what gave me the edge and stole it from her. I was three pounds, she was two-and-a-half—she had a pound for each day she lasted. The books say that twins can get really competitive, and maybe I'm the worst of the bunch. I'm the one who had to kick her twin's ass even at the life-or-death game.

Sometimes a really morbid part of me is sure the reason why Mom made me camp out at Mary's grave for so many of our birthdays is because she was hoping we'd trade places—that Mary would reach and snatch me right out of the arms of a summer's day, and then take her own turn on Earth. My mother never recovered from losing Mary. I think every time she looked at me, she was reminded of the face she didn't see, the one who was gone. Mary's the twin who never had the chances I do, just because I'm the one who's here. I'm almost sure that's why Mom distanced herself from me, then left us and took Jo, too. I think she sees me as selfish, and sees Jo as perfect somehow.

My mom blames me that Mary's gone, and I know it. But I wonder if it ever occurs to her that I didn't exactly get a free pass, either. Or does she honestly think that dealing with a disability is some kind of holiday? When I was born, I was pretty scrawny, too, and I had trouble breathing. So, some of my brain cells died. I breathe on my own, and speak, think and sing just fine, and I learned to walk with help. My movements can be slow and stiff, though. It took training and still takes work for me to coax my body to do some of the stuff most people take for granted—climbing stairs, putting on my shoes, using scissors.

Sometimes I catch myself being jealous of Jo, because she knew our mom before she got screwed up. She has memories of the real Irene Sinnallis, the one who existed before the weird, damaged version took over. But then I remember that I'm the one who got left with Dad—my solid, good father who raised me, put me first, and protected me like, well...like a mama bear. And I feel blessed. I miss Jo and I feel cheated, but there is silver lining here. I may have missed out on Jo, but Mary's always with me.

Anyone could be excused for thinking life got semi-normal after that, and in a way, it did. I've had some fun birthdays (although Lynne's right, I do still punish myself. I hate my own birthday.) I'm at the end of high school and at the top of my class in most subjects. I have an after-school job teaching riding lessons, and I'm not flipping burgers. I have friends and a life, and I only visit Mary's grave when I want to. But I think I have the weirdest family on the planet.

After Mom left, Yiayia Katina moved in, and she still lives with us. And just to make life even more interesting, Yiayia (Greek for Grandma) is Mom's mother, not Dad's.

She nearly fainted when she found out her own daughter had abandoned us, and before we knew it, she was lugging her bulging suitcase into the spare room and muttering about how Grandpa Theodore would roll over in his grave if he knew.

I gave her a dirty look for that one. I'd about had it with graves.

When she saw the look on my face, Yiayia flinched as if she had scared herself, and crossed the floor to me with the urgency of someone intent on turning down the heat under a boiling pot.

She didn't slap me, or lecture me about being an ungrateful smart ass, or announce the removal of my TV and dessert privileges, the way Mom would have done.

She gave me a hug. A real hug. One where I could fit, and be warm, and feel love in her bones.

When she straightened up, she took my face in her hands and said "I'm sorry, Naomi. I'm so sorry." I knew she meant it, and in that moment—eight years and a lifetime ago—in my nine-year-old brain, I wondered how it could be possible that my mother had come from this gentle woman.

I still don't know.

Yiayia is worried about Dad.

She says he needs a 'real woman' in his life. Every time he hears that, Dad laughs this big, booming laugh, as if he's just heard the biggest joke ever. Then he kisses the top of Kevin's head, ruffles his hair and salutes Yiayia. "I've got everything I need right here," he says, and I believe him. Yiayia rolls her eyes.

I'm remembering this as I close the front door behind me and hear my WheelTrans bus drive away. As I put my house keys back in my purse, home settles around me. Usually, whatever I'm returning from, this is the moment when the events I've missed here trickle in to me like condensed headlines: half of Yiayia's juicy phone conversation;

Dad pontificating about the flaws of whichever student essay he happens to be marking at the time; Kev figuring out a puzzle, babbling on to himself. They are routine, comfortable sounds, and I need them today, to fortify myself for going down the "Alice in Wonderland" rabbit hole I will face in a few short hours. I don't get what I need, though. I get a preview of the twilight zone instead: Yiayia arguing with Dad in the kitchen. I roll my wheelchair to the alcove behind the kitchen door and shrink back. My gut is twisting as I listen, and for no reason I can explain, I know with certainty that I don't want them to find out I'm back from riding yet. I'm thankful that Kev is in there with them, in his high chair, hitting his spoon against the tray. It's only because their voices are rising progressively that I can hear Yiayia and Dad over the banging.

"Charlie, honestly! Not every woman is Irene or Kelly."

"Katina, I have Kevin and Naomi to raise, and Joanna to worry about, too. This is clearly not the time to start any of this."

"That's garbage, and you know it. Naomi will be looking into universities this year, Kevin needs a mother, and Joanna is doing the best she can. It might do her some good to see you with someone who deserves you."

"Shit, Katina, leave it alone! You're the best mother Kevin can have, and that's it. Period. Relationships just don't work for me. I screwed up both times. I failed both Kelly and Irene, and I don't want to go there with someone else. End of story."

"Charlie!" Yiayia is going full blast now, and Kev is wailing and kicking. I can hear the rhythmic thump of his shoes against the bottom of the high chair tray. "You listen to me now. Irene and Kelly both failed *you*, do you understand me? Maybe you don't believe me about Kelly, but Irene is my daughter and yet, I'm saying it was her fault the whole thing fell apart, and I'm living here with you as I say it. She left you, remember? You stayed. She's the one who couldn't manage. And as for Kelly, that two-faced tramp who left you with a baby, for God's sake..."

I don't stick around to hear the rest.

First things first.

I park myself in front of the closet, yank open the door and survey my options. I know that, like it or not, I'm dressing for an audience. I've gotta look good. I can hear my heart beat as I run my hands across the clothes. Before I can start thinking too much, I spot the outfit I'm sure I'll end up wearing: my aquamarine blouse with the satin watery shimmer and the cap sleeves and my black pencil skirt. I take the clothes down, lay them across my lap, turn around and place them on the bed, trying to ignore my fluttering stomach.

For a moment, I consider what Lynne said earlier, that I don't have to see Irene tonight, if Jo really wanted to celebrate my birthday with me, she'd come by herself. For a moment, just a moment, I allow myself to flirt with the idea of canceling dinner with them and telling Lynne I'm free after all. It would be so easy.

But then the truth hits me like a left hook to my jaw.

I want to see Mom, too.

In my gut I know I still love her. This makes me angry, because I know she's done nothing to deserve my love, but it's as if we're still connected somehow. Despite her best efforts to make a savage, abrupt and final break from me, I can't make one from her. Each time I see her, I keep hoping that after everything, this will be the time Mom finds the part of her that wants to nurture me. She'll open her arms to me and say she wants a fresh start. I'll let her encircle me and we'll cry ourselves clean.

Shit. I'm screwed.

I pull open my bedside table drawer with more strength then I need, and find the black leather book and my favourite pen where I left them.

Dear Mary:

Happy birthday…I miss you. Do you remember me at all? I try to remember you sometimes, but it never happens when I try, only when I'm not thinking of you at all. Does that make any sense? Probably not. There are times when you're there, kinda like a name on the tip of my tongue, and then you're gone so fast—like an exhaled breath.

I wish you were here…you know, like I am, so we could talk. I wanna figure out how I feel. I want us to figure stuff out. Do you watch Dad, Yiayia Katina, Kev, Jo and Mom and me? Do you hate sharing us? Maybe you'd understand why I'm scared Dad will find someone who really loves him, who'll take him away from us, from me.

If Kelly had had the abortion she wanted, would you have been eager up there waiting for Kev? Would that have made it even? Sometimes I wonder, but I'm glad we've got him. There must be lots of other babies and little boys up there for you to…

By the way, did I tell you about what I've discovered about Kev? He seems UNABLE to grasp when he has property IDENTICAL to others. He cannot, for instance, calm down and understand that his life-size, outdoor toy car is an exact replica of his old one (which is also outside in the spring and summer, lined up next to the first, ready for whenever he has a friend over). This results in amazing hilarity, as he wants both things, (whether toy cars or, for instance, bagels). He can be on the porch playing with said car, and decide—whichever car he's sitting in—that he IMMEDIATELY wants the other. Also, on a trip to a high-end coffee shop, I recently discovered I'm not allowed to have my own bagel, because Kev needs one in both hands, and whichever one I'm holding, THAT'S the one he wants...NOW...He will SHRIEK if he doesn't get his way, to the detriment of said coffee excursion, which ended in Dad carrying Kev out under his arm, football style, while Yiayia pushed the empty stroller. Coffee break wasn't in the cards. If you can see this kid of ours, you must be LAUGHING...

Mary lives in my head. Just to be clear, I don't hear her voice, or any other voices. But I do see her sometimes. I know what she looks like; we're identical twins, after all. She's slimmer than me, and has a little less wave to her hair, but that's the stuff I hardly get to notice, because the Mary in my head is a girl of action. If I disappoint her (or my mental version of her) by making a move that's wrong for me, she'll pitch a fit. Just now, when I considered not going to dinner, I "saw" her, clear as day, smacking me upside the head, in classic "what am I going to do with you?" style...

Okay, you win, I'm going...

17

I write quickly in my journal. The sentence looks disjointed, with no context. But I (we?) know what I mean. It's a good thing no one else reads this...

I snap the journal shut as my bedroom door creaks open slowly, the sound of a twig bending under a weight. Kev's moon face peers at me through the widening crack, and my annoyance at being interrupted shrinks back to make room for him.

I smile, big and wide and true. "Come on in, buddy."

His little feet pad across the hardwood, and he beams at me, holding Robert Munsch out in front of him, his prize for waiting for me all day. "Book!" he says proudly, the consonants come out careful and strong, like guards.

I pat my lap. "Come up."

He hands the book up to me, climbs like a monkey without a second thought, settles in and leans back against my chest. His head is squishing my boobs, but I don't care.

I kiss his cheek and rock him gently as I read *Love You Forever*.

I'm careful, as I aim my wheelchair for the restaurant table. Careful to lock my brakes with poised wrists, hoping I'll fork my shrimp without wearing any lemon garlic sauce. My temperature is rising, and I'm suddenly itchy. I haven't noticed before how dark the inside of a Red Lobster is. The colour palette, the dark wood, the low lights—like the inside of a ship. I look at Mom and think, dear God, these nerves are going to make me seasick.

"How's your father?"

"Fine."

"How's Kev?"

"Kevin's fine. Happy. He has a good father and a good half-sister. An excellent Yiayia. He knows we'll never leave him or give up on him."

"I'm trying here, Naomi."

I watch Mom play with her food for a minute. She does that more than anyone I know. I take a shrimp, pop it in my mouth, and chew slowly, to rub it in, and look meaningfully at Jo, waiting for her to rescue me. No such luck. She's sitting beside Mom looking like she's undecided about whether to bite her nails or suck her thumb. The silence stretches like the prairies. I shrug. "Really, Irene? How am I supposed to know that? From all the time you've spent hiding out from me? I'm very impressed."

A quick, knowing look passes between Jo and Mom. I can't read it, but now I see Jo chewing her bottom lip. She does that when she's worried, and I feel instantly guilty. I don't want to freak her out, but what am I supposed to do, roll out the welcome mat for an absentee mother who's never even had the decency to explain why she left me in the first place?

"Is this how you want to spend your birthday?" Mom suddenly blurts. "Are we going to be like this forever? I don't have to take this!"

I'm sad as I look at her, her bleached roots, her cute little black dress that is so inappropriate my father would edit any descriptions of it out of a story, on principle. She looks like a skunk! I know she's hoping it's a sexy little number, and it is—just not on her. It makes her look like the wannabe that she is. She's given me the once-over, too, of course. She

19

likes my outfit, for one thing. For another, I can tell she's really proud of my spunk, but thinks I'm awfully snarky. That's okay. I hate her for making me act like someone I'm not. But I'm also enjoying this. Telling her off is cathartic. Happy birthday to me.

She's pushing her chair back, picking up her purse. I want to be sorry. I really do.

The hand that holds down her wrist and stops her is not mine.

"Actually, Mom, I think you do have to...take this, I mean. If Naomi wasn't mad at you, there would be something wrong with her. Sit down. She's going to open her present now. And we need to find a way to make some peace here. I still want us to go on that trip together this summer, and I don't want fights the whole time. The point is to bond, remember?"

I've nearly forgotten about the trip I had agreed to take with Mom and Jo in a few weeks. It is to be our "Girls Summer," driving through parts of Ontario and Quebec to spend time together. Obviously, I've been wrestling with myself about this family-time plan. Do I really want this? Do I want the stress that will be present, judging by the amount of tension between Mom and me already? But how can I not do this? Can I afford to avoid it, wishing for peace on one hand, but resisting the chance for it? Even as I imagine staying away, I know I cannot. It's impossible, and not just because I've never known a Greek to lie low. Also because I am not that person. Ever so faintly, sitting there, I sense Mary, calling me to my family.

I turn to Jo. "You're right," I say. "We'll make it work."

When I get home, the whole house is dark. It's not late, even though when Lynne picked me up after dinner, we drove around and talked for more than an hour. I still don't know what I'm going to do with all these feelings.

I drop my keys on the hall table, and the minute they jangle, the lights flick on.

They're all here, singing "Happy Birthday" at the top of their lungs: Yiayia, Dad, Kev, Lynne…and Jo!

Seventeen candles stand, sentinels on a huge chocolate cake. Rooted firm, dancing with light.

I can feel warmth spreading out from me, and I can't see anything through the blur of salty water flowing down from my eyes. It seems the candles and their warm flames wobble, so that all I can tell as I cry is that there is light on the other side of my tears.

Chapter Two
Made of Mistakes

Naomi

We're waiting at the ferry dock for the Thousand Islands boat cruise. Correction: I am waiting, while Mom and Jo line up to get snacks and take bathroom breaks. I am enjoying not being "on" for a few minutes, thinking of how I love this cruise, and can't wait to see the natural, 'miniature' beauty of a kingdom of trees and houses and sparkling water, nestled on tiny stamps of land. Everywhere I look on this waterfront, there are dogs and their owners—walking, running, even bicycling together. Little dogs in bicycle baskets or bigger ones going full steam alongside bikes, in hot pursuit of tossed balls or sticks, their ears pressed back in the wind...

When I was little, I wanted a dog. Not the way little kids want candy at the cash register, but the way they want love and food—the kind of stuff that you ache for when you're running on empty for long enough. But when I turned seven and asked Mom about it, she said something so jarring I can remember the hurt like you remember the terror of needing a whole bunch of stitches. It's waiting for it that's the worst and when it's over, you sort of pinch yourself, feeling glad it didn't kill you. But you don't forget the first time, the sinking, doomed what-happens-now feeling. That's how hearing Mom's answer to the dog question felt.

I've kept a few of the pages from the journal I had then, and I pull out some of those entries when I want to remember that no matter how hard some days are, they used to be a lot harder.

Yesterday I wasn't happy. I asked Mommy about a puppy, and she said we'll only get one when I learn to walk like other people. I asked her what if I can't be just like other people, but she didn't answer me.

Then I was looking out the window and I saw our neighbour laughing at a fat boy trying to skip rope. He couldn't skip right and he kept getting stuck, but it wasn't funny. I started to cry, and Joanna came in and Daddy came to hold me. They kept asking me what was wrong, but sometimes my feelings are too big for me.

Then Daddy asked Mommy what did you do and she said nothing. I wanted to tell her not to lie, but I was crying too hard.

I remember Mom trying to comfort me that day, picking me up and trying to stroke my head, but the pain was searing through my heart, and nothing she was saying could help me. She begged me to stop crying, to tell her why I was crying. She was saying everything but the right thing, doing everything but what she should have, and I was going off like a siren, my eyes shut to the world. Sobs and wails pushed through me in a wave of angry heat. I cried and cried, until her soothing turned to threats.

"If you don't stop crying, I'm going to put you down on the floor and walk away, or take you to your room."

I cried harder and could hardly breathe, imagining being left alone. I felt myself being lowered to the floor, so that suddenly cold linoleum stretched stiffly under me. I wished through all my fury that I could tell her how to do the right thing, how not to be mad at me or give up on me, even as my screams filled her eardrums. I wished I could tell them to let the anger pulse through me without judging me, that this was my way of processing the confusion of living in a world where only children who could walk were rewarded with pet dogs.

"What's going on?" Dad's voice. "What did you do?"

"Nothing!" Mom shrugged, helpless. "She won't stop."

Here is what I would have wanted. To be gathered in and held, no matter how much I screamed and fought. For someone to wait out my tears, to be my rock as I wept—solid, like a pounded shore. For someone to know, when it was over, that it hadn't been my fault.

Here is what I got.

I woke up hours later from an exhausted, dreamless sleep. My throat felt dry and hoarse, and no one told me what would happen after.

Mom and Dad didn't know how to look at me. They walked on eggshells, seeming shell-shocked. Jo looked at me like I had personally detonated the bomb of trauma and family conflict in her life.

I felt like I had bombed my own.

And then, there is this journal entry from a few months later, the same year:

All my dolls walk. I make them walk straight, and hold their heads up. It's so easy! I hold them with my hands, and we march across my bed or the floor, quick and tall. I talk to them and remind them to shift their weight and lift their feet high. My dolls don't like me telling them what to do, and Sara, the one with the red hair, she cries.

She's not brave, but I am. I don't cry in physiotherapy. My stretches are hard, and I'm trying to learn how to sit up, but the top half of me is weak. The bottom half is, too, but I'm going to walk with a walker soon. I'm working hard to hold myself up.

Don't tell anybody. Mommy holds me up sometimes, and we walk together. I'm really floppy, kinda like Raggedy Ann. Mommy and Daddy are paying a nice lady, Carol, to teach me how to be strong, and she says I've found two more dwarfs for Snow White. Floppy and Tipsy.

Carol makes me work hard, but she's funny. She makes jokes, and the time goes by. She would be mad at Mommy if she knew that Mommy makes me practice walking. Carol says my muscles aren't strong enough for that yet, but Mommy and me still do it.

I'm confused. I think Mommy likes Carol, but I'm not always sure. When Mommy holds me up to walk, after we take a few steps she gives me a kiss and says: "That's how much Carol knows!" She's always happy when I try to walk, but when she says that about Carol, she sounds mad at her. I don't know why. Carol is trying to help. I think she knows a lot. She calls me a tough lady.

I like being called a lady.

Sometimes I don't think Mommy likes me. I wonder if I've done something bad. I don't know what it is yet, but I'm thinking hard. Once, when my sister was little, she squeezed a whole tube of toothpaste all over the bathroom, and then she hid. She knew she was gonna get in trouble, and she cried when Daddy got mad. I don't remember that, because I wasn't born yet, but I've heard the story lots. This is different. Mommy makes me think I should hide until she yells, but she won't yell at me. She just looks mad. She looks really mad when Floppy and Tipsy show up. I wish they wouldn't come when Mommy's around, but they're always here, because I'm still weak.

I can't wait to grow up. There are lots of things I don't understand.

What did I do wrong?

So, if you want to talk about sins.

It's only fair to tell you that Mom was cool, too. It wasn't all her fault.

My mother fell in love with English. The first time she heard it—in a cinema during a subtitled version of the James Bond movie *Goldfinger*—it was in song, sung in a beautiful soprano voice that expanded to fill every space in the room. Her spine tingling, the hair on her arms standing on end, she determined to learn the language that had come to her first in the beauty of music. She determined to learn it until it crowded out the harsh sounds of Greek, the language that had made her feel she owed a massive apology to the world for being born a woman. Worse, a woman who could think.

The decision was not at that point conscious, nor could she in those young days actively, outwardly pinpoint the source of her discomfort with Greece. No one discussed feelings around her then, I suspect mostly because of some sense that to name their angst would get them nowhere. But she felt it, the way an animal may feel the pressure and hear the sounds of a storm long before the sky lights up the jagged, angry, divisive borders that make up lightning's geography. So, as children, Jo and I loved English with our mother, and learned Greek nearly as an afterthought.

On rainy days, my mom would read to us. I don't mean Mother Hubbard or Lambert, Ramona Quimby, or Harriet the Spy. I mean James Michener, Margaret Laurence, John Windham. So, in my childhood, most of my friends were from books. I'd heard about David Strom, Abner and Jerusha Hale, and Hagar Shipley by the time I was nine. Even before I could read *Hawaii, Stone Angel,* or *The Chrysalids*, I devoured their stories, their stubbornness, their difference and aloneness, their sorrows, mistakes, victories, redemption. I lost myself in their epic journeys as outsiders. I was with them as they were hit with harsh reality. I knew how that felt, and I drank them in.

With books around me, I wasn't alone. I wasn't the only one to betray and be betrayed. If my body didn't move with the ease of everyone else's, if every step, every ounce of muscle control took work, if my twin was dead and my mother left...well, she had given me books first.

In elementary school, I remember being totally obsessed with learning cursive writing. I loved it because it was artistic and smooth, and even though teachers taught the correctness of it—the exact roundness and clean lines and curled ends and flourish of the letters—we could each make the cursive alphabet our own. My g's slanted forward, the back of Nina Robinson's h's were upright soldiers, and Georgia Oliver's i's had no tails. In her trademark red pen, they looked like mini candy canes sliding on their backsides in her notebook. It didn't take long for us to tell each other apart in that class by our cursive writing. A signature.

My signature was neatness, no smudges and no mistakes. I hated mistakes, had no tolerance for them. When it came to my own, I was ruthless with myself.

"Just do the best you can," Ms. Rubin would tell me gently, her hand protectively on my shoulder. "I know that such careful writing might be hard for you."

I smiled and kept practicing until my friends could hardly tell my cursive and Ms. Rubin's apart.

Yiayia Katina would watch me write in my journal at the kitchen table, tearing pages out of my notebook each time I slipped up. She would shake her head and say, "Naomi, love, don't do that. Draw a flower and keep going. Growing up is made of mistakes."

But making a mistake into a flower, turning that smudge into a new leaf, forgiveness is in there somewhere. And it was me I didn't forgive.

Chapter Three
Beginning the Bridge

Naomi

"I'm not going!"

"Joanna Eleni Demas, you are going to come with your sister and me, and enjoy it. Are we clear?"

"You two can go. I love this chalet."

I almost tell her I'm with her on that one, but I'm supposed to be pretending I'm still asleep. It helps with the eavesdropping. But even with my eyes closed, I remember the rich wood that surrounds us, the beautiful sloped roof, and the wall that is almost entirely made up of window. I could write to Mary here. I wish Mom and Jo would just give it up and be peaceful tourists for five minutes. Don't they know they're missing out? When we thought of going to Quebec City, I imagined lots of time for Jo and me to wander these streets as sisters, drinking in the cobbled paths and French restaurants. It isn't quite working that way, with the tension between all of us that I can't deny, but it is still wonderful here.

Under the covers of my bed, I can only hear them. Despite no prince beside me, I feel a bit like Sleeping Beauty the morning after the kiss. Luxuriating is definitely not overrated. I woke up about five minutes ago, and after those few seconds of hovering in traveler's limbo when I wasn't sure where I was, I settled back into myself and waited for sleep to either come rushing back in, away from the edge, or else clear away altogether.

Although it's not entirely true that I have no prince. I wonder how Lancelot is doing at the barn without me, and I consider what must be happening there right now, if all is well and the routine is unbroken at A Gift Horse.

Charlotte owns the barn where I keep Lancelot, and she usually is the first one there. Charlotte is a real morning person. She says she prefers to do the morning feed. I think she likes talking to the horses on her own, though I don't think they do much listening to her at that hour. They are much more interested in the sound of grain hitting their feed buckets. At night check, you just make sure everyone is okay, that each horse has a bit of hay and enough water for the night. I always slip Lance a mint when I'm there at "bedtime." I joke with him that it makes the barn a hotel for him. Well it is. They get "room service" when they're fed morning and afternoon grain and they get "maid service" when they go outside for the day. (Or if they stay in for some reason, they still have to leave their stall long enough for it to be mucked out). When they get back, their stall is all "made up" with fresh water, clean bedding, and a meal of hay. But for him, it's not a hotel, it's his home.

What Mom says next snaps me out of my reverie. I lie facing the wall, away from them with my eyes closed, my breathing even, so that they will trust me to be sleeping and go on.

"I want Naomi to get that I was lost and floundering and made a huge mistake when I left and took you away. And now she won't forgive me, but what she won't understand is mothers don't get an instruction manual. I'm not God, or Mother Earth incarnate. I'm just me, just a person who did something stupid all those years ago because my reasoning was so twisted that I couldn't see straight."

"Why can't you say this to her?"

"I want to. I was planning to do it today. But she won't go anywhere without you, with just me. Don't you think that frustrates me?"

"Ma, if you talk to Naomi the way you talked to me, she won't rip your head off. She'll understand, really she will. If she didn't want to make things better, she wouldn't be with us right now. She just wants to know you're sorry and that you know you really hurt her. You've never really said you're sorry and you wanna fix it, you know. You've never said that."

Go Joanna!

I open my eyes, roll over, and hoist up on one elbow. I take a deep breath, and am vaguely aware that the earth in my corner of the world is shifting. I know it will shift further once I speak, so I do it quickly, like a nervous sky-diver taking a leap into thin air before she has a chance to think too much about the risks of trusting a parachute for the first time.

"Ma, let's find a place to talk," I say. "Just us."

The reaction from both of them is instantaneous, almost comical. They turn at the sound of my voice, and their eyes are huge with surprise, as though I've woken from the dead and spoken.

Jo is the first to compose herself. No surprise there. "Hi, Naomi! We...didn't know you were awake." Two heartbeats of silence, and then "What did you just say?"

"I said I'll go...with Mom, I mean. Whether you come or not, I'll go. We...haven't had any time alone, really. Not in a long time."

It's both the easiest and hardest thing I've done.

We don't end up going anyplace much at all, but instead, Mom and I sit at this tiny café, decorated in splashes of blue and yellow. I'm thinking that this has got to get easier somehow, and fast, because the tension is like a live wire running between us. The discomfort of it doesn't fit with this place, and I want it over, because it's causing spasms all the way up and down my back, crawling insects with pincers grasping. We've managed to eke out this time, just the two of us, and I want to put it to good use.

I am about to speak, just as Mom puts down her fork decidedly, a let's-cut-to-the-chase statement.

"I can't even begin to tell you how much I hope you'll forgive me for before. I hope you can try to understand that if I had it to do it all again..."

"I know, Mom," I say quietly.

She hasn't noticed, or else she isn't letting on, so I try again. I let "Mom" roll off my tongue with just the slightest bit of emphasis. This is the first time I've called her anything but "Irene," to her face since I was about ten. I'm surprised to find it's easy, like tying your laces when you're ready to learn how.

"Mom, do you know what I remember most often about you before you left?"

"No, tell me."

"I remember you crying. All the time. I used to try to tell myself that it was part of a dream, just to distance myself from how lost I would feel when you would cry about me, in front of me. I know it wasn't just me. I know it was Mary, too, and it's awful losing your baby. But you were so sad, Mom. You've always been so sad."

"Oh, God." Her eyes have grown huge, and she's suddenly alternating between rubbing the side of her neck over and over and shoving hair out of her face—one of her classic ticks. It's like those two moves are connected somehow, some funky nervous dance moves that flow one from the other, automatically. "You can't remember. There's just no way—"

I wait for her denial to make me angry. I expect to feel furious and indignant—angry because how could she think I wouldn't remember, when she was in tears so often? But indignation doesn't come. I realize in the moment that she had needed to believe I didn't remember, so she could convince herself that I haven't been hurt by the sheer intensity of her sorrow even for me, a daughter still living.

I stay calm. Nod as emphatically as I can, and know at the same time I need her to believe me. "I remember this one time, we were on that old beige living-room sofa, and I remember orange, warm light through the window. The sun was setting, and your face was wet. And I remember thinking 'Why is Mommy crying? I don't want Mommy to cry'. My thought was about your grief…even then I didn't want you to hurt. I still don't. I've just wanted…all I've wanted the whole time is for you to stop choosing Mary over me. I'm alive, Mom! Doesn't that count for something? I was never trying to take anything away from Mary. Never. She was already gone. But I'm not."

Mom's face is crumpling right in front of me, like a tablecloth bunched up in a child's fist. I can see her makeup run as I release my wheelchair's brakes and awkwardly try to make my way to her around the patio table.

I know everyone is staring and gossiping about the scene we're making: the blubbering mother, no doubt weeping for all she's worth about the poor girl in the wheelchair.

But for once I don't care. And for once I know what's true: Mom is just a person, has always been only herself— not Mother Earth embodied, not Mrs. Ingalls with the right thing always clear, or Maria von Trapp singing through the mountains despite a looming, awful war. Just Irene Sinnallis, who couldn't save her dead child and didn't know the two who lived would both learn to be just fine.

When I finally have my arms around her, I can feel her shaking, the epicentre of her grief reaching me so that, in an aftershock, I release my own tears. Mingling currents from the same ocean, we cry together and when at last she's done, her voice is heavy and still breaking as she whispers: "It wasn't a dream. What you remember was me crying for the mother I couldn't be to you. Being a mother is the most important job, and I couldn't do it anymore. Not for you."

Mom straightens up suddenly and, holding me firmly by the shoulders, she pushes me just far enough away from her that we are eye to eye. Her face glistens with tears. "No wonder you remember it. I was so sure I had failed you and that it would just keep happening. That was the first day I started to think I might have to leave you, for your own good. I'm so sorry. You turned out so well, and it's no thanks to me."

What can I say to that?

I don't know what to think, how to feel. I want to go home and never come back. But at the same time, I want to stay here, together, and never leave. How does that work, exactly? Your guess is as good as mine, probably better.

I remember the cold disconnects. This is the part that drives me away. But then there are the connects, the answers, the beginnings of the bridge Jo, Mom and I are building...

I don't know what to think or how to feel about our road trip being over.

We're nearly all the way home when Jo says it to me. "I think I'm gonna move in with you and Dad for a while."

We both see Mom flinch.

Chapter Four
Live Wire

Naomi

The sign he's holding up is simple: 'MUST GET HOME!' is all it says.

It's scrawled in felt-tip marker, and in this rain the red letters are bleeding into each other, weeping testimony to his emergency.

"Somebody needs to wring him out like a towel," Eva quips under her breath, staring out the window. "And if he's a towel, I'm available for wrapping."

"Shut up, Eva. We're not picking up hitchhikers tonight."

"Ah, Lynne, come on! Can't we have a little fun? We're supposed to be celebrating with Naomi here. How's she supposed to ever get a boyfriend if we don't show her how it's done? You're so friggin' uptight."

Before I can think of a decent comeback, before any of us are sure what's going on, Lynne swings the car to the shoulder and turns around in the driver's seat to face Eva. "Maybe I'm uptight, but you're a lousy drunk, and if we don't watch you, you'll turn into a lush and pick up a serial killer one of these—"The door on Eva's side of the car flies open. I didn't even see her touch the latch. Rain flings itself in my face as I watch her flail her arms at Mr. Emergency Sign Man. "Come on board, hot stuff!" she slurs.

Oh, crap.

"Thanks for this, man! I don't know you guys, but I don't care. You rock!"

He slams the door, and even in the dark I can see the puddle seeping into the upholstery of Lynne's cute little Honda. But hey, he's stranded and soaked. In his shoes, I would want a lift, too.

"Don't mention it," I say quickly, before Lynne can tell him this wasn't her idea, before Eva can make another comment about wringing out towels.

"My most excellent mother is going to kill me. Some dirt bags just lifted my new BMW. Well, hers, technically. Everything is always hers. So she gets one of her stuck-up little promotions, treats herself to a new set of wheels, and won't let me breathe on it for a year. Today she finally tells me I can take it for a spin as long as I'm home by 1 a.m., and..."

"And now you're gonna die slowly," I finish for him.

"Pretty much. I left that thing running for all of two minutes. No word of a lie. And poof! Those losers put the pedal to the metal, and now she's gonna have a bird! If you see on the news tomorrow that I've disappeared, look for me under my house, man."

Eva sways toward him and coos thickly, "I'll look out for you, baby. Where do you live? You're hot."

I give her a look that tells her someone may find *her* under her house, if she doesn't cut the bull. "Eva's really cool, *when she's sober*," I explain. "But we went out for dinner and drinks tonight because I just got back from this weird trip with my mom and sister. Imagine a road trip with three tense Greek women! Now, I get to decompress, so we're celebrating, and Eva knocked back a lake's worth of martinis. They're doing the talking right now. Sorry."

He shrugs, rolls his eyes in her direction, and leans ever so slightly toward me. Am I imagining it? "So why isn't your guy here?"

"Pardon?"

He tries again, just as it dawns on me that he was checking to see if I'm single. My laugh comes from way down in my gut, like he went mining to get it. "'Cuz there's no guy. Trust me, if there was one, I would've made sure he came on the trip with me. I could've used the buffer zone. That was *a lot* of family time for me."

"Ah, now family overload, I get. Welcome back to sanity…"

It takes me a minute to figure out he's fishing for my name. "Ah, it's Naomi. Welcome back, Naomi."

"Um, excuse me, party pooper that I am, but I kinda need to know where to drop you." Lynne is all business.

"Oh, sorry, I forgot. You can let me off at Rivercrest, please and thanks."

"Rivercrest? As in the hospital, Rivercrest, at this hour? What, are you contagious or something?" Lynne is still edgy.

His laugh surprises me, a deep rolling sound that makes me want to join in. "Oh God, no. That's a good one, but no.

My dad's one of the chaplains there, and he's got the night shift tonight. You guys can leave me there and he'll drive me home when he's done. Help me deal with Mom, hopefully, before he leaves again."

"Leaves?" I ask.

"Um, yeah. They're divorced."

"Sorry. I'm nosey when I'm tired."

"No worries. Hey, you got a pen?"

The note he scribbles and puts in my hand at the last minute is such a shock, it feels like a live wire. All caps, it seems urgent, just like MUST GET HOME!

NAOMI, CALL MATT, OR E-MAIL, ANYTIME… 647-555-3453

slightlylessthanagod@email.com

Oh, boy.

"I'm sorry about last night, Naomi."

Lying across my bed on the phone, I loop one of my curls around my finger and consider my options. I could tell her off for making a fool of herself, for putting us all at risk when she opened the door for Matt in the pouring rain. Lynne had been right, after all. He could have been anyone, with any intentions under the sun, and she just invited him on board as if Lynne's car was a dating service on wheels. Of all the nerve…

I could rip her a new one, but I also know she comes by her alcohol issues honestly, with that mother of hers. Sure, I could explode all over her. But I like him.

For a split second, I feel the short, sharp thrill of him leaning away from Eva and closer to me. What a jolt! And holding his number in my hand had been like touching an electric fence.

On the other hand, I can't make it all that easy.

"Sorry for what, exactly?"

"You know…"

"Eva, come on. You're gonna have to do better than that."

"You sound exactly like Lynne."

"Lynne's right."

"Ah, get off it. She wants me to start going to AA, for God's sake."

"You should try, Eva. You wouldn't have to go by yourself, you know. I'd come with you."

"Oh, that would be perfect. The drunk shows up with her wheelchair-bound friend, whom she undoubtedly put there with her irresponsible driving, of course. People assume things, Ny."

I can feel angry heat pushing through me. I roll over on my bed and put my palm to my suddenly hot cheek. "I'm not wheelchair-*bound*." I spit the phrase out like sour fruit. "Have you ever seen me tied to the wheelchair seat, bound by ropes? Don't I walk, with canes or a walker? Don't I ride horses? I use a wheelchair. I'm not bound to anything! Got it? And I'm tired of my whole worth being tied up in what I do, too. You don't have a right to steamroll me like this. And if you don't want to take responsibility for …"

"Oh, get off your precious high horse. Me drunk last night is the best thing that ever happened to you. If I wasn't a little off my game yesterday, you wouldn't have stood a chance with that hottie. Right now he doesn't have a clue that you *use* a wheelchair, Miss Hooked on Semantics. Just wait until he figures it out. He'll leave you in the dust, and you'll be begging to share my alcohol!"

My phone makes a very satisfying thunk against the wall. I had no idea it's so aerodynamic.

"Did you fall?"

It figures. I should have known they'd come running like a herd of elephants. "No, I didn't *fall*," I say, making sure the word sounds preposterous. "I'm fine. You guys are ridiculous! Even if I drop a book, you think it's me, cracking my head open!"

They're all here, Dad and Yiayia looking flustered and slightly angry, like the wind blew them through my door without their intent or permission. Kevin is hanging off Yiayia's hip, eyes wide, as if he's some kind of marsupial.

Dad's eyes follow the wreckage on the floor, my phone hurled across the room like a grenade. "What happened?" He's mystified.

I shrug, trying for aloof nonchalance. "I threw it." Give them the obvious and maybe they'll get a clue and go away. Yeah, right.

"Naomi, we aren't stupid. Out with it."

I sigh and grab onto the pole installed beside my bed to stand up and transfer into my wheelchair.

"Stand up tall," he instructs me as I move, as though he wasn't just begging me to spill my guts. I feel...reduced.

The tears don't just come, they burst. Prisoners storming a barricade. I watch my family watching me. I feel...caged.

How can I tell them about Eva's phone call, how much she's hurt me? Dad and Yiayia both tolerate her, but they don't like her. If I tell them what she said about Matt taking off scared if he knew the whole truth about me, they'll never speak to her again. (They don't even know about Matt yet! How do I deal with that little piece of business?) Dad says I should be proud of where I've come from and never let anyone make me feel less worthy because I have cerebral palsy. But then he treats me like, with all my training, I should be able to do everything physical in a way that looks "normal" (whatever that means), and that I should watch my own every move. I should, apparently, be able to erase every trace of what makes me different!

I know Dad doesn't mean it, but when he does that, I feel like a collection of moving parts, to be fixed. Who invented normal, anyway?

And how do I tell Matt, or any guy, about all this? They're all addicted to normal. Who's gonna take me as I am?

I want a boyfriend, but can I really expect one?

To me, coffee is the smell of progress.

I know it's weird. You're not sure if progress has a smell, are you? Don't be stupid. Of course it does. To some people it's the smell of money, or new clothes, or the carpet in the corner office.

So to me it's coffee. The really strong stuff. And if progress has a sound in my world, it's the gurgle of coffee brewing in the coffee maker. That's the aroma, the sound, and the punctuation of my childhood.

When I was about five, my father came into my room to tuck me in one night, sat down on the bed, and asked me if I wanted to learn to walk. I was puzzled. Wasn't I trying to do that already? That was what Carol was for, wasn't she? I told him that.

Yes, yes, he knew I was trying, and yes, Carol was a physiotherapist and her job was to help get me ready to walk. But she couldn't teach me everything all by herself.

This was news to me. As far as I could see, Carol could do anything.

But Dad explained that he was almost sure he'd figured out a new way to try and teach me walking. It was something that a lot of doctors didn't agree with, but to Dad it made a lot of sense. Did I trust him?

Yeah.

Would I give this idea a chance, even if it meant I had to work harder than ever?

What did he mean, harder than ever?

Well, he told me, when Joanna was a baby, she hadn't learned to walk right away either.

Really? This lit up my world, because if she hadn't known what to do right away, maybe there was hope for me.

Yes, really. First she had figured out how to roll over, and she did it lots and lots of times, until her brain and her muscles had really learned how. Then she learned how to sit up. Then to creep and crawl and move to get what she wanted on the floor. After that, she started grabbing the edges of sofas, tables, counters, and chairs, to stand up. She would try and try, and wobble. And then fall down and get up, until she felt steady enough to take her first steps. She hadn't just woken up one day and magically known how to walk. She had learned it, over a long time and in different stages—lots of small steps at a time. That was how every baby learned.

That was different from how Carol and Mom were trying to teach me. They were trying to skip all those steps and just do exercises that were supposed to make me strong enough to walk. And we were all trying very hard. But there was a problem, because I hadn't done lots and lots of everything else first. Did I understand?

I said I thought so. I had been sloppy and not learned everything right.

No, no, no. That wasn't it at all, Dad explained. I hadn't done anything wrong, and none of this was my fault. I hadn't learned those stages when other babies did because some of my brain had been hurt when I was born, when I had trouble breathing properly. And because that was true, the part of my brain that was supposed to know how to do all these things, the part that worked on movement and muscle control—it was called the midbrain, Dad said—that part had been injured. It hadn't gotten enough air at the very beginning of my life. That was the hard part.

The good news was that if we worked really hard for long enough, we could train other parts of my brain—the parts that had not been hurt—to take over for the ones that were too hurt to do their job. That was where this new therapy came in. My father would help me learn all the steps I had missed, and together we would retrain my brain to send the messages to my body that it needed to do the physical things it didn't know how to do yet.

It would be a little bit like teaching a bird that had fallen out of its nest how to fly. Did it sound like Daddy had a good plan?

And so we began.

Within a week, my father had built a sturdy table that I could lie on so that others could stand over me and move my limbs. We called it "patterning," because we were teaching my brain and body a pattern of movement. One person at my head, turning it while the rest of me was moved by volunteers—one at each arm and one at each leg, straightening and bending them in the creeping motion and rhythm. The neighbours came to help in droves, all day, every day. The coffee brewed.

And my life began to change.

My father built me a long padded wooden tunnel, with my favourite books and toys at one end, and so it was, after hundreds of hours' worth of patterning sessions, I was able to reproduce the movements I learned on the table, and crawl in the tunnel toward the things I loved. Not just things, but people, too. My father holding a plate of cherries—my favourite fruit. Joanna, wearing bunny ears. My mother, singing. "Amazing grace, how sweet the sound..."

Dad wasn't kidding when he said I would work harder than I ever had before. I crept, crawled, and was patterned for hours each day, with my family and the volunteering neighbours as my cheering squad. I climbed carpeted stairs on my hands and knees. He built me an overhead ladder, suspended from the ceiling in the den, so that as I learned to walk, I did it holding onto the rungs of that ladder, and wearing ski boots, to help align my feet.

Yes, I did learn to walk, with so much training it makes my head spin. But not the way we thought I would. Not the perfect way. But the possible way.

It turns out I could never muster the balance to walk without support. My balance, for walking at least, never developed enough for that, no matter how hard we worked. I use a walker or canes when I want to walk for short distances, and otherwise, my wheelchair. I'm like a hybrid.

I'm aware of how far I've come. I know that what we've managed to do in spite of my injury is a huge deal. All those years ago, my father was right and his plan worked. We've built detours in my brain, to bypass the injury and open new pathways, so that new connections were made, and other brain cells, like replacement workers, can do the work of the ones that are gone. We didn't fix everything, didn't manage to somehow blow every trace of my disability to bits. But how realistic would it be to expect that, honestly? Most days, it's enough for me that we've done what hardly anyone thought we could do.

Most of my doctors thought we were crazy, even called my father "brutal" for making me work so hard, training me to move correctly even if it's the toughest thing I've ever done. And yet, it blows my mind. So many "experts" have criticized Dad, but it's not like they themselves held out any hope for me. They told Dad to get on with his life and not commit so much to me, because there isn't much anyone can do about cerebral palsy anyway. But now that we beat the odds, and it's clear we didn't just fall for some harebrained scheme, all they can do is shake their heads and call me an anomaly.

It makes me laugh.

And it makes me mad that what most people see is Dad's sacrifice, not mine. Take Dr. Martin for instance.

"Your father is fabulous. Just fabulous, Naomi. He's given you so very much. You should be forever grateful."

"I'm very grateful, Dr. Martin. Who says I'm not?"

Dr. Martin adjusts his glasses, strokes his bald head. He looks suddenly uncomfortable and squirmy. He didn't expect to be asked to justify his assumption—the one that says disabled people, as a whole, are ungrateful whiners. "I just...want you to appreciate what's been done for you. Not every parent would go as far as your father has for the welfare of their children, you know."

I do, in fact, know. I know my father took his share of ridicule and scorn from the mainstream medical establishment for daring to go outside its bounds to help me. I know he went the whole possible distance to treat my tight muscles: acupuncture, osteopathy, hyperbaric oxygen therapy, stimulating my weak muscle groups with mild, intermittent battery-operated current through electrodes placed on my skin at night, while I slept. Biofeedback training to teach my muscles more about movement. Every approach to treatment that makes the least bit of sense, that would help me, and that I'm eligible for—conventional and nonconventional, government funded or private—we've done it. My father, my family, has taken the time and money to do an army of things to support my body.

But what about the rest of me?

Has he been negligent? No.

Emotionally absent? No.

Cruel? Never.

Loving? Always.

But does he realize, or does anyone who judges me and thinks I should bow at his feet, really clue into how committed I am? Could anyone have treated me if I didn't want to be treated, and wanted to do my part and more? Did they force me to do my exercises, put up with therapists and doctors, and being poked and prodded? None of these people balance my life for me: school, friends, being part of my funky family while working with horses, doing theatre *and* dealing with the full-time job that is taking care of my body? I don't think so.

Just once, I'd like to move out from behind Dad's shadow.

I won't ever do everything just like everyone else. Who wants to be like that, anyway, a clone? My movements will always be slow, stiff, even jerky, sometimes. I'll always have what amounts to the standing balance of a domino. But I'll also be creative, smart, resourceful, and intuitive. There's nothing like having to read your own body like a book and be at least ten steps ahead of every spasm, quirk and idiosyncrasy, to make me unbelievably sharp, keen, aware.

But try selling that one to the powers that be: The Upside of Disability. Good luck.

"Dr. Martin, my mother left us when I was eight. You don't need to tell me there are parents who don't have it in them to lay it on the line for their kids. I have one that does, and one that doesn't."

```
From: Naomi Demas
<funkylady@email.com>
To: Matt Dumond
<slightlylessthanagod@email.com>
Subject:
```

51

Hi, Matt: It's me, Naomi. Do you remember me, from when my friends and I picked you up in the rain? I don't believe I'm doing this! Oh, well. I've always believed in taking one risk every day. Are you there? I was thinking of you today, coming back from work (and at work, and before work and last night, and...)
But if you don't answer this, I'll understand.

N.

Chapter Five
Sisters

Joanna

For my whole life, I've been a third wheel.

Most people know how that feels. If you're single and you go out with your friend and her boyfriend who spend the whole time linked to each other and adding you on like a remainder in long division, you've felt it. Now imagine being the non-twin sibling in a twin situation. Third wheel all over the place. You know that crazy bond between twins that everybody's always talking about? How twins are often so close, they know each other like no one else ever could, so the rest of us poor schmucks better not even try to come close? Well, the life of a sibling outside the twin bond can feel very on-the-outside-looking-in. No matter how loved you are, how much being a regular sister still counts, you didn't share a womb with anyone, so you can't touch that private knowledge, that secret connection. I know how frustrating that is, and it's made forever more so when the twin you're up against is dead. They never got to live a life, make mistakes, or let anyone down. Just try living your life competing with a perfect ghost.

Naomi would be floored to hear this from me, because I probably sound something like her. She's always in the shadow of this twin she's never seen, who's kicking her ass in her own head as well as everyone else's. I get it. And I get it on an extra level, too. Having grown up apart means Naomi and I aren't nearly as close as I tell myself we would have been if we'd grown up together. But I also know there's more to our rift than that. I'm the sister who will never quite make the grade in Naomi's eyes, because I'm not her twin.

You know how, sometimes you're going along on this drab concrete sidewalk, and there's this flower poking out of the cement? It's beauty in a most unlikely place, and it takes you aback with its unexpected tenacity. You think "How did that get here? Nobody cared for it, watered it, but here it is anyway."

That's my relationship with Naomi.

And that's not the only casualty of my parents' separation. My relationship with my father is something else forged by sheer force of will. It shouldn't have been that way, and it wasn't at first.

I came out bellowing after eighteen hours of labour, looking like a scrawny red puppet at first.

Dad always says it was hard to imagine that the little being that punched the air with tiny fists and kicked aimlessly with miniature feet was going to talk on the phone, go to school, eat cereal, have jobs and go down water slides. He found it surreal, *unreal* how clean my slate was, how open my world. I could become anything from a marine biologist to a singer. He marvelled at how much would depend on me later. But at first everything depended on him.

His friends never let him live it down that while my mom dealt with an eighteen-wheeler-sized depression, he took care of me almost all by himself. "Come on, Charlie. A real man doesn't change diapers and clean spit-up. Get with it, buddy! What do you have a wife for?"

He said not a word.

He protected Mom, told no one about the time he came home to find me covered in food and shit, screeching alone in my baby chair while his wife cried bitterly in the living room.

"I'm afraid I'm going to kill her, Charlie. I'm really scared. I have these dreams…"

He just held her.

He said not a word.

"I let them call me 'Mr. Mom,'" he tells me when we talk about it these days. "That's what I was."

Dad didn't insist Mom get help. He told no one what she had said, or how she acted with me as a baby. He kept it a secret that she barely touched me, or that when she did, there was paralyzing fear in her eyes.

Only Dad's mother heard bits of his worries. She died before I turned two, so I don't remember her at all, but I wish I did. In all the stories Dad tells of her, she sounds so comforting. He told her that Irene woke from screaming nightmares of seeing little baby me disintegrating under her touch—and sometimes even just her gaze.

"It pass, Charlie," Dad's mother reassured him again and again, after these long, terrifying nights. The way she said his name in her heavy Greek accent over the phone, it sounded like Sharrlie, two inches from a girl's name.

"Every mother afraid to hurt baby. It come from love. I scarred when you small, Sharrlie." (With her thick r's, 'scared' sounded like 'scarred'.) He didn't correct her. He knew that it was a trick of the ear, but it made him feel oddly better, because if his mother's fears about him as he grew had scarred her, too, maybe there was hope for his wife, *my* mother. In the pit of his stomach, he knew that was what his beloved Irene was: scarred. He didn't know what to do, but he knew that much.

"What were you scared of, Ma?" he would ask.

"Dropping you, scratching you with diaper," (here he knew she meant 'diaper pin'), "feeding you wrong thing, teaching you wrong thing. Sharrlie, those days I scarred all the time. Ireni just like me. It pass."

"Promise?" he would insist.

"Your mother ever lie to you, Sharrlie?"

"Promise me, Mama." It was ridiculous, he must have known. What was he, six-years-old? Why did he need her to solve everything for him, to be right when he knew she wasn't? What was wrong with him?

But she always indulged him, "I promise," she would say, with feeling. He could almost feel her across the wires and distance, stroking his cheek. "It pass."

It did not pass.

Love is not love
which alters
when it alteration finds
or bends
with the remover to remove.

It is an ever fix'd mark
that looks on tempests
and is never shaken...

He quit his job at the school, to take care of us. Instead of teaching there, he tutored at home every weekday evening, year-round. During the day he rocked me to sleep reciting Shakespeare, Keats, Tennyson. Fed, changed, comforted, cuddled, and played with me. He cooked, washed, sterilized bottles. In the evenings he taught children who complained about their homework and their mothers—how overprotective they were, how they asked too many questions and tried too hard. He smiled, nodded. Passed no judgments. Gave no opinions.

Said not a word.

And watched Irene. He never let her shower alone, or disappear for long periods into rooms where she couldn't be watched, if only out of corner of his eye. If she was in the shower, he sat in the bathroom, on top of the closed toilet lid with me installed in a bassinet beside him. Some part of him was always aware of where Irene was and what she was doing. She slept repeatedly throughout the days, for hours at a stretch. Anxiety tickled through him, like the crawl of a fly on his skin. My cries had a longing to them, a pitch that screamed "Mommy!"—no matter how he tried to fill the void.

Mom would lie in bed, curled into the fetal position, sheets and blankets twisted around her. At the sound of Dad's pleas, she would groan, stare at him with equal parts of weakness and resentment, mumble "I can't," with faint, yet infuriating conviction, and flop back over. Her paralysis paralyzed him too, froze his logic and kept him immobile as a fossil crystallized in worry. A tiny seed of thought began to sprout, despite his best efforts to squash it. Should he leave, take me and go?

But that would leave his beloved Irene alone and lost. She would never come out of it if we packed our bags and were gone. Dad had, after all, said his vows.

But that didn't mean he had to stand around begging in this room, and watch her waste her chances. He would turn and walk out, leaving her in the lonely, ineffectual dark where she was lost.

Obviously, Mom did recover enough to give birth to Naomi and Mary, but not to save her marriage, or raise us well. I struggle with how Dad let Mom take me away. How could he think that was a good idea? Of course he was always involved and provided for us. He never actually left Mom or me alone, but he let her have her way. She decided she didn't want to stay and wanted to take me with her when she left, and he let her do it. She wanted the illusion that she was raising me alone, and he gave it to her.

Within a few months of moving away with Mom, I started getting bullied at school. I should have known. It was like the world suddenly knew I was vulnerable, sad and hurting, as if it was somehow open season on my emotions, and anyone who wanted to could pick on me without consequences. It started with two guys in my Grade Eight class who would taunt me on the bus, going to and from school, because my grades were too good. I would get on the bus, and Seth would have put gum on my seat, or, once, he'd graffitied it. The bus driver was helpless, and useless.

"He must like you," was all Mom said when I told her.

That didn't sit well with me. I've never thought that anyone who's attracted to you should put you down.

Mary

Be careful what you wish. I wanted a small window into Naomi's life when she was tiny, just about right when I died. I asked God to let me go back in time, so I could experience what it was like for my twin, but also for the whole family. Here is some of what I discovered.

From the start, Dad didn't like to talk about me.

Fathers aren't built for burying their daughters, but some of them are apparently forced to do it anyway. It's almost like some test for select members of the gender, to see how far the carefully handpicked lucky stiffs might be able to be pushed.

Dad prefers to focus on the living, and that doesn't make him cold and unfeeling. He's not detached; he's realistic and always has been. Facts are facts, and Naomi's the one right in front of him, the one he can see.

Mom, of course, fell apart when I died. It turned out that all of the postpartum drama after Joanna was just the opening act. At first they both cried, but there was a major difference between Mom and Dad in the way they grieved. She kept crying, while he eventually stopped and left me in the ground.

Naomi is his glass half-full. It's always been that way.

From the beginning, she was as bright as a button. Her eyes shone with curiosity and brilliance, and long before she could speak, it seemed to me that her commentary on the world would just up and leap out of those eyes...

But she couldn't sit up. Didn't creep or crawl or toddle around. And Mom and Dad felt like they would go crazy. No one would give them any answers. And when the answer— the official diagnosis—came, Naomi was two-and-a-half years old. They were beside themselves selves with worry. And the words 'Cerebral Palsy' fell on them like bombs.

The doctors told them that while Naomi was lucky to survive, she would probably not develop like other children. There was no telling what her life would be like. She had had trouble breathing after birth, and the lack of oxygen that killed me had translated to an 'unspecified degree' of brain injury for the twin who survived me. Naomi clearly had trouble moving and might have trouble speaking. Walking would be a struggle, and in fact would probably never happen at all, even with physiotherapy. She might have trouble with learning. She could speak and was not deaf or blind, but it was too early to tell how articulate she would be, or how well she would hear or see. She might be—and here the good doctor paused, straining for what tactful compassion he could muster—intellectually slow. But there were schools...

"Or she could be just fine, right? If we work with her, she could recover and have a super life, right?" Dad insisted.

"Y...Yes..." the doctor stammered. "But we shouldn't hold out for that."

Dad showed restraint and didn't point out that we didn't appear to be holding out for much of anything. I, however...

"What do you suggest can be done for her?" Dad asked.

"I would suggest letting the system care for her. There are facilities, options. Love her well, but focus on your first daughter. Get on with your life."

Mom, whose face was a crumpled paper bag of grief, pulled it together for a moment. "But she's not slow. I mean her body…it's…But her brain….She's so smart!"

Dad squeezed Mom's hand when the sobs took over once more, and put his arm around her like a shield. Somehow, he got the next words out.

"You say we should get on with our lives."

"Yes!" The doctor's response was emphatic. He sounded like a teacher, praising a student for grasping a concept.

"What about Naomi's life?"

"Well…We shouldn't—"

"Hold out for that?"

The doctor shrugged.

This is the history that drives Dad to fight for Naomi. How can he leave her in the hands of a system that offers only the sacrifice of her life for his? Naomi wonders how he can be so focused on her body, how he can tell her to straighten her posture at an obvious time of personal grief, but as he sees it, the real question is, how can he not, when her body's health is his most important investment?

I didn't say he's right…

Chapter Six
A Door Opens

Naomi

"Thank you."

I am late for class, zooming through the hallway door in my motorized wheelchair, past the lockers, so that they are a green blur. Saying thank you to whoever was holding the door open is second nature. First of all, I've been raised to be super polite, and besides, if he wasn't there holding it open for me, I would have had to resort to bulldozer tactics—plowing through the door with my wheelchair moving at top speed, books flying off my lap in all directions...CHAAARGE!

Charming, really. And not exactly comfortable. So, rush or no rush, I say "thank you."

But I have no idea who he is.

"You're...welcome..." It makes me do a double take to see that he's running beside me to keep up. Even Lynne doesn't do that.

"Are you training for a sprint or something?" I realize I recognize him from my English class, but only vaguely. I'm not even sure of his name.

He almost stops when I say that. "No. Why? Am I really fast?"

That makes me laugh out loud. "You're keeping up with this thing, aren't you? It runs on a battery, and unless you do, too, you're officially a good runner."

He beams. "It's just…I wanted to say thank you…for saying thank you, I mean. Most people don't notice. They think it's not cool to be awake or something."

I nod in complete understanding. I know how it feels to seem invisible. "You should see what I go through in malls or on busy streets with this thing." I indicate my wheelchair. "Nobody looks where they're going. All they look at is standing eye-level, which means someone like me doesn't exist until they walk right into me. And then I get the dirty look. It's depressing."

"Losers. What do they think you are, a piece of furniture?"

"Tell me about it! Hey, what's your name?" I'm really starting to like this guy. But now I'm really going to be late. He's still talking.

"There should be a law—"

"Hey listen, I've really gotta go now, but…"

"My name's Curtis. Where's your class? I'll carry your books."

I only half hear him, because suddenly, I really have to pee.

Dear Mary:

Bathrooms.

Reason #378 why sometimes I imagine you'd be glad you're dead.

I wonder sometimes if you're as connected to me up there as I feel to you. Can you sense me somehow, struggling with the door, because there is no one there to open it as I come through?

You've been dead for seventeen years, two months, three days. I never knew you not the way I know Jo, in the here-and-now world. But you're so real to me, it's freaky. Like I'll be watching something on TV and I'll turn around to make a comment, or see if you're laughing or crying, too. It doesn't matter who I'm sitting with, I still somehow catch myself searching for you.

And now, I'm sitting in the bathroom wondering what it would be like with you in here to help me. I picture you turning away once I'm on the toilet. Because that's what sisters do.

No, actually, Jo would barge into the bathroom just to piss me off. But you and I wouldn't have that kind of relationship. Would we?

I wonder what you'd tell me about that guy I just met out there.

Sometimes I wonder if it makes me seem creepy that I write to Mary as if she's alive…

Chapter Seven
Blast from the Past

Naomi

I find the letter on my dresser on Friday, the third week of school.

I don't throw it out. I take it to my room and slip it inside the cover of my diary—the one I write to Mary. Let her take care of it until I'm ready.

Ridiculous, but true.

I just want to be a girl loving the last of high school for a while.

It's a letter from Dad, but it's about Mom. It feels like he's speaking for her again, filling in her silence. It bugs me. It's weird, but when it comes to Mom, every little bit of letting her in is still hard. Two moves forward are not two moves forward, really. I start at zero every day and remake the decision to honour the progress we made this summer.

It's exhausting, and I don't want to deal with it right now.

Oh, never mind...it'll just eat me up, wondering about it.

Dear Naomi:

I know your mother has a lot to answer for about the past. It's obvious that you're unsettled about the family and about the way you've been treated. Of course you're angry about being abandoned by your mother. She's a difficult one to figure out and to love. (As her husband and your father who's watched you struggle with her on so many levels for so long, I really do sympathize.) You've been difficult, too, but I've come to realize that's your job. You're a teenager, which is enough to make anybody crazy, and you have a disability, which I know complicates your life even more.

I'm glad you spent time with your mother and Jo this summer; I think you made some headway in your relationships, and I know they are both relieved. But I can tell that the whole thing has left you unsettled; I think we all knew it would.

Your mother was in intensive therapy for obsessive compulsive disorder with a very insightful therapist Laura, whom we both trusted, but she didn't stick with it. When the process got hard, she fled from it. (Does that sound familiar?) But Laura used to say the only way to deal with this is to stare straight at it, and try to heal her life. OCD is an anxiety disorder. Obsessive thoughts drive compulsive actions (washing hands all the time, locking and unlocking the door one hundred times before leaving for work) because something in her brain believed her health, or the house, and the people she loves, won't be safe otherwise. (Can you see why she couldn't take care of you?) Please try not to blame her for that.

She hopes you'll keep opening your heart to her. We both do. You can talk to her anytime, just like always.

We love you. Really, we do.

Dad

Lynne slides the letter back across the patio table to me. "I never thought I'd hear myself say this, but good for her."

I watch the wind lift my friend's long hair from her shoulders, like a silk skirt billowing outward. It's always so easy to see that other people are beautiful. This is my longest friendship, my most steadfast friend—the kind who will sit on the porch as summer's breath goes cold, reading a letter she doesn't have to care about, so that I can sort myself out without the rest of the family knowing.

I sit forward in my wheelchair and put my elbows on the table, my chin in my hands. "I think she's making it up."

"Are you serious? Making what up, though?" Lynne's eyes grow wide. "You can't think she's faking the OCD?"

"No, not that part," I admit. "Actually, the OCD isn't news, and it explains a lot. I've sensed she has it for years. Dad didn't think I knew, but with all her symptoms it's pretty obvious, and I'm smart. I wouldn't mind learning more about it though. It's just—"

Lynne shivers. "Hurry up and fess up, Sherlock. I'm getting cold. And Ms. Williams has the flu and needs me to walk Cici."

"Again?" Lynne's neighbour, in her mid-seventies, has been catching every cold and flu available since her husband died last year.

I go on, talking faster. "Okay. Mom's hiding behind it. Again. Why didn't she stick to therapy before?"

"Therapy's rough, Ny. Not everyone can take it. You need to work on forgiving Irene, for your own sake as much as hers."

"Don't worry, I'm doing that. But I don't have to like it."

Lynne sighs audibly. "Ny, you know I love you, but you're being ridiculous about this."

"Whose side are you on?"

"Yours. Always yours. But when you get like this, you disappoint me. You're always saying you want your mom to grow up and set things straight, and then she starts trying and you're still complaining. I can't figure you out."

"Don't be mad at me, please. I didn't mean it."

"Yes, you did. But I'm not mad."

She is. I know she is. How can she not be?

Mary

Lynne can divide up the majority of her friendship with Naomi, and bookmark sections of time, according to the memory of homework assignments. When they were twelve, it was that novel study on *Bridge to Terabithia* and a unit on Inuit art. When they were thirteen, it was the fur trade, the Hudson's Bay Company, and a science fair project about nuclear energy. When they were fifteen, it was a major project on the causes of World War II and the Holocaust, and an in-depth analysis of John Wyndham's *Chrysalids.* (Written forever ago, that was. I'm gonna find Wyndham up here and tell him he's bloody well had his magic carpet ride and its past time he gave someone else a turn on the classroom bookshelf. Someone who knows what email is.) And last year—the Treaty of Versailles, *King Lear* (it's enough with old white men already!) and human responsibility for animal extinction. Speaking of 'The Big Finish.' If I had earthly faults, I would be jealous of Lynne for all the time she and Naomi get to spend together, the way they've bonded over so many years and situations. But I'm glad they have each other, and I know it hasn't been easy to be them.

All their years are punctuated by afternoons and evenings poring over books. Naomi's helped Lynne learn the geography of her learning disability, helped her manage its terrain, work it into the space and discipline of school, like a map drawn to scale. Naomi had been the instrument of Lynne's freedom from Special Ed, had cut her loose from the clutches of Mr. Bosch, that little humiliating man with the hair dyed orange and the plastic encouragements and patronizing kindness. In Grade Seven, when Mr. Bosch had told Lynne math was important for her so that she could work at McDonald's or the gas station and know she's counting money properly, Lynne's stomach fell so far, the drop physically hurt.

"What do you mean?" she'd asked, her voice hollow, barely above a whisper.

He'd been convinced by her question that she hadn't understood his words, so he went on to simplify his insult. "The jobs you can do don't pay well, sweetheart. When you manage to get one, you'll need to make sure you don't get yourself fired. We don't want you starving, now do we?"

Running out, leaving behind those books three grades below her and the stupid alphabet cards she hoped would go to hell, Lynne knocked over two chairs. It felt good.

But leaving, and refusing to go back, was one thing. Staying out, moving against the tide of teachers who believed and expected she would fail without Mr. Bosch's 'support'…that was another hurdle altogether.

Naomi is the reason Lynne learned how to keep herself out of Special Ed. Naomi has been her constant tutor, her always friend, her everything. That kind of loyalty, she needs three lifetimes to repay.

It was Lynne's learning disability that showed her what both she and Naomi would be up against in the world. It started with the *Bridge to Terabithia* novel study. They had both loved that book. They'd submerged themselves in Jess Aaron's character, in his feelings of being eclipsed by his sisters, misunderstood, bullied, and all but invisible in the world. They'd adored Leslie Burke, drank in her strength, the way she'd always known what to do, how to understand and support Jesse, the way she'd always felt free to imagine a world uniquely her own and then bring Jesse into it, teach him to make it real for himself, too. They had cheered for how unconventional she was—a tomboy, a rebel, a girl thriving against the grain, happy to be different.

They'd gotten into the habit of reading together each afternoon or evening—or rather, of Naomi reading to Lynne, either in school or in one of their living rooms or on the porch after dinner. Or else Naomi reading on the phone with Lynne, under the covers long after everyone thought she was asleep.

Naomi—who was thinking of Lynne as her own Leslie Burke—had not slept the night she had reached the part about Leslie's death. She'd stayed up, reading greedily under the covers—another covert operation, this one solo. She'd stayed up to finish the book, couldn't bear to go to sleep with the heavy knot of sadness in her chest. She knew that getting to the end wouldn't bring Leslie back, but she needed to find the nugget of hope that always lies beyond the ache in a story like this. She needed to find that place, the part where Jesse discovered he could go on without Leslie. The part where he grew sure that losing her hadn't been his fault, that her being gone had changed him, but her life, the fact of her and that she'd been alive and connected to him, had changed him more than her death.

I know Naomi's connection to that book is also part of her connection to me. She feels I left her the way Leslie left Jesse. But neither one of us had a choice.

When at last Naomi had felt ready, satisfied, calm, she fell asleep with the novel wedged under her pillow, and dreamed of Lynne, and of me.

The next day, waiting outside the school for the morning bell to ring, Naomi had been bursting to talk about the story with her best friend. She could picture Lynne glued to the book, methodically plodding through it as she ate her breakfast cereal, maybe even spilling bits of cornflakes or a few splotches of milk onto the pages as she sped madly through them. Naomi tried to picture no one noticing Lynne's mess—her being able to quickly, effectively, brush away all evidence of her absent-mindedness without anyone commenting on it. In Naomi's world, every mistake—a spill, for instance—was boiled down to her disability, and then analyzed to death: she would have had better control if she'd kept her wrists straight, if she'd maintained better posture, if her feet were planted firmly on the footrests. If, if, if.

"Hey, you. You look tired."

What was she, telepathic? Naomi watched Lynne drop down the school's cement wall, from standing to sitting, changing position as easily as water being poured from a glass to a bowl changed shape. She smiled through the jolt.

"Yeah, I'm tired. I finished it last night. Terabithia, I mean. Read all night, almost. It's really sad. But cool."

Naomi watched Lynne droop. "Oh."

Only then did she feel guilty. Only then did it occur to her that she should have waited, resisted the urge to get to the end without taking Lynne with her as she usually did. "I'm sorry," she said, knowing Lynne would know what she meant.

"It's okay. It's...Can you read to me from where we left off?"

"On the weekend. Tonight I've gotta do those stupid graphs."

Lynne raised her eyebrows. "Oops. I almost forgot about that thing."

"Must be nice."

It was a simple math assignment, really. The first step had been for each person in the class to record how their time was spent over the period of two weeks, and then figure out how many hours, and portions of hours, went toward each activity. Then they had to convert the results to fractions, decimals, and percentages, plus draw out line, pie, and bar graphs. Naomi's notes were depressing. She could see them in her mind's eye, laying where she'd left them on her desk.

Time in Two Weeks	(hrs)	(%)
Showers, etc.	6	1.8%
Eating	28	8.3%
Workouts	42	12.5%
Dressing/Undressing/ Grooming	21	6.3%
Homework	49	14.6%
Sleep	84	25.0%
Doctors	14	4.2%
Television	6	1.8%
Free time	1	0.3%

And the shitty thing had to be presented in front of the class, each detail of the math explained—how it was done, why it was accurate and correct.

"Want any help? I can work on the graphs with you. You'll be done in half the time, and then we can read together."

What she meant, Naomi knew, was that then she could read to Lynne, when the math was done. And Lynne was good at math, which was Naomi's own weak spot. Lynne could make the graphs clean and neat. Naomi's shaky eye-hand coordination meant that drawing charts, graphs, and diagrams was iffy, unsteady business. If she had to do this presentation in front of everyone, at least she could make sure the stuff looked decent. And she'd already done the math, and done it right, herself. Lynne would just 'be her hands,' and help her produce the visual aids.

"Sure. I could use a hand."

And the bell rang.

"Naomi, may I see you for a minute?" Our dad's voice cut across Naomi's narration of *Bridge to Terabithia*.

"We're kind of busy, Dad." Naomi's eyes rolled as she replied.

"I know you're busy. So if I'm calling you anyway, it's important."

Naomi glanced up at the stiff look on our father's face, looked at the tense angle of his stance in the doorway. "I'm coming."

Good move. That's what I would do. Move fast, oh twin of mine.

She checked her page then put the book down. "Be back in a minute," she told Lynne, trying to ignore the questions jostling for position in her friend's eyes as she pushed herself across the rug.

"Please excuse her, Lynne," our father said, nodding in her direction, almost as an afterthought.

"No problem. I can wait." Lynne picked up the novel from where Naomi had left it and began to flip through the pages in a focused way, but a weird kind of focused. Like she'd never seen paper before. Naomi was thinking that she looked like what she wanted to do most in all the world was bite her nails.

Our dad steered her around the corner and into the kitchen. "What are you doing, young lady?" The question hung between them, a stormy cloud. Naomi's thoughts ping-ponged. Don't answer. Be evasive. What he doesn't know won't hurt him. I willed her to realize that that hardly made sense. She wasn't doing anything wrong.

"I'm reading. We're reading together. What's wrong?"

"Lynne should be doing her own reading. She's older than you."

Naomi winced. They barely ever talked about Lynne having failed Grade Two and Grade Four, both before Naomi met her. "Dad, be fair!"

"I am being very fair. I'm being fair enough to remind you how long it takes for you to do your own homework. You don't need to be doing Lynne's, too."

My twin's heart skipped a beat. She looked down at her hands, the hands that at times of being put on the spot like this, felt like the agents of her betrayal—the hands that worked, wrote, and typed so much slower than her brain produced thoughts, answers, and ideas. What took everyone in her class or her grade about, say, an hour to do, took her about three. She loved the feeling of her thoughts whizzing around, so much so that it almost felt like she could hear the sparks go off sometimes. In many ways, school felt like slipping on an old pair of jeans—the kind so comfortable, so fitting to her shape that she could imagine them in the closet, posed in her own sitting position, without her body in them. School awakened her, made her mind race and tumble with the creative way she would do this or that presentation, the new way that someone's opinion made her think, the cool twist she would add to the project being assigned. She was forever disciplining her mind. Easy does it. I can't write that fast.

So our father had a point. But what about Lynne?

"Look, Dad," Naomi pointed out, "Lynne already helped me with my math. And this is my homework, too. We have to do this novel study, and—"

"Mr. Demas, I'm sorry." At the sound of Lynne's voice behind them, my sister felt an electric shock of dread pulse through her. She shot her friend a sharp look of warning. What are you doing, jumping off a cliff? But Lynne kept on talking.

"I know Naomi spends a lot of time helping me, but she doesn't do any of my work for me, I swear. We aren't doing anything wrong. It's just that when I try to read by myself...well, I can read fine, but the words don't add up to what they mean. All my effort goes toward stringing the words together, and the part of me that's supposed to concentrate on what I think of the words...it just shuts down. It's almost like there's no room for that part to work. But if someone, like Naomi, reads to me, it's like the plumber unplugged the faucet, and all my ideas are free to come out. I failed two grades because everyone was so stuck on me reading, they didn't notice that with a bit of help, I can be free to think. When I see words, it's like they're there, but they hardly reach me. I can't figure out what they're really saying. But when I hear them, I can learn from them. "

Silence filled the room—a silence that could either tilt the world toward disaster or set it upright, facing tomorrow. Either Dad would let them be, or all hell would break loose. Naomi knew her father was moral to a fault, and if he didn't believe that what the girls were doing was 'kosher' (people probably thought they were Jewish, the way he said that word all the time) the school might know by morning.

Naomi watched his face and felt light-headed. In heaven, I remember holding my breath.

The bear hug he gathered Naomi and Lynne into was sure and strong. Naomi could smell the wool of his sweater and feel the spasm building in her neck as he held her in a crushing embrace. "You've learned to hug like your mother-in-law," I wished I could tell him. There's a way to hold that makes up for a multitude of sins. But he was already talking. With my twin's ear crushed against his chest, his words were muffled, but they came through just the same.

"I'm proud of you both. Keep doing what you have to do. Keep doing right."

Naomi and Lynne exhaled.

"Who does homework for three-and-a-half hours every day?"

I watched as Naomi sat in front of the class ready to present her homework. Lynne had taped her colourful charts and graphs to the board and taken her seat.

"Even weekends!"

"What a liar! No one works that hard."

"Don't forget three hours at the doctor's office, man. She lives at the doctor's office. Twice a week."

"Maybe the doctor's a shrink."

"Maybe he's doing her homework. Maybe that's why she's such a friggin' brain. 'Cuz he is."

Right on the spot, Naomi was wishing to die. She was thinking that twelve years had been a good enough stint. Long enough. She didn't wish for the floor to open and swallow her; that would be painful, and she figured she'd been through enough. As the hoots and giggles multiplied, rabbit-style, through the room, she imagined the cool dark earth she would eventually blend into if mercy intervened and she was struck dead on the spot. She pictured the grass and flowers that would bloom over her, and found that oddly comforting. But lightning didn't strike, and neither did sudden death by embarrassment.

I watched as Naomi pinched herself, hard, until the hurt almost felt good. It was something, after all, that she could control. As luck would have it, she was very much alive.

Mr. Raj was doing his best at the front of the room, squawking about respect and quiet and being model citizens. Good luck, sir.

Busy with her out-of-body experience, Naomi didn't see the moment when the collective energy and will of her classmates split almost literally down the middle. She certainly felt the prickle and heat of anger, but couldn't separate what welled up inside her from the ugliness that oozed out of Jay and his clones, or the indignation and shock coming from her own friends, and from me. For Naomi, the whole atmosphere was fused into a mob mentality—that idiot loser mob that hated her for not fading away, failing, or lying about her life. The flicker that passed like a torch among her people, the moment when, as a group, they covered her back, was gone almost before it came. She missed it, but lines were drawn, decisions made, nonetheless.

Naomi didn't even see Lynne get out of her seat. She landed back into the confines of her own skin just in time to see her friend's thermos full of juice pouring out onto Jay's head.

"What the fuck, man—" he sputtered. "What the hell are you doing?"

"Making myself feel better, *man*."

Lynne didn't wait to be asked, or even observe her handiwork. She turned, smiled full blast in Naomi's direction, and took herself to the principal's office.

She's always been a girl after my own heart.

Lynne

The day I poured the grape juice all over that idiot, I remember waiting for half an hour on the bench outside Mrs. Tadman's door, imagining what I was missing as the rest of math class wore on. With satisfaction, I pictured the grape juice drying into a sticky mess all over Jay's clothes, in his hair, even into his socks and shoes. I wondered if Mr. Raj would dismiss him so that he could go home to wash up and change. I hoped not. I hoped he would have to sit in the crappy purple stuff all day.

The only problem putting a downer on my smug happiness was the idea that by dumping that juice, I might've actually made things worse for Naomi. It worried me that the class might pick on her more, because Jay and his posse were officially pissed. I remember smiling at the sound of those words. Pissed posse. Posse pissed.

Well, if they wanted to be babies, that was fine, actually. Because Naomi had a pissed posse, too.

"Okay, let's cut to the chase here. Mr. Raj already told me what happened. Why did you do it, Lynne?" Mrs. Tadman's face was serious.

"If he really told you what happened, you wouldn't be asking me that."

"He told me. Now I want to hear it from you, young lady. I have my reasons."

The way she said "young lady" undid me. She said it, not as though to tell me off, but as if I truly was a young lady, someone mature who had done the right thing.

Keep doing right, Mr. Demas had said. I started to cry.

"Jay and his friends...they treat Naomi like she's stupid... Like they want her to be stupid. Like just because she's using a wheelchair, other people must be doing her work. They made fun of her assignment and called her a liar...for telling the truth about how long stuff takes her. They made her sound like a desperate loser...the kind no one should ever trust when she gives her word."

Mrs. Tadman passed me her box of tissues. "Don't worry. I've heard enough," she said, walking around behind her desk, opening the middle drawer. "Here, have some of my personal miracle drug. Chocolate will make up for almost anything." She winked.

We began to talk. About how Naomi had it rough, but also had it good. About how some people would never really understand either Naomi or me in many ways, but about how both of us would grow past this day, this school, these problems, and build great lives. And that would be amazing revenge. The best.

"One day," the principal said, "you'll both look back on a time like this and remember it the way some older people see wrinkles. They're part of you, they're in the mirror if you look, but they don't stop you from doing much. They remind you where you've been, is all. And as for the lot of those boys, I'm going to haul them out of class myself, right now. They'll wish they stayed in bed this morning. And I'll speak to Naomi tomorrow."

Mrs. Tadman got up and headed for the door, handing me a small slip of paper. "Give this to your second period teacher. And if there's a next time with these kids, or any other ones at this school, just walk out of class and come and get me. Anything else is a waste of juice."

It's been six years, and still I remember that day as though only a flicker of time has passed. I don't have any wrinkles yet, but I can still feel the passage of time. An unstoppable contradiction—dizzyingly fast and maddeningly slow, fever pitch and rewind, sometimes almost in the same breath.

And still. And yet. Not fast or slow enough some days.

Since that first day in Mrs. Tadman's office, there have been others, both for me and Naomi. Not because we've gotten in trouble, but because, like race car drivers who stop to have their tanks filled in the pit, we need breaks. We need someone who just understands, who doesn't need to have the hard things explained to death. Both of us have friends our own age, but none of those friends have a plaque on the door, with the words 'I'm sorry if you're normal' stencilled onto it. Mrs. Tadman's office (eventually she told us to call her Lorena, in private) just felt like home. And these days, we have to be the only students about to graduate high school who still go back to our elementary school to visit the principal. Voluntarily, no less.

"Oh, don't worry about that thing, honey. Plants come here to die."

I jerk my eyes away from the wilting cactus, browning like a sepia-tone photograph in the corner, and laugh. "Yeah, but that takes work."

Lorena Tadman shrugs. "What, killing a cactus? It's easy. I watered it too much. What made you step in the time machine today?"

I think for a moment. "It's Naomi."

Lorena takes a sip of coffee. "What's happened?"

"Nothing happened. Maybe that's the problem."

"Stop talking in code and standing in the door like a stranger. Sit and tell me what's bothering you."

"Well, Naomi's mom is finally making an effort to communicate. She's confessed to having OCD, and Naomi's brushing it off and acting like it's a bald-faced lie."

"And it's not?"

"I don't think so. And that kind of thing takes guts to admit, you know?"

"I do know. Is that why you're crying?"

"I'm not crying."

Lorena doesn't say anything, just hands me a tissue. I wipe away a tear and stare at the damp spot on the tissue. "Okay. Fine. I'm crying. But it's because she doesn't get it. And that makes me wonder if she really gets me. You think you know a person, and then *poof...*"

"Lynne, I've known the two of you for a lot of years, and trust me, you get each other. That's not the problem."

"Maybe not. But I have a learning disability. And she's been, like, crazy supportive."

"You don't have to tell me. I was there," Lorena reminds me.

"Yeah, you were there. You were there when Naomi figured out that if I recorded my assignments, if I heard my own voice reading out loud or doing assignments by talking through them, I could work around my problem, and I didn't need Mr. Bosch. It wasn't simple, but we worked hard and we did it. She's a genius. But now I see her reaction to her mom's OCD, and I'm thinking: If Naomi's so convinced her mom's a fake because her problem is so-called 'invisible,' what does she think of me? My learning disability is invisible, too."

Lorena stays silent for a few moments. Then she begins telling me about the closed-door staff meeting five years earlier where my single mother, my teachers (including Mr. Bosch) and the guidance counsellors had discussed their recommendations for my future in high school. They had debated Special Ed and IEPs until my mother looked as if a countdown clock inside her was about to go off. She had sat fidgeting, chewing the top of her pen and tapping it against the table. Until…

"Lynne wants to go to university. So when she gets to high school, she's going to take courses to prepare her for that."

No question. No doubt. Just a statement of certainty. This will be.

"Mrs. Wood, that's not possible." Martin Bosch had looked clearly offended.

"Why?"

"Because your daughter has a learning disability. She failed two grades."

"Einstein failed Math."

Mr. Bosch had laughed. He actually laughed. Lorena shared with me her clear memory of wanting to get out of her chair, reach across the table and throttle him, but she had stayed in her seat and let him face my mother.

"Excuse me, but what is so funny?"

A very good question, Lorena had thought. Go Mrs. Wood.

Mr. Bosch controlled his inappropriate mirth, but only barely. It was as if any mention of brilliance when—in his mind—they were supposed to be discussing my 'lack thereof' was the very essence of hilarity. "I'm sorry...I'm sorry...It's...just...so...just so...ridiculous..."

"Excuse me, Martin, but we won't be flattening anyone's hope today. Are we clear?"

Mr. Bosch was suddenly serious. "I'm not trying to flatten anything, Lorena. I'm being realistic. I'm telling the truth."

My mother pounced. "If you want the truth, this is it. Lynne did fail two grades, six years ago. And since then, she's found a friend who's helped her learn to succeed and boost her confidence more than Special Ed ever did. She hasn't earned anything less than a B in three years. And she hasn't stepped a foot in your classroom for that long, either. You're not the one who's helped her. You never were. And she'll do fine in high school. Mark my words. That's the truth."

I've heard versions of this story plenty of times from my own mother, but Lorena's memories of the same event are pretty amazing. My then-principal had watched Martin Bosch's frustration build as all kinds of retorts fought for airtime on his face. Lorena had hoped, for his sake, that what ended up coming out of his mouth would be at least semi-professional. And she had hoped he remembered that Naomi, whom everyone knew was my saving grace, was zooming through middle school as a straight-A student, with the sole exception of Math. Lorena told me how she had wished—oh, how she had hoped—that his general idiocy would not cause him to seize this particular moment to make some disparaging reference to the fact that Naomi moved through the school in a wheelchair. She held her breath.

"Are you referring to Naomi Demas 'teaching Lynne to succeed'?" Mr. Bosch wanted to know.

"Of course."

He scoffed. "Oh, for God's sake! Talk about the blind leading the blind." Back then, I had opted out of Special Ed (which felt at the time like signing out of a hospital 'AMA' (Against Medical Advice) and Martin Bosch was gone the next year. Lorena Tadman worked her days at Terry Fox Elementary, waiting for news of both Naomi and me - two of the students she loved best. She didn't make a habit of siding with students who wanted to shake off academic support, but I had proven I could do it, and here I was now, ready to graduate high school with honours at the end of the year. I had told Lorena myself that my bookcase, and some of my dresser drawers are always full of my recorded essays, that my bedroom walls are covered in diagrams and study notes copied onto scrolls of poster paper in magic marker. And even as our circle of friends grows, Naomi and I have stayed fiercely loyal to each other. It hurts my heart that a fracture might be developing between us now, but I know that this is real life. If we can't work this out now, then that would mean our relationship has been wounded for quite some time—and perhaps not as strong in the first place as we had thought.

But that is impossible. Just in time, before my thoughts speed away from me in a very sad direction, I see Lorena take a deep breath, about to speak.

"Lynne, there is no way on earth that Naomi thinks you're a fake. I guarantee that."

I straighten up in my chair. "How can you be so sure?"

"Look, we can hardly expect Naomi not to struggle with her relationship with her mother. There's a lot of hurt between them, and damaged trust. Of all people, you know best how wounded she is over that. So now, everything Irene says to Naomi is difficult to believe, to take on faith. Right now Naomi's first instinct is to think anything that comes out of her mother's mouth is a betrayal. It's going to take a lot of effort from both of them to repair that connection, and it'll take time. It took a long time to break down this badly, and it'll take time to build again. You need to keep being patient. There will be days when Naomi feels closer to forgiving her mother, closer to understanding and accepting her, and there will be times when she backslides completely—three steps forward, five steps back. Sometimes she'll change her mind ten times a day. She's not sure what to think. And none of that has anything to do with you. You're not the one she has anger toward. You're not the one who abandoned her. It's fully understandable anger, but it's not about you. Got it?"

I bring my knees up to rest under my chin. It's what I do when I have lots on my mind. "Yeah, I think so."

"Good, because there's a bit more."

"What now?"

"Well, think about it. All of her life, Naomi's been busy proving what she can do."

"We both have," I say.

Lorena nods. "I think that's one of the reasons why you get along so well. But when it comes to her own mother, here is someone who's talking about what they can't do, about what has paralyzed them in the past and what is still threatening them. I think, to Naomi, it's a major turn-off. She sees it as another of her mother's excuses. And she might be figuring: 'Lynne and I have done stuff people never thought we could. What's her problem?'"

"That's really unfair."

"It is, but I think it might be in her head right now. She's going to have to figure this out by herself."

Chapter Eight
Battle

Naomi

I look at my watch, half to figure out exactly how long Dr. Morrison is keeping Dad and I waiting, and half to track in my mind where Lynne would be at this moment. She has a spare last period, and she's mentioned going to visit Lorena Tadman, which usually means Lynne is struggling with something. For the first time in a long time, I don't know what, though. It makes me nervous.

2:00: Forty-five minutes of waiting. Dad looks up at me from his magazine. "Dr. Morrison will come when she comes, sweetheart."

I roll my eyes. "She does this because she can."

"That may well be, but—"

"How is my princess today?"

"Hi, Dr. Morrison. I'm well, thank you. I want to tell her that I'm not her princess, but I don't have a right to be that much of a smartass. She's done a lot for me after all. There is no denying, though, that our relationship has changed a lot over the years. "How 'bout you?"

I was nine years old when I met Dr. Morrison. I had been a wounded child, fresh from my mother's leaving barely a year before. Anyone who called me a princess—who even sounded like they thought I might be beautiful and have a Prince Charming coming down the line—could do no wrong in my little girl eyes.

How I'd loved Dr. Morrison then! I couldn't get enough of her certainty, the self-assured glow that was part of her, the designer clothes, the ease with which she had told—no, promised—me and Dad that I would walk, with the help of a machine that stimulated my muscles at night, along with Dr. Morrison's particular cocktail of associated therapies.

I started out afraid of her. Here was this doctor—a genius, more like. It seemed she could perform miracles. There were patients of hers who walked after accidents, who learned (and earned) control over muscles they either never knew they had or never thought they would find again. With the help of a machine that sent battery current through weak muscles and worked to regenerate nerve-endings and neurological connections, there were people all around me at Dr. Morrison's who were getting their lives back—finding 'normal.' I wanted to be one of them so badly, my desire nearly choked me. To me, at nine, normal felt like The Holy Land, The Land of Milk and Honey and my personal Paradise Found, all rolled into one.

But one misstep and Dr. Morrison could take it all away.

She had become absolutely taken with me, and decided to make me part of the treatment project—not part of the main study, because that had been limited to clients with spinal cord injury or congenital spinal conditions like spina bifida—but the good doctor had started a new study with me as its sole star. The main study was for clients who dealt with non-neurological issues (the ones not resulting from the death of brain cells). I knew, even as a little girl, that if Dr. Morrison could prove that her approach repaired damage in those cases, she'd be up to her eyeballs in funding, research grants and referrals. She'd earn a super professional reputation and the credibility to help a tonne of people. That was Dr. Morrison's dream: the very summit of her ambition.

And then, she'd met me. And the dream had grown.

It hadn't been love at first sight on the doctor's part—I know that now. My father had heard about the groundbreaking new study, phoned Dr. Morrison's office, and basically begged them so many times to book his beloved daughter to see the doctor, they'd finally had two choices: give the girl an appointment, or sue her father for harassment.

Dr. Morrison had briefed one of her med students, Oliver Wolfe, about the nine year-old girl with the 3:30 p.m. appointment, who would be arriving with her father. "She isn't eligible for the study, but her father keeps calling here, crying and begging for an appointment. See what you can do to let them down easy. She's too old for the sample group."

I remember meeting Dr. Wolfe as though it happened yesterday. I remember his large, kind brown eyes and the way his gentle smile seemed always there, even when his face was serious.

I remember other things, too: feeling my bare feet against the cold floor as I walked with my walker so that he could observe my gait, focusing on everything Dad warned me to be careful about: stand tall, pick up feet, don't look down, put your bum in, lock your knees, smile.

I remember my sweaty palms and how terrified I was that they would betray me by sliding right off the handles of the walker. I remember the way my heart beat fast, like a terrified bird in my chest. I'd been sure Dr. Wolfe could hear it from across the room, that it would be the thing that gave me away as a fraud, that it would jump right clear of my chest and lie beating on the floor.

And I remember the moment Dr. Wolfe claimed the space in my heart that will always be his. Eight long years have passed, but that moment is forever engraved on my mind.

"You work really hard, don't you, Naomi?" It was a question, without being a question at all.

I had simply stared at him for a long moment, hardly believing the way his tone let me know he took me seriously and thought I was worth quite a lot; and the way he had communicated all that with just seven words.

"Say 'thank you,' Naomi," my father prompted, sounding embarrassed and apologetic. "She really is very eloquent, doctor. She's just forgotten her manners right about now."

Dr. Wolfe had laughed, not unkindly. "Oh, I don't think it has the least thing to do with manners, Mr. Demas. I think she feels so good right this instant, she doesn't quite know what to do with herself."

Finally, I found my voice.

"'Good' doesn't even come close to my expanse of feelings, Dr. Wolfe. Thank you for noticing how hard I work. Most people don't. They think if I was really working as hard as I could, I would be walking right now—and not just with a walker, but by myself, or at least without my dad having to walk behind me like a shadow when I'm on my walker. They think that all our work should have brought us that far by now, and if it hasn't, we must be doing something wrong, or I must be sleeping on the job. But I'm not. I take learning to walk very seriously. And you saw that so quickly. I'm very grateful. That's why I stood here so stunned at first. I must have looked wide-eyed, like an owl, and I still feel wide-eyed inside, surprised to be spoken to with such respect. Doctors don't usually address me that way, and so this is most refreshing, Dr. Wolfe. Actually, it's very interesting for me to think of owls, really. They are nocturnal animals. Did you know that? Of course you did. You're a doctor. Sorry. But I find it fascinating that they sleep during the day and hunt at night, when so many other animals are sleeping. I wonder if the diurnal animals, the ones who hunt during the day, misunderstand the nocturnal ones and think they're lazy. I wonder if they call them names. That would hurt. People have called us names, you know. Even doctors. They've called my father and me 'Siamese Twins,' just because my dad has to follow right behind me when I walk. But doctors have said I would never walk at all, and now that I do—with a bit of help—some of them make fun of us. It's very unfair. But I know you would never do that, would you, Dr. Wolfe?"

It had been Dr. Wolfe's turn to stand transfixed.

"How old are you, Naomi?"

"I'm nine years old. I'll be ten in the summer. But I feel a lot older than that, sometimes."

"I'm sure you do. You know, I have a daughter at home in Florida who is your age, and she has big brown eyes and lots of important things to say, just like you."

"You live in Florida?" I had gasped, my eyes dancing with visions of palm trees and beaches, seafood and Disney World. Dr. Wolfe watched me sit back in my wheelchair as I spoke, watched the mechanics of my movements as many doctors had done and many would do in the future. He wasn't the first, or the last, but he was one of the only ones who did his job and did it well, without making me feel as though he was building a catalogue of my flaws.

"My family is waiting for me in Florida, while I finish my residency here in Toronto," he explained. "I try to fly home and see them once a month, but it's hard. There is a lot of work to do here. So I'm glad you remind me so much of Mindy. It's like she's come to see me, for a while."

"You must miss your family very much."

My heart had skipped a beat at the way Dad's voice bent with sadness when he spoke those words. Even now, I remember thinking at that moment that if I let my mind even hover at thoughts of the way our family had splintered over that year, I would not just bend. I would break. So I steered my thoughts stubbornly away from my mother, or from tall beautiful Joanna, in just the way my grandmother held my face away from the television during a scary scene.

"I do miss them all very much. But then I think of what an honour it is to work with Dr. Morrison, and it makes missing them a bit easier. Not much, but just enough."

"Am I going to meet Dr. Morrison today?" I had been breathless with excitement, as though I was discussing the possibility of meeting God.

"She's in a meeting, but I'm going to go and get her right now."

At the time, all those years ago, I didn't know of the miracle that happened when Dr. Wolfe excused himself to get Dr. Morrison, despite a dire warning just hours earlier that he should do no such thing. Over time, Dr. Morrison's resistance to taking on my case, and her virtually immediate reversal of opinion upon meeting me as a little girl, became the stuff of legend at the clinic. After all her protests, the doctor didn't make me part of the existing study; she made me, in effect, a study unto myself: a one-child show, a phenomenon upon whom rested the entire burden of proof for Dr. Morrison's work on neurology and rehabilitation.

The logic went something like this: If Dr. Morrison could prove, through me, that her approach (electrical muscle stimulation, along with biofeedback training, physiotherapy, osteopathy, massage therapy, swimming, acupuncture, acupressure, reflexology, and yoga) could work together to teach the brain normal function, despite neurological brain injuries like mine for which conventional doctors held out little or no hope, then Dr. Morrison would quickly turn into the medical, scientific equivalent of a saint. If she could rehabilitate function in cases involving spinal defects and injuries, there would be a revolution. If she could make me walk without either my walker or my father—completely unaided—that would be nothing but eureka. At least if I could walk with my walker and without my father.

Yes, that at the very least.

The key, the bottom line, was me. The weight of Dr. Morrison's world sat squarely on my shoulders. If I succeeded, if I walked, all would be well. Hospital board members had focused on my case—the sweet child with the magnetic smile and the sad eyes. If I failed, the only gift that would come rolling in from the mainstream medical community—which already thought the doctor was crazy—would be I-told-you-so's.

I became Dr. Morrison's hot commodity. I recited poetry in front of her colleagues. I was the favourite at fundraisers of all sorts. I was the sweet-faced chatterbox everyone remembered and wanted to see cured. And the clock ticked.

But I never walked the way Dr. Morrison wanted and thus expected me to walk. The doctor never realized that my independent standing and walking balance was one area of my mid-brain that was far too injured to recover. I improved in a million ways: I grew stronger, more coordinated, gained more muscle bulk and muscle control. But none of that was good enough. None of it was what Dr. Morrison had promised her supporters she'd be able to do for the girl who had stolen their hearts.

The worst part was that the more the expected didn't happen for me, the less Dr. Morrison's successes with other conditions—sizeable as those successes were—seemed to matter to the medical community who was watching.

And the more that came true, the angrier Dr. Morrison became. At me.

And here I am, at seventeen, no less at the mercy of this doctor's sometimes-dripping-honey, sometimes-shooting-darts moods than I had been when I was nine.

"Let me ask you this, Mr. Demas. When is the last time you let Naomi fall?" Dr. Morrison's question jolts me out of my reverie and back into the present moment.

Uh-oh. Everybody duck. We're in the heart of Dartville.

My father clears his throat nervously. "I beg your pardon? What do you mean?"

"I mean, how is Naomi ever going to learn to stop relying on your presence behind her when she walks if you're always there? You're spoiling her rotten. Babies and children need to learn how to fall. That teaches them about where their bodies are in space, and trains balance. It teaches them how to deal with failure and disappointment."

My father begins opening and closing his fists in his lap as he listens. "Do you mean to tell me that I should let my seventeen-year-old daughter hit her head so that she can have experience in being disappointed? Are you kidding? She's had her fill, believe me. And as for failure, she faces that every time she faces a world that tells her that her best is never good enough."

Dr. Morrison speaks slowly and stiffly. "It's not my intention to crush anyone, Mr. Demas. You must remember that although Naomi is highly intelligent, it is as though her mid-brain—where physical movement originates—is slow, delayed. If we do not force her forward, she'll never walk on her own."

The doctor turns toward me for the first time since calling me 'princess,' as though she has only just realized her patient is still in the room. "Naomi, you have to learn to try, that's all. A bit of effort and you'll be running, darling. I promise." Dr. Morrison sits back in her chair, satisfied that she's made her point and that the discussion is effectively closed. But something inside me snaps, like a whip. "Dr. Morrison, I've done everything you've ever asked me to do. Every treatment. Every test. Every combination of the two. Just because you promised you would make me walk 'normally,' and that didn't happen, that doesn't mean you failed, or we failed. We just haven't gotten what we wanted when we made the original plan. And what is normal anyway, if it's not some ridiculous standard medicine made up so nobody has to face their fear of difference?"

"Excuse me?"

"My body has worked. It does work. My heart pumps. My blood flows through me. My lungs fill with air. My bones and muscles enable movement, adapt to spasticity and weakness, and help me find ways to function that work for me. My brain has built detours around my injury because of all the physical training I've done. I chew and swallow and speak and write and ride horses and stand and sit. And I even walk. My arms and hands work. Not like yours, but they work. My legs and feet work. Not like yours, but they work. And the reason most babies learn to walk is not because they've learned to fall. It's because their capacity for balance is uninjured and free to develop in conventional ways. You don't see any babies standing or walking by themselves before their bodies are ready to support them, do you? If I still need to be shadowed when I walk, it's not for lack of trying to get rid of the shadow. But I can't. That's just the way it is."

"You're giving up, Naomi. You're giving up on yourself."

"No, I am not. I'm facing facts. And I'm still more than willing to work and train, and stay fit and do all my therapy. But I'm not 'spoiled' for wanting to avoid falling on my head when I walk. No baby or child, no person at all, would even try doing that if every time they tried all they felt was absolute terror: the kind of terror that would freeze the blood in your veins, Dr. Morrison. That kind of terror doesn't come from being spoiled. It comes from being certain I'll fall. And I don't need any more injuries. I need to do whatever needs doing to protect my body while I challenge myself. Especially my head. Do you think it would do my brain any good to be smacked around? I won't risk it, and that makes me smart."

Dr. Morrison rises and begins to pace. "Naomi Demas, I have had many patients in my time, and most of them are so determined to make their bodies work, to be independent, they spend hours wrestling to do up their own bras, or put on their own socks. But not you. If you focused on your body, all day every day, you would have done the impossible. I'll always believe that."

I take a moment to look hard at Dr. Morrison. I think of the many sacrifices the doctor has made to make the clinic happen and stay open despite opposition in mainstream medicine. The place had been buzzing with rumours of closure. Referrals from other doctors have dwindled when the major hospital Dr. Morrison was associated with withdrew its backing because she wants to stop doing limited studies and offer the treatment on a wider scale. That decision has hurt on a lot of levels. But it's a gutsy one.

I haven't been cured, but I've improved—learned to train my own body, learned to make it work, learned fitness. Learned respect where others see only deficit.

"Dr. Morrison, success doesn't come from figuring out bras and socks, or whatever else. If I had hours to spend on it every day, I could learn those skills. But they won't get me into university next year, or give me a career, or solve the hurt in my life and my family. I need my brain and my heart for that. So I'll gladly work on my health, my fitness, my training. Just not at the expense of the big picture. I don't want to be on my deathbed thinking that I chased my tail my whole life."

"Leave my office, please," the doctor says.

Chapter Nine
Alone in the World

Naomi

A cemetery is a silent city.

When I was a little girl, coaxed, cajoled and sometimes coerced into spending birthdays here, I would daydream of Mary, descending from the sky (never rising from the ground, since I've always been spooked by the possibility of that) to meet me. I'd secretly hoped that those birthdays that connected us would turn into annual reunions, when Mary would materialize in a column of light and a fit of giggles to sprawl out on the picnic blanket Mom always brought so we could catch up on the past year: ours on Earth and hers in heaven. I don't think it would have hurt so much not having her with me if we could have had that one day together, in-the-flesh, each year.

In my head, we would play Hide-and-Seek behind the shrubbery and the gravestones, and Mary would never find it odd that I had to knee-walk or crawl to my hiding spot, instead of run. She would do the same, to make it fair. She would count extra-long for me and never grow impatient.

She would bring me bits of heaven—gems or chunks of gold from the streets. She would tell me she loved me and let me eat her birthday cake as well as mine, because she'd eaten one in heaven that was perfect, and she was full.

When we grew older, I would bring my husband to meet her. He would think we were only going to visit a grave, but then I would tell him to wait, to watch the sunrise, and he would see her coming and we would weep while she appeared over the horizon—beginning as a dash of light, a falling star, and turning into my sister, my suddenly living twin.

But it has never worked that way.

Sometimes I make lists of all the hurt Mary will never have to deal with. It helps, a little.

"I do that, too."

My heart skips a beat. I know that voice, or at least I feel as though I should be able to place it. I turn my wheelchair toward the sound.

"It's Curtis. You remember, right? I held the door open for you at school last week and you said thank you and that I was a fast runner. We got along great."

I shiver, but keep my thoughts to myself. I can't say exactly why, but it bothers me that he remembers our small exchange so well.

"Sorry, Curtis. You scared me for a sec, but I do remember. What are you doing here?"

"I kind of...followed you after school." Curtis sees the look on my face, and hurries past what he has just said, as if to erase it. "I'm visiting, too. Both my sisters are...here. They died when I was a baby. I talk to them out loud all the time, just like you."

"I hadn't realized I was talking out loud. And I'm sorry. That your sisters died, I mean."

"Can't be changed now. But it hurts, you know? Especially since all I have left of them is one box of their stuff." My heart sinks for him as his voice drifts. But then he continues, seeming to come back from his own little world. "I'm sorry too. About your..."

"My sister. I lost a sister."

Mary

There was only one piece of Curtis's past that I've been allowed to witness from heaven. I hover over the scene in the ultrasound clinic. It's strange, witnessing Curtis even before he's part of the outside world.

"Everything looks great in there. Do you want to know what you're carrying?"

Natalie looked around her at the baby posters, the calming blues, greens, purples, yellows on the wallpaper. She thought of all the happy mothers and supportive, excited husbands in the waiting room—the tidbits of safe, comfortable lives she would never have. She thought of the baby growing inside her, and how bringing it home to him would just be another one of her screw ups. If she was having another daughter, she would have to leave, and pronto.

"Is it a girl?"

"No, dear. You've got yourself a son." The nurse was beaming, her smooth, rich brown skin creased and dimpled by frequent exuberance. Natalie could tell she was expecting another one of the customary outpourings of joy that undoubtedly populated the majority of her workdays in the maternity ward.

Natalie's eyes filled with tears. Another abuser was on his way. And she hadn't bumped into this one in a bar. She was carrying him.

For a moment, the nurse mistook Natalie's cries as those of gratitude, happiness, relief. She'd seen her share of mothers come unstitched at the sound of a tiny, steady heartbeat, at the sight of hands and feet on the monitor. "It's overwhelming, isn't it? That baby in there, he's gonna be all yours in a few months."

That made Natalie cry harder. Great heaving sobs pushed through her and she shook from her core. "I don't know…I don't know…I…think I'm in trouble…"

"Why?"

"He…He…" Natalie had never said these words out loud, had lived so long with the secret that now it was like a bird trapped in a room, crazed with fear of and the instinct for freedom, both at once. "He hits us, me and the girls. I'm scared he'll make the baby just like him. He hates us and I don't know why."

She tried to hold back the rush of tears by sheer force of will, but it was no use—about as humanly impossible as reversing time to avoid meeting the father of her children. Impossible, no matter how much she wanted it to be true. The ocean itself was rising to overtake her face, and still she couldn't stop.

"Talk to me," the nurse said gently.

But there were no words big enough to encompass this. There were none at all. Words were lost underwater. Natalie's own Atlantis.

If she had been looking at the nurse then instead of locked in her personal flooded city of regret, Natalie would have seen the transformation of her face. Her joy didn't disappear, but it went behind a sort of screen of anger. She would have seen the moment of decision, when the nurse glanced around the room, double-checking that the door was shut. She would have seen her weigh the possibilities, weigh the risks and the chances. Natalie would have caught a glimpse of this woman's own past of despair. She would have seen the memory of abuse in her eyes. She would have seen her allow long-buried shards of panic to the surface, tiny glimpses of her own flight from hell. And Natalie would have seen the moment when enough was enough, when Glenore Alexander chose to tear the darkness down, and begin again.

She would have seen Glenore 'do the math'—Natalie's waifish, tired children in the waiting area, much too meek for their own good, obviously already bruised by life. There was the way the older one protected the younger, with quiet Mother Hen anxiety, and even fright. Glenore had caught all of that in a few moments—tiny fragments that came together now in a dark picture she had wanted desperately to be wrong about.

Natalie would have seen all of that—a topography of roads to this moment, when Glenore decided that, forget the risks, all her hard-won wisdom was for nothing if she didn't pass it on.

For good measure, Glenore took the chair normally reserved for loving husbands and placed it in front of the door. It was a wonder that no one had come in yet, to check on her wailing patient.

"All right, you listen to me. You don't have to stop crying 'til you're good and ready, but you need to know I've been down your road, oh, yes, I have. So I can tell you this. And all you've got to do is trust me, even just a little. Can you do that?"

Natalie nodded. Still no words.

"You and me, we've got to save you and those sweet babies. You need to run. You run, do you understand? Y'all can stay with me."

Glenore tried. She even secretly checked Natalie's file at the hospital, and visited the landlady, asking after them and hoping to find them and convince the little trembling family to come with her. But they were gone. The landlady, also concerned, hadn't the first idea where they went.

Glenore considered calling the police. But what would she tell them? That she had a bad feeling? That a patient of hers had cried on the ultrasound table? What was that to go on? And who would even believe her?

There's only one thing Curtis has from his mother, a letter to a mysterious stranger that Natalie has only addressed as *G*. The rest of his history comes from a trial transcript and a few newspaper articles. When it comes to family history, Curtis has only bare bones to work with...but in my humble opinion, no one has done more with so little. He's managed, bit by bit, sleuthing all the way, to piece this much together about the family he's lost:

G. had apparently offered to help Natalie leave when she was five months pregnant. His mother had poured out all her fears and her faint hopes to G.

Curtis often wonders what would have happened to them all if their mother had swallowed her pride and her fear and let Glenore help. But she didn't. She let herself be comforted, let Glenore's resolve wash over her, swore that she would leave The Sire, then picked herself up and went home to pack.

They did leave him, but they bounced from shelter to shelter as Natalie's belly grew and her legs swelled. And the more her body changed, morphed her into a fat, bloated blimp, the more she hated the baby. Months passed, months within which Natalie hardened. She held in her fear of the rats they found in the rooms they shared with women at the shelters. She held the constant pressure of the possibility that The Sire would show up, looking for his son. Not his wife, and certainly not his daughters, but his son.

Curtis learned to understand what their mother did next—he wrestles with it, but ultimately he grasps that what broke Natalie was the struggle to care for them alone, without a safety net or any certainty about the future. He understands now that she felt worthless and didn't know how to sustain her hope for something better. He knows that time spent removed from a poisonous reality can distort it, can create selective memory—memory that calls forth the scent of red roses, not the taste of blood from the beating that made The Sire bring the flowers home as a token of regret.

These were the ugly truths for which they—and Curtis—paid a price.

They went back to The Sire two weeks before Natalie gave birth to Curtis.

Everything was quiet.

He didn't even so much as pinch them at first, but within a month The Sire had killed both of his daughters and their mother in a legendary rage. Only Curtis survived, an infant instantly shuttled into foster care as his father went to prison.

So Curtis has been left essentially alone on the planet. It's no mystery how lost he is, how exhaustion and abandonment leaks from his bones.

He quivers on the edge of shattering.

When people construct buildings, they have to knock down trees to make room, clear away space, invade nature's territory. Left alone, nature is right on the doorstep. It's nature's Earth. People are the invaders. Difference scares people, but difference is like the trees. It belongs, and people are forever beating it back to build what doesn't freak them out, to build 'normal'—some elusive, slippery fictional standard that no one actually meets. They're resisting the lesson. But difference always comes back, because it's a teacher. That's a good thing, too. There would be no remodelling for people, otherwise. Naomi and Curtis are a litmus test—to see what the world is ready to respect.

Chapter Ten
Injury

To: Naomi Demas
<funkylady@email.com>
From: Matt Dumond
<slightlylessthanagod@email.com>
Subject:
Hi Naomi:

It's Matt. Sorry I didn't write back faster. Of course I remember you. I always remember sexy ladies who let me come in out of the rain! Is your friend sober yet? Boy, was she ever plastered—LOL!

I've been away, on a miserable trip to the Bahamas. Yes, you can so be miserable in the Bahamas. I should know. My mom comes from old money, so trust me: rich, miserable, manic-depressive, in denial (What mental illness? I don't see any...) and addicted to a nasty boyfriend makes for a shitty trip, even if you do get to miss the first ten days of your last year of high school.

```
Write soon. Tell me about yourself.
Matt
```

Naomi

A piercing shriek and thudding footsteps crash into the kitchen, through the back door. The unmistakable sound of my stepbrother wailing hits us all like heat.

"I told you to be gentle!" Lynne spits the words at Eva.

"I was!"

"She's hung over again, and she dislocated his elbow while they were playing," Lynne's accusation hangs there for a split second before Katina scoops Kevin up and runs for the car, his left arm a dangling sausage.

"Nami! Nami! Want Nami!" he sobs while being carried away.

I hate hospitals—the smells, the prefab food, the harsh lights, all the people wanting nothing more than home, or at least anywhere but there. I also hate the fresh, angry tension between Lynne—who is hiding out and counting backwards in the bathroom to cool off—and Eva.

"I love her, but I can't stand her drinking. I won't stand it. I can't look at her. Just knock on that bathroom door when they come get you for Kev. If I stay, I'll punch her."

Sitting across from me, Eva has watery, red-rimmed eyes, shaky hands and is wincing at the bright lights. "So, how much did you drink last night?"

Eva laughs sharply. "What's an alcoholics' favourite drink?"

"Eva, I'm in no mood for riddles."

"Trust me."

"Okay. So what is it?"

"MORE!"

I giggle, then stop short. "That's not funny."

"Oh, but it is. And true."

"Eva, you have to stop this. You won't get anywhere if you're drunk all the time. And I need my friend."

"You don't need me." The words are caustic, and with a heavy heap of sadness.

"Who told you that?"

"No one. I just know."

I open my mouth to respond, but at the same moment, Donna, Kevin's triage nurse approaches. "Excuse me, Naomi, we're ready for you. We've got him set, but it's really, really gonna hurt him. Prepare yourself, girl."

The sight of me only makes Kevin pause mid-sob. I enter—with Donna pushing my chair at top speed and Eva in tow—just as the two doctors, like arm-wrestlers readying for a match, are positioning themselves to deal with his elbow. Kevin shrieks with fresh gusto as they grab his right arm, push it in fast moves over his shoulder and twist it at a bizarre angle, forcing the elbow into a grudging reunion with its socket.

"Jesus loves me. This I know..."

I gently sing Kevin's favourite song, for his comfort and as a prayer sent up, up, up over the terror of his screams that threaten by sheer intensity to lift the hospital roof.

"For the Bible tells me so..." I continue resolutely through the bath of my own tears.

"We got it!" the shorter younger doctor announces. "I felt it pop back in. It's over, little man."

A few minutes later, the doctors have cleared away, like a mist. Kevin is eating cereal on my lap, holding the small Tupperware with one hand and feeding himself with the other. A fix for both his no-breakfast hunger, and a nod to the doctor's instructions to find a two-handed activity and confirm the elbow's function before we leave the hospital.

Equal parts relief and exhaustion are settling in around the room.

"Naomi, while Eva's drinking like this, I don't want her around your brother, do you understand? I don't want her near you either, but I know I would lose that fight with you."

"Yeah, you would. Dad, she so didn't mean for that to happen."

"I know she would never mean it, but bad accidents happen anyway. I don't want you letting her drive you anywhere either, until she sobers up. That girl should be in AA."

"I know. I offered to go with her."

I roll over, waiting for Dad to tuck in the covers. He stops in mid-motion. "Naomi, stop already with the taking on of the whole world. Eva's a big girl."

"Dad, her mom drinks. Her aunt is dead, and she raised her. She doesn't know her father. A lot of her friends drink too. She only has a few that are a good influence, and some of those are taking off. What am I supposed to do, let her rot?"

"You've already done more for her than most people would do."

"I'm not most people. Aren't you the one who's been telling me forever that it's not my fault my mom took off, that the wrong thing is easier to do, to get trapped into? It's not her fault she's trapped."

"Good night, Naomi. Love you."

"Think about it, Dad."

"Good night."

Maybe for you, I think.

I lie awake for a long time, thinking of Kevin's injury, of my parents and Jo and Yiayia, Eva and my mom, Curtis and his father, and about how the wrong choice is nearly always the easiest to make. Is that why trying to do right is so exhausting?

Naomi

Nothing, my lord.

Nothing?

Nothing.

Nothing comes from nothing. Speak again.

I can't understand that. I can't understand why Cordelia doesn't just play the game, claim the land her father means for her, and save him from the whole mess he causes himself by disowning her for silence. In fact, as a play, all of *King Lear* makes me anxious. The idea of the Fool really being the wise man in the play and trying to make the King see reason, the significance of the hovel and the storm, Gloucester's blindness, all of it just makes me wish that things could be fixed and all the blunders over with before everything explodes into unsalvageable disaster. It isn't that I don't understand the play; it's that I know it's a relentless tragedy, dominoes set to collapse in a heap, triggered by one touch, setting off another, setting off one more and one more...

I want to stop it, so much so that I can barely face reading the scenes or working through my assignments.

Come on, Naomi. Get a grip. It's a brilliant play; just appreciate the irony, I tell myself.

I don't want to just watch it go by with the feeling that I have to get out of its way, like a train with malfunctioning brakes. I need someone to help me find a way to see some purpose in the catastrophe, some reason why Shakespeare doesn't use all the same characters, all the same symbols and literary devices, but set things straight before what's left is Cordelia limp in her once-noble father's arms.

And suddenly there's Curtis.

"I don't see how this is a tragedy, Ms. Wyatt."

Our English teacher's eyebrows go up. I turn in my wheelchair to see him sitting back, relaxed.

"Talk about that a little, Curtis." Our teacher sounds intrigued.

"I don't think Cordelia was ever supposed to be here long, you know? She's a bit of an out-of-this-world babe. She was this perfect person, all love and no revenge. The way she died wasn't fair, but when she died she must have gone where she fit in. Someone like her would have suffocated with Goneril and Regan for sisters and such a clueless birdbrain for a father. It took everyone else getting killed and going blind and crazy to figure out that she was right and the Fool knew what he was talking about. By then she was in the wild blue yonder and the village of idiots had been set straight. Doesn't sound all that sad to me."

Before I can think too much, second-guess myself, I raise my hand. "Excuse me, but since when is death the only solution to nasty problems? And why is disability always a tragedy? I take that personally."

"So now you're blind, too?"

The sarcastic comment is a thrust javelin from the back of the room. Zach, the quarterback's younger brother is half-lying, half-sitting at his desk, huge feet splayed on either side.

"No, I'm not blind," I shoot back. "But if I were, I think I would eventually figure out how to understand it as a way to take in my world differently—through my other senses. I wouldn't appreciate being told, or having it implied, that I would be living a sorry, deprived life, as some kind of punishment for being clueless, getting it wrong, misreading my daughters. Whatever."

"So being a cripple isn't—"

"Zachary Mitchell! Get your books and meet me in the hall, this instant!" Ms. Wyatt thunders.

"Are you finished?" In a flash, Curtis has gotten up and positioned himself squarely in front of Zach.

"Yeah, nothin' serious, just good ol' healthy curios—"

Curtis

My fist met Zach's jaw.

I had a bad day. Okay, so I rearranged his face. Zach Lawrence could use some rearranging. I consider it a public service! And in a perfect world, everybody would leave me alone about it. Enough already. He opened his yapper, and I closed it for him. Simple. I wasn't looking for somebody to punch, but if he's going to run at the lip and insult someone's life, I'm going to have it in for him. It's not rocket science.

I did a good job of hauling off and pounding him, if I do say so myself. He had a loose tooth by the time I was done. The thing is, I wasn't done very quickly. I think I punched him four times! I remember counting in my head, punctuating the reasons.

The first two punches were for Naomi, who hardly knows I exist, but who doesn't deserve this idiot dissing her. My story being what it is, I know all about bullies and abusers, and how they can rob you of everything. One minute Lawrence is Mr. Harmless in High School, mouthing off, and the next he's pounding his wife. Nothing serious... The third punch was just for me, who has to take care of everything and grow up fast—with no one in my corner but some of my foster families. And the fourth one was just 'cuz I felt like it, so sue me.

That was last Wednesday.

And I'm sitting here now, after being suspended for three days over that shit-head, waiting for my appointment with some counsellor because I have 'anger issues.' No shit, Sherlock.

"Hi, Bodyguard. I had no idea you had it in you. But thanks."

I don't realize it at first, but when I see Naomi coming, I think I feel my back straighten. I smile, big and goofy.

"That wasn't just about me though, was it?" she asks.

"Nope. My dad was like him. Really nasty. He killed my mom and my sisters. I'm a bit pissed."

Naomi opens and closes her mouth, like a door on a faulty hinge.

"Leaves you kinda speechless, doesn't it?"

"Curtis, I'm so sorry," she finally manages. "You told me your sisters died, but I didn't know..."

"It's okay. Most people don't. It makes me blow my gasket sometimes, like you saw, and then I end up sittin' here missing classes 'cuz of anger management counselling. Mostly, they're not too hard on me. I'd say I 'managed' him fine. Maybe he'll learn his lesson and stay out of the slammer."

"Do you ever visit your dad?"

I shake my head. "He sends me long letters. I burn 'em."

Naomi

And there it is again, I think. "What is it with me and letters these days?"

"Pardon?" It isn't until I see Curtis' bewildered expression that I realize I've spoken that out loud.

"Um...Nothing...." I stammer. It isn't fair, after he's defended me, and after he told me so much about his life, but I can't figure out how to share my own struggles with someone I don't know well.

Instead I say, "You know, if you write down some of that anger, it might help. Ms. Wyatt is starting a writing group."

"I'm not writing anything down, and sharing it with strangers!" Curtis almost shoots out of his chair with anger. "The whole school does not need to know I have my own personal friggin' Boogie Man! And you better shut up about it! I shouldn't have told you."

I could slap myself, for suggesting group sharing. "Curtis, I'm a moron for saying that. But you have my word, my mouth is closed. Sit, please."

"Aren't you supposed to be in class?" Curtis grumbles as he sits, giving me a long look.

"My sister's picking me up. I have a riding lesson."

"Riding? What, motorcycles?..."

"No, para-dressage. I mean horses."

Curtis suddenly perks up. "My dad is terrified of horses. If I could learn to ride, I'd feel safer. I've always been scared he'll escape and come looking for me. He'd never look in a farm."

"Do you ride at all?"

Curtis looks sheepish. "I'm scared of horses, like him. I hate that about myself."

I smile. Finally something I can do for him. "I owe you one. Two if you count the stupid writing group idea." I look at him, hard. "Come with me to the stable. We can start next week."

"Why not today? I can skip anger management."

For a split second, I consider it, but then I think of him shooting out of his chair two minutes before.

I half-smile. "No, you can't."

Naomi

"Did you tell Curtis he's not your first class-room bodyguard?"

"Hadn't gotten to that part yet. Thanks, Jo." Beside my sister in the front seat, I roll my eyes.

"What?" From behind us in the car, Curtis sounds eagerly curious for any tidbit of information on my past. Suddenly, I wonder if helping him like this is a mistake. My stomach drops. I shoot Jo a don't-say-too-much look and wait for her to backtrack.

"Ah, it's not much, really. Just, once, someone in elementary school said some cruel stuff about Ny's Math project, and Lynne covered him in grape juice. It was a public service." Jo laughs.

"That's what I said," Curtis is laughing now, too—a nice sound, but short. Rusty. He doesn't do it much, I think.

"So you must be nervous, Curtis, about today." Jo changes the subject.

"I'm shaking," he confesses. "Talking helps."

"So let's talk about Rule Number One for being around horses," I suggest. "No fear."

"Then I might as well pack it in, go home now."

"That's not funny. You can be plenty scared. I was, when I started. And you need some fear, to keep you safe," I clarify. "You just have to push it down, make yourself stronger than the fear. Like how you're scared of your dad, but you don't let it lick you. You function. You do what you gotta do. And remember, horses aren't your dad. You'll learn to love them. You'll connect. Nothing like it, I promise."

I watch Curtis in the first few minutes at the stable, how he's gotten lulled by my routine. Me asking Jo to let us out at the big rolling door so I don't have to deal with the slush and the mud of the parking lot. Me getting into my chair and then setting the brakes so I can push the door open. The startlingly loud call of "Door!" as I do so. I usher Curtis in and warn him about Babs on our left as I wheel away to get changed. I warn him about the transition from the cold, fresh air into the overwhelming odour of animals that don't use litter boxes. Curtis is rooted to the concrete by the door, peering into the darkness of the first stall, watching for Babs.

Now he's more like uprooted, as a blast of hot air powered by a loud snort blows by his ear. He turns and backs into the cold stone wall. The air is coming from a very large brown nose now aimed at Curtis' face, like a rotating gun barrel.

I see the mortification on his face. I know in this moment that Curtis himself is thinking he screams like a girl.

Jo appears out of nowhere. "For God's sake Curtis, shut up!" she hisses, "Toby wouldn't hurt a fly."

"It tried to bite me!"

"No, she didn't. She was just checking you out. Keep your voice down, you'll scare the other horses."

"It was going to bite me." Curtis sounds a little quieter and less sure of himself this time. There's rustling and snorting all around us. "It was attacking me..." he trails off as I wheel around to his other side.

Instead of defending him, I ignore him completely and turn right into the open doorway of the stall.

"Toby, are you okay? Did he frighten you?" I reach up as the horse's head emerges over the single chain across the doorway. I give Toby a hug as the horse puts her head over my shoulder and starts to snuffle at my backpack.

"What do you mean 'is it okay'? Stay away from it!"

"Curtis, relax please. I told you, no fear." I continue scratching Toby's ear, which fills my whole hand, and finally I turn to him.

Curtis grumbles. "I should've never come. Dumb beasts!"

"Horses are very smart, I'll have you know," Jo snaps at him. "And in case you missed it, my sister's doing you a favour bringing you here, and she never gives up on people. Count your blessings, and don't be a baby. Grow up, already!"

Curtis opens and closes his fists. "I will never hit a woman...I will never hit a woman..." he mumbles under his breath.

"What's going on here?" Charlotte hisses.

The barn's owner, in full riding gear suddenly towers angrily over us. "You're spooking the horses!" She's glaring at Curtis, but I speak up.

"I'm sorry, Charlotte. This is Curtis, who I told you about. Toby just surprised him."

"Oh," Charlotte's demeanour instantly changes. "Well, keep it down. Jo, please don't leave him alone and make sure he stays in the lounge during Naomi's lesson."

"What did you tell her about me?" It's Curtis' turn to hiss, as Charlotte walks away.

"Only what I had to, to get you in," I say calmly.

"Like what?"

"Like, horses give you the creeps, but you want to learn to be around them. That you've been raised in foster care because your dad killed—"

"You didn't!"

Oh, shit! Why didn't I just shut it? I bite my lip, hard. "Look, Curtis, I'm sorry. It's hard. I had to...explain you somehow. You're not very..."

"Just say it. You think I'm weird," he hisses.

I look at him straight on. "I used to, yeah, at first."

Curtis' arms clap to his sides—slack and resigned. "You win. I'm a freak. What am I supposed to do?"

I soften instantly. "You're not a freak. You just haven't been around a lot of healthy people, or kind animals. You don't know what to do. But it doesn't have to stay that way. Fresh start?" I ask gently.

Curtis nods slowly. "Fresh start."

"I feel like a pack horse," he confesses, a mass of leather straps hanging from one shoulder, a saddle weighing down one forearm and a plastic stool dangling from his other hand.

"Oh, Curtis, you're not a pack horse," I offer coolly, my reassurance dripping with tease. "Even pack horses don't carry their own tack."

"Naomi, I'll be in for your tack in a sec," Deb lets me know, sticking her head into the tack room.

"Curtis has got it today Deb, thanks."

Deb raises her eyebrows ever so slightly. "Will he be doing the blanket too?"

"No, he's not ready to be that close to Lance." I'm careful to be honest, yet keep my voice easy.

"Okay, let me know," Deb's voice floats back around the corner as she walks away.

"All right, Curtis, you can relax. You're not riding today."

"What do you mean, I'm not riding? Then why did I come here?"

"If you're ever gonna ride Lance, or any other horse, you have to get your head straight first."

Lance stands in cross ties. Deb has just removed the blanket, folded it and hung it in the stall doorway, where I've parked myself. "Oh, my Sir, it was wet out today wasn't it? You had a good roll in the snow, did you? Did you make horse angels?" As I reach up, my horse's head drops so my hand cups his ear and rubs it. "Yuck," I exclaim softly, "There's even snow and dirt behind your ear! Now that takes work." I pick out a clod of dry mud and toss it to the ground. "It's a good thing we have Curtis to help get you cleaned up, isn't it, baby love?"

"Oh yeah, Curtis the lowly servant, that you're trying to prove things to about how cuddly you are with 'Lancey Boo'." Curtis scoffs. "Get real!"

"What are we going to do with him, Lance?" I respond, my voice never leaving the gentle register of horse-directed soothing talk as I turn my head to meet his eyes, my hand never leaving the horse's ear. "Curtis, get over yourself, please." It's almost a hiss. "Part of riding is tacking up your horse. The bigger part is having a connection with him. I talk to Lancelot like this all the time. He needs to know my voice. It keeps us connected and he's learned to respond to just my voice. If he trusts me and feels calm around me without getting all jarred by harshness, sudden moves and noise, he's more likely to do what I need him to do. Horses communicate with each other in lots of ways, and sound is one of them. They've also learned that human voice is part of how we communicate with them. Now, if you are serious, you can help me tack him up for my lesson. Getting Lance clean is a big part of it. And it's only fair. If he is going to carry me around, shouldn't he look his best? Right, sweetie?"

I lean my head against Lance's nose and he nuzzles my hair. "Seriously though, dirt under the girth can cause rubs and cuts, and brushing them is also a massage that gets their blood flowing."

"So open that tack box you brought for us, Curtis, and I'll show you which brushes to use."

Curtis

I can feel just a breath of a chance beginning. A chance not to shrink from my chances, to stop hating myself and the criminal my father's DNA might still morph me into, if I dare relax.

Just for today, I'm determined be *here*. Just for today, I won't think about it, won't care, won't flee from a world of people I might hurt, in spite of myself. I bend toward the plastic stool, which apparently is a 'tack box.' "What are you doing to me?" I grumble to Naomi. "Woman, this box thingy is more complicated than a makeup kit!"

Naomi laughs.

"Her seat is getting better," Jo comments, almost to herself.

"What do you mean, 'her seat'?" I don't want to advertise my utter ignorance of horses, despite knowing full well that it's not news to Naomi or Jo. But if I don't ask questions, I will be a horse-idiot forever, anyway. Might as well rip off the bandage.

For a moment, Jo seems surprised by my voice, as though she's been lost in the world of the glass-fronted upstairs lounge where we sit watching the lesson. I cast a wary glance in Casper's direction. The barn cat leaps from the floor to the back of the couch where I am, a flash of fur missing my face by inches, then perching as if she owns the space.

At Casper's performance, Jo snaps to attention. "Jeez, that stupid cat jumps out of nowhere all the time. Somebody gave that doofus the right name, he is a ghost-cat. He drives me nuts."

I am secretly relieved that Jo's not about to treat this spooky animal to more cooing and strange praise. I give conversation another shot. "What's this about Ny's seat?"

"It means her balance is better, more secure on Lance's back. Sitting on a horse is a lot like riding a bike, the way you keep your balance, and if you go over too far on the horse, lose your centre, that's part of how falls happen. The trick is to learn to hold balance while the horse is moving. It's called 'dynamic balance,' a balance that's always ready for change, always nuanced and responding to the horse. Staying loose is important when you're riding. Get stiff and you lose shock absorption in your joints. Horses read your tension, and when there's no relaxed 'give' in the body, it's harder to carry you. If you're stiff, you're more likely to get dumped, go for a dive. You know."

I nod. I do know. It sounds like my life story.

"She makes it look friggin' easy."

"She does that. It takes practice."

A surprisingly comfortable silence settles over us as we watch Naomi and Lancelot move around the ring. They aren't just staying on the path along the wall. They move in circles and they ride down the middle. They stop and start and change speeds. Naomi doesn't say much and always keeps her eyes looking where she and her horse are going with a look of fierce concentration. Sometimes she nods and occasionally grimaces in apparent frustration, but more often there are big smiles and quick pats for Lancelot. She's just pulled the horse up to confer with Deb, her coach, who's walked into the centre of the arena. Apparently all of this has just been a warm-up.

The whole atmosphere right now is calming, friendly, gentle. I remind myself I'm only watching, not yet riding, yet I'm impressed with the easy feeling suddenly in my gut, an almost totally foreign sensation that's swept me up unawares, especially in the vicinity of horses. That's why Jo's next words are as unexpected as a gunshot in a quiet forest.

"You're not the only one, you know," Jo tells me carefully. "With stuff you don't wanna talk about, I mean."

I turn and stare at her, stopping myself just short of expressing my shock out loud. Is she really confiding in *me*?

"It's true. Our mom has OCD. She left the family, and of the two of us, I was the only one who grew up with her. She would go through really functional times. You know, working at a hairdressing salon, cooking, laundry, helping with homework…that stuff. At those times, it was easier to go along with her weird habits, like washing loads and loads of laundry over and over again, making sure each different kind of food never touched each other in the fridge, the cupboards, the stove, or on the table in platters, plates and bowls. Everything had to be super organized, categorized, labelled. When she functioned, I could almost convince myself she was just…I don't know…weird, original. But then she had these times when she was so stuck ritualizing, she couldn't work, could barely move. The only one who saved us then was my dad—he would fill the bank account, make sure we had enough for whatever we—"

"Don't be such a lazy ass!" Jo's sudden exclamation catches me off-guard, but she's staring into the arena now.

"Wha—?" I mutter in confusion.

"Lancelot. For such a good horse, he can be a lazy bum sometimes."

I can hear the coach's muffled shouts through the glass, but can't make out any words. I don't notice any difference, but a look of grim determination has come over Naomi's face when she next turns toward the lounge. She flicks the small whip she's holding at Lance's shoulder and he spurts forward, faster than he had been moving. "There! She's got him back," Jo comments with more than a little pride. "I swear, 'Laze-a-lot' would rather curl up in a corner and watch than have to canter. But Naomi knows how to keep him going."

Chapter Eleven
Connection

Hi Matt:

I know exactly how it feels to be pissed off and sad when people expect you to be happy. While spending time with my mom and sister this past summer, I had a very bittersweet experience. But then again, I expected it to be downright awful, so the fact that I had any fun at all is a bonus. (You should know I'm also a twin, but my twin died very soon after we were born.) I'm not a spooky person, but she's still a big part of me, and if that freaks you out, no offense, but there's the door... (You did say I should tell you about myself, remember?)

I have a complicated little family. Actually, a few years ago I went to Greece and met my complete herd of aunts, uncles and cousins, and now I realize we're not so small. I'm glad to know the people I come

from, it's just, Greece isn't set
up for a tourist in a wheelchair.
Whew, that wasn't so hard. To
tell you, I mean. It's not that
I'm hiding it. It's the opposite,
actually. People kind of expect
me to have all kinds of hang-ups
about my disability, to wish I was
different, to have this hate on for
not being 'normal,' whatever that
means. But I'm not that person.
And I'm not a person who doesn't
tell you for the longest time
and enjoys keeping a secret just
because, over email, she could.
I won't do that. Being disabled
is part of me, part of my life,
part of my story and my body, and
I don't have regrets about that.
I just dread dealing with people
who go into shock over the whole
thing, and start treating me as
if I exist to inspire them, or to
overcome my difference. I cringe
when people act like it's nothing
but something in my way, and I'm
defined by the quality of detour
I create. Did you ever sing that
camp song? "Can't go over it, gotta
get under it. Can't get under it,
gotta get around it...Can't go
around it, gotta get through it!"
When I was younger, we used to
sing that at camp all the time—
Easter Seals camp, where we were
all disabled. And every time the
counsellors sang it with us, it
felt like that was their message:

"Listen up kids, here's what to do
with your big bad disabilities."
And even then, I wanted to ask,
what if you don't go under it, or
over it, or around it, or through
it? What if it's part of you, and
what if that's not a problem?
But I never said that out loud,
then. Now I would though, and I
am. When you met me, my wheelchair
was in Lynne's trunk, and I got a
huge kick out of you liking me, so
I was a little woozy on the thrill
(and two martinis) and it didn't
come up. So now I built up coming
out with it as this big deal, this
deal-breaker. And it is. Not my
disability, your reaction to it. I
don't want to deal with a guy who
has to 'look past' my difference.
Let's just get that clear. Any guy
worth my time has to celebrate it
as part of me. I haven't got time
for anything less. I was putting
off telling you because for as long
as I didn't, I could dream of you
as someone who gets all this. But
if you're not, I need to know now.
If you are that guy, I'm a catch.
Otherwise, I'm busy.
N

Hi Naomi...
WOW, you don't mince words, do
you? That's okay, I'm glad. Now I
know I'll be getting the straight
goods from you. I'm good with that,
considering it doesn't happen

Christina Minaki

often in my life. I already find
you refreshing. Yeah, like I told
you, the Bahamas with my mom was
a disaster, but I had to go. Mom
said her friend Ethel (who names
their kid Ethel, anyway? It sounds
like a thorny bush!) was bringing
her twin boys, so it was time for
us to have mother-son time, too.
She was already making a list of
'quality time activities.' I saw
it in her purse. (Okay, I stole a
fifty one day. She's made of money,
she can take it.) I've applied
to Harvard, and she's offered to
make it all-expenses paid, unless
I piss her off. Turning down the
trip would definitely piss her off.
And I figured any money spent on
my tuition is not being spent on
shoes. So, it was the Bahamas for
me.
My best answer about whether I'm
'that guy' or not is I don't know.
I want to be. My mom wouldn't win
any Parent of the Year awards, but
my dad is awesome, and people are
always saying that I'm like him.
I hope so. I'm hoping to head for
Harvard, so I'm no lazy-ass. And
I've been taking the bus to church
by myself since I was thirteen.
I don't know much about disability—not the way you know it. But
I want to learn, and I like you.
Does that count?
It's your call. If you don't
write back, I'll consider that my

answer, no hard feelings. But I hope I passed.
Matt

Hi Matt:
My dad is awesome, too, so we have that in common. My mom's not exactly too much of a winner, but she's slowly growing on me. (That's a long story, for later.) God is a big part of my life, so kudos to you for hoofing it to church of your own volition for so many years. No kudos for stealing the fifty, though. (Have you been falling asleep during sermons lately, or something?!)
Congratulations on Harvard, that's so cool! I know you're not in yet, but it's a huge deal even to apply. I dream of grad school at Harvard, but one thing at a time. As Rachel Lynde would say, "You appear to be hinged in the middle, but you may turn out all right." Let's keep getting to know each other, and go from there. Friends first, okay?
N

Me again:
I can't keep this to myself, so I'm writing back because I can't tell anyone else yet. My theatre class was supposed to be putting on a production of Dirty Rotten Scoundrels this year. (Have you seen the movie?) But now I hear there's a change in plans and

we're doing another show instead, and no one is saying which one. Last year, our musical was Hair, and I was a hippy. (No nudity in our rendition, sorry...) It was fun, and it worked out fine, but I felt like an afterthought. The decision about how to cast me wasn't made until four days before opening night. I was biting my nails.

I promised myself I'd never go through that again, but I've stuck around. Does that make me a pushover?

Naomi:

You're not the only one who feels a lot like an afterthought. My mom's seeing someone. Of course, I'm the last to know, and I have no say (long story). But I guess I should be grateful because it means she's gonna lay off me for at least a while. And wanting a part in the play doesn't make you bad, even though I know it really goes against your convictions. Not if you love theatre that much. I guess you'd have to, to put up with being an afterthought. Maybe you should drop out? I'm just sayin'...

M

Matt:

Um, no, I'm not dropping out. I love theatre. In most parts of the world, working as a team is so against-the-grain. (I'm aware that there are work groups all over the place, but even then it's usually a team in name only—it really ends up being all about what each person did to gain credit for themselves.) But in the theatre, if everyone doesn't come together and really make it work for the sake of the whole show, nothing works, for anyone. So we do come together, and a lot of us are real friends. I'm not giving that up anytime soon. Also, this theatre program is an actual class, for credit. Not just extra-curricular. You don't sound enthused about your mom's catch. Well, here's hoping he takes you by surprise. Gotta go for now. My turn to watch my baby brother, and he's full of beans.

N.

P.S. I'm feeling marginally better about the theatre thing. Nothing official yet, but rumour has it that we're getting the rights for Annie. It shouldn't be too hard to cast me as a disabled orphan, no?

Dear N:

No, it shouldn't. I'm sure disabled people of all kinds were abandoned all over the place during the Depression. But if things don't go well with the casting, don't put up with it. That's what I have to say.

And speaking of feisty little boys, when I was four I had this superhero fixation. I wore Batman, Superman and Spiderman costumes EVERYWHERE, and it was a BATTLE to get me to wear anything else. My Batman one had this big long zipper in the back that you had to undo to get it off. So one morning, my dad walks into the kitchen and finds me boogeying with my costume on, and he says: "That's a great dance, Matt!"

And I say: "I'm NOT dancing! I have to PEEEEEEE!!!! HELP MEEEEEEE!!!"

Your laugh of the day, Madame...

M

Dear Matt:

You were a hilarious kid!

My turn to give you a laugh...

Kev (after announcing he sorely misses Daddy, but doesn't want a hug from anyone else) "I'm sad."

[Insert majorly conflicted face]

Me: Then give Mr. Penguin a big hug, Kevie. He needs a cuddle. Where he's from, it's very cold.

Kev: (squeezing Mr. Penguin tight) I know!

Me: (seizing a teachable moment) Where do penguins live, baby boy? Do you know?

Kev: [Insert mildly impatient 'I just told you I know' face] In the fwidge.

N

Chapter Twelve
Peace Talks

Naomi

"Kevin! You stop that and get down from there! You're going to go BOOM!"

The urgency in Jo's voice makes me turn away from my computer screen and propel myself into the kitchen. I arrive in time to see my brother cuddled on Jo's lap, sobbing. I head straight for them, lean forward in my chair and stroke his hair. His curls lie as though pasted down, wet and smelly with sweat. I can see the exaggerated rise and fall of his chest as it heaves through tears.

"What happened, Kev Baby Love? Did you hurt yourself?"

Above his head, Jo rolls her eyes. "He was spinning on the kitchen chair again. I caught him just before he fell. Now he's having a meltdown because I cramped his style."

"And because he's shocked and scared and probably dizzy. Welcome to growing up. It's tough stuff."

"You have an answer for everything, don't you?"

"Excuse me?"

"It just doesn't surprise me that you understand tantrums, that's all."

I blink, shocked. "What's that supposed to mean?"

"It means I remember your meltdowns well, dear."

"It doesn't take much to carry me back."

I know I've never been a child of war, in the conventional sense.

Whatever my family's deep issues, whatever the compound fractures between us, I always know I am loved. I've never been in the middle of a war zone. Sure, I've experienced plenty of ignorance, prejudice, stereotyping and misunderstanding on the basis of my disability, but I've never heard a gun or bomb go off, or seen anyone tortured or killed—let alone someone I know and love.

But I do understand chaos intimately well, and how it feels to have the wind taken out of your sails when doctors, therapists and 'authority figures' have so little hope for your life. Hope is such a clincher. I can do so much when I feel it alive and breathing beside me, yet so little seems possible when it's ripped away from me. I never forgot that truth; it's with me every day, and I'm not about to become a wallflower.

When I was little, clouds of dark depression pressed down on me—bursts of anger and inexpressible frustration, the inescapable knowledge that my feelings were 'too big for me.' There was always a foreboding notion that I, personally, had done something very wrong to end up in this 'mess' everyone wanted so badly to fix.

No, I wasn't constantly angry, sad, and in turmoil. In fact, I had many happy times, even in the midst of the mess.

Everyone acknowledged my exceptional language and communication skills that reached far above my chronological age and what was often described as 'profound intelligence.' But those gifts had also backfired on me, at the time and in the present, because I was often judged for not simply stopping my outbursts and discussing my feelings with the amazing maturity I had at my disposal even as a child. (At the time, telling me to "just stop" was the equivalent of telling an anorexic teenager to "just eat.") I knew that my outbursts were causing tension, yet there was little I could do. I tried to 'simply' stop. In fact, following an outburst, I would look at the wreckage of hurt around me and swear I would never lose it again. But it never worked, anymore than it would work to try to reason with a tsunami. So my credibility was damaged, because however much I yearned to keep my word, my massive hurt and anxiety would be triggered, would surge, and would make a liar out of me, time after time. These episodes were like huge waves that passed through, caused havoc, and then receded.

Of course, my relationship with Joanna is one of the ones that has been hurt the most by this. I know that. How can that not be true when we were separated while so young, and left to assume things, only knowing bits and pieces about each other?

And, of course, Jo will remember the explosions she saw and heard before Irene took her away. That isn't a surprise. But to use my past against me, out of the blue, because I understand my brother's tears?

"That's not fair, Jo."

I watch Kev scoot off Jo's lap. "I'm sorry, Naomi. I have to be honest. I'm still mad at you. If you hadn't been such a tantrummer then, maybe Mom wouldn't have decided to leave. You were so mature when you were small. Like a little lawyer...How does a kid that mature cry instead of talk? I think you drove her away, with all your meltdowns."

"I couldn't..." I want to flee—to take off and put the whole thing to bed. This confrontation, Dr. Morrison, my worries about theatre class, memories of my family splitting apart, my concerns and doubts about Matt. But I know that fleeing runs in the family. I don't want to be that person.

"Look at the mess we're all in because we left," Jo continues, running over my words as if I haven't spoken.

"That's not my fault. It wasn't then, and it's not now. And I thought you were on my side about this."

Jo steps around Kevin as she crosses from the living room into the kitchen, begins emptying the counter of dishes and filling the dishwasher.

"Don't walk away from me. That's not fair, either." I begin to make my way over to the sink.

"I am on your side. It's just..."

"What?" I ask, leaning forward to put my brakes on so that my chair won't move while Kevin fiddles with it underneath me.

"Well, you're not a kid anymore, and you and Dad still fight. You still blow up."

"He's up in my business all the time, Jo. What Mom did made you and me adults too early. He just assumes you've got stuff figured out, but that I haven't. He thinks he has to live forever, or else I'm gonna flunk being in charge of my life. You would explode, too. You know, when you haven't been there to watch a fight start, and you walk in as I'm losing it, of course I look like an ungrateful instigator. But when we end up like that, it's because he's put me in a situation where I can't avoid arguing. That's all."

"Is that what happened this morning?"

This morning...This morning...? I let my mind reverse over the day. This morning feels like last year.

"He wants me to do Botox treatments now, big needles of toxic bacteria into my spastic muscles, so the stuff can put them out of commission for six months and we can use the time to retrain without spasticity. And after six months, we have to do it all again. Oh, and I have to sign a cute little contract that says I won't sue if I have an allergic reaction, or if the muscles we relax into oblivion decide they like it there and never function again."

"Oh, crap," Jo whispers.

"My point exactly. But Dad thinks this is a viable option."

"What are you gonna do?"

"Not Botox. And Jo?"

"Yeah?"

"I know sometimes our fights are a horror show. And I'm sorry. It's...I'm in trouble if I lose it, but if I don't...if I hold it all in..."

"You'll reach the moment when you can't take anymore, and then you'll erupt and end up covered in lava, like Pompeii."

I nod. "You know, once, when I was about twelve, I had to stay in the hospital for a week, and Dad made sure I had Dr. Morrison's muscle stimulator with me. He left all the nurses with instructions for putting it on specific muscle groups at night. He gave them all the details, except he forgot to tell them that sometimes, unless you use skin tape properly—and even sometimes when you do—the electrodes come off. And if I roll over onto an electrode with battery current still going through it, it hurts enough to make me scream. He should have explained this and maybe demonstrated the problem to a couple of nurses, but he didn't."

"Let me guess. You got in shit for bellowing in the middle of the night?"

"Oh yes, I did. There was one nurse who was super bitchy and yelled at me for sounding like I was in dire straits. I tried to explain how much it hurt, and she 'explained,' at volume, how she didn't very much care. I started to cry, and vowed I would never call out to the nurses' station when that woman was on night shift. And I avoided her during the day, too."

"And?"

"And the next time it happened, she was right in my room, helping someone else go to the bathroom, but I didn't say a word. I whimpered and suffered and managed to find the controls and turn off the current. But by then, I'd peed on the bed. I slept in it, and in the morning she yelled at me for it. But then another nurse yelled at her for yelling at me. Told her she couldn't have it both ways. If she had made it so that I would rather sleep in pee, caused by being jolted awake, than face her wrath, then that was her problem."

"So what happened?"

"The sweet nurse with all the spunk got me into clean clothes and told me, while we were in the bathroom, to never let anyone treat me like crap because I have strong opinions, or because I need help that isn't always convenient, or that others don't understand. I never forgot what she said. And the bitchy nurse got fired within six months. I don't know why specifically, but I can guess."

"So can I." Jo dries her hands with a dish towel, appearing thoughtful.

"Naomi? Does Dad make you feel like that?"

"Only sometimes. But I wouldn't be who I am or where I am without him, and I really, really love him, Jo. But I don't let him get away with the really unfair stuff for very long."

"Good."

"That's why we fight. You see my problem."

Jo nods. "Go to bed. You need sleep. I bet you're gonna need to have another row with him tomorrow. Night, Naomi."

"Night. Can you get Baby Love up from underneath my chair so I can move, please?"

"And that reminds me, you gotta go to school in this chair tomorrow. Dad told me to tell you your motorized one has a flat."

I close my bedroom door carefully, and move quietly over to my desk.

My creative writing assignment, still unfinished on my desk, draws me in like a magnet:

Many people seemed to forget that however mature I was, I had still been a child trying to get my head around my disability and difference, which so many framed as only a huge and tragic problem. Attempting to wrestle my identity out of those years, in that atmosphere was not only difficult and complex, but also bewildering and upsetting. My father had often been reassured that I was too young to be grieving. One of the most woeful errors in judgment made by the 'experts' (and there were many such errors) was their conviction that I was too young to understand the 'gravity' of my disabled reality, and therefore couldn't possibly be having emotional reactions to it. Those 'professionals' never realized that their inability and unwillingness to imagine anything other than a sad future for me was creating my emotional upheaval. If the medical establishment thought I would fail, who was I to argue? So instead, I did the only other 'safe' thing I could: I exploded at the people who loved me. My parents were told (and not gently) to take me home and "learn how to control (i.e., subdue) me." They were also told—and warned—that "all disabled people are selfish!"

What little counselling I received felt belittling. No one took me seriously and made me feel heard, convinced me that it wasn't my responsibility to feel guilty.

Reading a page of my paper randomly like this makes me feel disjointed, or rather, double-jointed, the way it is when people realize I can bend my fingers the way so few people can. My reflections make so much sense to me distilled this way. But going against the grain was not popular business; it made me incredibly lonely sometimes. Why hadn't I been able to express my feelings this way before? Why hadn't I fought harder and better to be understood? Why is it easy to hand a reflective personal narrative like this to my creative writing teacher, but impossible to show it to my father? Yet I know why. The fear of being judged by him, of him using my story against me, as he often does when we're fighting, is like Botox for my courage: a paralytic.

"Write about some formative experiences of your childhood. And don't make it easy on yourself. Put yourself out there. Don't tell me about the time ice cream landed on your favourite dress when you were five, unless that somehow affected the trajectory of your life."

I wince as a car-wreck of a memory slams into me...

"Did you have fun complaining about your life today?"

The question had cracked like thunder on my ears, in the fall of the year I was eleven. It filled me with the electricity of shock. The words felt like something Irene would have said. To hear them from Sydney, one of my father's colleagues and good friends, had broadsided me. I can remember looking around me in Sydney's car, half expecting to see Irene in the backseat.

"I don't complain about my life at counselling."

"No, I forgot. You only complain during tantrums. You know, the way you pitch fits, I don't blame your mom for leaving."

That was the moment I swore I would never go back to counselling, if that was what people were assuming I was doing in my sessions.

Even now as a young adult, I find I have anger, resentments and pain I don't know what to do about. I, who pride myself on being a communicator, find there are times and issues, conflicts and arguments, which turn on great surges of old and new pain, shut down my words, and bring back hurt and tears.

Every once in a while, I think seriously of going back to counselling, trying again with a counsellor I would choose for myself this time, someone who would let me wrestle with my feelings, with the injustice I've faced and the injustice still coming at me—even from my own sister. Maybe that'll make it easier to face Irene, too. But it'll have to be on my own terms. I wonder if I can find a disabled counsellor. But would it follow that just because we would have a disability in common, it'll be the right fit? I hate the way so many people often assume that disabled people connect magically, just because our disability is common ground. No two experiences of even a shared disability are, in fact, identical, and no two people react to even an identical circumstance the same way.

There is something more than vaguely oppressive about the whole thing, like as soon as there is a disability, the right to choose—a counsellor, a support system, whatever—vanishes.

I take a deep breath and keep reading my essay, fighting down the insecurity that it's awful, all wrong, too much of a risk, and too much exposure.

My teenage years were tumultuous. (Imagine puberty and teenage body image developing alongside doctors who saw my body as 'wrong,' 'broken' and in need of 'repair.') Imagine a foreboding forecast where many of my doctors and other medical professionals assumed that puberty would be the time my body would lose physical abilities I had worked extremely hard to gain—like the ability to stand and bear my own body weight.

Worst of all, adolescence is usually a time when teens begin to separate themselves from parents and family and start the task of figuring out the world on their own. 'It's a time of independence' is a popular refrain in Western culture; young people are supposed to strike out on their own. Ironically, at a time when young people are 'finding themselves' (which can be at once invigorating, infuriating, bewildering and intoxicating), more than ever they need an established network of loving support and advice. But society tells them at every turn they should be leaving that network behind at the stage they've reached, and building a new one independently.

Nowhere do these unquestioned contradictions abound more than in the lives of disabled teens and young adults. Low expectations are a huge problem faced by disabled people. Society expects very little of us. When, at the age of eighteen, we are unceremoniously pushed out of the mainstream institutions that have coddled us, belittled us and reinforced the mentality of disability as nothing more or other than pure problem of limitation and lack, we face a 'real world' for which few truly prepared us. It is assumed either that we will do very little for and with ourselves, or else we feel pressure to singlehandedly climb every ladder and scale every wall to change the world. The gap that exists is enormous. From the point of adolescence, we are left virtually alone to take on the world, and underachievement can rapidly become a self-fulfilling prophecy. Why are we not better prepared and equipped? Why is the widely-held assumption that we must do it alone or not at all?

I was never asked by physios or OTs whether I was feeling accomplished, happy, or fulfilled in my life. The question was always: "Are you living alone yet?" "Do you still need help putting on your socks?" Why is exclusion and isolation idealized as the ultimate goal for disabled people, under the guise of independence? Why is interdependence not valued? The truth, after all, is that we are all interdependent. We all need each other. Independence is a fallacy to which society foolishly clings...

Here's a newsflash: We are ALL interdependent, and the more we fool ourselves that we are not, that we can do it all on our own, the more we hurt ourselves. Self-sufficiency is a myth and a trap. The more we fall for it, the more danger we face. Think of this: When is the last time an executive (or most of the rest of us) hunted and slaughtered her/his own meat, built a fire to cook dinner, chased down and sheared her/his own sheep to make clothes, beat his/her own laundry clean down by the river, or rode a horse to work? We rely on countless modern conveniences that we take for granted—the butcher, the grocery store, the mall, the washing machine, the car, the stove/microwave. Many parents have housekeepers and nannies, or daycare workers and a handy list of after-hours babysitters. But those are 'acceptable', mainstream dependencies, about which many of us have the luxury to barely think twice. Just because a disabled person relies on a different, and/or bigger team does not make him/her inferior, pitiful, or incapable.

"Naomi Demas, you open this door RIGHT NOW!!"

I scan my desk and cover my unfinished essay with the biggest book I can find.

"Coming, Dad."

"Right NOW, Naomi."

The minute the door is open a crack, my father edges himself inside and closes it.

"What is it, Dad?"

"Do you know what your sister is doing right now?"

"Jo?"

My father rolls his eyes. "No, Mary. Of course Jo. Who do you think?"

"What is with everyone right now? Okay, fine, what's she doing?"

"She's downstairs on the phone with Lynne, complaining about how ridiculous my Botox suggestion is, and what I'm doing to you."

"Good for her."

"Don't talk to me that way!"

"Dad, calm down. I didn't mean it the way it came out. It's just, sorry, but your plan is ridiculous."

I watch Dad begin to pace. "You know," he mutters, "Dr. Morrison is right. You do have a mouth!"

"That's a low blow. Especially after you saw her treat me that way. You can't tell me you think she's right?"

"I think your mouth got us kicked out, and now we're managing your disability alone. You made it so we have nowhere to go to solve this, Naomi. And when I grasp at the Botox solution that could possibly help you, you complain to your sister, like I've done something awful, and now she's tattling to your friend. In case you hadn't noticed, I like to keep things in this family pri—"

"Oh, yeah, Dad, you love your privacy, don't you? It doesn't matter to you that all these precious secrets and all this pain is eating you and me—all of us—up. It doesn't matter to you that I'm frustrated enough to feel like a shaken Coke bottle, ready to explode, as long as it's all in the family! Well, Lynne is part of the family I chose, and I've had few choices!"

"Oh, and I've had so many, have I?"

"I never said you did!" I yell. "But you've had more than me! I never asked for how hard things are!"

"See? There you are! I've always searched for ways to help. That's how I am. I can't turn it off, I'm still trying to find ways, to find treatments to fix what's hard, and you—"

"STOP!! STOP RIGHT THERE!!!!" Angry tears stream down my face. "You don't get it! You're trying to fix the wrong thing! THIS," I gasp, pounding my wheelchair's armrest for emphasis, "is not my problem! I'm not in pain because of this! You don't need to grasp for solutions anymore, as if my disability is a problem. As if I'M a problem. That's my pain, right there!"

My father looks hurt. "We're on the same team, Naomi. I've been beside you the whole time. Don't be insensitive about this."

"No, I'm not insensitive, not at all! What I am is proud of my brain and the funky way it's wired. I'm proud of where I am and how I have sweated to get here, of how I have to sweat, all the time. I'm proud of the work it takes, and that I prove we can't do life alone. I'm proud that other than God himself, I'm the expert on me. Not the doctors who guess, and judge or dismiss, and scratch their heads, and think I'd rather go through any lists of treatments, rather than be me. I'm proud that I know I'm enough, as I am. I'm happy as myself, and I know what I want. I'm not interested in turning myself inside out anymore. I want to go on, Dad, and build my life. I want to be a career woman, a mover and a changer, without believing there is something wrong and backward and inconvenient about me. What all those doctors want to change so damn badly is part of me, as I am. If they want to change something useful, they should change the way they don't take that in."

"Working for independence the way Dr. Morrison wants you to isn't all bad. It'll mean you won't need caregivers. Won't that be kind of cool?"

"You still don't get it, Dad."

"I'm trying." He stands there, looking at me meaningfully.

Here's the deal with the caregiver thing. It's not that I don't know I need help, that I need someone in the role of an assistant sometimes. But it's the way the word is used that makes me so upset. It's as if the word 'caregiver' attached to me, to my disability, automatically brings down my value. It's like I'm a dilapidated house on an otherwise high-quality street, like I do nothing but receive, contribute nothing but need to the world.

I wrestle down my frustration, and try to wrack my brain about what might really be going on with Dad. Is it another argument with Kelly over Kev? A problem with work? Worries about Mom?

Or is it what it sounds and feels like—frustrations with me? I try another tack.

"I always remember what you say about what I'm worth, how I should never forget my value, Dad. I know you don't mean to hurt me, but sometimes you really do. This is one of those times."

He looks at me searchingly. "I don't want to turn into a drill sergeant, Naomi. Watching you struggle is hard, and sometimes being tough is my only protection when your struggle hurts me. The Botox suggestion is just me being a fixer. You're one too you know, in a different way."

That night I lie awake long after he leaves, pulling together threads of poetry:

We slice impossibility through the middle
and clear a path for me
you can hear me running
and the power of my stride in your dreams keeps
you awake at night.
You wake and crash
I wake and kiss the day.

I've been to dark places
clawed my way along cold walls
thrashed through churning of shallow sleep
and found a way out through the roof
climbing toward the sun.

To you, right angles are failure
straight upward lines success
I know how you measure time
how you define
the scales of justice
I know you think we have failed

154

and that's so wrong.
Still waters run deep.

We fight again
and I feel the ground split as you float
away.
You are a dot.
I want to reach you, but
my outstretched hands thrash only air
we speak hot arrows and cry
in foreign tongues

I fell in love with life and learned
to reach out
I feed my heart
while you've said
I waste time
and need to work on
straight upward
lines.
We are parallel lines
and I wonder how so close together
we grew so
far.

Pain is an unpredictable artist
who does strange work on love
your love is duty
mine is softer than have to
I'm angry and I love you and Father forgive him he
knows not what he does

words run deep together

you think I want you to forget
difference
when you look at me
but i want you to remember
to bless what made me
come out strong.

I don't cast distinction as problem
it makes me rich
and how I wish
you could grasp
that I've taken down walls
built love instead

when I travel deep
that's where I go
to the kingdom of growth and giving
that came to be
because you challenge me
to bless and still change
your legacy

I watch you sleep
the way you did when I was small
the pillow has signed
your face
with the red pen of imprint.
You are a folded statue
and your sculptor has come to visit
reshaped the tense lines of waking hours

with the vacation of dreams.
I push guilt away and make a deal with God
that He may cast me on the stage of your slumber
long enough to say thank you
and tell you I am happy
and will be so long after your sounds of my running
have faded
into day

Chapter Thirteen
Collision

Naomi

Kev: "I want juice!"

Dad: "We only have water, love."

Kev: "I want juice! Water's boring!!"

Dad: "That's okay, if you don't want your water, you'll be thirsty today at daycare because that's all we have, buddy."

Kev changes his tune: "Water, please."

"That's better."

He plays hard ball, Dad does. Kev might as well find out now.

From my motorized wheelchair, it's easy to take stability for granted, to assume that my chair will stay where I put it. One morning in my manual chair, and all of that ease vaporizes. Darn flat tire, I grumble inwardly. Transferring in the school bathroom is always precarious this way. The support bar on the wall is at the perfect height to be useful when I'm in my motorized chair, which has a higher seat. But my manual chair is lower, which means the bar is too high to use with confidence. I manage, but I leave the bathroom thinking of how wrong it is to put support bars in bathrooms without consulting the people who need them about what works or doesn't. One size does not fit all.

Getting through the school is another issue—the long hallways that usually speed by are drudgery whenever there isn't a friend around to take over. Every uphill slant suddenly registers in my shoulders. The only upside to forgetting basically everything at home this morning is the lack of weight on the back of my chair. And here, at the top of the steep slanted aisles in the auditorium where my theatre classes are held and where the final production will be, is the first spot I can stop to rest. Class is starting. We'll be doing vocal warm ups soon, and I'll be able to relax my shoulders, forget about the argument at home, and focus on my voice.

I close my eyes and breathe deeply, counting backwards from one hundred.

"You look relaxed. Not like someone who was all tied up in knots last night."

I open my eyes to find my father holding my bag. "Oh! Thanks for bringing that, Dad. I didn't wanna call about it, nothing's due today, so it wasn't really an emergency. But it's nice to have my stuff."

"You're welcome. Your laptop is in the backpack." He hooks the bag onto the wheelchair handles, and is gone.

I think about turning around to go after him. Eva is at the bottom of her aisle, by the risers. If I call out to her and get a lift out to the hall, we can probably catch him. Then I can ask Eva to leave us alone and I can try to set things right. He seemed so hurt, walking away.

It'll be easy, I think, beginning to wave at Eva below. Our eyes meet.

"'Scuse me."

It happens so fast, I don't even see who squeezed past me in the aisle. One minute, I'm parked on the flat section of ground before the slant in the aisle begins, and the next, the person edging past me has pushed me too far, over the edge, onto the huge slope.

Momentum takes over. There's no way to stop it.

I'm moving, at breakneck speed, toward the bottom of the aisle, toward the huge black risers against the stage that will rearrange my face, my teeth. My life. I realize with horror that my only buffer is Eva.

Eva locks her knees.

The momentum of my crash into Eva at the bottom of the aisle sends her flying into the risers. The image of Eva on her back, a stunned upended turtle, is the last one I see before the sobs engulf me.

Amita Kamta was a fellow hippy in last year's production of *Hair*. She's beautiful in a green-eyed, dimpled, exotic sort of way that makes a lot of guys want to put their girlfriends in saris—not unlike girls wanting to put their guys in uniforms.

Without saying a word, she takes over when I become incoherent. I'm not sure how she gets to me, or even where she'd been in the auditorium before, but suddenly Amita is there, hugging me close and tight while the shock sets in and I begin to shake. Suddenly there's a second Naomi-self hovering over the scene, so that I can see myself from above, as though perched high on the auditorium wall as the lava of hot tears spills over.

In the girls' bathroom, Amita helps me lean into the sink and wet my face with cold water. The cold splashes revive me and bring out fresh sobs.

"I didn't mean...I didn't...Oh my God!"

"Nobody thinks you meant it," Amita says gently. "It was a freak accident. And Eva loves you. She chose not to get out of the way. None of this is your fault."

My face feels raw and bloated. Can I ever even hope to explain to Amita how guilt feels like my birthright—how it seems my father is mad at me for trying to make my own choices, how Jo seems to remember only outbursts, how my family history seems to cast my disability as a villain, as some kind of bad karma.

"Love puts others first, even when it hurts. That's what Eva did. She loves you," Amita continues.

She makes it sound so simple. But my stomach still hurts at the idea of the bruises already flickering on Eva's body and the bump on her head, blooming like morbid Christmas lights. And I hurt, too, because I know something more about how Jo is feeling, how it must have seemed, so often in her life with Irene, that she was alone. That Dad and Yiayia have chosen me and not Jo—had chosen to get in front of the risers in my life, but let Jo crash.

It isn't true. Dad had set up a bank account for the two of them that always had money in it. He and Yiayia have been a part of their lives in every other way they were allowed to be. They wedge themselves into whatever space Irene and Jo will let them have in their lives while Irene tries to hide her illness and the reasons for its hold, and Jo lets her do it.

But, I figure, to Jo it doesn't matter how hard we had tried, and are trying. The reality is she was the one under Irene's roof, handling the day-to-day life with her.

"Thanks Amita." My voice is suddenly a whisper as the bathroom door swings open. Amita's cousin Nazrene, also in theatre, pokes her head in quickly. "Naomi, you okay?" she asks, but doesn't wait for an answer. "You guys better get back in there. Final decision's been made, they just announced it. The show this year's *West Side Story*."

The week goes by in a trickle, but preparing for my audition keeps me focused. By day there is plenty of guilt, and in my dreams there are flashbacks of the auditorium collision, but Eva keeps assuring me she'll live.

"Just rock the audition for me, okay?"

Finally, the day comes.

"Miss Jordan, I really feel that Anybody's is the perfect role for me to adapt in the show. You've told us that *West Side* is all about racial tensions, misunderstandings, hatred, prejudice. It would make sense for a disabled character of those times to feel her own anger and want to express it from within the Jets."

The director leans back, exchanging a brief, nearly imperceptible glance with Mr. Albanese, the dance teacher. Giving me a tight smile, she nods. "We note your point. Let's see your audition, and we'll discuss."

Amita, acting opposite me as Riff, takes all the anger I channel into Anybody's role. I shove. I shout. I pump my fist. And when it's time to lunge for Riff, I grab Amita by the neck of her t-shirt and yank, until we are nose to nose.

At the end of the audition, I'm out of breath, and Amita herself looks floored.

Jordan and Albanese straighten after having their heads bent close in whispered consultation.

"Thank you, Amita," Ms. Jordan smiles warmly. "Since this is Naomi's audition, you can go now while we speak to Naomi alone, please."

"Catch you after, Ny," Amita says, with a wink that means 'you've got that in the bag,' and she walks off-stage.

When she's gone, Ms. Jordan speaks first. "Please come into the auditorium from the other side, and meet us down here, in the audience. We'll see you in a moment."

"No problem." I drive my motorized chair quickly, still riding the high of that moment, still feeling Anybody's power coursing through me.

Maybe this is why Eva gets drunk—for this buzz, this rush. But theatre is better. Theatre is a rush you earn.

"Congratulations, Naomi, on a job well done. A very powerful audition. You're very talented."

"Thank you." There's a 'but' coming, I think, scanning face to face. Albanese takes over suddenly. "We...just don't think we can cast you this year."

"Why?" It comes out as a whisper.

"It's nothing personal," Jordan jumps into the relay race. "We like you. You were a great hippy last year, and—"

"What's different this year?" I skip any reference to 'all due respect.'

"Last year, casting you as a hippie was easy. Lots of hippies had war injuries. But *West Side Story* takes place in New York of the '50s. A gang member in a wheelchair? Naomi, really—"

"She's not a gang member," I shoot back. "She wants to be one. And her anger is a perfect reflection of all the prejudice around her in New York. This can really work."

"We'll be the judge of that."

"It'll be no different than colour-blind casting." I spit out the term, hating it, as if race was a blemish whose best hope lies in being ignored. But the spirit of the term is what I need to invoke here—that if the role of Tevye, for instance, in a production of *Fiddler on the Roof* is best played by a black guy, they have no right to withhold the role from him and discriminate.

"Naomi, the decision is final. And we would have thought, after your freak accident..."

I'm speechless. So they're going to hide behind a one-time fiasco that never would've happened if I hadn't been stuck—for one rare day—in a light-weight wheelchair I hardly use at school...How about insisting that I always come to theatre classes and productions in my motorized wheelchair? How about finding another way?

Fat chance, apparently.

"We hope you'll still be part of the SickKids Telethon with us, though. And we hope you understand."

I feel electrocuted, operating on adrenalin. I remember the utter humiliation of being an afterthought in my grade school *Sound of Music* production. No way will I let history repeat itself here. "I understand completely, when I'm being frozen out of the production, and used for charity, both at once. I understand when high school has become something to live through—with my head down against the wind. I'll be dropping this class today. I hope you understand, and are satisfied."

They act as innocent as doves, but I'm not fooled. I want to tell them that those 'innocent decisions'—every building with no elevator or accessible bathroom or ramp, every classroom or pool or mall or hotel with barriers to me is like a silent slap, an eraser, a barricade meant to exclude me, or pretend I was never there. "Oh, so sorry. We weren't trying to keep you out. We just never thought you would expect or want to come, or stay. But you can come. We never said you couldn't. Just let us know when you're ready to handle the stairs and the bathroom and the pool and the mall exactly as they are. They were built for normal people, and majority wins. Oops! So sorry."

I storm off at full speed, feeling my chair's power under me working to replace what has just been sapped out of me.

Chapter Fourteen
A Lot on the Line

Naomi

My dreams of Mary return that night. I roll into bed exhausted from the day, and thinking I would either fall deep into dreamless, heavy sleep or have nightmares. I don't see the dream as much as feel and hear it. A laugh, like a church bell. The next night it is a musical note, a rich strong singing voice holding that note as though for years. Though I see no face, hear no words, receive no instructions, I know.

My twin has my attention.

"Do you guys ever dream of Mary?" I work to make my voice sound light, breezy and nonchalant. Just an everyday question anyone would ask, between bites of banana at Sunday breakfast.

"No." Jo's denial is quick, short and sharp. "She's your twin, not mine."

I gulp down my hurt, thinking of how my sister can swing around like a bat—and with the same drastic, painful wallop. Just yesterday, she had been defending me. Now she smacks me over the head.

"I do, sometimes," our father says gently. "Eat up. We're late."

Like most of my life, church is a complicated space for me. I love the peace of it, the feeling that there's a place where I can sit without anything else to do except be with God. Nothing else expected. Except when it comes to me, there's always so much more on the line. After all, isn't that true, for me, everywhere?

As the toe of my shoe catches again on the stairs up to the pews, I gulp back the lump in my throat. I shift my weight carefully and strive to yank my foot up and over the lip of the stair. I feel Dad's arm tighten around me, and I'm determined not to look at him. I know what I'll see if I do. Disappointment. Frustration. Anxiety at the real or imagined staring around us.

It doesn't matter how hard I try, how much physical training I work to incorporate, it's always the same. My physical differences—I refuse to call them flaws, even if *he* does—are always here. Dad catches them, like fish. Someone needs to tell him about Heisenberg's Uncertainty Principle: that in the act of observing, the observer immediately, unconsciously, changes the behaviour and action of the one observed.

So many times, so often on these very stairs, I realize there's a third twin in my life. This one is not dead at all, but instead she's a shadow living with my father always. My father sees this strange other girl, this mirror image, all the time when he looks at me…She's the twin I would have been. The one who moves fast, stands tall, has smooth moves and no spasms. She has clean lines—no twists and pulls, no choppiness. No spills, no complications. And she's always here. She's Karen Kain to my Tin Man.

But Karen Kain has bunions and back problems and she's written so well about the National Ballet and its warts, all the stress and strain that goes into the erasure of effort on the ballet stage, the illusion of smooth. It's all a beautiful mask.

And I've always thought of Tin Man not as rusty, but as—"Hurry up!" Dad says in a sharp undertone. "You move like molasses!"

"Yeah, well, modern dance takes time."

Finally in my seat, I scan the pews, looking for Eva, hoping my eyes will catch that bag—bulging, lipstick-red, no doubt holding its clandestine receptacles of alcohol.

My father squeezes my hand, not reassuringly. "Focus," he whispers, mid-hymn.

"Eva's late," I whisper back. Dad's eyebrows shoot up. "You invited her here?"

I ignore him and go back resolutely to singing. *Create in me a clean heart, oh God. Renew a right spirit within me.* I half-sing, half-pray.

God, you are God because You survive Your believers. Please, dear God, don't let her show up drunk.

His answer comes right away, jolting me. If she does, will you love her less?

Oh, sweet Jesus, no.

Except, yes.

I feel her first, and I turn as she sways from pew to pew, holding on to each edge as she comes forward. The cracking ice of harsh whispers follows her.

Eva grabs the side of my chair. "Sorry I'm late. I woke up dizzy." She slouches into the pew. "I ache all over."

What dear Lord, am I going to do now? I continue praying, but for what? For instant sobriety? For a live, immediate AA intervention? For wisdom?

For a hole in the floor?

"I'm glad you're here." Jo puts a firm arm around Eva. "Just listen. We'll talk after."

Thank heaven for small mercies, that first, Eva is a happy drunk this morning. Second, I have lots of experience being one of the last to leave crowded rooms in my wheelchair. And third, the whispers stop as quickly as they started, as though someone has turned off a faucet with a quick, definite twist.

Back at home, Yiayia stands in my bedroom doorway.

"What's wrong, Yiayia?"

Katina is flushed with worry. "It's Eva. She had an accident. She broke her leg."

Oh, God. Help.

All I can think of, as Yiayia drives is, this could work. If I can warn the nurses about Eva's mother and her uncanny ability to smuggle alcohol into anywhere...This can work...

Chapter Fifteen
Thin Ice

Naomi

The Emergency nurses' station is a beehive of uniforms coming and going, snippets of chatter, medical charts and clipboards being snapped open and shut, hospital wheelchairs and rolling beds being pushed by.

I shift in my own wheelchair, to the most poised, ready-for-battle position possible, infinitely glad I've had the presence of mind to transfer to my motorized wheelchair before dashing out. Something about being pushed by my grandmother does not exude 'woman-in-charge.' Even as I weave into the crowd, coaxing my wheelchair around obstacles and away from ankles, I mentally swat myself for playing the game. Why, after all, shouldn't I be taken seriously with an aging grandmother in tow? As a duo, will we always be a target for ableism and ageism?

As we first arrive, I catch our reflection in a security mirror. Yiayia Katina so proud, claiming every last advantage from her high heels and tailored suit.

It's easy to forget how old Yiayia is, with all the effort she puts into her appearance. It's the way she moves too, as though she's tilted into motion and always in a hurry to get somewhere.

The halls of the Emergency ward are lined with wheel-chairs and cots, the people occupying them somehow shrunken by the onslaught of illness or injury. I watch a young woman wincing in pain as she adjusts herself on a cot, and a man of at least eighty regarding his I.V. drip with something close to contempt as it pierces his onion-paper skin.

I smile at him. "Have you been waiting long?"

He rolls his eyes and laughs. "Not in comparison to the Canadian Shield, love. It's all a matter of perspective. My son is off yelling at someone about making me wait five hours for a bed, but what I really want is the tubes and needles gone."

I'm not sure what to say to that. Promising it will happen soon doesn't seem like my business, so I only nod, reassuringly.

Yiayia is making tsk-ing noises of disapproval, whether at the state of health and fashion disarray before her, or at my pause in progress toward the Information desk, I'm not sure and don't ask.

"I'm going to Greece," she mutters suddenly under her breath.

Ah, it's nostalgia then. Whenever Katina is reminded of her age, the fragility of life, and of time flowing past, she begins wanting Greece and her sister. And while in Greece, she soon wants nothing more than to touch down in Canada. Alas, the lot of the immigrant as Solomon's baby.

"You should go, Yiayia," I say carefully, as though testing the temperature of a lake tentatively, toe first.

Katina says nothing.

I don't wait to be asked. "I'm looking for Eva Cavanaugh," I tell the stout nurse who has just hung up the phone. "She's just been brought in. Drunk-driving accident."

The nurse—'Christine' is stitched on her white coat—raises her eyebrows and checks her clipboard. She smiles wide, her white teeth a sharp contrast with her dark skin, and a dimple accenting her left cheek. She confers quietly with another nurse.

The second one approaches me. "Are you family?"

"I'm her sister," I say quickly, keeping the 'not by blood' qualifier to myself, and wishing I was still speaking to Christine. No such luck. Nothing any good ever comes from a nurse named Ethel. But there's a first time for everything. "And this is our grandmother." I look boldly at Ethel, inwardly daring her to disagree.

She smiles a little, but still looks doubtful. "We have record of an Eva Cavanaugh, who has a broken femur. But it's not a drunk-driving accident."

"What kind of accident are we talking about?" Katina all but pounces.

Christine reappears, edging her suspicious colleague out of the way. "Excuse my friend here. She knows when her sister sneezes, and doesn't know how the other half lives. Your Eva's had a skating accident."

173

"But you don't even skate. What were you thinking?"

"No, it doesn't hurt, unless I move it. Thanks for asking," Eva remarks dryly from the bed.

I look away, sure I can feel in my own gut the intrusive ache of the I.V. and catheter tubes snaking out of Eva's body.

"Did you bring Lynne with you?" Eva asks.

"No. I only came with Katina. Why?"

"I can feel Lynne judging me from here, that's why."

"She's worried about you. I am, too. We love you, you know."

Eva says nothing.

"What happened?"

"I was pregnant, Ny." she tells me. "It was just one night, with a guy I had just met. When I found out, I freaked. I was hoping...I tried to...and it worked. I miscarried."

Eva goes on to explain how she felt on the ice, inching along that clear, smooth line between joy and danger, flying and crash. How she had both wanted and dreaded the fall that had cleared her slate. When they had checked and found no heartbeat, Eva had felt both fear and relief for the second time the same day—once in the cold of the ice rink and once with the ultrasound table beneath her and the jelly on her abdomen.

I hold my head in my hands and squeeze my eyes shut, wishing I could do the same with my ears, but knowing I can't afford it. "Who is he?"

"I don't know. I was at a party, and my memory blacked out. Last thing I remember, I was sitting with him, knocking back tequila shots, laughing at some joke of his. After that, I'm missing a whole chunk."

I cringe, imagining the demoralizing feeling of snapping in and out of the scenes and experiences of your own life because you're so drunk, your brain shuts off. I don't want to think of how often this happens to Eva. Once would be bad enough, but if you're drunk all the time...With effort, I shake off the picture in my mind and force myself to keep listening.

"Then what happened?" I ask.

"Then I missed my period. Twice. And the pregnancy test I took was positive. I thought it would be better...I thought...I'm a screw-up, not a mother. I don't want to be like *my* mother. I was sure falling on skates would...get rid of it, and for once in my life, I was right. How d'you like that irony?" She laughs bitterly.

"That baby was supposed to live. You know full well how I feel about dead babies."

"Yeah, I don't know how I could I forget that you know everything. And everything is about you." Eva tries to roll away from me, then winces as the pain strikes her in a searing punch.

"Don't talk to me like that," I warn her, quiet with anger. "I've got you covered, but you have to talk to me, let me in. That's the deal."

Eva sighs so deeply it seems she is emptying herself of everything. Abortion by air, I think bitterly, and wait, refusing to fill the expanse of silence myself.

Finally, the words are little more than a whisper. I understand this much: Eva has no energy for anything more. "There was tequila, and I'd already drunk wine at home." She sobs and groans, dipping in and out of tears as though she has been set loose in a storm-ravaged open ocean. When she can breathe again, the words are hoarse, ripped free at a great cost. "I'll never drink again."

I've heard that before. Hangover remorse. How Eva had drank her last alcoholic drop, how she'll finish the rest of school with top grades, how she'll never embarrass herself or anyone else again. There is always a chasm between the person Eva wants to be—the choices she wants to make—and what ends up happening in actuality. People are always telling me I can't force Eva to do the right thing, to get help she doesn't want. They tell me I give her chances she doesn't seize. But of one thing, I'm sure: alcohol is running, and ruining, my friend's life. It has a hold on her. She won't be able to make a different choice until she detoxes long enough to clear her mind.

I stare at Eva, my own eyes wet. "Don't worry, you won't."

Suddenly, panic seizes Eva afresh. Her eyes grow wide. "Ny, you can't tell the nurses. You can't tell anyone here what I tried to do, what I wished for. They'll put me in the Psych ward. They'll drug me. They'll tie me down, never let me out...Please, Ny. If you love me, like you said..."

My life just keeps getting better. Less complicated by the minute. I wipe away my tears quickly with the back of my hand, knowing my face will remain raw with grief no matter how I cover it.

"Eva, they have to know that you're—"

"That I'm an alcoholic. You can say it."

I hesitate for only a breath, knowing that stumbling over the words will serve no one. Not wanting it to exist changes nothing. How many times, watching me negotiate with my body's weaknesses, has my father yelped "I don't want it to be this way!" It makes me want to rage, whenever this happens. "But it is this way!" I retort. "And it's not all hard. And I'm glad I'm me. I'm glad for everything that makes me myself. And when, at every turn, you make me defend the way things are for me, I have no room to admit when it is hard."

I will not do that to Eva. I will not be afraid of the words. I will not be afraid of the whole story.

"Fine. Yes, you are an alcoholic. They have to know that. It might change the way they handle your leg—the surgery, the painkillers. And they have to know you were pregnant."

"They know all that already. They just don't know I did it on purpose…" The words stick in Eva's throat, and another surge of sobs wracks the two of us.

"Hi girls…"

Katina pauses at the sight of both of us crying. "Ah, the two of you!"

I start at my grandmother's sudden, exasperated tone.

"No tears!" she orders. "You, you'll have surgery, you'll be better soon," she proclaims, as though in prophecy, in Eva's direction. "No reason to make each other cry. So you're hungry and you can't eat until after the operation. So what? You'll live. By tomorrow, they'll fix you."

Eva and I exchange a knowing glance. If only it were that easy. I almost want to laugh.

Well, if I have anything to say about it, Eva and I will not lose. A battle maybe, but not the war. Anyone willing to give up on Eva does not know the woman who saw a wheelchair coming down a huge incline at her, and locked her knees.

Now it's my turn. I face my grandmother. "We're done crying now."

I look meaningfully at Eva, lean over to squeeze my friend's hand, and close my fist around our secret.

"Eva will be in surgery as soon as she can be fit in," Nurse Christine explains patiently. "She's getting transferred up to the Ortho floor within the hour, so that's something. But it all depends on whether or not a more pressing surgery comes into Emerg. She'll be kept as comfortable as possible while she waits."

An image of toxic medications coursing through Eva's bloodstream immediately lodges into my brain.

As if having read my mind, Christine nods seriously. "We've put her on a Fentanyl patch for now. She's going to need a lot of physio after the surgery, and because of her health, recovery's going to be a long road."

I nod and smile in the right places, liking this Christine woman more every time she opens her mouth.

I take a deep breath and hold my gumption close. "I'm scared about her being on Fentanyl," I confess. "She's already an alcoholic. With an addictive drug like Fentanyl in the mix, she'll be in a whole new mess."

I watch Christine's eyes grow wide and realize the nurse doesn't know the truth.

"Eva said she told you, but you didn't know she's an alcoholic, did you?"

On the way home, my mind races, trying to find a new way to reach Eva, a way to help her realize this injury can mean a fresh start. I'm caught again in full-blown solver mode. But I am a solver, I rationalize, as my van bounces along, the metal of the folded ramp squeaking at every bump. I'm built for this. I was born fighting.

It had started because, outside of my father and grandmother, people generally didn't expect me to take on much in life. Self-care and physio were to be the best I could hope to reach. Dr. Morrison has tattooed an inferiority complex onto me, but it had started long before the doctor's arrival. Really, it isn't even something I can blame solely on my mother's and Jo's, or Mary's, absences. My sadness just serves to make an already-present injustice more noticeable.

Maybe there really is no way to help Eva, if she isn't willing to do the hard work of real recovery. And now, Eva's injury means she's in the hands of doctors. If they do their job, she'll have good supports in place before she's discharged. That means I can relax a little about Eva. But what if she pushes all the help away, the way she has so far? What if no one believes in her enough? What if they give up on her?

What if...

In my lap, my fists clench and a braid of spasticity goes up my back. But then, I remind myself, when people expect so little, maybe those low, no-pressure expectations are actually what frees me to be a come-from-behind surprise.

In Grade Eight, the school put on *The Sound of Music*. I had auditioned to be a nun in the choir and had gotten the part.

And then been left out. Totally.

I learned the songs, quicker than everyone else, even, but no one had adapted the choreography even a little, so that I could be part of the chorus from my wheelchair. There had been a ramp up to the stage, but because I couldn't leave the stage quickly for the scenes that only included the leads, Ms. Blake decided it would be distracting for me to stay onstage longer. So I was left on the floor in the corner below the stage for the whole show, to sing alone and apart from all the other voices.

My whole family was in the audience, including Irene and Jo, Yiayia and a whole crew of neighbours watching me do almost nothing but use my boring alto voice to sing the songs in the dark, in my ridiculous nun costume. Stuck in the same spot the whole time, making up bits of dancing myself where I could.

How many times had I wished for Ms. Sherman, my English teacher from the year before. She would never have allowed me to feel left out. She would have made me feel like part of the show, different and proud, but no better or worse than anyone else. She would have made me feel like a piece of the puzzle—a small piece, but a piece just the same. A puzzle with one bit missing still wasn't done, was it? Was it?

But Ms. Sherman had moved to a different school, just before I had been humiliated.

It was like I was in the show without being there at all. And the show had run for four nights. The worst part was, I had to come back three more times. I had wanted to sing so badly, and be part of something big.

"You're not going back," Dad had barked later that first night, back at home when the disgusting show was over. Everyone else had either gone home, or had gone to bed looking sick, but neither me nor my father could even pretend to sleep, so we stayed up and had it out, our argument complete with the sound effects of the dirty dinner dishes being roughed up in the sudsy sink.

"I am, too!" I had shot back, my voice shaking, swollen with ignored tears.

Dad had slammed another pot down and spun away from the sink to face me. His voice was barely a whisper and his mouth hung open. "Why in the world would you want to?"

"I wanna sing, Daddy."

That was all.

After that first night, I had convinced myself something, something would be different for the other three. A teacher would realize I felt forgotten, show me more moves, and find a way for me to really be a part of the group, not in the corner.

But nothing changed.

So I had talked to one of the teachers in charge of the show after the second night.

"No one sees me there in the corner," I began. "I hardly do anything!"

"I'm sorry, Naomi, but the show is the baby," is all Ms. Blake had said.

For hours, I had wondered what that was supposed to mean. The show was just a show, not a baby. People made the show work. Real people. But a little voice had told me exactly what Ms. Blake had meant. It took too much time, work, and imagination to make someone in a wheelchair really part of the cast, especially an everyday, plain alto who was only one of the chorus.

Ms. Blake was more interested in the sopranos and soloists, people who sang the notes that hung crisp and clear in the air and spread over the room like the ring of a church bell. In a way, I could hardly blame her.

But somewhere along the way, I made myself believe that most of the world thought like Ms. Blake, that I ought to stay home and leave the world alone, not expecting anyone to spend any effort on me. As if my participation would be a favour, as if I wasn't part of real life at all.

Maybe that's it. Maybe all this saving Eva from herself, supporting Lynne and trying to figure out my family is a shot at claiming my place in life. If all life's a stage...

But there's something to be said for doing the right thing because it's the right thing. Can I really leave Eva drunk and, having lost a baby (whatever the circumstances) while I play Miss High and Mighty on the right side of the tracks? It's no different than all those surgeons who had wanted to cut me open, snip my tight hamstrings when I was younger, with no notion that it's my spastic muscles giving my body the resistance it needs to move and work against gravity, holding me firm. By instinct, I had hated those doctors, with their cold hands, metal instruments, and doomsday prognoses. By instinct, my father fended them off, even without understanding what I've always known. My body functions like an orchestra, with the conductor settling feuds, modulating rhythm, tempo and pitch. With that fine-tuning going on live inside me, how can I pretend life isn't messy, nuanced and complicated? If I cut Eva loose in a free-fall, what makes me any different from those scalpel-happy surgeons?

That's the thing about spasticity.

There's the lie that says it means a lack of bodily control. But spasticity demands nothing but control. It means a life-long dialogue between muscles and brain—communication with knots, quivers, and jolts, to smooth things out, to plan and prepare next moves, to strategize out of rough spots.

Now I'm trying to prepare the way and smooth the path for Eva. Speaking of transferrable skills…

The verse of Corinthians that makes it all clear floats to the top of my mind:

If I speak with human eloquence and angelic ecstasy but don't love, I'm nothing but the creaking of a rusty gate.

If I speak God's Word with power, revealing all his mysteries and making everything plain as day, and if I have faith that says to a mountain, 'Jump,' and it jumps, but I don't love, I'm nothing.

If I give everything I own to the poor and even go to the stake to be burned as a martyr, but I don't love, I've gotten nowhere.

So, no matter what I say, what I believe, and what I do, I'm bankrupt without love.

"When I was your age, I did everything I could to stay out of trouble. When Theodore and I were married, all we wanted was no trouble. Only peace. That girl doesn't give you any peace."

Yiayia stops talking as she turns onto our street, her Greek trailing off. She doesn't have to continue. I know exactly what she means. She agrees with everyone else, believes I'm wildly trying to save the world by saving Eva and Curtis. And she believes I have no business trying.

Well, I've made sure that nurse Christine knows about Eva's addiction. I've been clear about that. I didn't tell that Eva lost the baby on purpose, but that's the only secret I'm keeping.

And a promise is a promise.

Jo

Naomi's right, church is a place—really, the most important place—where you should be able to come as you are. But to show up swaying drunk in God's house? I just don't know...Isn't that a big signal of what Eva thinks of my sister inviting her? If that doesn't say 'I don't want to be here,' I give up.

I'm a doer. I don't sit around considering things, second-guessing my instincts, dipping myself in the ocean one toe at a time. When I see something I want or need, I move. So I don't understand people who are half in (or less) and half out (or more). Either you recognize an attempt at rescue, and grab the rope, accept it, or you don't. This morning, I think Eva said 'I don't.' But still Naomi is fighting for her, heading straight for heartbreak.

I fought for our mother that way, and if I'm going to be honest, I'm still reeling.

Moving in with Dad after the trip this summer has me so very torn. Here is our family almost entirely back together, and yet, what it took, and how it hurts! And the price is leaving Mom by herself.

I couldn't take it anymore.

I remember I was still dragging the suitcase behind me when Dad laid down his objections.

"Where's your mom right now?" he asked.

"At home." I looked away. "Where can I put this?"

"Well, you've got some choices." He shifted uneasily. "You can share with Naomi until we get things...figured out. Or, you can sleep in my study." His hesitation during the last sentence was scarcely a breath long, as though if he spoke fast, I wouldn't do the math.

"It's okay, Dad. I'll put this in Ny's room for now. We'll figure the rest out later." I headed down the hall.

"Jo?"

"Yes, Dad."

"You can't leave your mom alone like this, permanently. We'll have to discuss this later."

I spun around then. My suitcase crashed to the floor. "No, Dad, let's deal with it now, 'cuz let me tell you, I've been living with Mom for more than ten years. I need a break. I didn't have a choice before. I have one now, and I'm taking it. I'm not going clubbing every night, or getting wasted, or running away, or street racing to get your attention. I just want the rest of my family. That's all, Dad. It's not much. Bring her here. Go ahead. But I'm not going back."

I could tell my honesty had blasted him like a gush of icy rain. Good, I thought. Let him sit with the thought of his daughter trying to get his attention by breaking windows or wrapping her car around a pole.

"I'm sorry, Joanna, that it's been so hard on you."

I shrugged, said nothing and picked up my suitcase.

A big reality check was in order for him. It was long overdue.

In some ways, it still is.

>Dear Naomi:
>I haven't told Dad about the last straw with Mom.
>So…picture this.
>I find her one day, sitting in the living room, alone, with the lights off. I perch on the edge of the chair opposite her. I try to sound calm. "What are you doing, Mom? You can't just sit staring like this."
>"I can do what I want. Where've you been?"
>"Church."
>"You think that's gonna solve everything or something?"
>I take a deep breath, pray for strength. "Not everything," I say, already tired.
>In a heartbeat, she changes the subject.
>"Are you going to write those cheques for me, or not?"
>I cringe, feeling as though I want to fold inward. This had begun a few months before, her asking me to fill out cheques for her that she would shakily sign. Each time I do it, Ny, it's with a queasy dread, as though every bit I take over is something she might never again do herself.
>"Mom, do you have trouble writing them out yourself?"

She stands quickly. "If you won't help, then just go. You never want to help me!"

Some things never change. Her temper, as always, is mercurial. It's a wonder I survived with her for this long.

I know I should have brought her back here with me. I should've insisted. I should've dragged her to the doctor, told him to send her to specialists, told him that I'm afraid that something new is wrong.

But I didn't have the nerve. I only had enough guts to save myself. Does that make me a selfish coward? Don't answer that.

Jo

Chapter Sixteen
Confessions

Curtis

"You are doing great, Curtis. How about you let go of the saddle now?"

"How about I stay on this thing instead?"

"Keep your weight on your sit-bones and move your hands to your thighs. You'll be fine. All you have to do is relax and ride. Laurel will keep Wolfgang at a walk on the lunge line."

Is Naomi nuts? And when the beast goes nuts and dumps me, what's she going to do about it, sit above me and laugh? She's already at least a head taller than me, astride Lancelot who's standing just outside the circle.

Thinking of the height, I look down. Mistake! I grip the front of the saddle tighter.

"Look where your horse is headed. Look between his ears."

That's hard to do when those ears are facing back at me. Wolfgang is peering over his shoulder at his obviously clueless rider, perhaps considering whether I am worthy of occupying his saddle.

"Laurel, keep him on the bit."

Laurel flicks the long whip and Wolfgang swings his head to the front and takes off.

"Nice walk, Laurel, keep him there."

Walking? With the bumping under my butt, I must be going faster than that! I look ahead to see what this beast is going to run through with me on it.

"Okay, Curtis. That's good. Keep your chin up like that. Relax. Relax into the saddle. Laurel has Wolfgang."

Naomi falls silent as Wolfgang takes me around Laurel, and I begin to feel a rhythm in this chaos of sensation.

"That's it, Curtis. Just let yourself flow with the movement. It was on a horse that I first felt a smooth walking motion, without the pressure of trying to produce it myself. If you can just get yourself to relax, it'll start to feel good."

It doesn't feel like walking to me, but I'm not going to open my mouth.

"Let's try taking one hand off the saddle and giving Wolfgang a pat on his neck. He is doing very well."

"Yeah, he is," I mutter.

"You are, too. I know how you feel, you know. Lessons can be intimidating for me, too."

"Yeah, but you get to do this on Lancelot," I point out. "You get to be on your very own animal. No wonder you're all comfy."

Naomi rolls her eyes. "That's because I'm handling your lesson, and I can move better in the sand of the ring on a horse than I can in my chair, smart ass. It took me years to get this confident."

She clears her throat meaningfully. "I know what I'm talking about. Just release one hand, and give him a pat on his neck."

I inch my right hand forward and scratch at the short brown fur with two fingers. I don't dare look at where my hand is going. Because below it is a long way down.

"Come on Curtis, use your whole hand. Keep going."

Steadfastly staring forward into nothing, I feel my hand leave the now sweaty, hard leather of the saddle, and flatten out on the fuzzy warm neck.

"Good stuff! Now, don't think too much. Just lift your hand and reach your arm straight out to the side. Just trust me."

I gulp. I'm really doing it.

"Don't laugh at me."

Naomi covers her mouth, her eyes still twinkling. "Sorry Curtis, it's just, you're walking looks like a diagram in one of my horse books. It's labelled 'Spots That Will Be Sore.'"

"You're hilarious."

"I try. Did you soak with Epsom salts like I told you?"

"No, I forgot and had a bubble bath. Of course I soaked."

"In what, lying potion? You can put it off, but no more horses until you do. And it would be such a shame to waste time when you've made such progress."

"My foster brothers'll never get over it. I may as well soak in bubble bath while listening to opera. You mean to tell me I bussed it all the way here for nothing?"

Naomi shrugs, then thinks for a brief moment. "Not for nothing. I caught Kev climbing up on a chair to undo the lock on the front door this morning. Freaked him right out with the yelling. So he's sulking in the loft, hoping someone will find him and agree about how awful I am. Can't do that part. It undermines my authority. Plus, I'm going to the hospital from here to visit Eva. So, you're hired. Seems like a job you'll enjoy. Do you know how to get to the loft? It takes a bit of doing."

Naomi

With Curtis gone, I refocus my mind on the second scheduled lesson of the day. I'll be working with thirteen year-old Aurillia, who has a head injury because of a major car accident. She's a real daredevil who loves the freedom of riding horses, but considers it her right to work her horse into a lather as she reclaims her pre-accident addiction to adventure. Aurillia always reminds me of the difference between my own disability experience, living with it since birth, as compared to coming to it later in life.

And Aurillia's parents remind me that some parents actually have what it takes.

"She was telling us that she was going to jump today," Mrs. Kustin leans over to murmur in my ear as she appears to be rummaging in her handbag. We are watching Aurillia groom Cleo in the cross-ties.

"Aura, I'm just going to get my water bottle." I call out to my student, and turn my chair toward the tack room.

Aurillia nods without turning from reaching up to Cleo's withers with the curry comb.

"I'll give you a lift," says Mrs. Kustin, as she smoothly falls in behind my chair and grasps the push handles.

When we reach the relative privacy of the tack room, Mrs. Kustin circles around my wheelchair to face me. "You know what I just told you about Aurie being in one of her moods? Keep that between us, please."

I look sincerely into her face. "Of course."

"I just wanted to give you a heads up. She's in her 'I'm gonna jump a unicorn at Spruce Meadows' mood.'" Mrs. K laughs.

I half-laugh myself. The Kustins are so pragmatic about everything that has happened to Aurillia because of the accident, all the ways her injuries have changed her and her life and the things required of the people who love her. I often catch myself wishing I could transplant some of their coping mechanisms to so many of the families I know who are stuck being so sad about having disabilities in their lives.

The Kustins seem to know how to let their daughter grieve what used to be without letting her miss the gift of her new life. Aurillia has always loved risk. But horse-jumping would be something of a death wish for her. Trotting poles with her horse will be the closest she can safely get now. That exercise reminds the horse to be aware of his body and control his feet, and when the poles are laid in tricky patterns, they give Aurillia the satisfying rush of a challenge without letting the rush go dangerously far.

Aurillia hates having enough time for her thoughts, so she keeps herself spinning, out-maneuvering her memories. And Aurillia's parents? Well, they pay me 'the big bucks' to make their daughter think…

"Naomi, Aurillia has Cleo ready." Charlotte's son David shows up in the tack room.

"Have you checked her tack?" I ask him.

"It's fine," comes the unenthusiastic non-answer.

"David, please check it over properly. If I can't trust you to do it, I'll have to do it myself, and it will just keep us all here longer." I use my don't-mess-with-me voice. Am I going to have to get Charlotte to replace David as my assistant? This is a safety issue. And Aurillia is already trying to push boundaries. The last thing she needs is to have a fall because of a loose girth.

"Do it by the book, David." I follow and watch David look at and touch each buckle and strap of the bridle as he makes sure it's secure and fitting properly. I double-check that the bit is riding in Cleo's mouth properly ('two wrinkles of the cheek,' came Charlotte's voice in my head). It's Cleo's bridle, so it's always adjusted for her, but it never hurts to check, especially when David's head doesn't seem to be in the game. He moves to the saddle and feels under the front of it. He's checking for wrinkles in the saddle pad, and the spot where the saddle rests relative to the horse's shoulder. He moves to her rear and eyes the symmetry of the saddle, that it's not canted one way or the other.

Aurillia is not hiding her impatience as she sits in her chair by Cleo's head and holds the reins so Cleo doesn't decide to walk off during this closer-than-usual inspection. 'By the book' means that David has to indicate each thing he's checking by touching it, so that I can tell that he's checked it. When I train someone as my assistant, we talk through it, too, but this is faster. Lately, I've been relying on my own eyes, trusting that both Aurillia and David are being as safety conscious as I've trained them to be. But with David's attitude today and Aurillia's natural thrill addiction, I'm not going to risk it.

He checks the girth, making it obvious that he considers this a needless repetition of something he's already done. It looks fine.

"Okay, David, please warm him up."

David takes the reins from Aurillia and waits for us girls to wheel to the ramp up to the mounting block, and then he leads Cleo to the arena door and slides it open. As he and the horse turn onto the arena to walk around and warm up, I catch a glimpse of the set-up in the area. Where the trotting poles are supposed to be set up on the far quarter line, instead there are two uprights supporting a horizontal pole about a foot off the ground.

"Aurillia," I say her name like a warning. "What did you do?"

"Nothing."

"You're not allowed to jump, Aurillia. It's too dangerous."

She shrugs. "Rules are made to be broken."

I position myself carefully in front of Aurillia, blocking my student's path. "I won't start your lesson today until you're honest about why you want to jump so badly."

Aurillia tosses her head. "My parents pay you to teach me."

"Your parents pay me to keep you safe when you're here."

At the word 'safe', Aurillia bursts into tears. "There's no such thing for me anymore, except on horses," she says. "If you take that away from me—"

"I'm not taking anything away, I promise. Aurillia, have I ever told you the first law of thermodynamics?"

Aurillia shakes her head, wordless.

"Nothing is lost, only changed."

"That's not true," Aurillia says steadily. "I'll never be the same again, ever." Tears squeeze out of her eyes.

"No, that's the truth, you won't. And I don't want to make light of that, make it sound like you haven't given up anything. I know you're sad. I would be, too. And I don't know what it's like to have had a trauma like yours."

"That's right, you don't." Defiance.

"But I do know what it's like to have stuff happen that changes who you are forever. You won't ever be that person again, the person you would've been if your scars had never come. But you'll be someone different. You won't have the life you would've had, but somehow, life will be good again. You won't get that if you just do nothing and wait for it, but…"

"That's why I wanna jump my horse. To get my life back."

"Taking that kind of risk isn't the way, Aurillia. You still have your horse, and every time you ride, even if it's a different kind of ride then you would've had before, you win."

Aurillia smiles, just ever so little. "Only changed," she says quietly.

"Exactly."

Curtis

My head emerges. I am like a groundhog popping out of a hole. As I gingerly climb the steep steps in the back of the feed room, the feeling of my surroundings changes. Still distinctly 'farm,' but now grassy and dusty, less 'animal.' I'm facing a wall of hay bales. It's not just the smell, the air even tastes of it.

"Kev?" I call out as I step on to the ancient wood floor of the barn.

Nothing.

"Kevin?"

Silence.

I take a deep breath and use the tactic I've heard works every time. "Kevin Apostoli Demas, where are you?"

"Don't call me that."

Jackpot.

I turn away from the hay wall. It's dim and bright at the same time in here. I can see motes of dancing dust in the air, and ever so faintly, I can hear: "Sir Topham Hat is not going to like this, Bert. You can't just leave whenever Bash and Dash embarrass you. It's against the rules of the train yard."

What the...?

My foot catches on the uneven loft floor, and I almost go flying. There's a tiny giggle. So he can see me, I think. My mean double-crossing mind suddenly shifts into high gear, as creaks from hinges and floorboards pop around me. This could be the perfect place to hide someone. If my father ever comes for me, I might not be found for days, weeks... Does everyone's mind do this, or just the paranoid children of criminals?

What am I doing here? Maybe I really am crazy, using horses as some bizarre exposure therapy to prove I'm not exactly who I really am: my deranged, angry father's son. Why do I even work in this barn? I'll never be able to outsmart my father, much less use a horse to do it.

I turn to go, feeling like a trapped animal, attempting a failed escape.

"I'm up here," says the little voice. I turn back ...for Naomi...

I try to peer up into the rafters. It's disconcerting—big and dark and shadowy. Anything can be hiding in there.

I remember to check my footing before I start toward what looks like a shed within the loft. "Okay Kev, where are you?"

"I'm up here," repeats the little voice. I feel rather like Wilbur trying to track down Charlotte and her web for the first time.

To the left of the shed is another stack of hay bales. A head is peering at me from behind one just about at my eye level.

"There you are! Who were you talking to, kiddo?"

"My trains. I'm not little."

"I didn't call you little."

"That's what 'kiddo' means."

"Okay, Big Guy."

"Big Guy still means you think I'm little, but you talk opposites."

"You're tough, you know that?"

Kev shrugs. "Can't help it."

I step up on a hay bale and lean over another to see Kevin nestled among the bales. I prop my elbows on the bale and plop my chin on my fists, trying to look comfortable, half-in and half-out of Kevin's sanctuary.

"What are you doing up here all by yourself?"

"There's no screaming. It's quiet here. Nobody's mad. It's mean to yell. Ny was mean."

"I know Naomi yelled at you, but she yelled because she saw that what you were doing was very dangerous. Sometimes when we're scared, we yell, and being yelled at feels awful. But so does being scared that something bad would happen to you because you fell off a chair, or because you went outside alone and got hurt."

"I don't like her."

"Sometimes I don't like her either. You don't have to like her. But you do have to love her."

Kev exclaims. "I don't like 'have to'. It's bossy."

"I don't like 'have to', either. I don't have to love your sister. I just do. There's lots of stuff about her to love, even if you don't like everything."

If there are any other words on the planet that I will ever wish I could take back more, I don't have any idea what they are. I can't believe what I've just said out loud. My only saving grace is that I'm here in the friendly dark, with a kid. It's safe, I reassure myself. Kev will never tell. My secret is still safe.

Although I won't dare tell Kev to keep a secret. That would be making the information like forbidden fruit. It's not like no one knows, I remind myself. This crush is like an open secret. And you haven't been acting in love with her. If anything, you snap at her every time she turns around.

Darn. I'm just not used to everyday kids. In my foster care world, every kid around me is weird. They hide under tables and chairs. They bite. They scratch. They take vows of silence. They steal and hoard food. They're runners, a lot of them, like I became. We all do odd things with the fear and abuse and poverty that brings us to the storage bin of misfits that is foster care.

Sure, I made friends in the system. Real friends, sometimes. But friends are hard to keep when you move around so much, when you're busy being a runner or when you hardly trust yourself and what you might become.

Kev is different, though. Maybe it's because I can trust that the system's revolving door won't snatch the kid away. Maybe it's that he's a kid, like I was when I needed solid ground most. Maybe it's all his smarts that are disarming.

Probably all of the above. Whatever the reason, the secret of my more-than-a-crush is out. And for the first time in my life, protecting my relationships with both Naomi and her little half-brother is more important than keeping feelings to myself.

What do you know? I'm growing up.

"So, are you gonna turn into a horse now?" Kev is asking.

"What do you mean?" How am I ever going to keep up with this kid, anyway?

Kev shrugs, as though this were the simplest, most obvious logic ever. "You love her, she loves horses. So..."

I burst out laughing. To my relief, Kev laughs with me.

So, it's official. I'm stuck with horses now, after all. Like it or lump it. I'll have to figure out liking it.

Chapter Seventeen
Blacklisted

Eva

"Will you let me…help you at all?"

I stare ahead at the window and consider the Last Supper in stained glass. Jesus with the Twelve, together for the last time before the betrayal.

Today is the first time I've been able to drag myself all the way here to the chapel from my hospital bed. Until now this chaplain came to my hospital room. Two days after the surgery, a physio and two aides had me out of bed, leaning on a huge walker, taking careful steps. After moving only about thirty feet, I was exhausted and covered in sweat. And there's more than physio to exhaust me. Sure enough, there've been visits from social workers and counsellors of various shapes and sizes. The chaplain, Gavin Dumond, has sat with me four times so far, trying to get somewhere with me.

But I know it's hopeless.

"I'm not sure anyone can help me," I tell him flatly.

"Well, will you let me try?"

I give him a short, tired laugh at that, and proceed to look this chaplain up and down, unashamedly regarding his huge, eager, peaceful green eyes. "I don't have a good history with people wanting to help."

He nods, as if this makes a world of sense to him. "People can be tremendously disappointing. That's why God—"

"God has a lot of explaining to do!" I snap.

I expect a lecture—about God working in mysterious ways, learning patience, everything working for good, or any combination of the three. Instead, he leans back against the pew. "I'm sorry," he says. "Sometimes I'm a little quick with the solutions. But if you'll let me, I'd like to listen."

No one has ever once apologized to me before, for the way things have gone, for the way life hurts.

I begin to talk.

My first memory of my mother without my Dad, is her standing under a tree in the backyard and shaking her fist at heaven. I was about three, and the picture stuck.

I have only snatches of memories of my father, but those are bright and clear. Holding an ice cream out to me, lifting me on his shoulders so that I could see the bride I'd been sure was a fairy, throwing me up in the air and catching me while I shrieked with laughter and my mother shrieked in fear.

"Alberto! You'll drop her! Oh, God, bring her down safe!"

Back then, when Mom said "Oh God" she was referring to the Almighty Himself—no blaspheming anywhere. Mom and Dad were amazing missionaries who served God, loved people, and talked to the Trinity about everything. If Dad hadn't died in Peru, I would have been raised there, with my awesome parents and a healthy mom whose relationship with alcohol would have stopped at communion wine. But that's not the way it worked out. The minute that car hit my father, our lives were spinning on black ice.

Church was a strange way for me to rebel against my mother, but it worked. When other kids were fooling around, I was playing the church piano, singing hymns.

"Where do you think you're going?"

I had finished rolling up my red sweater and was stuffing it in my gym bag. I faced my mother, straight on. "Church retreat, with the youth group."

I remember being ready to do battle, ready to stare down the tears that so often spilled during moments like this. But there were no tears that time, only a surprising, sober pragmatism from my mother.

"Your father would be ashamed of me."

I said nothing. What had there been to say? I could hardly argue with that.

"I'm not really an atheist, you know."

"That's good." I checked the contents of my bag and zipped it up.

"God is there all right. I'm just furious with Him. We're not on speaking terms."

"Isn't that dangerous, Mom?"

I thought of all the sermons I was hearing in church, about the God I met when I read my Bible and prayed. He was loving and patient, but how long could Mom keep doing this? Would I always be the mature one? Would I not be a teenager who could rebel and expect my mother to catch me?

"What, is not speaking to Him dangerous? No, it's quiet."

"What about when He turns up the volume to get your attention?"

Silence.

"Gotta go, Mom. Stay sober while I'm gone."

On the second night of camp, it rained. Not just a little bit of rain, but torrents. Campfire was cancelled, and instead, us girls huddled in our cabins, watching lightning flash.

I had watched the sky open, and was thinking of my mother at home, probably settling into her bottle of wine as the silence of our empty apartment tucked itself around her. I wondered how getting drunk would feel, if I tried it. Would control slip away or make a dash for the exits as soon as I took, say, my third sip? Would I be a 'happy drunk' or would I turn nasty and cruel? Would it feel good to be bitchy, to release the control I had stuffed in place around the troubles in my mind?

"Hold still," Fay admonished. "I'm going to get nail polish everywhere but your toes, if you keep squirming."

"I won't get you in trouble for not colouring in the lines," I promised, with a small laugh.

"I'm bored," Fay admitted. "I wish the rain would stop."

"Let's go raid the boys' cabin." Muffled shouts, spews of laughter and deeper voices had made it clear moments before that the boys were awake and probably in the midst of a pillow fight.

"Put our flashlights under our chins and freak 'em out!"

"Oh, yeah, that'll do it," Fay quipped. "What are we, five?" She finished my last toe.

"Knock on their door and French the first guy who opens it." There hadn't even been a thought proceeding that statement. It was out of my mouth before the idea was even consciously formed. Drunk without the alcohol.

The girls stared at me, some in shock, some with an odd mix of admiration and dread at the trouble that would follow such a prank.

"Girl, what've you been smoking?" Alexa's eyes grew wide. "We'll all be grounded for, like, months when we get back."

After that, the atmosphere changed in church, as if someone had fiddled with a thermostat and gotten it stuck in the cool position. Invitations to my friend's houses after services trickled down. Alexa's parents began messaging her away from me with their eyes whenever we managed to snatch a few minutes together. The phone stopped ringing.

"Alexa, what did I do?" I finished putting a price tag on a plate of peanut butter cookies for the Christmas fundraiser.

She shrugged. "What d'you mean?"

"Ever since the retreat, it's been like people are mad at me. Like I'm in trouble or something."

"You're not in trouble." Alexa looked away.

"Come on," I whispered urgently. "Get real. It's like someone's secured the perimeter around me these days. It wasn't so bad right after, but now every week it feels worse. Did I turn into a crime scene?"

"Not exactly." Alexa shook her head.

"You know something."

Alexa sighed deeply, giving in. "It was Fay."

"What about Fay?"

"Remember at the cabin when we were bored, talking about the boys?"

"Yeah."

"Remember how you said we should surprise them and kiss the guy that opens the door?"

"Yeah..."

"Well, Fay kinda went home and told her mother, who told Grace's mom who told Bella's dad, who told my mom. People are saying you're bad news now, that it's bad enough your mom drinks..."

Like the sun coming out late in the day, the implications of what 'bad news' meant in this church crowd began to dawn on me.

It was official; I was blacklisted.

I was fascinated, in a strange, uncomfortable way. How very odd that a church, the House of God, where people were to be the light of the world and the hands and feet of the Gospel, was the place where condemnation seemed to come so easily. My alcoholism didn't come from anger. It came from confusion, and a curiosity, a sadness, a will to administer a test—could alcohol make me forget?

"I was so shocked and hurt. How could the church freeze me out for mentioning kissing a boy? And I was tired," I tell Gavin Dumond simply. "Tired of resisting the temptation all the time, when alcohol was everywhere at home. When even church abandoned me, I lost it." I shrug, remembering. "It was a relief, the first time I took a drink, like, question answered, *this* is what it's like. I never imagined drinking would lead me to this, that I would end up so much like my mother, that it would end this way."

"Your life is not over yet, Eva," Gavin says gently.

"But it is!" I explode. "I've lost a baby. I've lost so many friends there's almost no one who hasn't given up on me. I have no father. My mom's been grieving ever since I can remember. What's left?"

Gavin exhales deeply and takes a moment to consider my words. "Eva, alcoholism is hard. But you're not a bad person. You have a disease. I've seen a lot of people recover from many painful things"

I stare at my leg. "I...know what you're trying to do... tell me I'm not all bad, I'm human, I'm forgivable. But my situation is..." I break off, fumbling, at a loss for words. "My Aunt Sylvia would support me, but she's dead. Did I mention that she died of cancer a year-and-a-half after she moved in to protect me?"

Gavin raises his eyebrows, shakes his head.

"Yeah, people who care about me get hurt or die. I only have one loyal friend, Naomi. She's in a wheelchair, has a screwed up life, too. I was right years ago, in church. I'm like a crime scene. That's still true. So I couldn't have kept a baby like that—carried it, kept it safe. I can't promise I'd keep anyone safe."

Mary

No one happens by and wonders what Naomi's doing in the alcove of the hospital chapel.

She is alone and mostly hidden from view, letting the chapel's acoustics carry Eva's conversation with Gavin to her. She hadn't meant to eavesdrop. As her twin, I would know that even if I hadn't watched the nurses on the Ortho floor tell her Eva was in the chapel when she came to visit.

She's come in her motorized wheelchair. (After what happened at the top of the aisle in theatre class, I doubt if she'll ever 'go manual' again.) So motoring on and off the huge hospital elevator and down the long hallways alone is easy. Naomi's feeling free as she covers the route to the chapel, and I'm wishing people could witness this in her, the woman-in-charge posture, and the confidence, before they declare that disabled people who use wheelchairs are confined to them. My twin can't help feeling sorry for people stuck in their ableism. (And I can't help but agree.) Sometimes it's a case of vindictiveness. But sometimes the ignorance is so entrenched it appears to be business as usual, nothing unjust, 'just the way things are.' That's almost scarier than the things people realize are wrong. Slaps that come out of left field hurt more than the ones you can predict are on their way.

I want to give her a hug. Oh, I want to give her such a hug.

"Eva, think," Gavin continues. "Your friend Naomi, she won't get to be a mom. With her limitations, parenting just isn't in the cards. But you, you can do this. We're not going to leave you like this, we won't discharge you without support. You can get clean and finish your education, get married, have kids. Your mom's mistakes don't have to be yours. And with God's help, you can do what Naomi can't. When you are weak, God is strong. Especially when you're weak. Hang on tight. If you change your choices, break the hold of addiction, the next baby you have, you'll be proud to keep." Immediately I fume. What does Gavin mean 'parenting isn't in the cards for my twin?' For her sake, I want to smack him.

Naomi

No one lives, works or parents alone. It takes a village to raise a child. Everyone says those words, but I don't think they mean them. Apparently, I'm not allowed to need a village for my hypothetical kid, and that makes no sense at all. I am co-raising Kevin after all. This Gavin person doesn't know that, and I doubt it would matter if he did. But it should. I'm good for Kevin. Good for people. Good for Eva. Good for kids.

I want to tell them that. Shout it, actually.

But instead I hold my peace in the alcove. And I seethe.

Not very many people are ready to imagine a world where parenting isn't confined to its little box. Isn't it ironic that my theatre director, and even a chaplain think of someone like me as suffering and incapable, but it hasn't occurred to them that *they're* suffering in their narrowness— the choices they make about how they treat me also mean they're depriving themselves of a deeper, better experience in life. What does it say about them that they can hardly imagine me onstage, or with a child? So I would need help and support. So what? So does every mother.

There's a vase on a windowsill beside me. As I prepare to drive away, I can no longer resist. I drive over to the vase first and nudge it over the edge. I imagine Gavin's shocked face when the crash draws his attention, just before I am out of sight.

I'm finally leaving the hospital when I see him, through the glass on the other side of the automatic doors. He's paused, standing still in the moment it takes for his presence to register and the doors to respond. It's been hard to swallow past the lump in my throat, after what I overheard in the chapel. I had been looking for Eva and ended up not seeing her at all. Instead, I heard her story, which makes my ears ring, and then I heard a stranger pass judgment on me. I want to go home.

But now I can hear my heart in my chest.

All of us are made up of energy, atoms, protons, neutrons, electrons, and I can feel mine surging toward Matt. It's like it was in the car all those months ago, only now we have just enough history so we're not falling into empty space, shocked by the rush of the surge.

At least now, my voice doesn't fail me. "What are you doing here?"

"My dad's the chaplain here. Your emails stopped."

What do I say now? It's not you, it's me. My life's a mess. My heart is breaking. All very 'Damsel in Distress.' All about me.

"How's your mom?"

"Still talking about our bonding in the Bahamas, but she doesn't trust me with her car again yet."

"Sorry."

Matt shrugs. "No biggie. I can take a bus."

In the tiny sliver of silence that follows, I know I have a choice: give him something real now, or let the silence stretch and carry him away.

I make my choice. "I dropped theatre. You were right."

Matt's eyes grow wide. "I'm sorry." He says the words with just the right weight, like they're so much more than "what you say at a time like this."

"It's not your fault." I look straight at him. "Just, nothing's worked out this year." I feign nonchalance, try for a shrug, but what comes out is a sudden shiver, as if all the betrayal has made me cold.

Right away, his jacket is around my shoulders. "My dad's the chaplain here," Matt says, again. He has no idea he's rubbing it in. "He can smooth anything over, and I want you to meet him. Come on, he just had an appointment right in the chapel. I'll bet he's still there."

As I wait for my WheelTrans, it's impossible not to be glad for how easy it was to get out of that one. My words ring in my head: "I can't go meet your dad. I have WheelTrans due in ten minutes. I have to be early, and I can't leave my spot. Even if they're two hours late."

Matt is disappointed, but he covers it well, and gives me a hug. I wonder now if he misread my avoiding his father as avoiding him, and I'm freshly angry. This man, this chaplain, no less, has judged me and sickened me and perhaps delivered my fledgling relationship its dying blow. In a flash, I understand how people's failings have dropped Eva off a cliff and made her bitter. The only difference between her and me in this context is I understand that moments like this don't reflect who God is, only that he's right about how flawed people are. "Father, forgive them..."

"If you have to wait, so do I." Lost in my thoughts, Matt has snuck up on me. I wasn't expecting him to be back. We had said goodbye. "Will you always surprise me?" I ask, as I register that he's brought me coffee. I beam at him.

He doesn't answer me. He just puts our coffees down on the widest edge of the planter I'm parked beside, and kisses me.

People always say, if a kiss works, it changes everything, like fireworks in the middle of a quiet night, like a gourmet chef in a boring kitchen. But in my world, that kiss doesn't change anything. A change would be if we didn't know there was attraction, or love, or trust, but then found it despite ourselves. Not the case here. No, it doesn't change anything. It makes things happen, an action whose time was on its way, and had finally come. Yeast in bread. Matt, coffee, a kiss, and me.

And now all we want to do is kiss. So it's all we do.

Half an hour later, we don't even hear my bus pulling up.

Our coffees are cold when we drink them, as the bus crawls toward home (I've never been happier about how long that process can take), and we talk.

I don't tell him anything about what I know, what his father said. We've gone from zero to sixty in the space of half an hour and I want to keep speeding forward, not stalling, or worse, moving in reverse.

Matt's taken to picking me up after school, and driving us out to parks. We kiss in the car, mostly. We gave it a shot on a bench. Too much staring. Me on his lap, with my empty chair beside the bench is apparently too much for the public psyche. We provide the voyeurism, they explode with questions we can feel. Which one needs the chair? What's he doing with her? Is he taking advantage of her? What's she doing with him? I'm used to all manner of people and how they think (or not). But I don't want them scaring Matt away. And who needs a park bench, when you have access to a car with a sun roof? I mean, really.

"We should stop hiding and tell our families. We have something here, don't we?"

I turn to stare at him. He is concentrating on the traffic on the way home.

"Sure we do, but are you kidding?"

He looks at me briefly then his eyes return to the road. "No, I'm serious, aren't you?"

I squeeze the hand of his that I'm holding. "Of course I'm serious about us. And I'm serious about waiting some more before our parents find out. I want it to be 'just us' for a while longer, Matt."

"Are you ashamed, Ny?"

"No!" I exclaim, emphatically. "No." I say again, looking at him intensely. I want to punctuate that with another kiss, but he's still driving. I keep talking. "Remember the park bench, how people stared?" I ask.

He nods, rolls his eyes.

I want to tell him that the staring makes me want to shout "Yes! We're on a date! I'm the one who needs the chair, and he's good with that. He didn't settle for me. He chose me, and I'm a catch! Take that!" But I don't say any of it, and I'm glad we've chosen privacy. I don't want anyone telling us to get a room. I don't want to get a room. I was raised in church, and I actually believe we should wait. A long, long time. White dress, tux and minister first. I'm serious. Haven't told Matt that, but it's early days yet. But not so early that I don't silently pray *Please God, don't let his dad marry us.* And then I'm shocked at the thought.

Out loud I say: "I just think we need some more time. We need to be stronger before it's our parents staring. That's all." *That's all for now.*

He turns off the highway, pulls over, and we kiss. I breathe a sigh of relief that I've bought some time.

I don't have to tell Matt I'm scared. I don't have to face his father. Not yet.

Gavin Dumond can wait.

Curtis

I shouldn't be getting on Lancelot's back.

He's fine with me leading him around the ring to warm up. I'm warming up fast—with fear. He hardly shifts as I push my hand under the saddle the way I've seen Charlotte do as she checks whether the girth is tight enough. He seems almost bored as I pull down the stirrups and adjust the leather straps to the right length the way Naomi showed me. As I lead him to the mounting block in the corner of the arena, he starts to get interested though, and not in a good way.

As I start up the steps, instead of Lancelot continuing to walk beside me, the reins pull tight. I look back over my shoulder to see Lancelot's neck stretched and his eyes rolling. His hooves are firmly planted in the sand. I take a breath and back down the steps until his head is back where it should be. I feel silly as I chirp "Walk on" and march up the steps again. To my surprise, he starts forward. Not so much to my surprise, he keeps going until the reins burn out of my hands. As they spring free, they snag on the hand

214

rail in front of me. As they catch, he snorts and tries to dance away. With his head held by the reins, the darn horse swings his body around and snorts. He jerks his head and backs up, causing the reins to come free and snap back at him, right into his own face. He rears.

Horses are big. And though Lancelot is no slouch, there are horses in the barn that loom much larger than him. But not at this moment. Even from the top of the mounting block, I feel two inches high as his front hooves mill in the air above my head.

Lancelot finally lands, and stands puffing and blowing, his head hanging down. He stretches his neck forward and rolls his eyes. I back down the steps and try again. This time he keeps going. The reins pull out of my hands and then snag for just a second on the hand rail. Lancelot jerks them free as he spins his body. I start to breathe again. But I don't move. I stay frozen. Everything is unnaturally calm, except the harsh rasp of Lancelot's laboured breathing. But gradually that subsides as well.

Talk about signs, and misreading them. I should back off, but...no. If I'm ever stuck sharing air with my psycho father, mastering my fear of a heavy-breathing horse-beast could be the best skill ever. So, I sit down and wait on the mounting block. Eventually Lancelot is breathing normally and just stands there watching me, watching him.

I go over to him and he leans his head into my hand as I rub his ear. Perfect. I'm a poor substitute for Naomi's connection with him. She doesn't like other people riding him anyway. If she knew I was riding him for the first time alone in here, she would knock me out of the saddle herself.

I urge Lancelot back to stand beside the mounting block. He's facing the opposite way, but what do I know? How am I supposed to know that you never do it that way? That he should never be mounted when he's facing the arena door. The door that I've left open. I almost trot up the steps and slip the reins over his head. He's standing close enough for me to swing my leg straight over and sit down. So I do that. That's when he decides he's had enough. That's when he announces that he would rather be in his stall than anywhere else. As my butt hits the leather of the saddle, my foot is being dragged along the mounting block and then down the steps. This isn't right. I'm supposed to be above Lancelot. I'm holding onto the front of the saddle like they had told me to until I feel settled, but I am not settling. I am sliding. Still in the saddle, I'm sliding down Lancelot's side in slow motion. When my left knee comes up over his back, I give up and let go. I'm spitting sand as Lancelot breaks into a trot. With the saddle hanging off his side, he misjudges his clearance and scrapes the saddle on the edge of the door as he turns into the barn and disappears.

I guess the girth wasn't tight enough...

PART TWO
TRIAL BY FIRE

Chapter Eighteen
Complications

Naomi

One look at Lancelot, and I know Curtis has been around him, if not on him...again. He's edgy in the cross ties, and it's taking a stream of cooing and stroking just for him to let Charlotte clean out his hooves.

Charlotte is right, I know. Lancelot is the best horse in the barn for Curtis. He's a dressage horse, and dressage is all about a calm, clear and trusting connection between horse and rider. Lancelot is a trooper, so well suited to that bond that riding him is like flying, dancing and sailing. We read each other the way a pilot and co-pilot know their plane, the way dance partners read each other's bodies, or the way a sailor knows the wind. And Lancelot knows how to control his movements—a calm sway when I'm frustrated, a power surge when all I want is to move.

Lancelot is the horse for Curtis to learn riding and trust. I agree with that. But in the weeks since Curtis fell off him and ended up concussed, I can read a change in my horse. It's as if he's got anger he needs to burn off, as if he's frustrated in a whole new way. Charlotte tells me Lance is fine, and he gets lots of TLC, but I know what's in front of me, as far as I'm concerned, and Lance has never given us attitude, never seemed on edge this often.

I press my palm gently along his flank, instinctively checking for scratches, bumps, welts, a flinch of discomfort—anything to tell me if Curtis has hurt him in any way.

Charlotte pauses her work on his hoof. "I brushed him two hours ago, Naomi. He's fine."

I pull my hand back quickly. "I was just..."

Charlotte holds my gaze steadily. "I know what you're doing. And I'm telling you, Curtis is good to Lance. Would I allow anyone to hurt him, or any of these horses? Seriously, ask yourself."

There can be no debate there. And after all, Curtis stole the after-hours security code from my own wallet. If it is anyone's fault that Curtis had spooked Lancelot during his first ride, and then gotten himself hurt, it is my own. But still.

"You'll feel better if you come and watch Curtis look after Lance, you know."

"I can't." My answer to that is quick, emphatic.

"Aren't you guys friends?"

"Sort of. It's complicated."

Charlotte shakes her head. "It must be. What happened between you two?"

I pause in my search for the carrot in the bag attached to my armrest. "Well, it's nothing you don't know already. It's just...he dug around in my wallet and stole my entry code for the barn. He mounted my horse without permission, he rode him and he put himself at risk. He broke my trust, and yours. What if something awful had happened—some huge injury to him or Lancelot when he fell? There wouldn't be enough insurance in the world! I feel like such an idiot. How can I ever take his word on anything now? How did he even pull this off?"

"Could someone in your family have let something slip?"

"Not a chance. No one would have mentioned my code around him. You know how private we are. There's no question in my mind that he snooped around in my purse. What kind of morals are those, anyway?"

"I don't know, Naomi. But I do know he hasn't had the same chance to build moral stability with his history. Or any stability at all, what with being bounced around in foster care. I can promise you he didn't intend to fall off Lance and spook him. He was probably just super eager to prove to himself and to you that he can ride, that he's determined and that he's worth your time. He loves you, you know."

I laugh out loud at that. "What kind of bizarre way is that to show it?"

"I promise you, Curtis is not getting off consequence-free. He won't be riding Lance, or any other horse until he proves he's learned from this. And I can't know his mind for sure," Charlotte admits. "But I do know that you guys can get through this. If you communicate, you can turn a bad thing to good."

Naomi
I am a colossal idiot.
I can't bear to tell Charlotte what I've done to Curtis.

I was enraged after what he did with Lance—sneaking into the barn, using my tack to ride Lance, falling off. There were a zillion ways he could have hurt my horse, himself, or both of them so much worse than he did. And there are the million ways he broke my trust. I had so much anger, I just wanted to hurt him as he'd hurt me.

I dug around in his backpack and found the stuffed penguin he carries in his bag, like a baby dragging a blankie behind him in the dirt. It used to be his sister's; I forget which one. But it's from the box of keepsakes he told me about. He always has it with him, and sometimes in a spare moment when he doesn't realize I'm watching, I've seen him pull it out and stare at it.

So there I was, furious. Just wanting to take something from him that mattered...the way he could have hurt the barn and my Lance.

I took a pair of scissors and started snipping up that penguin, waiting for revenge to feel sweet. But as soon as I saw bits of white stuffing flying, guilt set in. I started thinking of how I would feel if someone did that to something of Mary's. I stopped in my tracks and started trying to stuff the penguin's violated innards back into the hole my scissors had made.

The damage didn't look like much, I thought, cramming the stuffed animal back in his bag where I had found it.

Maybe Curtis will never realize anyone has touched his keepsake. Maybe he won't ever know the truth about how awful I've been, how the adrenalin of revenge has left me drained. But I know, and I won't forget.

If he does figure it out, maybe that will help him realize his sisters' stuff is just things, that none of those little bits will bring them back. Maybe then he can set them free. Maybe this will actually help.

What a load of bull.

There is no manual for letting your sister go. And when she's your twin, that process is an extra eternity's worth of heart-wrenching. I've read up on twins and how the twin relationship is understood to work (and this reading process is a weird, exquisite torture, but I feel it's something I need to do). Here's some stuff I've figured out so far.

Enhanced empathy makes twin-hood wonderful. You have someone beside you who's on your side, who's most probably going to understand things your way before anyone else's. They will share, rather than declare something—or even someone—entirely their own.

It's not always that simple. Sometimes it's a hybrid of bond and turbo-charged, rivalry-based contradiction. If love can be so powerful, so can conflict, even hate. The idea of using my knowledge of Mary against her, if she'd lived, turns my stomach. But I can speak for myself. Toddlers have to learn the art of sharing. There are meltdowns about toys, clothes, books. Jealousy over friends, privileges, grades, jobs. But for twins, enhanced empathy means we don't readily understand why people don't share—why the world doesn't work the way it does between twins (or in our case, the way it would have worked in the microcosm between Mary and me) if we were together.

Empathy isn't all roses, though. I sometimes catch myself imagining how it would feel to have had Mary in my corner all the time. Would she feel it in her gut when someone hurts me? Would I feel it if she were hurt? Would my physiotherapy sessions mean she would feel lactic acid burning through her own muscles? If that were true, I think she'd be a super fan of the fact that I'm the rarest of birds when it comes to cerebral palsy, since I've never had surgery. Because if I had, and if she felt that, too—if our connection meant she somehow experienced my post-op and recovery pain—I don't think I could handle that. (And I don't think I could handle being plugged in to her that way, either.) I imagine her having to learn to control her anger when Dad misunderstands or blows up at me, when Eva hurt Kev's elbow... And there would be me smouldering when Mom shuts her out.

Our heartbreaks give as good as they get, pack a double punch. Two for her, four for me.

I talk to her out loud sometimes.

I am imagining Mary and me as a team, our idea of aloneness built as alone-together, a sort of two-in-one. I picture us talking ourselves hoarse. At home in the kitchen, talking until the sun goes down, and long after...talking so long, we don't even realize we're still going without lights on.

I realize I've never talked to her in real time and had her answer me.

In the Bible, Mary let go of Jesus, first when he, as God's son, had to put God the Father and His ministry on Earth before her. Then she let go of Him again when He hung nailed and sacrificed on the cross. Abraham was ready and willing to let go of Isaac. Moses let go, first of his nobility and confidence, then of the idea that there was nothing

224

he could do about his own People's oppression—the idea that God could or would use nothing of him to end the Israelites' slavery in Egypt.

He let go of that, too.

And I must let go of my beloved twin. My Mary. My Maria. Mine.

Mine always, yet not mine at all.

Chapter Nineteen
The Course of a Storm

Naomi

I love university. First semester is amazing!

I don't have to apologize for being smart, and I can study what I want. Thursday is my creative writing class, and I could stay here all week. I hope it doesn't show on my face that I'm already imagining my first novel. Matt would probably be annoyed if he knew the dreamy face I have on right now, and that I'm not sitting here imagining him. It's not actually writing the novel I'm thinking of, it's the new-book smell all over the place when it comes off the press, the reviews in the paper, the speeches, the awards, the royalty cheques. And all for doing what I love: making words work on paper. Creating worlds of characters, drama and problems that don't get solved for the longest time, and some that never do.

It's what I was born to do.

"Find out what your main character needs and loves most in their lives, and take it away. Find out what they want most badly, and make sure they don't get it, at least not easily."

Those were Professor Ogden's first words to us, on the first day of class two weeks ago, and I liked him right away.

He started that way, and then talked about raising the stakes ever higher when we write, putting more and more on the line for our characters as we build their story.

"We have to love them," he continued, "and make sure readers love them, so that it matters when circumstances go wrong and get ever-more complicated."

Ogden's words are ringing in my ears as I get in the door after school. I am busy in my head, examining and rejecting high-stakes scenarios for next week's assignment, when I roll into the living room. The television is on, and a rerun of *Everybody Loves Raymond* has started. Frank and Marie have just crashed their car into Ray and Debra's front room, but no one around me is paying attention to comedy at the moment.

"Jo, she's your mother and she's sick. We have to do what we have to do for her."

"She's always been sick, and I'm always in the crossfire. I just moved back here, Dad!"

She's so emphatic, Jo's arms are flapping, as though she were at a park bench scaring away pigeons. I feel for her, I do. My own stomach is dropping at Dad's words that Mom might be even less well than usual. I don't want to imagine what that might mean, and I realize for the first time, I am worried purely for her. Maybe it's just a flicker, and my selflessness will be gone in a moment, replaced with derogatory thoughts and comments about how she will, in short order, be turning everyone upside down again.

I wait for them. They don't come.

Instead, I hear my own voice. "What's going on, Dad?"

There was a time when my being calm about Mom would've stopped everyone cold. But Jo keeps on going, as though she hasn't heard me. "If she's coming back, I'm leaving," she says simply, with finality.

"Is that how I treated you when you came back?" Dad wants to know. "Did I turn you away because of how complicated life would be with you here and your mother alone, still refusing us?"

"But that's the—" Jo interjects.

"But nothing," Dad says. "We are a family, and we will act like one. I'm moving your mother in, and taking her straight to the doctor. Something isn't right with her."

At that Jo explodes, a thrown grenade. "It's always her you're worried about. Never me. There were so many mornings I couldn't get her out of bed because she didn't want to face another day of compulsions. And she had them, Dad, even in bed. She had this rule that she couldn't get up if she didn't roll over twelve times first, or turn her lamp on and off twelve times. I never even friggin' understood what it was with the twelve thing."

Dad sat frozen for a moment, stunned—not unlike Raymond as he watched his parents' car plough into the living room on the screen.

"The disciples," Dad says, his voice sounding as though it came from far off somewhere. "She used to say that if God had patience for them, there might be hope for her."

"What's wrong with Mom now, Dad?" I ask the question, thinking of how desperate she must feel, following strange compulsions that feel as inevitable as rain.

"I think your mother has Alzheimer's."

There's this thing called 'co-bedding.' Doctors often prescribe it for babies who are failing to thrive. They put two or three of them together in a crib, or a large incubator—depending on the situation—and somehow being together increases the chance of bringing on recovery for all. Being close enough to touch, having someone there for comfort, makes all the difference.

"What are you doing?" Jo turns her tear-streaked face toward me as she hears the pop of my footrest's lever directly beside the futon where she's lying.

I don't answer directly. "Help me transfer," I say gently instead, indicating the spot beside her.

"Why?" But she's already up, offering me her arms and helping me pivot the way that I would using the support pole and bars in my own bedroom.

The transfer is choppy, but it works. I try not to think of how Jo would do it if she were me, or how Mary would do it, if she were alive.

This is me, as I am, and I'm here. I pull my legs up and over.

For a while after she gets back in beside me and I grab her hand, we are silent, but it's not long before I break it.

"How did we let it get like this, Jo?"

Thankfully, she doesn't waste time pretending not to have a clue what I'm talking about. When she says "I don't know," she's answering the question I actually asked, about why we argue, and barely know each other, and why we were divided and isolated so long on the trajectory of separate lives.

"What I don't know is, how you survived with Mom and didn't bail," I tell her honestly. For the first time it strikes me how much Jo and Eva are alike, only Jo got out with her integrity.

"I don't know that, either. I always knew you and Dad and Yiayia were there, so I could take it. And she always supported me the best she could, found a way to go to work. I got the Reitman's job as soon as I could work, so that I could put myself through university, if Dad couldn't, and in case I didn't get scholarships. I took school and work seriously as my only way out, and learned to hack it on my own. I'm okay. She screwed me up, but I'm okay."

"She screwed us all up."

"But we're okay?"

"Or getting there," I admit.

"Naomi?"

"Yeah."

"What if Dad's right?"

There's more silence, both of us, I know, imagining Alzheimer's stealing our mother from us, so that she'd be gone a second time—with so much unsaid, so little understood among us. I think of all my hanging, unanswered questions. My stomach hurts.

"We'll stick together. We'll figure it out. But you can't leave again, Jo."

"I know…" she admits.

Suddenly, she laughs sarcastically. "It figures," she says.

"What figures?"

"If Mom has Alzheimer's, she's checking out just as we start working on this stuff."

I nod, say nothing. There's no answer to that.

This time Jo is the one who breaks the silence. "I think he is right, Naomi."

I turn over on my side, look at her steadily. "Why?"

"It's why I came back to live here. I saw some signs of... changes in her. I was scared, didn't want to be alone with her anymore."

"What kind of signs?"

"She stopped being able to decide what to eat. She'd stare into the fridge for hours if I let her, almost like she didn't know how to combine a snack anymore. I had to help her."

"Uh-oh."

Both of us say nothing for a long time, unsure of how to change the subject, but knowing we have to, because there is nothing we can do about this one. It's hard to describe the helpless feeling, like there's a train on our direct path, but no way to stop it and no way to get out of the way fast enough. However quickly we move, the train will be quicker.

"I have a boyfriend, Naomi. Really serious."

I'm unspeakably thankful that Jo has spoken—so filled with almost irrational gladness: it takes a moment even to register what's been said. But I catch up. I'm right behind her.

"Does Dad know?"

"Yeah."

Jo has someone who really loves her. My heart flutters.

"I've met someone, too." It's the first time I've said it out loud, made it real.

"When?"

"It's been a while, but it still feels new."

"Does Dad know?"

"Nope."

"He's gonna have a cow, you know."

"Yup. Maybe it won't last."

"What makes you say that?"

"His dad already doesn't like me, and I don't like him."

"Have you met him?"

"No. Don't ask."

"Okay." A minute passes, maybe two. Then: "Is the guy worth all this?"

"It's early days yet, but I think so."

Jo squeezes my hand. "He better be."

Talk about high stakes.

In a million years, I would never have guessed that the first time I met my sister's other half, he would be cooking for us, but here he is, in our kitchen making scalloped potatoes, pork roast, and herbed veggies. I catch myself staring at him as though he might disappear.

He's telling me how he met Jo, at a singles' church potluck. She was wearing this gorgeous green dress. He waited all evening to get the nerve to go up to her and ask her out, and it never came. So the next Sunday, he looked all over for her in church, couldn't find her even though he spent the whole service scanning the place. It took three weeks, but finally he saw her wearing that dress again. He walked up to her, knelt down in the aisle and asked her to lunch. They never looked back.

He's moving around, opening and closing cupboards and drawers, familiarizing himself with the space while I chop salad vegetables and stare at his back. I wonder if Jo does this, worrying that he'll vaporize right in front of her.

"You can do that all day, you know, Naomi. It doesn't bother me. Your sister does it all the time."

I look down. "Sorry, Sam."

"No worries. Is there something you wanna know?"

I think of what I know about my parents. How, once, everything had seemed so solid, so sure. And then...

"Do you really love her? I mean, really," I emphasize. "Because, you gotta know, in this family, there's been a lot of leaving—a lifetime's worth, almost. And we all need to be done with leaving. Doing it, and having it done to us. It needs to be over, and we need to do some staying, and have staying power around us. So, if you've got leaving in your bones, you've come to the wrong place, Sam."

Sam finds a flat spoon and tastes the marinade, nodding to himself, taking his time. He reaches back in the drawer, finds another spoon, and dips an edge into the pan. "Here, try this."

I let the flavour unfurl on my tongue. Dijon, sugar, steak sauce, garlic, rosemary. "That's good stuff!" I exclaim.

Sam watches my face register its appreciation. "I've been cooking full meals by myself since I was nine. I'm the eldest, so I took over and cared for my brothers and sister when our father died, and my mom had to work three jobs. I don't leave. I want to marry your sister. And I take my vows very seriously. Yes, I love Jo. And I understand her. I understand how much she sacrificed in taking care of her mom, your mom. I respect her, and I won't leave."

"Then you can stay." We both smile at that. Sam takes in my approval, seems to savour it. I watch him pause in genuine pleasure for that moment, and like him even more for it.

"You're planning a big salad, right?" I ask.

Sam turns from his work, surveying the cutting board and counter covered in chopped tomatoes, green and red pepper, cucumber, and celery. He nods, "I am now. Thanks for cutting all that up."

"Anything else I can do?"

"Jo says if I hand you down the dishes, you can set the table for me?"

It was counterintuitive, really, how my spasticity makes so much fine motor difficult, yet some things that would seem impossible like cursive writing, vegetable chopping, balancing plates and cutlery on my lap, then arranging them just so on the table, are fun for me. "Yeah, I can set it. I'm surprised she remembers that."

"She thinks of you often, remembers lots of things." Sam pauses, seeming to consider his words carefully before taking a risk. "She's glad to have her sister back, Naomi."

"So am I. But she needs to know I'm still not always a picnic. And call me Ny, Sam."

"Picnics aren't perfect, either. There are bugs."

We both laugh at that. "It's more work for you, me setting the table. And slower," I point out, putting a plate down on my father's spot and returning to the bank of drawers at the counter to collect forks and knives to ferry over on my lap.

He shrugs. "So where's the fire? It's not a race. Do it at your pace. If you've got the patience to do it, I've got the patience to wait."

"You're going to make me cry, Sam."

He shrugs again. "Jo says you don't let yourself. Cry enough, I mean."

"She tells you everything, doesn't she?"

"Let me answer your question with another question. "What do you think I'm doing here, cooking dinner for your family while your dad is having a hellish time at his ex-wife's doctor's office?"

So it's official. He does know everything.

"I have no idea," I confess.

"Do you see Jo anywhere?"

"I've been wondering about that."

"I'm going to ask all of you if I can marry her."

"I vote yes."

"You're sweet. And speaking of voting 'yes', I need to tell you I know your friend Eva, and my parents knew her parents, when we were small."

My eyebrows shoot up.

"Before my dad died, both my parents were missionaries in Peru. Both Eva's parents were wonderful, so sweet. My mom always said her father's words dripped honey. And her mother was the straightest arrow. So devoted to that man. I don't blame her for losing it, with him gone. But...at the same time, I can't believe how she is now."

"I wish I knew her then," I say sincerely.

"She was wonderful. Everybody's mother. And I want to tell you I think it's great, how patient you're being with Eva.

Jo doesn't agree, she thinks you're overdoing it with support, but she'll come around. I'm working on it. Not too much, of course, or she might run from me screaming, and I want her to say yes."

"She will."

"How do you know?"

"Because she isn't stupid. Sam?"

"Yeah?"

"Are you inviting Eva and her mom to the wedding?"

"I don't know," he tells me honestly. "First I need a bride."

"You'll have one. I'm just curious, because I have this friend..."

"Of course you can invite your boyfriend. I hope you do. You'll need a date, won't you?"

"Oh, yeah, I'm inviting Matt for sure, but it's not him I'm talking about. There's this other guy..."

"Ah," Sam chuckles. "A love triangle."

My eyes grow wide. "Oh, no...it's not like that. I'm not in love with Curtis at all. It's..."

"Oh, it's Curtis!" Sam exclaims. "Don't worry. I know what you're getting at. Jo told me about him. Go ahead. Invite him. See if he'll come. He's probably never been to a family wedding, which could hurt, or be just right. You never know. But for you, he'll show up."

"We don't even always get along, you know. I'm even mad at him right now, for hijacking my horse. It's a long story. I didn't even know I was gonna ask to invite him, until right now. I surprised myself. But I get him, you know? As a friend. And it's weird. I think he gets me, too. But he's not in love with me, Sam."

"Oh, please. I only hope he doesn't give Matt a black eye."

We don't talk about Irene's diagnosis tonight. Tonight there are toasts, hugs, laughter, congratulations and joy. It's impossible not to notice how Mom sits there quietly, happy but 'checked out,' too. But then, for whole minutes at a stretch, I forget the new worries about her, and I watch Dad forget, too. In fact, we manage not to talk about it at all, for a very long time. But there are differences I notice right away, between my mom and dad. Maybe they're so clear because I'm hyper-aware of having Mom in the house again, so my attention bee-lines in that direction and brings me face-to-face with the deterioration we're all afraid of, like a scratch or cut that hurts more once you know it's there…

I notice what Jo said she'd seen before: Dad having to guide Mom through the basics of choosing a snack, or doing the dishes. I watch Irene stall and stare at food choices or at Dad's routine at the sink with the supper dishes.

Dad starts out patient. "No, Irene. Like this…Circular motion. No, you missed a spot, use your palm, press in. That's it, don't give up. NO, soft fingers, soft fingers, soft fingers. Don't go stiff, relax. I said RELAX!"

"Dad, calm down. That isn't gonna help."

"Naomi, it's *dishes*. How did this happen? How did we get so that she sits alone in the living room with the lights off and can't write cheques, make snacks, do dishes? She blanks out at the doctor's office. How could this happen, when she knew she's always had us?"

Mom looks ready to blow, like she has lots she could say, given the chance. Thus is the moment I know life is changing forever—the moment when I slide into being my mother's voice.

"Don't do that, Dad. Don't talk about her like she's not here, like she can't hear you. Maybe it happened *because* she knew she had us, because she wanted to fix things on her own and not need help. Maybe she figured she could afford to thrash around, because we'd have her back when it got too hard. Denial's powerful. Maybe she felt herself changing and didn't want it to be. Maybe she thought if she ignored it, it would disappear."

"Well, honestly! How does it seem like that went?"

"We're here now." That's all Mom says. Her words are barely above a whisper, but they feel quietly important enough to shift everything, like the beat of a butterfly wing changing the course of a storm.

Take me as I am. This is me, as I am, and I am here.

Dad and I exchange glances. I don't know what he realizes or decides at exactly this moment, but I know what I'm sure about: Nothing is ever really only one thing: all sorrow, no joy, all catastrophe, with no healing, all tragedy and robbery, no blessing. So whatever is happening to my mother, however she's changing, it's going to mean learning to come together and love someone new. And if there's a train coming to carry us away, at least there will be that gift on it, along with the pain.

It is after dinner when the doorbell rings. Girl Guide cookies, I think.

Matt's voice at the door. I freeze.

I listen as though pinned to my spot as Matt explains to my father that we are dating. I listen as he begins to extol my virtue.

"How come this is the first I'm hearing of this?"

"Naomi didn't feel ready. She wanted to wait to tell you, sir."

"Well, that's a little underhanded."

"She's not underhanded, sir. She's the best person I know," he asserts. "I've never met anyone like her, and I would like you to approve of us. I just want you to know, I'm a good guy and you've raised a good daughter, and her disability doesn't mean dating won't work. We've only been together for a couple of months, but…"

My father jolts. "Excuse me, young man, did you say a couple of *months*?"

"I wanted to tell you, but…"

"What are you doing here, Matt?" I interject. "Dad, we're just gonna go talk outside for a minute, okay?"

As soon as we're outside, I light into him. "Where do you get off barging in like this, and telling my father something we agreed would wait, Matt? You shouldn't be here now."

"We didn't agree on anything. You wanted to wait and I didn't. I care and I'm serious about you."

"I know you do, and I know you are, but you don't really understand."

"I do understand."

"No, you don't. Stop clomping around like Big Foot. Tonight was not supposed to be about me. My sister's getting engaged and her boyfriend came to ask for our blessing. That was what tonight was. That and the news that my mom has Alzheimer's. It's both the best and the worst night. We have enough to digest, without you barging in at the most inappropriate moment…"

"I don't clomp."

"But you assumed. You presumed that my dad's issues with us as a couple would be about my disability, when it's your father who's got serious issues with me being disabled. Serious, man! He's an idiot, if you must know."

"Excuse me?"

"Just ask your dad what he said about a certain Naomi when he was counselling a certain Eva in the hospital chapel, about her drinking. Ask him, and then you'll know why I say we have issues. I didn't want my dad to know until we fix those."

It goes downhill from there, and that isn't the way I had wanted Matt to find out about his father's judgment of me, sight unseen. I also don't enjoy my family's reaction to Matt's visit. My father is so disappointed in me for being silent about him, I want to cry.

"You had no right to ambush Jo and Sam's evening like that. We have enough going on, and going *wrong*, in this family, without you keeping secrets."

"I'm sorry about that, Dad. I really, really am. I didn't mean to ambush anything. I was ambushed, too. I had no idea Matt was going to do that. Really."

Dad looks at me warningly. "Just make sure Matt behaves himself at the party next weekend."

It seems Dad bought an entire Greek bakery's worth of pastries and cake for Jo and Sam's engagement party. There's souvlaki and moussaka and a ton of Greek salad and lemon potatoes, even before you see the dessert table. With so much food, the party atmosphere that gets us all Greek dancing is part joy, part calorie-burning strategy...

I love it. I love my family's happiness and the glow of Jo and Sam together. Lynne and Eva even seem to be happy in the same room, talking and laughing and learning Greek dance moves. Life is good, and I barely sit out any dances. This is perfect practice for the wedding. I soak in the moment.

The party is an open-house atmosphere with a steady flow of relatives, friends and neighbours coming by to congratulate the couple. Dad is run off his feet, answering the doorbell so many times, he often doesn't make it back to the living room before it rings again.

"You take over," he tells me over the music on his way past me.

"Let's just go sit and talk close to the door," Lynne suggests to me and Eva. "It'll save us the back and forth trips."

So we are right there when Matt arrives. There's a suppressed air of excitement as he steps past Lynne holding the door for him.

"I got into Harvard!"

My frustration with Matt evaporates at the delight in his eyes, his face flushed with the thrill. Our problems can wait. This is such a happy day; his joy will fit right in.

"Oh, Matt," I exclaim. "That's amazing! That's the very, very best news. I'm so, so happy for you!" As I lift my hands to embrace him, he leans and...grabs Eva instead. Her skirt flares as he twirls her around.

I freeze. Time slows down. It must have, because Lynne hasn't let go of the door, and I can't take a breath. As Matt and Eva finish their spin and come to rest facing me and leaning on each other, I finally exhale. And then time restarts as Matt reaches to squeeze my still upraised hands.

"Thanks," he says a little breathlessly. "I'm proud of me, too."

There hasn't been any time to think.

I am being loved half to death—pinched, petted, kissed—by my thia Lydia (they're all 'thia' or 'theo,' Aunt or Uncle) when a visual image grabs me, and I can't let it go. In a flash, I'm remembering my favourite stuffed animal, a caramel-coloured puppy with large brown spots that I christened with droplets of water from a Dixie cup and dragged around for five years, insisting that he actually answered to Tache. (Yes, I knew even then that *tache* is French for 'spot.') After years of loving abuses, poor Tache had no eyes and had been stained by food, crayons, and dirt.

"It's a good thing Tache found you," my father would say. "You're the one I would want taking care of me if I went blind at thirty-five."

I haven't thought of Tache for years, but I know now how he must have felt, how bittersweet to be roughed up by the complications of affection and love.

"Mi stenehoryese pethakimou." Don't be sad, my child.

My thia Sophia is standing beside me.

"I'm not sad," I say. It comes out slowly, like the delay in a long distance call from half a world away. I think in English, of course, and have to speak in Greek here, so it takes a minute.

243

She gives me a pointed sideways look that lets me know I'm not fooling her, that she saw what happened at the door. Then she squeezes my hand. I want to squirm, but something in her warm grasp holds me there.

"Maybe a little?" she coaxes in Greek.

I wait a moment. "Maybe a little."

"I was once beautiful girl," she says, and her English startles me. "I was to marry handsome man in village. Teacher. His name Spiro." Her face brightens at the memory. "But before wedding is fire in kitchen, so…face not beautiful, no wedding."

I gasp a little, and stare at her face, at the puckered skin, the huge scar on her right cheek. It makes me see flames. I look at her now and try to see clear skin, try to envision what would have been if she could undo the accident. I see her laughing with children around her, with a husband who loves her, pouring her wine. In my mind's eye, he toasts her and their glasses touch, glass lips in a wedding's echo. Wine bounces a little, but never spills.

Her name is Sophia Alexandria. It takes my breath away how well that name suits her, because Sophia means wisdom. And Alexandria hits at my heart, makes me think of the ancient Greek library that burned down, but survived history. The name fits. Wisdom living through flames.

"Mi kanis etsi," she tells me suddenly. 'Don't do that.'

I'm startled. Do what…How did she know?

"Spiro was idiot. He lose best wife," she says, sounding sure, looking at me hard. "Remember."

Chapter Twenty
Spinning Away

Naomi

"Where did Matt go?" I ask.

I find Lynne exiting the washroom about twenty minutes later, the next time I can manage to extricate myself from the throng of Greek relatives.

She gives me a funny look. "I don't know and I don't care, and neither should you. I have half a mind to throw that ridiculous flirt out of here for you."

"What?"

Lynne is unapologetic. "I want to defend my best friend, who clearly won't defend herself."

"Please don't kick them out. I don't want a scene."

"I won't say anything, but I want to, that's for sure. You're gonna let him get away with it."

"He didn't do anything."

"Oh, come on, Ny. Is having a boyfriend so important to you that you'll let him disrespect you and say nothing? Think about it. He gets to do whatever he wants and he still gets *you*. But what do you get?"

"I don't want him to leave me, Lynne," I say quietly.

"If he's acting like this, Ny, he's already left."

For years, long before she'd even met Sam, there's been this flattering murmur around my sister, and candid talk of the streams of lovesick suitors that all our relatives, near and far, imagine must be beating a dent into our door. I've never begrudged my sister her beauty. Before Sam, Jo had two steady boyfriends who couldn't keep their hands off her olive skin or out of her long chestnut hair. She's wise and brilliant and subtle, a real genius at math, and she carries herself like a picture of grace. She walks into a room and holds its attention in silence, and she doesn't need a ball gown. I love that about her. It's not the admiration for her that has me feeling like a piano out of tune, always just a fraction of pitch away from producing the right kind of music to enchant. That's not what bugs me; it's the badly concealed pity on the subject of my own chances where guys are concerned. It seems a foregone conclusion to most of my relatives that I'll always be single, that no one will have me because I don't 'walk with the crowd.' They assume there will be no boys for me.

Okay, truth.

Ever since I was a preteen, I've worried that they might be right. But I've also known in my gut that I'm worth more than believing I'll always be alone.

It's not news to me that my story about boys and men will be different than most. Around me in school, girls are dating and having an obviously fantastic time flexing the muscle of attraction so easily. They seem to fashion their place on the arm of a date as quickly as they would snatch

a pair of sexy new shoes. Watching them, laughing hysteri-
cally or encircled snugly in the space under his arm, I've felt
only half envious, only half longing for that spot. The other
half (I admit it) is almost smug, because I know something they don't. I can sense with uncanny accuracy, how
many—or, really, how few—such relationships are real, in
the lasting, committed, loving sense. The numbers are not
good; favourite shoes, after all, are not only made, but also
lost, ruined, or quickly replaced.

Lynne is right; I want more than that. I want to have
my heart taken seriously, to have a space under the arm of
someone who will give that space to me as mine, not so
that I can own it, or him, but so that I know we're real
partners—not just convenient, good enough until someone
better or sexier comes along.

From knowing my landscape, I know I'm years—in some
cases lifetimes—ahead of most of the others. And that's why
I'm putting up with Matt right now. Because he's a good
guy. Maybe he just needs time to grow up.

There's something else, too. I don't want to be alone. I'm
so tired of having to prove myself. It's shallow and stupid and
'unbecoming,' as Dad would say, but having a boyfriend has
helped me relax and know that someone is attracted to me,
so it's confirmation that I must be worth it. The idea was,
with Matt in my life, I could stop trying to prove everything
all the time. That, at least, was the plan. But what do I do
now, since he's proven that I still have to prove myself? I've
had to do that all my life, and I'm tired of it.

Even with my own extended family, my own Greek
relatives, I saw quickly that to most of them, for the longest

time, weakness in legs was instantly synonymous with weakness in brain. Growing up, I wanted to scream "I don't move like you, but I can think just fine!" I've seen many relatives both discuss me and address me while staring at my legs, and I've felt something akin to the indignation that amply-bosomed women must experience when their breasts precede them into a room. My struggles to express myself fully in Greek did not help this prejudice any. The language would fall off my tongue in staccato spurts, and my knowledge of my relatives' preconceived notions of me, their misunderstandings about my lack of mental capacity, used to severely stunt the fluidity of my performance. Whenever I tried to have a conversation in Greek with someone who made me nervous, I felt as if I was operating in slow motion, in a nightmare where my tongue went on strike as the conduit for the perfectly lucid thoughts waiting impatiently to be cut loose from my brain. Using my parents as translators never worked, either. When I would choose to respond in English to the Greek around me, I could see disbelief rearing its ugly head on my listener's face. If the responses Mom or Dad gave on my behalf in Greek were a direct translation of what streamed out of my mouth, then these people had to seriously entertain the notion that I was intelligent, after all. I observed as many faces struggled with this dilemma, watched the revolutionary synapses of such a notion attempt and fail to spark in their heads. I watched this and felt the salvation of humour's tickle, the irony that it was my intellect being doubted when it was them unable to understand.

It's not so bad anymore, as I get older, as I follow my cousins into university, and as their parents see us chatting at family gatherings, clumped together talking about mutual experiences, puzzling over the dilemmas of higher education. Also, a lot of my extended family has learned more English than they used to know, so now they understand that my words are mine. But the insecurity of their doubts, their patronizing and infantilizing, has never left me.

It's not just them, either. Every time I go out into the world and a stranger on the street assumes I come with an intellectual deficit (and that if I do, I'm automatically worth less), that translates to more pressure in me and on me... to say just the right thing to change their minds, to dispel myths and reconfigure assumptions about disabled lives...

How can I explain?

In school, I'm the one with the answers bobbing up and down in my head, but I always have to be sure my answer is perfect, not only right, but arranged precisely before I raise my hand. I can't, won't, draw attention to myself and then make a mistake. When I do, I retreat—question myself and my confidence. I know there are expectations loaded up in me. I feel the presence and pressure of my category, 'disabled girl.' My success or failure has tangled in it, implied in it, the successes and failures of all like me. If I win, stereotypes will float away like torn tissues on the wind. If I fail, I will be just another one who fits the assumptions, and everyone's chances of being appreciated for potential, instead of pitied for weakness, will go down with mine.

Everything, everything, hangs in the balance, every time I open my mouth. No, I'm not a little mouse who never speaks in class. I don't throw myself at silence to protect myself, but I choose my stones. I break silences carefully and well. Everywhere I look on my school record there are As, but none of them have prepared me for a moment like this—a moment when the guy I trust the most shocks me. A moment when words, for all the planets of possibility they normally open, fail me.

Why don't I get hopping mad at Matt? For one thing, I love him, and in that moment, as he floored me with his insensitivity, I froze in absolute shock. For another, I don't want to dump him and fight over this. He didn't mean it. Grabbing Eva instead of me and spinning her around like that was probably a spur of the moment expression of exuberance. Getting me to stand up is a production. Spinning her around was simple. Easy. Fast.

It's not his fault. And it's not like I don't get a lot from him. We have a bond. He's told me things he's never told anyone. And I remember how, just the other day, he had defended our relationship to my father. When it happened, I was annoyed at his tactics and we fought, but now I cling to that moment like a blanket. No one can take that away. And even Lynne doesn't understand what a relief it is to go out in the world with him on my arm...In one visual image, I reach the world with a statement that I'm at rest. The proving can be over because I have him, a regular guy. But is it over, or did Matt just prove, by spinning with another girl, that the proving has only just begun?

"Eat, eat!" The third aunt around the circle of chairs is pointing expectantly at my untouched plate, piled high. She is not pretty, but she is strong. She stands firmly and her thin frame seems to have sprouted from productive, dependable earth. Her body is a ripple of muscle built by the hard work of building a life in a new country. Not every woman at this party looks like her in an exact sense. Some have wider frames, some rounder bodies and less angular faces. Others flash easier smiles and are younger behind the eyes. But in this moment, I realize these are the women I come from, all with so much work and history in their bones. There's a lot their no-nonsense ways can teach me.

"Yes, thia, I'm eating," I promise, and I begin to make good on this. I can't control Matt's actions, but I can get back to basics and take care of myself. Eating is the perfect thing to do right now, important, but also methodical and routine.

I don't have to think anymore.

The minute I finish eating, as if on cue, I am surrounded. The time for being pensive is over.

"Come, dance!" Sophia sweeps up next to me and pulls my arm gently, as Jo, quick and confident in her nefarious tactics, snaps my belt undone and my footrests out of the way.

"No, no! I don't—" I try to protest, but I'm out-flanked, outnumbered.

We walk slowly over and join the women, linked in a circle by a chain of arms. I am slow and behind the beat, but Sophia and Jo show me the routine of stepping forward, back, and to the side, the small hops, bends, and kicks. They are patient, and the three of us form our own link, our own small huddle. We laugh and work, work and laugh, and as usual, my brain picks up the moves and rhythm quick as fire, my body slow as winter.

I make a million mistakes and sweat like a lumberjack, but here, just here in the huddle, it doesn't matter.

Over the pulse of music, Jo whispers strategically right into my ear. "You don't dance, my ass."

When the dancing is over, I'm happy but exhausted. My head is pounding. I can't wait to get to bed and stick my nose back into the novel I'm reading, *The Poisonwood Bible*. I'm addicted. All my life, my disability has been a thing to get through, get past, get over. And now, I've been ushered into the mind of Ada Price, a girl thrown into the Congo right before independence. She actually loves her disability—LOVES it. I can't get enough of Ada. I'm actually eating her words when I read them, and it feels like hardly realizing you've been starving until you have food in front of you.

After the roller coaster of my day, I need some of that food badly tonight.

Chapter Twenty-One
The Other Woman

Naomi

"This one goes with your hair."

Seconds ago, my eyes were drawn to the same red flame hanging off that mannequin, and now I can't tear them away.

It doesn't matter that Dad doesn't like it. I still want it.

I reach out and feel the cool, soft, satin-smooth water between my fingers.

Like a fickle spotlight, Dad has moved on already. Even if I couldn't hear it, I would still have felt it. I can script what he is nattering on about.

"It's too bad it's not for you, really. You have to think about what it'll look like when you're sitting down."

"It'll look gorgeous, Dad," I counter, loving how the dress flows, easy as a ripple, to right below my knees. "Matt says I have hot legs."

Dad takes full advantage of looking down at me. "Matthew doesn't get a vote," he says flatly.

"My boyfriend does too get a vote," I snap. "Unless you're planning to be my date at this wedding, I'm going to try it on."

"You look great, darlin'," the saleslady coos. "Just be careful. You could stop traffic in this dress!"

"Thank you," I beam, shooting my father a look that says "See?"

I focus on my image in the mirror, thinking how the silky skirt will fan out on the dance floor, Matt's arm firmly encircling my waist. In this dress, he'll only have eyes for me.

He will.

Dad and I walk out of the small bank of change rooms to come face to face with a nosey shopper.

It's like something out of Theatre of the Absurd.

I, in my low-cut flame of a red dress, am standing with my walker, enjoying my reflection. My wheelchair stands empty in the change room and Dad is beside me, fishing for words as a skinny, wiry woman exclaims about how lovely I am, "You're so beautiful, love, aren't you?" she croons, patting my cheek. "She's so precious!" she extolls, in Dad's direction. "Are you her father? Well aren't you both just so brave! There's just no telling why these things happen, now is there? We just have to be brave, don't we? And really, love, is this dress appropriate? We wouldn't want anyone to get the wrong idea, now would we?"

On that point, I have the good sense to clamp my mouth shut and keep the truth to myself. It's none of this stupid lady's business how I want to look at this wedding! How do some clueless strangers end up thinking it's a good idea to broadside a person in a wheelchair or using a walker with public displays of 'sympathy' like this? It's so insulting, it's painful…

"I think he's ashamed of me," I whisper to Matt, setting the truth free between us as we lie curled close together on my backyard hammock.

"Who, your dad?"

"No, the green-eyed monster. Of course, my dad."

He pulls me closer. "Naomi, you're smart, you're rocking university, you're hot, you crack your friends up all the time, you've got the patience of Job, and you have a stud for a boyfriend, if I do say so myself. How could your father be ashamed of you? There's just no way."

I sigh—a deep, tired, frustrated sigh. It feels like all the air I took in—an army of oxygen—has been parachuted down into my chest to scrounge for answers and proof. I can explain about the dress shopping, but the idea of rehashing that scene makes me want to cry. That would mean telling him the whole story, and I just don't have it in me to go there, and speak everything out loud.

So instead, I say only, "What you mean is there's just no way *you're* ashamed of me, and that's not the same thing, Matt. You know it."

"Okay, so enlighten me. What is there to be ashamed of?"

I raise myself up on one elbow and look at him, hard. "Roll over and look at what's sitting empty on the front porch right now."

Matt stays where he is and groans. "Forget your wheel-chair right now. It has nothing to do with…"

"Bullshit. It has everything to do with this. You asked me why my Dad's ashamed, and that's the answer, like it or not. And he's driving me nuts about this wedding, you know. Absolutely out of my mind. Haven't you noticed, or are you too busy flirting with Eva these days?"

Matt's eyes spark then. "Flirting with Eva, Naomi? You're kidding! I don't flirt. And you should talk, my girl. You're the one who invited Curtis to your sister's wedding!"

I'm flabbergasted. "That's not because I flirt with him, or because I want to. You're my boyfriend, and my date for this wedding, and I'm very clear on that. I invited Curtis to the wedding because he's never been to one, in his whole life. He has no family, Matt. There's no one in his life to include him in a celebration like this. Can you imagine never having had that experience?"

Matt just grunts.

"Don't be mean, Matt. I'm dating you, but that doesn't mean I won't show basic kindness to another guy. And that does mean you have to accept me, as I am. It's enough that I have to accept my dad's hang-ups about my disability. He's my father and he's fought for me his whole life. He's allowed to have his issues and be infuriating sometimes. He didn't ask for all the hard things in his life, but he takes them on anyway and he's been in my corner forever, the best way he knows how to be. But I don't need this from you. You made a choice."

"Can you please be angry about one thing at a time?"

"I am angry about one thing. It's the same thing, your problem and Dad's. You hate that I'm different. You wanna hide from it, like it's something to make disappear instead of something that's part of me. You just said it yourself, Matt. You said 'forget about your wheelchair,' like I can just fling it aside and pick the times that my disability affects me, the times when it shows or doesn't show. Well, I can't do that."

"You can't, or you won't?"

I shift and study where the hammock's material has dug in and left its mark, making my arm look strange. "Both," I say. "Take me as I am, and cut out the stupid jealousy. You're better than that."

"You can't blame me for not liking Curtis. You're jealous about Eva, remember?"

"You *flirt* with Eva, remember?"

Matt is silent.

"I don't know what I'm going to do with that sister of yours," Dad muses as he serves our stir-fry. "Who in their right mind chooses bright red and bright blue as wedding colours, can you tell me that? What happened to green and gold, or purple and yellow, or… "

"Well, Jo is the bride, Dad," I remind him as I sign off on an email briefing Matt on the wedding tux expedition scheduled for next week. "And the colours are royal blue and red. I like that. Besides, it's up to Jo and Sam, not you or me."

"Yes, but this is a wedding, not the Fourth of July."

I roll my eyes. "Oh, Dad. This is not your business. Let it be."

"Don't be sassy, Naomi." He puts down his knife and looks at me quizzically, raising an eyebrow. "Are you okay?"

"Sort of.. Not really, but I will be. I'm going to my room. I'll eat later." I turn my wheelchair toward the back hallway and begin to roll myself away from my dad.

"Phone Matthew back first."

"I'll call him later."

I can feel Dad's eyes staring at my neck. "Did you two have a fight again?"

I say nothing.

He's sloshed.

The truth hits me, and pain zings through my forehead as I watch Matt make a fool of himself on the dance floor—with Eva in his arms. I sit bolt upright, raise my chin almost imperceptibly, and paste a pleasant close-mouthed half-smile onto my face. Just a few minutes ago, I'd been beaming a real smile as I watched my sister and brother-in-law sweep across the dance floor, in their first dance as a mesmerizing, regal married couple. But now...

I force myself to look at Matt and Eva, feeling both lightheaded and oddly clear, at once. There will be no more 'soft place to fall,' no more of me cushioning the blows he deserves. As I watch him fondling Eva, holding her butt in his hands like firm grapefruit and, yes, nuzzling her neck as the slow song progresses, I know this is it. I'll wait until he's sober, (a tiny courtesy that I might even rethink) and declare myself done with him.

We are *so* over.

Around me, sympathetic looks are settling in my direction, and because of them, I stop scrutinizing Matt's mess for a moment and instead let my gaze roam the room—a few seconds for the wait staff bustling around the tables like eager, high-speed penguins, then a few to admire the red roses Jo had chosen as centrepieces. A few more—dear God, my heart hurts—to beam at the enlarged framed photo at the entrance to the banquet hall. Jo and Sam holding each other. They fit, like exact puzzle pieces.

And finally, back again I go, like a driver rubber-necking to gawk at a burning car, to glare at my once-beloved with his slut. Only half an hour ago, I'd been dancing with him, had twirled with him—the skirt of my red dress flaring out as I had dreamed it would—and held him close while, over the loud speakers, Frank Sinatra crooned about champagne being no thrill at all.

The irony of those lyrics strikes me now as I watch Matt and Eva.

Matt's been nursing drinks all night. When he'd gotten wobbly enough that he could no longer dance with me while augmenting my somewhat shaky balance, I'd told him to stop drinking, said my feet were tired, and sat back in my wheelchair to watch my world fall apart.

I can't help but wonder what I've done wrong.

Had I expected too much of Matt? Was it a lot to ask, lifting my wheelchair in and out of his trunk when we drove together, accepting that I can walk, but not far or long, that I move more slowly than the Evas and Jos of the world, that when we danced, my half wasn't the easy, slinky, flowing motion fitting the definition of sexy that Matt might have chosen?

But he chose me, and when I warned him that the two of us getting together wouldn't be all picnic, he'd said he didn't want a picnic. He wanted me.

Christina Minaki

So what`s happened to that, now?

I give myself a mental once-over—electric smile, white, straight teeth, ample boobs, healthy skin, buff arms, long legs, also buff from merciless adapted workouts. I know I'm physically beautiful, with a big heart and my own opinions—the whole package, really. My focused mental mind can win arguments with my physical one, and after years of practice, I manage to get used to heading those negotiations while doing everything else, including falling into—and now out of—love. Not bad.

I'm worth it, damn it. I'm worth the effort!

And I thought Matt was, too.

"I'm so sorry about him, Naomi."

Kendra, a fellow bridesmaid sits down beside me, and for a moment we both watch the horror show still unfolding on the dance floor. There's a techno beat now beginning to thud through the banquet hall, and all around, people boogie and sway. My eyes are glued to one set of bodies— their every move a suggestion.

"Never mind. I don't care."

"Yeah," Kendra guffaws. "Tell me another one."

"I'm not lying," I say, a little sharply.

"Your sister is gonna come over in a minute to talk to you. She and your Dad have been plotting about how to throttle them."

"I don't need the help."

"What do you need?"

"I need Jo and Sam to have a blast on their day and leave those two to me. Is she okay right now?"

"What do you think?"

260

I lean back in my wheelchair. "Before, you know, I wanted to be someone else. Another woman," I laugh, a little angrily. "Someone with another body, one that can move like that," I say, pointing to the dancers. "But now I just want it to be okay to be me. There has to be a guy out there somewhere who's ready for that. Don't you think?"

"I don't think. I know. And in the meantime, I also know what you need. Let's go shake our booties. Show 'em how it's done, no?"

Curtis

I want nothing more than to get up and punch that piece of shit.

Look at you, I think bitterly, making an ass of your sorry self with Eva, in front of Naomi and her family. You have no friggin' shame. If I had Naomi as my girlfriend, she would feel respected every day of the week, I vow. Sure, you're drunk. You'll hide behind that tomorrow for sure—maybe for the rest of your life, even. You have a girl like Naomi and you are so friggin' full of yourself, you think you can just drop her for an evening and then pick up again where you left off. Anyone who actually deserves her would make damn sure she knows that whatever he was doing, he was hers and she matters. You don't make her feel small. You don't make her watch you get busy with someone else, at her sister's *wedding*.

If I could sear Matt with my eyes, I would.

That idiot takes so much for granted, he makes me sick.

I'm fuming. Matt's not the one with no family, because someone took them away from him. And he doesn't understand how much I would give to be him. I cherish this

261

wedding, and the girl Matt's devastating right now, so much that I'll keep every single photo and memento of this day. I'll keep them all, and I don't care if that makes me seem pathetic. That's how rare a day like this is for me, while Matt's calendar is so full of happy days he'll combust from the gluttony.

I really can't stand that guy.

I sit on my hands, so I won't use them.

Screw that, I think suddenly.....What goes in, must come out. If there's one thing that I know about drunks, it's how true that saying is. Matt will be pissing like a race horse soon enough.

I head to the men's room to wait.

As he pulls open the door, Matt is slurring out the words to the Sinatra slow song that he and Eva were making out to on the dance floor.

Totally unconcerned, totally relaxed, totally an asshole.

The stinging words I've prepared fail me. This idiot's not gonna get it. He's not going to hear, let alone understand.

But I need to kick something, so the trash can takes the fall instead. I'm not about to draw blood at Jo's wedding.

Matt sloshes through the doorway. "You okay man? Do you need some help?"

"Shut up, shit head, I'm not the one who needs help. *You* don't deserve Naomi."

Matt's bent toward the fallen trash lid before the words register. He throws himself at me and I step back, letting him crash to his hands and knees on the ceramic tile.

"Who does she deserve? You?" Matt snarls.

"Why the hell not?"

"Oh, please," Matt scoffs thickly.

"At least I'm man enough for her," I shoot back.

Matt tries to get to his feet, but loses his balance.

I leave him on the floor without a backward glance.

"This isn't over!" Matt hollers, as the bathroom door swings shut.

"Oh, I'm shaking." I almost laugh.

Naomi

"Naomi, you have an exam tomorrow. Get up, please."

I pull my quilt back up to my chin and groan. "I'm not working on anything today."

Dad kisses my forehead. "Sulking won't bring Matt back."

That wakes me up faster than coffee. "I don't *want* Matt back."

"I know, honey. Just remember, he's a teenage boy trying to figure out his life. He messed up in a big way, but guys do that. When I was his age, I was an idiot a lot of the time."

"Are you excusing him?"

Dad is shocked. "Dear God, no! I just don't want to see you hurt, that's all. I want you to realize that what happened yesterday was about Matt. It had nothing to do with you. Don't blame yourself. But the best revenge is getting up and getting on with your life."

I roll over in bed and sit up. "I don't give up, Dad. I danced at the wedding and gave my speech for Jo and Sam because I love them and life goes on. And tomorrow, I'll ace my exam and get back to my workouts. But today, I'm going to be unreasonable and sad, if that's all right with you."

I flop back down and pull the covers up again, with finality.

I hate being unfocused in class. I should be listening to this lecture on The Treaty of Versailles, especially since it's so interesting. Dr. Gustav is talking about how, instead of brokering the peace everyone wanted so badly after World War One, the Treaty ended up making international matters worse. I'm not tuning out because I don't get that. I think maybe it's because I do.

I let these facts wash over me, trying to imagine all of those leaders fighting it out, a strange extended family at odds. Gustav is explaining how, in the aftermath of World War One, Hitler trained his German troops in secret, and then made invasions into territory and with weapons clearly prohibited by the Treaty.

Okay, so I am listening.

I turn my head as the door to the room opens. I can never get used to people showing up late for lectures. Some people in my class are single moms, a couple more with tough stuff going on, like dying parents, a couple of cases of really bad mono, and a few who are putting themselves through with no tuition help at all, working bizarre shifts. I don't need to be told that everyone has a story, that you can't tell by osmosis what someone is carrying or working through, or how they're hurting. Cars stall. Babies cry. I know this.

But there are people who float in here any old time, rejoicing that there is no late slip and no attendance sheet, as if this is first-come-first-served seating and because they're paying tuition, they can decide how they roll. That drives me nuts.

I shouldn't even be thinking about slackers. I'm distracted today, which makes me mad. I haven't been myself since the wedding.

The wedding.

Just like that, I'm remembering Eva and her drunkenness, which takes me back to Matt's behaviour, which leads straight to the string of emails I see behind my eyes whenever I blink now.

> From: Matt Dumond
> <slightlylessthanagod@email.com>
> To: Gavin Dumond <g.dumond@
> email.com>, Naomi
> Demas <funkylady@email.com>
> Subject:
> I had a horrible experience in
> class a couple of weeks ago. I've
> kept it a secret until now, but
> it's messed with my mind. I have to
> talk to someone, but I don't want
> to tell anyone about it but you.
> In my media class, my teacher, Mr.
> Shabir, did this experiment with
> us. He handed out glamour head-
> shots of girls and guys, to all of
> us. We passed them around and read
> the detailed bio that came with
> each one, and after that we were
> told to put each photo in one of
> two piles, based on what we knew
> about the models in them: one pile
> for people we would likely date,
> and one for people we would like
> as friends.
> In round one, most of the photos
> ended up in the 'date' pile—these
> were pretty impressive people,

Dad. Then Shabir sends around full-length photos of the same people—still glamour shots, but now we could see different details left out of the first round. Disability details, as they applied to each model—wheelchairs, walkers, guide dogs.

And just like that, all the photos ended up in the 'friend' pile. There were three people who didn't change their minds.

None of them were me, Dad.

I have a disabled girlfriend, but none of them were me.

How am I gonna face Ny, Dad?

The truth is I should've never gone to class that day. It's changed me. It's changed the way I see her, the way I feel when I look at her. And I made a fool of myself at her sister's wedding, Dad. I was dancing with this friend of hers, and even when I was drunk, I knew I would never be able to move like that with Naomi. I was totally stuck on that, and I acted like a moron.

I don't know what I'm going to do.

Matt

From: Gavin Dumond
<g.dumond@email.com>
To: Matt Dumond slightlylessthana-god@email.com; funkylady@email.com
Subject:
Son, did you mean to include Naomi here?

```
From: Matt Dumond
<slightlylessthanagod@email.com>
To: Gavin Dumond
<g.dumond@email.com>
Subject:
Oh shit. I'm so used to e-mailing
her. Shit. Shit. Shit.
From:                       Naomi
Demas <funkylady@email.com>
To: Matt Dumond
<slightlylessthanagod@email.com>
I have nothing nice to say in
response to this, so I will say
nothing. For now. You are sooooo
much less than God.
```

Mary

I can't kill him. It's against the rules. I would like to, though. Just a little, just to teach him a lesson. But then he'd be up here.

Or not.

Let's see...Flood. Pestilence. Locusts...

Nah.

I love my sister enough to let her chew him up and spit him out herself.

Naomi

I'm wondering at what mean, nasty weapons the tangents of the mind can be, when the door opens again.

So much for paying attention in class.

I imagine my double-take to be comical. What's *he* doing here? Why is he here?

But I can't deny that it's Matt, striding toward me. Matt, who doesn't go to my campus, who knows full well I'm furious with him.

But this is very much our pattern, I realize, coming in and out of each other's foreground. He comes toward me with a small note in his hand.

I half-smile, remembering Matt holding that first sign. "Must get home."

You were home, I think. And you lost me. My smile disappears as I consider the new note he's just handed me. *We need to talk. Please.*

"What do you want?"

"I can explain."

"I don't think so. I have another class in an hour, and I don't want to spend that time talking to you. You've distracted me enough already."

"You have to listen to me."

"Excuse me?"

"It wasn't my fault."

"Yes it was."

"How can you be so sure, if you don't listen to me?"

I look at my watch, pointedly. "Talk."

It had been Matt's father's idea.

"Do you know what you're getting into, son?"

"What do you mean?"

"I'm sure she's lovely, this Naomi."

"She is..." Matt's voice trailed off in a what's-your-point tone, as he raked the latest leaf pile into a bag.

"You have to understand, it's not a parent's dream that their child will bring home a disabled girlfriend, son."

Matt paused. "I'm not your child anymore, and I haven't brought her home yet, Dad."

"I know," Gavin conceded. "It's only that she's had a difficult life already. When you're a couple, her problems become yours."

"I've had a hard life, too."

Gavin sighed, exasperated. "All I ask is for you to think about the reality of it, not just the good in her. There're lots she can't do that someone without her...limitations—"

"Aren't you supposed to be a chaplain, Dad?"

"Yes, and I've seen a lot of suffering, Matt."

"We all have limitations. And you haven't asked me what makes her so great."

His father softened immediately. "Oh, I know she's great, Matt. You don't fall for just anyone, or defend someone mediocre this way."

"Exactly. She doesn't give up on people, Dad. She has this friend who's a drinker, Eva, that most other people have freaked out on and backed away from, but not her. Her family's been through tonnes, but they're facing it."

"What did you say her friend's name was?"

"Eva. Why?"

Gavin shook his head, as though trying to dislodge something. "Nothing. Never mind…"

"Whatever you're thinking, Naomi's not like that. She's not the picture in your head…"

"Just promise me you'll think, okay?"

"You know you're not helping me to like your dad, right?"

"He's a good guy. It's his job that makes him think like that, his history with all kinds of hurting people…I didn't agree with him, Ny."

"So how did you go from that to.—"

"He got me thinking. And the more I thought about it—"

"You thought that getting drunk at my sister's wedding and draping yourself all over my friend - the recovering alcoholic, no less—on the dance floor was a good idea? You know better, Matt. You know what Eva's been through. How could you feed the fire like that? Are you seriously sitting here telling me this? If this is your idea of making peace, it's worse than the Treaty of Versailles!"

"What does ancient history have to do with us trying to make up?"

"Neither attempt worked, Matt. And it's not ancient history. You're such an idiot."

"Look, I felt guilty right away. So guilty I was almost sick."

"Good."

He sags back in the chair, deflated. Suddenly he flashes anger. "I said I was sorry, okay? I got drunk to forget that day in class and everything. I think of it and dancing at the wedding whenever I look at you now."

I flinch. "Oh, that's lovely. Just lovely," I groan.

But Matt keeps on going. "Even my mom told me I can do better, that she doesn't want to see me with 'damaged goods.' And now they're making me doubt everything, Ny!"

"DON'T call me Ny. Only people who love me are allowed to do that, you bastard!" The tears stream hot down my face.

"I do love you! I do!"

"You do not!"

"I wanted to forget being confused and just..."

"If you were so confused and you wanted to be sure again and be free, you should have wanted me! Not a drink, a dance floor and Eva!"

"So break up with me then, since you're so disgusted."

My eyes grow wide. "Oh, don't you dare! You're not getting off so easy! *You* are gonna break up with *me*. And I want to hear you defend your pathetic reasons! Was that your tactic by the way—act like such a fool that I would get rid of you, and save you the trouble of being an adult?" Was that your plan, genius?"

"No, it wasn't my plan. But if you want to be furious with someone, why don't you get furious with Sam? He's the one who invited Eva."

"He invited Eva out of loyalty to the childhood they shared together, loyalty to the people her parents used to be. Loyalty. Something you apparently know nothing about. Sam is not my problem, Matt. He's not a problem at all. He was a loving groom, by his wife's side. It's you who has a problem, man! You allowed one stupid assignment in media class to change everything. No one else did that but you, and you have no one else to blame. If underneath everything, you had those hang-ups, then we were headed for a cliff anyway! Don't be shy, Matt Dumond, tell me how you really feel!"

"I don't know how I feel!" Matt shouts, as people turn to stare.

"Well, I know how I feel," I say, through clenched teeth. "I feel like you've let me down. You've dropped me from the highest height, Matt. You're not who I thought you were, at all. And another thing," I shoot back at him angrily. "You're so resentful of Curtis. You didn't want him at the wedding, and yet you're the one who acted like the biggest jerk! Curtis has nothing in the world, Matt, just one, single, solitary box of stuff from his sad past. But he cares about people who care about him, and he shows it. You have everything, but you've treated me like shit. You don't want to admit it, but he's a much better man than you."

Matt stands abruptly, and stalks away, fuming. So much for making peace.

Suddenly he turns back toward me. "I've really had it with this Curtis guy," he sputters. "And would I ever love five minutes alone with that box..."

I skip class, and cry all the way home, until my cheeks are raw.

"Can I do anything for you?" the WheelTrans driver wants to know. I shake my head wordlessly, marvelling that, with the exception of my relationship combusting, the day has been shockingly smooth. My bus had been waiting for me, when for the most part it's the other way around. Today I figure that my relationship on fire must be injustice enough, because the ride is smooth and quiet. Miracle of miracles, there's no other passenger on the bus and the driver accepts it when, in answer to his question, I only shake my head. I am left to cry quietly.

Matt called me damaged goods. Okay, technically, his mother did. But he acted like she was right.

Is he expecting me to feel better because it was that stupid class that changed everything? If that was enough to sway him, wasn't trouble coming anyway?

He knew how much it would hurt me, and what I would think of being reduced this way, and he still did it. He didn't talk to me first about his fears and didn't consider investigating all the ways we could work through our weaknesses together (as if it was news to him that he had them, too). He didn't talk to me after seeing those photos and wrestle with me about how they changed his thinking. He didn't try hard enough to fight the doubts and explore how we could use each of our strengths to balance the things he was worried about in me.

No. Instead he wrote me off. Literally.

I can feel the force of my tears.

It doesn't help that I already have a headache from crying, and from the sighing, squealing and hissing noises of the bus. Opening the front door, the squealing starts up again. This time, it's little brother squeals.

Immediately, Dad is passing me with, "I have to get to the hardware store and Kelly is late. Curtis said he could stay with you and Kev. I'll be back in a half hour or so."

I finally enunciate "Curtis?" but the whisper meets a closing door.

So when I see Curtis at my front door, it gives me a very disjointed feeling, as though I've rolled into a Sesame Street segment—which one of these doesn't fit in this picture?

Part of facing trauma when you're too young for it is learning where to put it, learning to tuck it away somewhere so you can deal with it later, turn it over in your hands, face its sounds, stare it down when and where it's safe. I wasn't all that good at that growing up, which is why I had so many meltdowns at all the wrong times, in all the wrong places. It's the basic mechanics: water + pressure overload = flood. If you solve for x, substituting frustration or hurt or anger for pressure overload , x still equals flood, in case you're wondering.

I'm an expert now. Quickly, I put my hurts away, my jagged stones, and close my mental drawer.

"Nami, Nami, Nami!" Suddenly, Kev comes hurtling toward me in the doorway at highway speed, nearly tripping over his own feet in his haste to get to me. "Nami's home!" he exclaims. "Nami! Nami's home!"

"Whoa! Slow down, buddy." Kev is starting a second circle around my chair when I get my arms out and pull him to me. He starts scaling my chair into my lap. I drop a kiss on the top of his head and meet Curtis' eyes.

"What are you doing here?"

My tone must be sharper than I intend, since Kev answers as Curtis freezes in his tracks.

"He's the giant. We're playing Ride the Giant. Curtis is a good giant."

Curtis' mouth quirks at that. "I also came to talk to you," he says softly.

My head reminds me of the day I've had and I look at Curtis ruefully, as Kev scrambles back to down.

"I'm not sure how that's going to work, Curtis, with Kev so full of beans."

After another hour of rough and tumble, Curtis' whole story comes out as Kev pushes his trains around the living room floor.

Afraid of the mistrust between us ever since he fell off Lance, Curtis had gotten Charlotte to drive him to my house to smooth things over. I'll say this for Curtis: he knows the way to my heart, so he started playing with Kev.

"I just felt like such a loser 'cuz I never explained what happened the day I snuck in and rode Lance. You invited me to Jo's wedding and I came, but I've never had the guts to tell you what I was thinking that day. I thought, if Kev likes me, you'll listen."

I'm thinking of a certain stuffed penguin belonging to Curtis that I've damaged, and I feel so guilty, I can hardly breathe. I want to tell him he hasn't been the only one keeping secrets. But I still can't bring myself to confess, to tell him I make awful mistakes too. The words won't come out, and if they did, they would make me sound psycho. Curtis has had enough of that.

With that, the very last of the tension between us about Lance dissolves.

Curtis' accident on Lancelot's back had been just that— an accident, involving a well-meaning rider, confused about horses. And after all the underhanded goings-on that've been happening to me lately, Curtis' hurting heart reaches me.

He tells me that one of his foster fathers had been an awful drinker, and his son Andy had learned to escape to their barn during his dad's rages. Their horse, Ollie, watched over him, letting him curl up and sleep close by in his stall.

But Curtis had been more afraid of Ollie than his foster father.

"I think part of me believed I deserved the beatings, so I stayed and took them. But it's always bothered me that I was afraid of Ollie. He was such a sweet horse. He used to lie down in the hay to keep Andy warm and safe. I knew it and I was jealous, but too terrified to share the space."

"And you thought you deserved to be beaten because...?" I wonder aloud as we sit in the kitchen, watching Kevin play.

"I didn't save my sisters, or my mom."

"You were a baby when they were killed," I remind him.

"Doesn't matter, in my head. I'm really twisted, aren't I?"

"Ah, get in line."

"You're not, though."

"I'm not what?"

"Twisted."

That makes me burst out laughing. "We're all twisted Curtis, somehow or other."

Curtis nods. "I would never hurt Lancelot, you know. I only wanted to ride him so badly 'cuz he's the most like Ollie."

"I get it. And you must have known I wasn't so furious anymore. I invited you to my sister's wedding, didn't I?"

That settled it.

Kev is standing with the neighbour across the street, protectively clutching his memorized toy train catalogue, and energetically describing each and every toy therein with such enthusiasm that the occasional spasm of knowledge, declared at volume, reaches us. His mother, Kelly, has chosen this particular evening to show herself, which means

I'm not free to call Lynne and lick the wounds of my day in peace.

"You left our son alone" Kelly's in a rage, and as I watch her pace back and forth on the driveway, puffing on her cigarette, I'm reminded of nothing more than one of Kev's Thomas the Tank Engine DVD's with all those trains chugging on missions in Sodor.

"I didn't leave him alone," Dad corrects, his voice on edge. "I left him with Naomi. And she had Curtis as backup."

"Oh, lovely," Kelly shoots back. "You leave him to a foster child's supervision?"

"Curtis isn't a child," I snap. "And I was supervising."

"Supervising from your chair—like that's going to keep him safe."

"Like you keep him safe with your smoking? And my wheelchair helps me move fast, which helps me babysit. Sometimes you really don't think, Kelly."

"Are you going to let her talk to me like that?" Kelly rounds on Dad. "I told you that you don't discipline her, and look at the back-talk you're getting now." She shakes her head. "If you're not tough, you get that one there! How's that working for you?"

Here's the thing about Dad: he may explode at me regularly, but when I'm under attack, he knows how to rally. He knows the truth full well. This is one of those times.

"Let me tell you about this one over here!" He clamps a hand on my shoulder for supportive emphasis. "Naomi has supported this family through huge stresses. She's an amazing half-sister for Kev. She makes up for your absence every day, keeps me sane when it comes to Irene, and keeps herself on the straight and narrow. I don't know what I would do without her, my mother-in-law, and Joanna. And if I complained, in our quiet, secret moments as I've been trying to manage frustrations, I never meant to put her down, or send you the message that it's okay to refer to my daughter as 'that one there.' It's not. It never is."

Chapter Twenty-Two
A Blessed Mess

Curtis

Morality is something I've learned in reverse. As I cowered when my drunk foster father verbally berated my foster mom, I swore I would always respect women. When my foster brother stole his teacher's purse and then dropped her keys down a sewer grate, I promised myself I would not steal. And then there was the other bombshell, the one that struck me in the heart, almost deeper than the murders themselves. My mother had almost left me with my father and escaped just with my sisters. I didn't need the trial transcripts to figure that out. I have a letter to prove it—a letter the police had found among my mother's few possessions, in her own scrawled handwriting. As far as anyone can tell, it was a letter never sent, to a woman my mother only ever called G. But G was obviously someone my mother trusted. That makes her a rare bird.

I keep the letter in my box, and I have this part memorized:

There are times I think seriously of taking the girls and leaving Curtis behind with his father. Julius only cares about his son anyway. I think he even hates the girls. If I don't take Curtis, I don't think Julius will come after us. And I'll be spared watching my boy turn into that man. But can I bear to turn away from the tiny, sweet face of my baby boy? I start thinking I have to, and then I watch him sleep and I know I CAN'T do it. Either we all go, or nobody goes. That's it.

I only met you that one day, but I wonder what you would tell me to do. I wonder if Julius will kill us. I have no one to talk to, so I start thinking crazy.

If my mother had left me and saved herself and the others… Well, it blows my mind to think of how different things would've been for her, for the girls. They would all be alive, if I hadn't been in the way. I have proof of that, in the letter.

I've bounced around foster care a lot. I don't often find a place where I stay for very long. It was easier when I was small, when I could be classified as cute in the chubby-cheeked, chubby-elbowed sort of way. I had places to stay for long stretches then, a couple of families who really seemed to understand me, and I was on the adoption track, too. The adoption track is actually the designated spot for a kid like me, who's been in the system since I was a baby, without parents who could contest the adoption. I'd been considered low-risk, which cracks me up now. Low-risk means that with one parent dead, the other in prison, and virtually no relatives, there would be no one to challenge the new parents because they wanted custody of me. I have no family at all (except for, it turns out, two aunts who disowned my mother when she married The Sire). They made it clear, when they were contacted about me, that they were not about to thaw themselves out for me. So there would be no messy court dates with my jilted biological relatives.

I've been close to being adopted twice. The first time I was not yet jaded, at just exactly Kev's age, nearly five. The memory has a misty, pastel quality in my head, of two people who had hugged me often, even in the brief time they were in my life.

When I turned five, I started having gargantuan tantrums.

And I became an epic saboteur.

I became mean to my assortment of foster parents, and foster brothers and sisters. Most especially the ones in the process of being adopted by anyone.

And I became known in the system as 'a runner.' I didn't mean to freak anyone out. At those times, I was just moving on, before anyone else moved me, before it hurt too much.

It's why I love Kev and want more than anything to protect his innocence. It's why I want to get over my fear of horses—animals misunderstood and misread by a lot of people.

In the short time I've been at Lancelot's barn, I've figured out this much: horses are kinda like foster kids. There are polite ones, rude ones, mischief-makers and hell-raisers, and the ones who know full well how to play the system. To understand these particular horses, think of the little girl who breaks the neighbour's window, blames it on the neighbours' kid, and gets away with it because she knows how to bat her eyelashes. I also know that Charlotte runs a tight ship. The horses are well looked after and the barn is swept and organized. These are the constants.

So when I come in to find Prison Break: Equine Edition, I know this is not business as usual.

First, the stench hit me. The stench of a barn that is decidedly unclean, and so its odours not in check. I know that for whatever reason, I will be cleaning horse poop for hours, and I wonder, for a few seconds, if one or a few of them are sick.

Not so much. One or a few of them are loose.

"What did you guys DO?" I wince. "The one day that Charlotte gets me to open the barn instead of her. Thanks so much!"

It's a wild mess. Stools kicked over. The barn's large sturdy boom box knocked to the floor, whinnying unsettled horses everywhere, even the ones still in their stalls.

I'm not proud of it, but I cower. A few noses are pointed my way over stall guards and there's snuffling and snorting from closed stalls. I am definitely freaking out, but I push that way down. *Rule number one - no fear.* Naomi's voice rings in my ears. Avoiding Toby's questing nose, I walk farther into the barn and turn on the lights. As the fluorescents flicker reluctantly, I can see it isn't just horse shit, but whole bales of hay. What the...? How did they get into the hay stall?

Lancelot's stall is empty! I grab the stall guard and find the broken hook attached to the loose end. I stare into the stall, but no horse appears. If he's not in front of me, he could be behind me. That shakes me out of my momentary haze, and I continue my horse count. Rascal's door is open;

it should be closed. Another empty stall. I look over Orion's stall guard. Empty. That's three unaccounted for.

"All right, you enormous idiots, where are you?" not loud but very, very clear.

Breathe.

Carefully, surveying damage, I make my way to the other end of the barn. I don't have any proof yet as to how this happened, but instinctively, I want to throttle David. Passive-aggressively being careless, leaving Rascal's stall door open. I can see it now. Rascal, bored at night, looking for a challenge, a good time and some rebellion, had managed to get loose.

And the hay stall? Does David want to kill a horse? They eat. They also breathe and poop and sleep, but primarily they eat. So give them a stall full of the hay, and they think they're in heaven. Until they overeat and stuff themselves sick. That's colic and it's deadly. That's why the hay stall door stays closed and latched, dumb ass.

I sneak a peek and locate Lancelot in a standoff with Rascal. There's a wheelbarrow there, on its side. What the hell? David is going to catch shit for that one. Wheelbarrows are supposed to be locked away overnight.

Lancelot is not a happy horse. I don't need any specific horse knowledge to know that. He's backed into the corner, all stiff and almost shivering. He rolls his eyes at Rascal and me, as I quietly attach a lead to Rascal's halter. Lance can't seem to stay still, but as he shifts forward, Rascal snorts and Lance shrinks back into his corner again.

Not good.

Breathe, Curtis, I tell myself. You're just leading a horse, there's nothing amazing happening here. I urge Rascal back before I turn him around. He isn't terribly interested in moving, but once I start turning him, he goes willingly enough. Around the corner, I nearly lose my footing in a smear of horse turds. My foot slides and I automatically pull on the lead for support.

Suddenly, my foot is under Rascal's hoof. I yell. He stops exactly where he is. I try to retract my foot, but his hoof stays planted. Eye to eye, I am not at all politically correct as I haul on the rope. He stares at me in complete incomprehension.

Breathe, I repeat silently.

"Walk on," I try to chirp the command the way Charlotte does when she's lunging him.

And he does!

His nose is buried in the hay even before I let his stall door slam behind him.

I sag on the door and stare at my foot. Thank God for steel toed boots, but still it hurts. Putting it out of my mind, I go looking for Lance.

Naomi

I open the barn door and my heart sinks. Brooms in the aisle, baling string, hay and horse muck mixed and strewn about. The lights are on, so I know somebody other than the equine miscreants is here.

I listen intently and hear a young male voice murmuring soothing noises coming from the back of the barn. Good, David is handling it, I think. Not wanting to spook either him or the horses, I roll softly toward the voice.

"Okay, Lancey, it's okay. The idiot is gone." I smile at the profanity camouflaged in the reassuring tone. "It's just me…" he continues.

I give a small start. Not David. Curtis. Can it be? Shocking or not, it is. I hear a soft clanking and peek around the corner to see Curtis slowly righting a wheelbarrow and backing it away from Lancelot. The soothing invective continues unabated. Lancelot is standing stiff in the corner, staring at Curtis. I ease back around the corner myself. I really don't want to startle anyone now.

Good job, Curtis! You go! I cheer silently, and listen.

Time seems to stop, all other sounds fall away. Just the soothing murmur and progressively quieter snuffles and snorts from Lance. Then, finally, a huge rush of air as Lancelot sighs and Curtis declares "Good boy, let's just walk on." The sharp ring of horseshoes on concrete shakes me awake and I retreat.

I see them pass with Curtis holding a lead rope looped around Lancelot's neck. I smile to myself, so proud of him. When Lance's door shuts with a clang, I reach back, opening and closing the people door, to signal my presence.

Curtis

Lance attacks his hay the way children attack wrapping paper. He tears at it, and it comes away in ripped tufts. If I'd not been so busy nursing my blasted horse-stomped foot, I might have laughed at the sight.

"Why does this place look like Kev's bedroom?" Naomi appears in the aisle as I sag onto a convenient bench.

I clamp my mouth shut, because I've learned early on that the easiest way to get into trouble is to talk yourself into it, and the best hope in a bad situation is to clam up.

"Well, which horse got out?"

Naomi just lifts an eyebrow at me. She expects an answer and it looks like she's going to wait for it.

"Lancelot." Short, sweet and back to silent.

"Lance did this? No way."

"And Orion."

"And..." she prompts when I don't continue.

"And Rascal."

"Who got them back into their stalls?"

Another silent standoff. I break first. "Orion ran past me and I got him in there." I gesture at Rascal's stall, though Orion is too short to be seen through the closed door. "Then Lance screamed. He was backed into a corner behind a wheelbarrow. Lance was so scared and I had to..."

You're forgetting to shut up, idiot. As quickly as the gush of words has released, I clamp down on it.

"So who was on night check last night? Let me guess —David."

No answer required there, just a frowning nod as I busy myself with easing my throbbing foot out of my boot.

"I'm proud of you, Curtis."

"Thanks," I mumble. Then, almost to myself: "I wonder if my mom would be proud of me..."

Naomi's hearing is too good to miss that. "Of course she would be," she answers. "Now, what's with your foot?" she asks, and I love her for the ordinariness of the question.

"Rascal stood on it."

"Let me have a look."

"It's fine." I cringe, bringing it closer in as I massage it, as though to protect it from her interference.

She shrugs. "If you can touch it and squeeze it and fiddle with it, it's probably not broken. Try wiggling your toes."

She watches my face carefully as I do it. "If you put your shoe back on, it won't swell as much. Then we can feed the horses and start cleaning up this mess."

Chapter Twenty-Three
Hinged in the Middle

Naomi

I hug my grandmother close, careful not to squeeze too tight, but hoping to leave an imprint of myself to fill in the spaces of sorrow Irene's decline is leaving behind. The other night, my mother rang the doorbell and woke us all, remaining tight-lipped ever since about what had driven her outside at 3:30 a.m.

She hadn't wandered off, not really. The shock of sudden cold had woken her straight up out of whatever sleepwalking stupor she was in, and she rang the doorbell right away, to be let back in.

But the terror has already settled into all of us.

It hasn't happened before or since, but right after that episode Katina's ticket was booked and her bags were packed.

"Don't stay away too long," I say quietly now.

"Do not be silly," Katina admonishes gently. "It's not a one-way ticket."

I smile slightly. Katina is still Katina, whatever else is changing. Funny in a stubborn way. "Please don't run away. We need you more if we're losing her."

My yiayia straightens and holds my face in her hands. "I will be back," she promises sincerely. "Home is where the heart is." Tears wait in her eyes. "Be strong while I am gone."

I watch her hug the others and I pray that this trip is not a result of homing instinct, by which people and animals seek the place of their birth shortly before they die.

Yes, home is where the heart is, I think to myself. But which home are you talking about, Yiayia?

Dad begins slamming cupboards and banging plates as soon as we return from the airport. Dinner is an affair of both sounds and silence—plates, glasses and cutlery meeting surfaces in a harsh cacophony. Then there's the muttering, grumbling.

"She left!" Dad thunders over his food, unceremoniously beheading his broccoli.

"You knew she was leaving. You picked up her ticket for her, Dad."

"Yes, but I didn't think she'd actually go through with it and leave."

"It's only a month. She'll check in every day and come back the minute Mom gets worse."

"Oh, that makes me feel just great! That's so much better..." he seethes.

Kevin's face begins to crumple, like red origami.

"Dad..." I issue a warning. Then I keep talking. I can't bring Yiayia back any faster, but I can be the solver in other ways. Again. "Don't worry, Dad. While Yiayia is gone, whenever daycare doesn't cover us and the babysitter can't make it, I can take Kev to the barn for some of my shifts. I'll check with Charlotte, but she loves him, and he has fun there. He plays for hours in the loft. He knows how to stay out of people's way."

"That'll work," Dad concedes, nodding. Then he continues his rant, almost as if there hasn't been an interruption. "Katina's done this before, you know," he goes on bitterly. "She reaches her limit and heads off to Greece. She did it when your mom and I hit the rocks, before we split up. She told Irene she expected her to stay and honour her vows, and that she was not going to have a daughter abandon a child. She had thundered, 'You, with a husband who loves you, you have no excuse!' And then she flew off while Irene and I battled it out those last few months. Did you know that when Katina moved in with that enormous suitcase, she was coming back from Greece?"

I shake my head. "I didn't know that," I admit quietly, not sure if I should point out that even stayers flee sometimes. But I say nothing.

"That's right. She's not as much of a stayer as you might think. Everyone is always leaving us, Naomi. We have to look after ourselves. There are people who create gaps and absences, and those who fill them. Your yiayia is hinged in the middle."

Curtis

Not for the first time, I stop just short of cursing Charlotte's miniature poodle, Tank. The name is purely ironic, I know. There's nothing gargantuan or threatening about Tank, with his small frame covered in wool and his heart craving affection. But he lacks all self-preservation, because he can't conceive of a dangerous scenario in which a human might not be able to save him, get him out of harm's way, and cuddle him in the process.

Tank's favourite pastime in the arena is to chase the Gator, the machine we use to smooth out the sand, which he streaks after with abandon. On a good day, I find I'm able to coax Tank to sit beside me on the Gator. Not today, so I'm forced to stop and start the machine, which will mean lumpy, uneven sand for the horses and riders. "Tank, you're such an idiot," I mutter, giving up and turning off the engine. I'll have to get a lead rope and tie him onto the Gator. That means starting over again, and making sure the little doofus doesn't try to jump off and hang himself.

As soon as relative quiet resettles over the arena, I notice Charlotte striding toward me. She's waving at me, and for one sickening moment, I feel sure I've actually hit or run over Tank, and missed hearing the horrid crush of bones over the roar of the motor.

Just now, just in time, Tank comes bounding toward Charlotte from the other side of the arena. She bends to scoop him up, as I exhale with relief.

Charlotte regards me closely. "Curtis, I have something I'd like to talk to you about. Would you come to the house and have dinner with us, please?"

I'm sure I'm in trouble, that I'll be fired, that Charlotte would say she feels awful about it, but she has to do what she has to do. She can't have someone at the stable riding horses without permission, who's never learned proper horse skills or social skills, or...

At the barn, people are expected to be responsible around children and animals, and I've already almost hurt a horse and a dog.

"It's okay, I understand. I'll just get my stuff and go."

Charlotte's eyes widen. "Get your stuff and go?" she repeats, incredulous. "Curtis, you're not fired."

"Oh."

Charlotte sighs. "David and I don't want you to be nervous about the visit. Quite the opposite, actually." She shifts her weight, and for the first time it occurs to me that she might be nervous herself.

"It's just...we know that when you turn eighteen, foster care will spit you out. And we thought you should know you'll always have a job here. There's a cottage at the back of our property. It's fully equipped, you can live there, have your privacy and your life, but we would look out for you. We just wanted to discuss this idea over dinner."

I stand still, stunned.

Naomi

Kev, beside me at the kitchen table, eating a pear with the skin on:

"I have something in my teeth. Need to brush and floss."

"We don't have your toothbrush or floss here, sweetie pie. We'll tell Daddy and he'll do it for you later."

There's a pensive pause, then: "I'm a big boy now. I'm not gonna cry this year." I know he means at daycare.

"It's okay to cry, darling."

He shakes his head decisively, as if this is a decision made, a New Year's resolution he's sure to keep. "No crying. I'll take my bag and lunch box, and I'll go."

I am lamenting the speed and efficiency with which we teach children to stifle emotions, when Kev drops the bomb. "Is Daddy gonna leave us?"

A sick shock spreads through me, and with a fierce shove I push it down. Kevin comes first. I turn my wheelchair so that I'm facing him straight on, and I hold his gaze. "Daddy and I will never leave you, Kevin," I say, as steadily as I can while I work to get the words past the lump in my throat. "Sometimes sad things happen that people can't change, but we will protect you always, every time we can."

I know I'm speaking far over his head, but I feel I have to explain that if we die or otherwise become separated, we won't mean to.

"Why is Daddy sad?"

In the moment, I don't know how to explain that without causing more damage, so I don't. Instead, I say: "He won't be sad for long, not with a little boy like you to love, I promise. And for now, there's KISS MONSTER!!"

Dad doesn't know what he's going to do about Kelly. She doesn't agree with the way Kevin's being raised, which is funny, because she's the one who left him with us. Now she's saying he's being neglected, because Dad is so focused on me and Mom.

Newsflash: I don't need my father to be hyper-focused on me. I'm going to be a career woman. I'm my own woman and he knows it. But he learned that by watching me, not by listening to the throngs of idiots who told us the best I could hope for was to be a receptionist. No offense to great receptionists everywhere, but I'm no receptionist. I'll be an educator, a speaker, a teacher, a lawyer. Maybe a journalist.

Some manner of game changer. Someone who works to stop neglect of all sorts, not someone who perpetuates it. What would Kelly have us do with Mom, leave her wandering the streets? Not on my watch.

And Kev is not neglected. His family has its share of scars, but he's learning that love boils down to action, and that we fight for each other. We love him.

And we'd fight for him, without a thought for preserving ourselves.

Speaking of which, with Yiayia in Greece and Irene back with us, appearances are almost as if nothing in our family ever fell apart in the first place. We are together again, all but Jo, under the same roof. If Kelly thinks our family wouldn't have a gaping hole in it without Kev, she's wrong.

Speaking of gaping holes and losses…

How can I accept my mother's awful stillness? The way she can sit on the sofa, watch television for hours, not want to do anything. All her drive has been syphoned out of her. And this is not depression. I've seen her in depression.

It's something worse. But not Alzheimer's.

I know, everyone says that when they don't want the truth. Except I'm right.

She doesn't wander off, or lose track of time, or forget who we are or where she is. I know the argument is that if she has Alzheimer's that kind of decline is coming, but what if it isn't? She still perks up during conversations—has the right reactions to what happens around her—wants to help and cooperate, laughs and cries appropriately.

Well, all but once. When it counted most.

Dad blames himself, for her diagnosis. Really, what else is new?

He took her to Hope Springs Memorial, because that's where the Alzheimer's specialists are, and that's what Dr. Donovan suspected from the very first.

The nurse who did the test was lovely and kind, and everything was fine, until the questions started coming.

"What day is it, Irene?"

"It's Wednesday," she offered helpfully.

"Which month is it?"

"October." Irene was getting suspicious now.

The questions continued, gently phrased, but they came nonetheless. Who was the Premier? The Prime Minister? Could she look at the clock on the wall (not digital) and tell what time it was? Could she move the hands on the cardboard clock so that they would read 10:10?

She got the political questions and the time questions wrong, and no one could miss that the more quizzed she felt, the more she hardened, toward the nurses and, especially, to Dad. He was, after all, the one presenting her to the sharks, who clearly smelled blood in the water. I know something about how she felt, since I've been judged by doctors and all kinds of medical people all my life. I wasn't there that day, but we've talked about it so much now, I can picture the scene clear as glass.

It didn't take long for the doctor to arrive, consult with the nurse who had done the test and announce, out loud and in Irene's presence, that the issue was Alzheimer's.

Dad's eyes grew wide. "Not in front of her!" he exclaimed, indicating Irene.

The doctor paused for only seconds, then smiled sadly at him. "You're suffering because of this news, but you need to know that for your ex-wife—"

"My wife," he corrected emphatically. If Alzheimer's was here to take her memory, then it would give something too. The family together.

The doctor was no doubt thinking that Dad reclaiming his wife when she was clearly falling apart was only more proof of denial. "For her," he continued, "the disease comes with apathy. The news of her diagnosis doesn't bother her like it bothers you."

He indicated Irene's face—no tears, no storm of indignation—as clear evidence of how right he was, and handed Dad a prescription from the pocket of his lab coat.

"Fill this, just as soon as you can. Trust me."

Dad was going to trust the doctor. Actually, he was going to be good, go to the pharmacy and fill the darn thing, the word apathy ringing in his head.

And then the meltdown came.

"Don't you ever take me there again! I'm never, ever going back!" Irene exploded. But not until they were in the car, on the way home.

Apathy? Yeah, right!

Mary

I know there is a legion of people who deny their Alzheimer's. Denial is the first reaction to diagnosis. Who wants to face their entry into a reality where the mind breaks away from the world like a jigsaw puzzle first put together and then broken apart? When Daddy took Irene for that stupid test, there was a family coming out of a room labelled

'Quiet Reflection.' The man was in his fifties, tall and slim, with salt and pepper hair, a bulbous nose and a firm jaw.

His family was crying, their faces like bloated jellyfish.

Now, my family had turned into them. But they didn't need Quiet Reflection. I wanted to reach down through the clouds and steer them away from being morose. I wanted to yell at them "Cafeteria, you need the cafeteria!" They needed to remember they are a family first. Together in sad times and happy times. And doesn't hospital cafeteria food deserve a better goal in life? So I say "Food fight!"

Irene's cognition may be getting tangled and muddled, but mine is clear. I know—the way she started losing words. Calling a chair a table, answering the question "Do you want ice cream?" with the word 'blue...' Irene doesn't have Alzheimer's...not just because I don't want her to have it, not just because from up here I *know,* but also because it doesn't fit. It's also more than that; it's that something else fits better.

Daddy knows from his pile of research that aphasia can explain Irene's frustration with language, something she never had before. The way she gets edgy and flustered because she knows exactly who a person is to her—the emotional connections in her brain are still whole—but she's losing names and other identifiers. On a good day, during a good moment, she still calls a bank a bank. But other times, it's 'the money place.' The other day, Irene came to Daddy asking "Our girl? Our girl?"

"I'm not sure where Jo is, honey. She's married now, so Sam takes care of her. They went to work earlier, I know that..."

Irene shook her head. "Our girl!" she exclaimed.

Did she mean me? Before, it seemed she always meant me. Instinctively, I saw Daddy look around, hoping Naomi was not sitting in the living room doorway, overhearing what would certainly be another continent-sized disappointment for her.

Unless...

"Do you mean *Naomi?*" he asked. Relief flooded Irene's face, then leapt to his and multiplied like loaves and fish in Jesus' hands. Naomi, *finally* the wanted one.

Irene beamed.

The big stroke happens the next week. Mom wakes up from a nap covered in sweat, and limping.

Dad is getting used to the slide. Losing words, reading, writing. Not being able to finish, or even start simple tasks without instructions. But this...?

In his heart he knew it was coming. I could see the knowledge inside him. What he couldn't predict is how life with Irene back under his roof will begin to feel like they never separated or divorced. Her dementia and whatever is causing it has brought with it a strange coming together. It's as though, in being taken back to its essential frame, Irene's mind shows that love doesn't fall apart when the mind's mystery increases, when words fail and communication changes. That doesn't happen anymore than a moulting bird stops being a bird or moulted feathers, when discarded, stop being beautiful.

It's a strange dance they're doing now. Mom follows Dad everywhere—washing dishes, raking leaves, washing the car, cleaning out the garage. She's become his loyal shadow, and it's as though she's trying to make up for lost time and past abandonments.

Dad used to completely agree with the Shakespearean line "love is not love which alters when it alteration finds." He's ashamed of that now, because he knows how fluid a commitment to love needs to be. The commitment, once made, is what should remain, but the nuances of the meaning of that commitment must be flexible in the extreme. As people change, and those that love them commit to doing and being what they need in the reality of each moment, love, real love, grows to make facing reality possible. Dad's learning that. He's been learning it in increments all his life, but now he's aware of it.

I'm proud of him. I wish I could tell him that.

Naomi

Dear Matt:

I stare at the words on my computer screen, almost cross out 'Dear,' then reconsider. Despite the volcanic eruption that was the end of our dating relationship, I still care about him. And, I have to admit, I can't ignore that he cares about me and is trying to make amends. Failing, but trying.

Matt hasn't gotten up the nerve to call me since our Break-up Blowout, but the e-mails keep coming. It makes sense, when I think about it, because everything between us started over e-mail. Maybe he's hoping that over the next weeks and months, my mind will cancel out the problems between us and move back to the days of our first correspondence.

There's little hope of that.

And this one is making me furious.

First of all, it's a forwarded e-mail. I hate forwards clogging up the arteries of my inbox. Doesn't he know that? Has he ever even met me?

Second of all, the forward is a paraphrase of the biblical miracle, in the Gospel of John, where Jesus heals the man who hadn't walked in thirty-eight years, near the pool at Bethesda.

I've heard the story of that miracle so many times. Jesus coming upon the man by the pool, and asking him if he wants to be healed. And the man's answer: "I have no one to take me down to the pool when it stirs."

So often this is interpreted as complaining on the man's part—as evading Jesus' question by whining about his lot in life and his loneliness, instead. But I don't read that at all. What I picture, through the same words, is a man telling Jesus what his problem is.

When you don't walk and people trample past you for thirty-eight years to get to the pool, without ever stopping to help you get there yourself, it changes you, hurts you, makes you cynical, shows you the 'me first' tendencies of the world. I understand the guy is nowhere close to complaining—he's stating facts, pointing straight at the brokenness of the world. He has probably become self-absorbed, yes. After years of watching everyone rush past, step on him (probably literally), he's lost faith in God, in hope.

If the guy had paused after Jesus' question, and said, "You know, the last thirty-eight years haven't been all sob story, all the time. There's been a richness here, a chance to build bonds and get to know others at the pool, and grow together and pray and learn together. Jesus, I'm so glad to see you, we've been waiting for you! You're such an artist, for giving us such gems to balance the times of struggle! Every time I turn around there's more to learn and more ministering to do. I recognize it's You behind this! And now You're here, God in the flesh...Do with me what You will. I'm in Your Hands. "

That would have been a whole different conversation, a different healing.

But that isn't how the man answers Jesus. He said: "I've been alone, ignored. And I can't get to the water by myself, to access the healing."

So many times, I've sat in my pew or my wheelchair quietly while ministers talked about how Jesus had restored the man's 'independence.' People have a strange and dangerous love affair with independence, with self-sufficiency as the great ideal, as though we've arrived if and when we can prove (or at least convince ourselves) that we don't need anyone but ourselves. God doesn't operate that way.

Beautiful, isn't it?

But not the way this forward makes it sound.

I stare at the screen and consider the paraphrase of the story—the 'whining' man, healed by God, whose disability was a manifestation of God's anger at sin. And at the bottom of the forward, this advice: *Make sure you want to be healed.*

I start firing off a response about the many forms healing can take, and about my take on that little scene in the Bible, but I stop short. I don't want to sound angry, but if I keep going, I will. I don't want to *be* angry.

Matt means well. He wants me to be happy. I know he wants my disability to go away, so we can be a couple without his parents' judgment, and let's face it, without his own. At that thought, my anger bubbles up again, because it's not okay for him to want that, to want from me what I can't be, what I wouldn't want to be. How can he say he loves me if in the next breath he says "I love everything about you, but this'? How am I supposed to feel? The truth is I am who I am, a person with all the qualities of character and personality he claimed to love—*because* of how my disability has combined with other factors to shape me. He can't have the essence of me without it. Yet the irony is that if I was my exact self and also, say, a leaping, somersaulting cheerleader, there would be no opposition, no wedding embarrassments, no "I love you, but not enough" break-up fight. But that contrast is a reflection of his problem with the reality of me, not mine with myself. If life for me were different in the way that his hang-ups make all-important, would we have gotten married, had a brood of kids, never raised our voices?

Most likely not.

But I wonder this, too: what if I were exactly me, but he was the one who changed—became progressive and gutsy and understood that God has healed me by not letting me become a person wishing to be someone else? What if Matt understood that God always heals, just not the same way twice, not always in a conventional, physical, predictable way? FYI: There's not much about God that's either conventional or predictable. What if Matt had been the kind of guy I wanted him to be—the kind who understands that you don't rectify prejudice, oppression, and the discrimination of ableism by telling a disabled person to fix themselves, anymore than you can (or should) fix racism by telling a Black or First Nations person to become white? If Matt understood that, now, at nineteen, nearly twenty, I wouldn't be wondering what he sees when he looks at me, or at which exact moments of our times together he was wishing for an unreachable version of me. I suddenly know how women might feel when they catch their loves watching porn—the awful dread that despite best efforts, measuring up will always be a mirage.

And I question if he sent the forward because he thinks walking is what I want? That I should want a cure? Or because he believes God's only version of healing is granting the ability to get up and walk away? Is Matt somehow justifying dumping me because he's afraid my future will turn out like the Bethesda guy before Jesus showed up?

I'm suddenly cold.

I want to tell him the God I know expects people not to flinch and balk, but to stay, and find their purpose.

Maybe I'm overreacting. After all, I'm assuming what Matt was thinking when he forwarded me that message. But after the way he was acting when I dumped him, I'm making an educated assumption.

> Dear Matt:
> Have you ever wondered why Jesus didn't heal everybody at the pool? The place was full of disabled people, after all. He could have staged a healing bonanza. It was within His power. So why not? I believe it was because disability has a purpose. My life, as it is, has a purpose. This is me, as I

```
am, and I am here. End of story.
Or maybe, just the beginning.
N.
```

Jo

"She won't talk to me about it. So I don't know how she's doing."

"What d'you mean, she won't?"

"I'm not Mary," I say simply, trying to cover the pain.

"Oh, babe, I'm sorry. Can I help, I mean with the lasagna?"

I love my husband for the second half of that sentence, for knowing there's nothing he can do about me and Ny, at least not right now. For not trying to instantly heal something that's taken years to morph into what it is.

"No," I say quickly. "It's done, basically. It just has to come out and cool."

Halfway to the counter, the hot lasagna dish in my oven-mitted hands, I trip, sending lasagna flying in every direction.

Sam is up in a flash, cradling me as I cry. "It's all right, love, we'll order pizza," he comforts. "It's all good, we'll fix it."

"How can it be all good? It's a mess!" I sob.

Sam kisses my forehead, then holds me firmly by the shoulders and looks me directly in the eye. "If it wasn't a mess, we wouldn't be able to clean it up together."

Now my tears are of relief.

Maybe it's the cathartic act of cleaning the food from the floor, the stove, the rug, even the walls. But maybe, most likely, it's the absolute proof of Sam on his knees beside me as we scrub and wash and gather bits of shattered ceramic, strands of cheese, splashes of sauce and chunks of meat and vegetables.

Whatever the reasons, I begin to open up about my splintered family as I never have before. I talk and work. He listens and works, keeping his gentle supportive responses to the minimum, for fear of staunching this new flow of words.

As the mess is cleaned up, the past comes alive and out of my mouth, streaming with the surprised eagerness of air or water rushing through any opening at all.

Even after the separation, our parents tried to keep Naomi and I together. Movies on Saturday afternoons, sleepovers on Friday nights, ice cream and trips to the library or bookstore after school in the middle of the week. Mom and Dad often tried even to do some of those things together, as if the split between them had never happened— as if, for a matter of a few hours, we were all together again, and not in the sense of patchwork, but whole.

"Ny and my mother were always wishing I was Mary. I was never the sister either of them wanted. I could feel it. Still can." I say, matter-of-factly. "And Mom and Dad were so bewildering, it didn't help that they both had a completely different attitude about their relationship. To Dad, the split never happened. To Mom, it was the marriage she seemed to try to erase, or at least that's how it came across."

One night we'd gone to Swiss Chalet for dinner—quarter chicken dinners all around. Dad was in a purple dress shirt and black dress pants; Ny in her finest—a deep blue dress, a red scrunchie in her hair and red Mary Janes. I wasn't sure if Ny looked so polished because she felt like it, or because she wanted to prove she was fine without us and felt proud in her dress.

Even sitting close together around the table, it was as though we were split down the middle—Dad and Ny, dressed and polished. Mom and I looking tired and bruised under our smiles.

"Dad, I have to go to the bathroom," Naomi said quietly as the waitress retreated after taking our orders.

"You'll have to hold it, love. I can't take you, not here."

I saw the pained look on my sister's face. "I'll take her, Dad."

Instantly, both of our parents sized up the two of us—Naomi's ten years to my fourteen, the various permutations of possible disaster. They each weighed this against Naomi's discomfort and my confidence. "Be careful," they both cautioned, simultaneously.

Suddenly, a look of surprise passed between our parents, as though caught off-guard by being in sync.

"I can do it, Dad," I promised. "Ny won't fall. We'll be fine."

And we were. I was patient and protected Naomi's balance, paid close attention when Naomi gave me instructions, "Guard my hips, please, make sure they don't swing too far to the left...Please hold my arm when I lower to the toilet, the bar is in a really awkward position."

A lady or two came and left while we were in the cubicle. Toilets flushed, water ran, and a few times there was the snap of the paper towel dispenser. But by the time we moved from privacy to open space, we were alone.

Naomi was otherwise quiet, pensive as we worked together on transfers, the awkward door and doorway, negotiating hand washes when the wheelchair didn't fit under the sink, when Naomi couldn't reach the soap dispenser bolted to the wall at standing, not sitting level.

The mirror was too high for Naomi to see below her hairline. It was as though she had no face at all, as if, however we tried to see 'eye to eye,' there was a cut-off that made symbiosis a challenge...As we returned to our table and came into earshot, the waitress was putting down our plates.

"For you..." she said to Dad, "and for your wife," she announced, each plate hitting the table with friendly flare.

"Thank you," Dad beamed at her as Naomi parked her chair and I sat back down in mine.

"I'm not his wife," Irene said quickly. "I'm his ex now." It was the exact opposite of the earlier scene, an undoing of the synchronicity of just a few minutes before.

The waitress, Holly, her name tag read, was a pile of apologies. We felt we had to be, too.

Mom could hardly eat. I could see her at war with her food, trying to make sure her chicken didn't touch her fries and nothing touched her creamy coleslaw. The slightly crooked tablecloth made her cringe.

I looked at her and saw my responsibility and my failure, at once. I thought I saw on Naomi's face at the time that she felt it, too, but now I'm really not sure.

We've never talked about it.

I've learned to be afraid of many things because of the particular fabric of my life: not surprisingly, death and abandonment chief among my fears. But my mother's

OCD repeating itself in me has never figured into the mix, even though it would make complete sense if it did.

The truth is, what I craved most growing up was mess in my physical space, an irresponsible move, an unmade bed with crumpled sheets and clothes dumped on the floor, disorganized binders and backpack, Any of those things would've made my mother lose it, and were to be avoided at all costs. But a messy school desk where I couldn't find anything, full of wads of crumpled paper, chewed ballpoint pens and broken pencils—that, I could've gotten away with, if away from home.

"But you never acted on that wish?" Sam asks now, giving me a gentle kiss.

"I was scared that if I took the lid off, gave myself that kind of escape valve, I would never get it back on securely enough, and then my rebellion would start leaking at home. It wasn't worth hurting Mom."

There were times Irene came completely undone—the night a mouse shooting across her bedroom floor turned her raw, inside-out and exposed. Watching my mother then reminded me of taking the insoles out of my shoes and bringing out their innards.

She'd sat, rocking back and forth, with her comforter over her head, weeping. "Get it out, get it out, get it out, get it OUT!! The only living thing in my room should be me," she had wailed. "I can't DO this. OH MY GOD!"

I had stayed up all night, setting traps laced with peanut butter and cheese, and singing to Mom, who lay on the fortress of her bed refusing to move until the creature had been removed.

Neither of us slept.

"Maybe Ny's just done with the roller coaster her life's been. Maybe she thinks that with everything I've been through, I'd bring too much mess back into her life. I don't know."

Sam stares at me for a long moment, clearly shocked by the intensity of my experience. He shakes his head. "You bring so much more than mess, Jo. And I don't think Naomi means to shut you out," he reasons. "She's just busy licking her wounds, is all. She hasn't had proper access to a living, breathing sister, not really. So maybe she doesn't know how to tell you she's hurting."

"After the big split," I continue, "when Mom took me with her, Dad would come and pick me up, and we'd drop gifts off for Ny. I'd leave my doll on the porch for her, or one of my favourite books, or my stuffed animal kitten. A few days later, he'd bring Ny to me, and she'd take her turn. She left me cookies, and a beaded necklace she made, a bracelet, a Cinderella video, a puzzle she had refused to share when we were together. We gave each other our favourite things, traded them for the words we couldn't say. I still want to do that, you know. Give her my favourite things, only now they're words."

Sam gives me another kiss. "Tell her that," he says simply.

We kept it up, the leaving of gifts for each other, long past the point where we needed a go-between. The gifts, of course, changed to reflect shifting maturity as we grew, a small print of a painting one was sure the other would love, favourite novels each thought the other should read, a handmade barrette in the shape of a butterfly, a caterpillar keychain that would light up when you squeezed it. The caterpillar and butterfly gifts were given together and are, to date, my favourite thing from Ny, most especially because of the note attached, that read, *Not ready yet, but soon. Not finished changing.*

Surely, she's ready now?

I throw three of my favourite novels, books that'll give us plenty to discuss, into my car, and drive. I hope they'll do the job of carrying Naomi away from her hurts. Yes, ready or not, books will be our bridge.

I drive on, determined.

Naomi

"Matt says he wants a chance to explain," Dad tells me, with just a hint of cynicism attached to the word *explain*, as he hands me the phone, to do with as I will.

We tried that already, I think to myself. What I'll do, I decide in the few seconds it takes me to seize the cordless phone's receiver, is pitch it with great gusto across the kitchen. The throw, and resulting crash, makes me feel better than I have since before Jo's wedding.

My father walks deliberately across the kitchen and retrieves the phone from where it's fallen, just under the large window. "Wanna do that again?" he asks.

It's after the next throw that the tears come, in a great gush of heaving sobs.

"I want...I want...I want..." the words come out muffled against Dad's shoulder.

"What do you want, sweetheart?"

"I want Jo. She probably won't even talk to me, you know."

"Why on earth would you say that, Naomi? She's your sister."

"I knew, Dad. I knew what living with Mom was like. I should've supported Jo. But I was so busy being mad at Mom for leaving, that I managed to abandon Jo when she was stuck in the middle. When she needed me most, I wasn't there."

"That wasn't your fault, Naomi."

"Oh yeah, Dad?" I fight back a surge of tears. "Then whose was it?"

"Mine. When your mother chose...what she chose..." he says carefully, "I felt I had to respect it. I thought it would be worse if she stayed and resented us her whole life. I let her take Jo with her, hoping Jo would give her a reason to hold on to her sanity. I was so wrong but Jo knew she could come home anytime she wanted. I made sure they both knew this was always home."

"I wanted it to be different, Dad. I wanted the whole thing to be different."

"I know. Me, too. So let's start now."

"Oh, from now on, if she needs me, you'll have to hold me down."

"That's it. That's the way to make up for lost time."

"Ditto on this end, too." Jo suddenly stands in the kitchen doorway, her presence shocking both Dad and I.

"Where did you come from?" Dad blubbers.

Jo raises her eyebrows. "Don't you know? They beam me up now, Dad."

She walks forward, put her arms around me from behind, having tossed a few novels onto the table. "All right, what can I do, Ny?"

"Just be here."

"Where else would I be?"

Chapter Twenty-Four
Letting Go

Naomi

Lynne and I sit together, hashing out problems over cake.

"Ny, the big question is, do you want Eva here, really? After everything, do you want her mess and drama back in your life? Think of the wedding, for one thing. Remember how she embarrassed you."

"She's like a piece of glass under my skin, Lynne. I can't forget her. I can't just be resigned about it and move on and let her sleep in the bed she made. I can't do it. And she would want to be here if she knew how sick Irene is. She deserves a chance to see my mom, just like we all do. Eva needs closure this time. She hardly ever gets any."

"I know." Lynne cuts another slice of the coconut layer cake that sits between us. "I just wonder if you'd be so pre-occupied if it was me who was off 'finding myself.'"

"That's not fair. You're here."

"How very 'Prodigal Son' of you."

"Very funny."

"It's true. The father in the parable wants the son who ran away. He wants him so badly, he spends forever pining for him and does this dance of joy when he comes back, but the steadfast son—"

"I don't take you for granted, Lynne. Neither does the father in the parable, who's a metaphor for God, in case you forgot. I'm not God, and I'm not perfect or always right, but you know why I'm not worried about us, as in you and me?"

"Pray tell."

"Because of times like this. Because we talk. Because we can argue and have it out, and we're still us. We can disagree, and we do, but you won't disappear and do anything stupid like cut me out. And I won't do it to you. We wrestle things out. And we show up. We're stayers. Eva, not so much." I exhale audibly, exasperated and spent.

"You know what I picture when I think of Eva living in the country now with some cousin?"

I say nothing.

"I see gravel lot parties and car surfing, and meet-you-in-the-ravine drink-a-thons. I see trouble. I don't feel better."

"It's Eva. Of course you don't feel better, Lynne. So what are we gonna do? Sweep in there and remove her free will? I just don't know. I'm at a total loss with her, but I don't wanna give up."

"If you really want me to, I'll go get her tomorrow."

"You're the best friend in the world, Lynne. I love you."

"I know. I love you, too. Eat your cake."

Mary

"She didn't exactly choose the outback of beyond out of a wealth of options. She had nowhere left to go." Lynne is reminding herself aloud, mentally checking off the lack of choices as another of Eva's predictable failures. I know what Lynne's thinking as she drives along, of course—that this rescue is another reflection of chances badly spent, no better than a swig of alcohol up, up, away and into oblivion.

"Not so fast. You promised." I watch the moment Lynne hears Naomi's voice in her head.

Well, that's the truth. Lynne had committed to treating Eva with kindness. "Shoot for love," Ny had advised. But Lynne's resistance to this is palpable. To her, love is too much to ask, so far. Love is like a muscle, Lynne was thinking, and muscles get tired of overwork with little to no payback. *Love is like a muscle?* Disappointment floods Lynne, as it should. Disappointment in herself, and she is disappointing me, too. No other person in Lynne's life can bring out that cynical, tired reaction, only Eva. In most cases, she would tell someone off for being so cynical.

My twin, my Naomi, makes Lynne trust love. Why else, after all, has she taken this road trip to a blink-and you'll-miss-it town to snatch Eva back?

As concrete, steel and stone give way to farmland, water and church spires in the distance, Lynne tries to think of what she'll say when next she speaks to Eva, once she wakes up, now that the two of them are alone in the car. She imagines yelling at Eva, dragging her home, forcing her to be a clean support to Naomi, who—Lord only knows why—wants Eva beside her almost more than anyone.

Lynne is thinking people always want the one they shouldn't have, the one they can't rescue.

"You snore like a buzz saw, Lynne says out loud, although she knows that those words will do nothing to wake Eva, deeply asleep as she is in the passenger seat beside Lynne. "How can you sleep at a time like this?"

"I'm not sleeping."

Lynne jolts and imagines herself hitting the car's roof, a popped champagne cork.

"You weren't supposed to hear that."

"It's not like I didn't know you're mad at me." Lynne can hear the shrug in Eva's voice.

"Geez, don't act like you care or anything."

"If I didn't care, I wouldn't be coming back with you."

"That's right, you'd still be back in Eden over there."

"Shut up!" Eva explodes. "That's the first Eden I've ever had. It makes me think…" Eva's voice trails off, her sentence disappearing like a balloon released to open sky.

"It makes you think what?"

There's a long silence, long enough to make Lynne believe there will be no answer. Fine. Be that way.

"That God still loves me."

It's Lynne's turn to be silent, to think of what she'd seen in only the few hours she'd been in Eva's refuge—a beautiful, sprawling home, green space, a honey-coloured poodle puppy, a cousin who sang while she worked in the bright kitchen. If Lynne had been Eva, if she'd not had a healthy mother, if she needed a place to get clean, and finally found one, she wouldn't want to come home either.

Lynne considers turning around and taking Eva back, but can't force herself to make the car perform that move. If Eva's father hadn't died, if her mother had been stronger and alcohol-free, if Eva's aunt and ally hadn't gotten cancer, if the church hadn't pushed her out, if, if, if...how would Eva be different?

You would think that I, Mary Demas, living in Heaven as I do, would have answers to some of these questions, but the simple truth is I don't. So much hinges on the choices we make, on what we do with what happens, on whether we talk to God and listen for the responses. I don't have the answers either, about what will or what would have happened. But I know God puts people in our lives on purpose. I'm watching Lynne and thinking, "Eva has a real chance here."

I wonder what she'll do with it.

In a flash, Lynne glimpses in her mind the version of Eva that Naomi is hanging onto and willing to fight for against almost all odds, the friend who locked her knees at the bottom of the auditorium aisle, who stayed put to save Ny when she saw a collision coming straight for her. She saw the friend who agonized when Kev got hurt because of a hangover, a friend who would show up in church even if bad memories and hurt meant it took being drunk to get her there.

Lynne flashes back to Eva as she'd been when they had met her, in grade school. The year of Grade Six, Naomi had fallen out of a living room chair and deeply bruised her leg. She'd not been allowed to put weight on that leg for eight weeks, and she'd been ordered to get out of her wheelchair and stretch her legs out at every break during the school day. That meant indoor recess and lunch, and Eva had volunteered even before Lynne to stay inside with Naomi, so she wouldn't be bored. That's when the real bonding had happened between them—talking, laughing at inside jokes, goofing off as only twelve-year-olds can...

It hurts Lynne to remember Eva this way—beautiful, pre-addiction Eva. Lynne doesn't allow herself to go there often, and when she does it's bittersweet pain. When she does, she has to concede that she understands why Naomi is fighting so hard for her friend. For their friend.

It's like that weird drawing: when looking at it from one angle, it was an old woman, from another, a young girl.

Look one way, see Eva the drunk. Look another...

Lynne pulls over and takes the note for Eva out of her pocket:

```
I just want to tell you you're an idiot...
but I still love you, you know. You don't have
to come to stay. Just please come. My mom is
slipping away.
N
```

"Why are we stopped?"

"No reason. Just give me a sec."

"You're not gonna kick me out, are you?"

To her own surprise, Lynne laughs. "Nah, it's nice to know you're afraid of me and everything, but I don't hate you that much."

"You shouldn't hate me at all, you know."

"It's not you; it's your addiction, Eva."

"My addiction's not my fault," Eva says defensively.

Lynne carefully ignores that. "You know, when Vikings hit a new shore, they made this huge show of commitment," Lynne says. "The kind of commitment that meant there was no turning back."

Eva turns in her seat to face Lynne, half her face covered in shadow, the other in light.

"What kind of commitment?"

"They would burn their boats." Lynne states simply. "Eliminate the way out, once the choice was made."

"But they could just build more boats, if someone or some people really wanted to go."

"True. But the burnt boats were a symbol, a declaration—a promise. To stick with their decision, to stay where they were needed, to do what had been agreed needed to be done."

"I can't promise anything, Lynne."

"Naomi needs you, Eva. Naomi's committed that way to people she loves. She's been committed that way to her family, to me, to you. She needs that commitment back now."

"I just got clean, found a place that feels like home, that feels safe. If I leave, go back to where everything happened, I don't know if I can hold on. I don't know anything for sure."

"I know. But wherever you're living, you can try."

"I can try." Eva admits weakly.

"That's a good place to start. That's all I ask. That's all Naomi would ask. And you'll be back with your cousin. Your exit strategy doesn't have to go up in smoke."

"But you just said it does."

"And you just said you could always build another boat."

Naomi

South

Although I am made of equal parts sky
and earth, this is home—this soaring. I
spread my wings and gather in the rivers
that the stiff bones of winter will soon
stretch over with a frame for the thick
skin of ice. I am happy that I know, somewhere in my own bones, that the winter
can do what it likes with the skin of life,
but stillness never penetrates the soul of
these. I coast over the trees that I knew
this spring, and I know that green will lie
low and play the game of absence, but
then will return. So will I.

I know this when I must move, fly far
and for long, and there are long nights
and thin sleep, with one eye open. Still,
I move. Still, I fly. Even thin sleep has
dreams. I dream of winter unfrozen, of
warm wind, and the caress of sun—sun
of rich gold, not weakened by the lean
of Earth away from heat. I dream, and I
know soon reality will match this.

I have come this way before.

I wrote this for Mom. She's in the hospital now.
There's this thing I know now about lines—the boundaries we draw. We keep pushing them away.

We think we know where the thing is we can't handle, the thing that is so much to bear it will knock us over and hold us down if we try to cross it.

When we're young, we think when we're old we'll feel spent and be ready to go gently into the night.

When we're not disabled, we might think that if we become so, life will be as good as over, only to realize when we get there—that life is sweet, and it's our idea of the power of each moment to make it so, that's changed.

I've heard people say all the time that needing help with care is a game-changer, that they wouldn't want to need sponge baths and help with feeding, dressing, moving, everyday household stuff. But a lot of the time, when we reach those moments, the moments whose arrival we were sure meant giving up and having nothing left, we find we're not going to quit, that there's much left to live for and purpose left to find.

I get back from school to find Dad crying. Nobody prepares you for seeing that.

"I can't anymore!" he sobs. I can't mop up anymore of your mother's urine, follow her around, catching the pieces of her falling away. I'm putting her in Grace Lodge, Naomi."

So I write *South* hoping Mom will find her way home, or at least manage to find slices of home in Grace Lodge, in our visits, in our vigilance, in our love.

I have to do something with this feeling, with all my loss. Mom qualifies as disabled now, too, so now there are even more reasons why my politics is personal.

Dear Mary:

Your absence is a presence. You know how, sometimes, best friends meet as babies, stay friends for a lifetime, and realize at some point as they get older that they don't remember meeting? Well, I don't remember meeting you. We never did actually meet, I guess. But I imagine a nurse or two, when we were together in adjoining incubators, talking to us about each other, encouraging us to survive so that we could take over the world.

Did you hear those nurses? Did they say, "Mary, this is Naomi. Give it everything you've got, babe, because she's going to need you to fight for her and beside her?" I used to be mad at you sometimes, thinking you somehow didn't fight hard enough to stay with me, to stay with us, to live. But I forgive you, because I realize you had a battle on your tiny hands that was stronger than you—that in fighting to stay for me, you were fighting a force like a deadly storm. God called you home, you got swept away. End of story. You didn't have a choice. And given a choice, I wouldn't take heaven from you.

My creative writing prof will probably write a note on the story I finished today, asking if I'm doing okay. It's happened before, like when I handed in that big piece about my childhood—the one I first drafted in high school. Well, I polished the heck out of it and gave it to Ogden as my 'high stakes' assignment. After all, my depression almost cost me everything.

Ogden thinks I should enter that long expository essay on my stormy experience with depression into a contest or something, that what I have to say should be out in the world, so more people can learn from it. But he hasn't met our father, our uber-private family. Lynne found out about our Botox fight (from Jo, not even from me), and he was furious. I can just imagine the trouble I would get into if I won a contest, got my essay published in *Writer's Digest* or something. Or *Reader's Digest*! The potential fallout boggles my mind. I think of how much Dad would 'enjoy' my emotional struggles in print. He would immediately worry about being judged as a parent if I went public. I can hardly blame him.

The truth is I'm not sure how I would feel about it. I feel exposed enough just writing this stuff for Ogden's class. But it's part of working all my feelings out, part of putting words to my sense of loss and my realization about our story, about forgiveness, about Mary. And it doesn't matter whether I'm writing fiction or fact about my life. The emotional truth is the same. I think I owe it to myself, and to my twin, not to stop. I think that's what she would tell me, if she could.

When I missed my WheelTrans bus today, I had to call Dad to come and get me from campus. While I was waiting, Ogden passed me in the hall, told me he'd been wanting to talk to me about considering the Journalism program when I'll have to declare my major next year.

"I don't know, sir," I confessed. "I have pretty major reservations about journalism, about a specialty that would ask me to take myself out of the stories I tell. Maybe I've been watching too much *Oprah*, but I really think I need to be using my life in whatever I do. I don't want to hide my voice behind other people's stories, Professor Ogden."

"Oh, Naomi," Ogden smiled, "journalists don't hide. That's the best part. They can be some of the bravest people. They put it all out there to get the story and tell it."

"I'm sure that's true, sir. But the media doesn't always get stories right. My father had to push them away when I was little, when Easter Seals wanted me to be 'Tammy'—the face of fundraising and 'inspiration' for them. He turned them down, because he knew that they would use my disability to tug on people's heartstrings, because everyone is taught to believe disability is a sad story. To this day, I'm thankful to him every time I see one of those charity donation boxes, with the requisite picture on the front. You know, the beaming kid with the wheelchair or walker, and the caption that spouts garbage like, "All Sally wants to do is walk. Help her dreams come true.""

"And Sally doesn't want to walk?" Ogden was curious.

"If she does, it's because other people have set it up in her mind as The Great Goal, the Holy Grail, almost The Thing That Makes Her Human. And her disability, to most of the world, is The Thing to Be Pitied. It's the media that perpetuates that, and I won't be part of it."

"It's your decision," Ogden conceded. "But I think you're a born journalist. In a few years, I see you with your own column. Honestly.

"See you in class."

"You know, I would give my own legs if it meant you would walk," Dad told me, after he had picked up my stranded self. We were waiting at the railroad tracks for a steel caterpillar of a cargo train to make its lumbering way along. I told him about what Ogden said, and then I took a deep breath and told him about the writing I had handed in, about my past.

"I wouldn't want you to give up body parts for me," I said. "I wouldn't let you, Dad." I was so disturbed, thinking of him mutilating himself for my good. "I owe you for all you've done as my father, but you don't owe me that. I wouldn't want it." I told him that, flat out, Mary, and he took it. He kissed my cheek while we waited, and there was comfortable silence all the way home after that.

We're growing up.

All of this cycles through my mind before my pen carefully starts moving again.

Speaking of things I owe, I think I owe you an apology, Mary. I was going through all the letters I've written to you over the years (I flip through them sometimes) and I found an entry about all the pain you've missed. Is that the same thing as being glad you're gone? Please tell me no.

But I think I owe Matt an apology, too. He's not the only one who gets broadsided by his own mind. And I have to tell him what I've realized: that we're both right, and both wrong. I can't deny that, especially after the e-mail he sent me yesterday.

```
To: Naomi Demas
<funkylady@email.com>
From: Matt Dumond
<slightlylessthanagod@email.com>
Subject:
I know how hurt you were by what
happened, and all that hurt has to
go somewhere. I'm glad you have
people who support you, to help
```

you make room for the ones you
love (or loved) who damaged your
trust and spent your patience. But
I can't understand why Eva gets
so many chances with you, and
I don't.

So here's what I have to say about
my own weaknesses:

I am impatient. Mostly, I do as
much as I can the easy way, as
fast and painlessly as I can, and
I avoid risk. I'm terrified of
heights, you know. I didn't even
like climbing up on a chair to
reach the cookie cupboard when I
was little. You, though, always
find a way to do what needs doing.
You don't overthink things and
stop yourself before you start,
and you finish what you started,
no matter how long it takes you. I
guess I'm not that guy...the guy I
most wanted to be for you.

Also, I listen to my father too
much, even when I know he's wrong
about something or someone, like
he was wrong about doubting you.

Just wanted you to know that I get
it. Also, unless you don't want me
to, I'd really like to visit your
mom. I still love you, Ny. Yes, I
called you Ny—your name, to people
who love you. And I'm not taking
it back.

A while ago, in a sober moment,
Eva also told me about that Viking
tradition. She's sorry she can't
be a 'burn the boats' person in

```
your life right now. But I can.
I want to be, and I believe in
second chances. I won't ask for a
third. I won't need one.
I am like you that way.
Matt
```

Naomi

My head hits the pillow, and immediately, I wake to another pillow being thrown at me.

"Look lively, sis!"

Mary's voice is just like mine, but yet not. I don't know how to describe it, really, except to say she's just different enough to sound like her, while I sound like me. I rise up on my elbow and wallop her with the pillow she just sent careening at me. She grabs another pillow, and back and forth we go, until I begin to cry. Except I don't really cry so much as feel the sorrow in my throat begin to rise.

She's beside me on the bed, and I'm not sure how she got there. I look at her, see myself staring back at me, and I know we're both taking each other in.

I am dreaming, I know it, even from within my dream. I don't know what's real, or what I or she will remember, or what took her so long. But I know I cannot be silent.

"You left me," I sob. "I've been lost."

"No, you haven't." She doesn't touch me, even though she's close enough to hug. But her voice is a kiss. "You've known where we each were, all the time. And people leave with intention, Ny. I had no such thing."

"No, you can't play with your friends. Eat your grass. There's even nice clover for you over there, Lance. Go

329

chomp on it so Curtis doesn't have to go at it with the weed whacker. He shouldn't be allowed near those things. "Don't look at me like that. You know full well that if I let you near your horse friends you'll find a way to rub that ear, or let Twist chomp on it. Again!" I twitch the lead shank attached to his halter, to indicate the base of the oak tree that's giving us shade. "And I know you don't want to be stuck in the barn when everyone comes for the day on the farm. But you won't be healed in time, so you'll have to stay in. I'll just have to make sure we always leave one horse friend in there with you for company. That's the best I can do. Now behave yourself."

Lance almost looks abashed as he drops his head to the clover blooming against the trunk. He tears three huge bites of luscious greenery off at the roots in quick succession. As he chews through the mouthful, he stares longingly again at his paddock mates grazing beyond the fence. The bandage on his ear is stark white against his gleaming coat. I reach over and stroke his neck. He leans into my hand, then blows out a large snort and goes back to the clover.

"That's it. Eat up. You're my good, sweet boy, Lance. Ny loves you."

Mary

I'm watching the sun start to go down, wishing I could stop time on Earth for my sister. We are so happy in heaven that you might think it would be monotonous, but that joy is in everything here, and it's always new. No one is ever bored. No one has to wish for something to go wrong so we can spice things up and have a little fun.

You know the way the fireball sun drops inch by inch below the horizon, in an incremental sinking until it's gone? Well, we sing it down, and you should hear our voices harmonizing in splashes of colour. You should hear our song and our dance actually producing the movement of the sun. Doesn't mean that everything is perfect, because even perfection is subjective. Not *everything* changes here, if you can't dance on Earth... Let's just say it's a good thing the sun is not a talent show judge. You wouldn't believe our exuberance. It's not work, it's a party. If you could feel it on Earth, it would make the whole place shake, and everyone would be shaking their booties, whether they understood why or not.

Here's the thing about shaking your booty, though.

What people feel in their best, most freeing moment of life, that's a tiny morsel of what goes on here. I wish I could take a fraction of this peaceful, single-minded happiness and give it to my sister right now, as a shield against what's coming to her.

But I can't. I wish I could stop time on Naomi's planet just long enough to still and reverse the trajectory of the trouble on its way. I wish I could stop the sun going down on this day for her, because when tomorrow comes, well...

Naomi

I suddenly flash on a memory of my ninth summer, with Cabbage Patch Kids being all the rage, and Katina checking every Eaton's, The Bay and Toys R Us until she found the last two dolls, one for me and one for Jo. Then she took three buses to get to the store, and returned with determination three times her size, hefting each doll. To carry them, she had broken each doll's huge box packaging, and then carried the dolls in one large cloth bag.

"They wanted to meet you so badly, they worked to be free of the boxes so that when we reached home, you could hold them quicker," she had explained to Jo and I, both of us wide-eyed.

"Why didn't you let me drive you?" Dad wanted to know, as Yiayia limped with fatigue.

"Because they need a mom, a woman who comes through for them and doesn't demand things be always easy."

And she'd done that. Every day.

Asleep in the chair beside Mom's bed, Yiayia appears far more diminished than when she's awake. At least, when awake, I can still feel her spunk and her drive, know that the engine of her spirit is still running, see the glint in her eye that tells us her clock is ticking and she's not done yet. But, eyes closed in sleep, she is incredibly still and seems smaller somehow. The rise and fall of her chest is an ebbing tide.

Unbidden, my mind locks on the memory of the last time I was in this hospital—the bizarre cocktail of indignation and horror as I overheard myself being judged by a man I had never met, followed by the elation of my first kiss, followed by the roller coaster of emotions that come part and parcel with Matt and his father. And Eva...

I shift my gaze up from my ailing, beloved mother to the empty space across the bed from me where I wish she was. "Irene's still here," I say quietly. "And you? Where in the world have you been, Eva?" My voice is steady, an edge of steel in the clear words.

Dad often says I'm easy on everyone but him, that I save all my stubbornness to fling in his direction and reserve softness and patience for everyone else. The truth is, there are few others who use up my patience the way he does, few who can push my buttons with the same targeted efficiency. Let's face it, as my trainer, he knows my physical weaknesses like a farmer appraising the offerings at a cattle auction. And he moves so quickly compared to me—with a swiftness and smoothness he expects me to produce consistently within my body the way I do in my mind. Despite my reality, it's as though he's both experienced rancher and rapid-fire auctioneer. But my body is really the only tension between us, the single flint stone that keeps the possibility of fire ever close. And the love between us as daughter and father is what controls it.

I know my father both loves and hates the job he has chosen—to be simultaneously my parent and trainer. He loves teaching me the discipline and focus of coordinating my body and hates critiquing me, with the impatience and even harshness that can result. And I hate that the gulf between us is about the very body that I love and appreciate for its ways and for being mine.

But we make a real effort, Dad and I. We're stayers. We make it work. Underneath it all, we're friends. I help him with Kev, with Mom, with the up and down and in and out that is Kelly. He wanted to flay Matt. I stopped him. Every injustice I face hurts him. My success makes him dancing-in-the-rain happy. We argue, we work it out. We commit.

Yesterday, I watched Dad, standing over Mom and crying. Not the misty non-tears associated with 'the man-cry,' but real sobs. Afterward, I watched him stand with Yiayia in the hall outside Mom's room. He kept saying thank you over and over, with the gratitude of a man whose mother-in-law rescued his children and sanity, and helped him be sure he was not alone with it all. I left them to their moment, and resolved to tell him he's done the same for me.

There is suddenly a commotion in the hospital hallway and the unmistakeable scrambling hustle of alarmed nurses, and I'm pulled back to now. Something about the quality of the noise pulls me away from Mom's bed. What I find around the corner sends chills up my spine. Did I summon her here with my thoughts? I can't help but wonder.

Eva is unsteadily lumbering down the hospital hallway, teetering like a toddler, careening this way and that. "NAO!" she slurs at the sight of me, her voice blurry. "I'VE MISSSSSSSED YOU!"

Two of the nurses wordlessly come to stand beside me, shielding the entrance to Mom's room, while another two attach themselves to Eva, steadying her.

"NAOOOOOOOOO, DON'T GOOOOO!" Eva wails as security is called, her face contorted with pleading as I turn away. Even at her height of drunkenness, I think this small move has caught her attention because some part of her knows I won't turn back.

Hospitals don't allow for much lying. The real stuff of who you are is laid bare in halls and rooms like this. Are you the one at bedside, or the one high-tailing it to the door?

I know I may never see Eva again past this moment. I won't go rescuing her as she drowns, and be punched and drowned in the attempt.

At some time later, I will find some final tears for this, for her.

But for now I finish the trip back to Mom's bed, and hold her hand.

Mary

"Is there anything I can do for you, Mr. Demas?"

Our dad's eyes widen as he turns toward the door. "What are you doing here, Matt? Naomi wouldn't want you here. It's a good thing she's in the cafeteria with her sister."

Matt shrugs, looking sad and unsure of himself. He holds out a large greasy paper bag. "I brought you guys burgers and fries. Is there anything else I can do, sir? I really want to help, and I have my car."

Our father looks at Matt hard, gauging his sincerity against his past wrongs, against what Naomi's reaction will be, against all the ways they really do need help...

Suddenly, a nurse is in the doorway. "Mr. Demas, Dr. Armstrong wanted me to let you know that he'll be available to discuss your wife's blood tests, but he has a few other patients to see first. Please don't go anywhere."

Daddy nods. "Thank you for letting me know, Cheryl."

When the nurse has gone, he turns to Matt with new scrutiny. "Can I trust you to pick up Kev from the barn...?"

Naomi

I pensively stir my apple cider with a cinnamon stick and Jo glances at me sideways.

"Are you okay?"

"What, with being here?"

She looks around her in the hospital cafeteria. "Yeah, that and Eva."

I shrug, as offhandedly as I can. "I don't care. I've got bigger problems than her right now. She's made it clear she doesn't want to be here, so I have to let her go. I haven't got time for this. I have to get it together so we can explain to Kev that Mom is sick. It's time to huddle together. That's all I've got in me."

Jo nods, but it is Lynne who answers beginning to nibble on her cinnamon stick as though it is a cigar. "Fair enough," she muses, but I know they don't believe me at all. They shouldn't. I watch them watching me, carefully. They says nothing. I say nothing. They sit as Job's friends sat on three of the smartest days of their lives, before they passed judgment.

Finally Lynne drops her head and mumbles, "Eva was sober when I drove her here. I would never have brought her with me if she was drunk. We talked in the car. She was sober, I swear."

A search of Eva's backpack had revealed, in part, the sad truth of what happened. Said backpack had not been filled with supplies for her stay away from home—clothes, toiletries, snacks, a water bottle. None of that. Instead, there were only three large plastic bottles filled with cheap wine and one of vodka, partly empty, nestled around cans of beer. Her only concession to the routine realities of travel is one outfit, rolled up tight among the cans, with a toothbrush in its folds.

"She drank in the bathroom," Lynne realizes incredulously. "Once she got here, I mean."

That image just will not be shaken out of my head: Eva knocking back the vodka straight from the bottle.

Did she justify it by thinking she was back in the city, away from the vicinity of her attempted recovery, and therefore 'free' to binge? Was she triggered by the stress of being at the hospital, driven to start up again? Or has there never been any recovery, at all?

I don't really want to know.

Chapter Twenty-Five
What if…

Naomi

Dear Ny:

I can't help Mary dying. That's over and done, has been for a long time. But I can give you myself, my sisterhood, my friendship. And I intend to do just that…you're stuck with me now!

You know, Mary died in my life, too. I didn't lose a twin, but I lost a sister. And for what it's worth, I want to be a sister to the one I have left.

When Mary died, I didn't sleep, I didn't eat. I thought that if she couldn't, I shouldn't, either. I felt guilty when I did sleep or eat, because she was gone. I was young, but not so young that I didn't feel the loss, and take it hard. Five can feel like fifty, sometimes. Not news to you, I know.

By the way, I've done some reading on OCD. More than some, actually. I've spent quality hours in the library where I can see Mom in the pages as clearly as you can see this letter in front of you now. I would sit and read, sometimes bawling my eyes out because in reading about other people's struggles with OCD, I understood what Mom faced.

So here's what I know now.

When you have OCD, compulsions come in certain flavours that all stem from the brain's inability to close a repetitive loop, designed in part to deal, in some strange way, with the general uncertainty of living. So some part of Mom has always believed she's some horrible person and that a mess up on her part could unleash catastrophe—for people she loved or for anyone at all. Every compulsion that plagued her began with a single question: 'what if?' What if she didn't drive around the block for hours, retracing her steps to make sure she hadn't hit any people, dogs, cats or squirrels? I can't even tell you the number of times she'd call me from a pay phone (me having arrived home from school to find no snack or dinner ready and having made mac and cheese for myself) and beg me to come and get her from some intersection, curb, street corner, park, or parking lot.

This was obviously happening long before I could drive. I would have to take the call, calm her down, then take a bus or taxi to wherever she was in the city, break the hold of whatever was going on and coax her home.

"I'm going to tell Dad, Mom," I announced more than once, on the way back from these excursions. "We need help. I can't keep doing this. I'm just a kid. I've got homework."

She would beg and cry, and tell me she felt responsible for all the things that could go wrong if she saw the possibility of something that could hurt someone and didn't do anything to stop it—if she didn't scour any stretches of ground for perceived hazards and save the world from them.

"An abandoned Smartie some kid dropped in the grass in the park is not a hazard, Mom."

"That's the thing!" Mom would exclaim, tears in her eyes. "What if some sicko put the Smartie on the grass, so some innocent kid would pick it up and poison herself?"

"Mom, you need help."

"No!" she would shriek. "No hospitals, please!" Now the tears would flow, and she would plead and bargain. If I didn't tell Dad, she would stop doing this crazy stuff. ("That's the thing, Joanna, I know it's crazy. It's just...") She swore she would stop wandering around, trying to save the world. "I'll only do this stuff at home (as if turning a light switch on and off thirty times or pushing her chair in and out nine times before and after she used it in a game of Repeat or Bust would save us all and be so much saner than acting as the Smartie police, but hey...)

I do wonder how she managed to work at all. But as a hairdresser, she was cool, calm, collected, in control. Hair, she could do. Maybe it was because she could tie hairdressing's package with a neat little bow. Be done and paid, from start to finish, in a matter of minutes, or hours. She could tell herself it would be over, her job done, her customer gone and unavailable for obsessing, so very, very soon.

But before work, after work, behind closed doors, it was such a different story.

Then there were the times it was so bad, she couldn't work. That's when the money Dad always made sure was in the account came in really handy. At those times, the 'what ifs' were endless. Anytime she figured her way out of one, there was another one waiting.

What if Mary had died as payback for some unconfessed, unforgiven sin of hers?

What if the only thing she could do to save you was stay away from you?

What if the only way for her to save herself was to have me with her?

So her OCD was her brain's manifestation of trying to keep the horror away.

If you ever want to talk about the rest of this, about all the time we've missed, I'm here anytime, and I'm done with secrets, too. Why am I telling you this? Because I'm like you in ways you might not realize. I'm not sorry you're disabled. Never have been.

I'm just glad you're here.

You'll see.

Love,

Jo

I put down the letter and stare at my sister, bug-eyed, food forgotten. "How come you never told us how bad it was? If Dad knew, he would have never let that…" My voice trails off, because of course, Dad *had* known. He'd known full well. He'd lived with Irene for years. He'd intervened and checked in almost every other day. He'd rescued Jo repeatedly. He had to know.

"I'm so sorry," is all I can say.

Jo shrugs. It can't be helped, her body language says. "He came every day, or every other day," Jo reminds me unnecessarily. "He stayed with us for hours sometimes. He took me away from it a lot. That's how we would see each other, remember?"

I nod. It's true, I know. There had even been sleepovers, like the one when we had stayed up late talking and eaten ourselves sick, gorging on chocolate chip cookies, and then we threw up in the wee hours of the morning together. Like many of our memories, this one is bittersweet, because after that night Mom's obsessive mind convinced her it was bad for Jo to be with me. Jo had gotten sick near me, therefore letting us be together was a horrid idea, a sure and imminent sign of calamity. Thus began the years of leaving gifts at each other's doors and seeing each other very sparingly. The cycle didn't change substantially unless relatives visited from Greece—and not fully until after Jo made her own decision to move back in with us.

"Naomi and Joanna Demas, please go to H Wing immediately." The words come booming at us through the cafeteria's loudspeaker intercom.

H Wing? But Mom is in B Wing. Isn't H Wing the burn unit? What the...

We take off in a blur.

Chapter Twenty-Six
Under the Apple Chariot

Kevin

"Mommy, you can't play magic dragon anymore. Nami said so."

"I know, kiddo."

"But you're still playing. You're playing now." I watch the smoke flowing out of Mommy's mouth, and then climbing slowly in puffs toward the sky. Puff the Magic Dragon.

"Soon I won't anymore."

"When?"

"After you stay at the farm next week, Mommy won't ever play dragon again."

My eyes get big. I didn't think about after. All year, I'm excited about the summer party at the barn where Nami works. Everyone who works there is always there, and a whole bunch of kids get to go, kids who ride horses at the barn, and their families. There's always hide-and-seek in the long grass, baking pies, playing in the hayloft, fishing in the creek, and, oh…the best part is the apple chariot races. It's hard to believe there's such a thing as *after* the party. But

I know that going to the barn is like Christmas; it comes and then goes away, but it'll always be back. That makes me feel better.

"Are you coming to the barn this year, Mommy? It's so much fun!"

"No, baby. Mommy doesn't belong at the farm. But you'll have a great time. You always do. How 'bout those races you always tell me about? You love those."

I wonder if I'm old enough to push a chariot by myself this year. I'm FIVE now.

"Kevin, you shouldn't watch Mommy play dragon. Go inside and play, okay? I'll be there in a few minutes."

"Why?"

"Because smoke isn't good for you to breathe."

I gather my favourite fire truck and my lion from the grass and stand up.

"Mommy?"

"Yeah?"

"Will it be hard for you to stop playing dragon?"

"I think so, big guy, but I have to stop anyway."

"That's what Nami says."

"Nami's right. Go inside please, honey."

"Yeah. But Mommy?"

"Yes Kevin."

"Is it kinda like how I have to stop sucking my thumb before I start kindygarden?"

"Something like that."

"Okay. Mommy?"

"What is it?"

"When you stop smoking, I'll stop sucking my thumb, okay?"

She kneels so I can see her close, kisses the top of my head, and tickles my stomach. I giggle.

"You've got a deal, my man." Handshake.

She smells like smoke and mint chewing gum. Grown-up smell.

"Ready. Set. Go!" We're off. I run *fast!*. I keep the wheel of the chariot churning in front of me and watch as the wheel eats more and more of the space between me and the shed. It's like watching Cookie Monster munch cookies until there are none left. I can hear the other kids laughing from inside their chariots as their wheels bump over the grass. Do they have to shriek like that? Is it really that exciting? Next time I'm riding in my chariot, and someone can push me, too.

The idea of having apple chariot races at the barn was mine in the first place. Every year Charlotte lets us pick apples from the trees around the paddocks. She says the horses love this part of the year, when their everyday food comes with some fresh apples. Everyone else gets to take home some apples too. Everybody gets a chariot to fill. Even I get one. And every time enough time passes for one Sesame Street, we stop picking and filling and race to the shed, pushing our chariots full of apples without spilling any. Whoever gets to the shed fastest wins, and their prize is to pick the next thing to do. Some kid in a wheelchair usually wins, but that's because those kids are kinda allowed to cheat. Somebody always has to drive their chariots for them. Now some girl's chariot is stuck in the grass, and I can see that David stopped driving it and is yelling at everyone behind me. I know they won't let me help, so I just keep on running until I'm close enough to the shed to touch the wall.

"I won! I won! I won! I won! I won!" I call out. "I wanna go fishing in the creek now, everybody!"

But the girl is still stuck, and I don't even know if anyone's heard me.

No fair. I didn't even spill one, but nobody's paying attention to me.

David

Stupid, pain in the ass, demented race, I think, as I stand in the grass in the middle of all the mess. There are apples rolling everywhere, apples that landed on top of Olivia when the wheelbarrow tipped on the rock and sent her flying. There she is now, sprawled on the grass with blood pouring out of her bottom lip. That's going to be one fat lip tomorrow, shit brain, I tell myself. And then you're going to die. My mom's gonna have my head. And the lip will be the least of my worries. There'll be bruises, I'm sure. I can see scratches already on Olivia's arms, and I've seen spots all over her legs that promise to turn black and blue and green and yellow like a morbid version of Christmas lights. And the bump on her head. Oh, my God, it's swelling already. Ice. She needs ice. It's like the fucking wheelbarrow threw up, spewing this little thrill junky, out. She had been riding in there with her apples and laughing like a happy drunk.

I should've stood my ground and not let her ride in there, no matter how she released the waterworks. But Mom had jerked open the screen door the minute she heard the princess wail and bellowed at me to let her do what everyone else was doing, without even checking what that was. Not Mom's most professional moment as a barn owner, working with disabled kids. She had assumed giving in was a good idea. But I have no right to talk, because I listened. I transferred Olivia out of her wheelchair and into the wheelbarrow—the chariot, she calls it—ignoring the ominous lurch of my stomach. I knew full well that what she wanted to do was not the same as everyone else. No one was riding *in* their wheelbarrows; everyone else in the race was pushing them. If my mother had known that letting Olivia be part of the race at all meant she would be rocked around in a wheelbarrow, there would have been no race for her.

Curtis is going to get hell for this. I'm going to kick his sorry ass. Not only does he work here, he even *lives* here! He should be here, taking care of this, instead of setting up the stupid scavenger hunt for later. I could've done that, and Curtis could've done this. He's the one who's good with kids.

If Curtis were here, probably none of this would have happened. He would have put his foot down with Olivia and said she couldn't be in the race. Wouldn't he? Well, even if he let her, at least Curtis has been working with her lately and knows more about how Olivia's body works, or doesn't. I don't have a clue what her Cerebral-Whatever is. I hardly know Olivia. I'm not even sure whose kid she is. I feel squirmy.

I can't get the sight of her out of my head, bouncing on top of those apples before she fell. She couldn't sit right. She hadn't been sitting at all, really. More like lying with her upper body scooped in a C shape and her legs, rigid and straight, kicking out in front of her while she shrieked. I wasn't even able to tell at first if she was shrieking with laughter or fear. Why didn't I just stop?

Screw this. I'm going to find Curtis.

Kevin

I swing the big screen door open and stand inside. I feel a little better. Last year I couldn't even reach the handle! All the big people are moving around the kitchen—only Nami and Daddy aren't here.

I wish they were. I wish Daddy hadn't dropped me off at the barn and left me. I know Daddy's going to the hospital again. I'm tired of so much sickie.

I'm mad, too.

I run to Charlotte at the kitchen sink and tug on her arm. "I won the apple chariot race, but..."

She takes one look at me, scoops me up and kisses my forehead. A big kiss, not one of those little pecks I get from Daddy when he's in a hurry at home. I start to tell her that I've won the race and how nobody paid attention when I won and...

"What a good boy you are, Kevin. I'm very proud of you."

I'm not finished. "Come play with me!"

"Don't whine, pup. I'm making the big dinner for everyone. It'll be yummy in your tummy and it'll be ready soon, but I can't play right now. Later." She puts me down facing the door.

"I'm not a puppy," She doesn't even hear me.

I go back outside.

I don't want to join any games. The big kids always leave me out after a while. They aren't doing what I want anyway, and that isn't fair. I won the race, but they're acting like it doesn't matter. Nobody notices me or plays fair like before. Nami would fix this. But she isn't here either.

I want to tell Curtis, but I can't find him. I can hear one of the big kids calling the others to play Frisbee.

Olivia's chariot is empty. I can see her lying on a blanket and crying, two grownups fussing over her.

I want to be in the loft by myself. There's another chariot up there, and I want to hide under it, alone in my own secret place. Everyone's leaving me all alone anyway...

I'll lie down up there in the loft, under the chariot and play quietly with my trains. I turn and head for the barn. I wonder how long it'll take for everyone to miss me.

Matt

"Where is Kevin?"

Curtis startles at the sound of my voice, and almost drops the box he is holding.

"What the hell are *you* doing here?"

"Where's Kev?"

"I'm not telling you."

"Look, Mr. Full of Myself, I'm trying really hard not to knock you out here. Mr. Demas sent me to pick Kev up so—"

"No way he gave you that responsible job."

My hands are fists, my voice like steel. "Don't make me pound you, buddy."

David finds us on the gravel path just outside the barn, in a tangle of punches, thrashing and cursing. He hauls me off Curtis. It's a shame. I was really going for it. "Break it up, guys!" David hollers. He grabs Curtis by a fistful of shirt.

"Listen, Curtis, you gotta cool it and come with me. Olivia got hurt and my mom's blowing her top. She's saying heads are gonna roll. If you wanna keep your job…"

Curtis and David run. They don't even look back at me.

I wait for them to disappear.

Jackpot! Here's the shitty thing. Curtis jumped when he saw me standing in the barn's doorway. He'd jumped and put the box back in one jerky movement.

He's made a little nest of his stuff here in the corner. And right in the middle of things, two hard corners are sticking out from under Curtis' jacket. There it is. The box.

It makes me feel strange inside, gives me a weird out-of-body feeling in my bones to see so many things kept inside it from Jo's wedding. There are pictures, even an engraved package of matches. *Joanna and Samuel…June 23rd, 2001,* it reads. And none of this has anything to do with Curtis' own family, yet he's acting like they *belong* to him. Ny, Jo, all of them.

'They belonged to you once, and you screwed that one up. And this stuff you're snooping around in isn't yours. Yet here you are.' My conscience needles me.

I'm never sure why everyone calls the conscience a 'little' voice. There's nothing little about it. It's big and bossy and loud…and just now, a real pain. It's not my fault I lost them. Naomi refused to give me a second chance. What am I supposed to do, beg? And of course I have a right to look through this stuff. Curtis insulted me at the wedding. He insulted me first, anyway. But that sounds hollow. Shitty conscience.

To shut it up and busy myself, I open the box and sort through what's inside.

I shouldn't be doing this, I tell myself, as I come across a slightly damaged stuffed penguin (what the heck is the idiot keeping toys for, anyway?), and faded pictures of a smiling woman and two laughing little girls. This is clearly not Naomi's stuff, and that makes me feel better for a minute. I should stop snooping. My conscience is going off like a siren. But then I see Jo's wedding invitation mixed in with the other crap, and I'm mad all over again. What's this guy playing steal-a-family for, really? Is he some kind of sicko stalker?

I should leave him a message loud and clear. Let him know that I'm onto him and whatever stupid shit he's trying to pull. And suddenly, the other stuff that wasn't Ny's doesn't make me feel better anymore, either. Just because it isn't hers doesn't mean it rightfully belongs to Curtis, after all.

Hasn't Curtis been in foster care because his father was a murderer?

Just like that, my blood runs cold. Well, that does it. My boom box of a conscience can just shut up, because I'm not snooping. I'm doing the right thing, protecting Ny and her family.

Keep your friends close and your enemies closer.

Curtis will know he's being watched. I'm keeping tabs on him, and his stalker plan is not okay. I'll light up these memories of his, and even use the wedding matches from the precious box to do it... The next time Curtis opens this box, expecting to see all this crap of his, he'll find nothing but a pile of ashes instead.

I start by lighting the wedding invitation. Why not? I wish that whole dance floor, bathroom fight fiasco had never happened, after all. I watch the flames eat first the edges and then the whole invitation in orange-black consumption. I'm mesmerized as the ashes from the card drop onto the box. There's a short letter. Just one page, written in a hurry, with a couple of tear-stains on it. *Dear G…I don't know if you remember me….*

I'm not sure why that makes me pause for just a heartbeat. But it's too late for second thoughts now. I light a photo, this time dropping the match into the stuffing of the penguin. Lighting another match, I go after one photo… Two…This is fun, in a weird way.

Until…

Oh, shit! Ny trusts Curtis to look after Kev. She trusts that crazy loon.

Oh, *shit!*

Distracted by that thought, I hold onto a match for too long and do a good job burning my own finger. I curse again.

Heedless of the match now, I stick my throbbing finger in my mouth, slam the lid on the stupid thing and shove it back into its dark hole with a penguin wing sticking out.

Go walk it off, I tell myself. It's what Dad always tells me to do whenever I need to calm down. I'll go and take a walk before I find Kev and take him back.

I have no business being around the kid in this mood, anyway. Not with every second word in my head being a curse. Yeah, I'll take a walk and figure out what to do next with this Curtis moron.

Cradling my throbbing finger, I storm out of the barn.

Mary

Kevin jumps out of sleep. He can hear screams and crying everywhere, but he can't move. He's gotten under the chariot, but can't get back out. He can hear people calling him, and he's calling back, but no one can hear.

From under the chariot, he can see feet and the colour orange. And he can smell smoke, like when Mommy plays magic dragon. But now the smell is everywhere, thick and strong and close.

All of a sudden, Kevin knows that his mommy has really become Puff the Magic Dragon. She's finally come to get him, and she'll save him, the way Elizabeth, the princess wearing paper, had saved the mean prince in that book Nami reads to him sometimes. Now Kevin is sure all he has to do is wait. But it's hard to breathe and he remembers what Mommy said about smoke being bad for him.

So Kevin stops wiggling under the chariot. He lies back down, sucks his thumb, and waits for his mommy to come.

I look away.

Curtis

"Look, smoke!" That's David's voice. We all turn toward the barn.

"Not smoke, fire!" Charlotte's voice rises, "Lance!" Her panic pierces my ears, and I take off toward the barn. There's no thought, only movement.

But thought returns somehow, in nonsensical fragments. I've never *run* into the barn before, I realize, with a small flash of pride.

I duck under the chain hung across the door into the dimness of the barn. I sense flickering light from the hay stall but concentrate on the nickering sound that battles that of the crackling fire. I unhook Lance's stall guard almost without slowing. The three snap hooks of Orion's slow me down but Orion is right there, ready for freedom. I throw the stall guard to the side and pull on Orion's little halter. It isn't necessary. The fat Shetland pony is already heading back the way I came.

I can't believe how loud the crackling is becoming, drowning out Orion's hoof beats. There's no thought of water, of working to stop the flames, only of getting out. I'm following Orion's fine example when I realize that Lance is still in his stall! The idiot is standing with his nose to the back corner as if ignoring the situation will make it disappear. I reach for Lancelot's halter to drag him out but my hand closes on nothing and slips empty down Lance's face. I forgot the reason Lance is inside on such a fine day (and without a halter) is his injured ear, nipped in a play fight in the paddock with the others. It's become infected and Lance can't be trusted, outside on his own, not to rub it open and make it worse. Like most horses, he hates to be separated from his herd, so he and one other horse (a rotating cast) have been in 'detention' for the past few days, except for strictly supervised excursions for grazing and his regular schooling. Orion drew the short straw today.

Instead I pull a lead rope from the front of the stall and fling it over Lance's neck, heedless of the heavy metal clip that barks my knuckles as I grab for it under the horse's chin and yank his head around. I almost scream in frustration as Lance stops in the door, rolling his eyes in panic. Thank God I haven't opened my mouth, because in this instant, I hear a different sound, a human sound, the small sound of a small, frightened child. I look up. I can see nothing but I know instantly who the small human is.

Kev. Hiding in the loft, in the spot where I found him sulking and playing with his trains. Months, and an eternity, ago.

What are you doing there, child? A string of under-breath curses flow, and still I don't stop moving.

Move. Only move, I order myself. No one is dying today. "I'm coming, Kev!" I call as loud as I can, even though only the flames will hear.

When I look back, I know I will never be able to describe what I did next—even to myself. In my head, there are only shreds and fragments, images but no connections: yanking the horse out of the stall, smacking his rump to keep him going, the smoky aisle, the closed trapdoor in the ceiling, feet above my head. Did I jump? Did I climb? It must have been a combination, because next was the rough floor of the loft, below a ceiling of smoke not 12 inches above as I was levering myself through the open hole. The hole meant for dropping bales of hay from above, not lifting me from below. I roll onto the rough, dusty floor, out of the ferocious gust of air that comes with me. I gulp the dry, smoky air, trying to orient myself. That post. That way. I commando-crawl, heedless as I scrape elbows and knees and toes on the uneven floor of worn planks. That wall. Around the bags of horse bedding. And into nothingness. There is floor and smoke. Smoke and floor. Keep crawling. I run headfirst into something. The built-in ladder. Too far!

"Kev!" I mean to shout but it comes out as a croak. No answer. Spinning to the right, I pause to check my bearings. I have to get this right or I'll be circling forever. Now. This direction. Keeping my hands out front as far as I can I nearly cry when I touch solid hay. The bales. Now up. Into the solid wall of smoke. Deep breath. I'm crouched up on all fours, when I freeze. A whimper to my left, and not above, I drop flat again in relief. Two crawls and what was that? The tire of a wheelbarrow.

"Kev" I croak and my head is engulfed by a small body.

Hang on. Hang on. Hang on. Only hang on.

A command. A wish. A fervent prayer for us both.

Chapter Twenty-Seven
Broken Open

Naomi

I once thought it was difficult dealing with Mom in Grace Lodge and then Rivercrest Hospital's palliative care unit. Those troubles seem so far away as to be mist, now that Curtis and Kev are in the same hospital's burn unit. Everything that once seemed a monumental worry has evaporated, and all my prayers and hopes are centred on the people in these beds. Our days pass in waiting—for nurses and doctors to come, for painful, necessary shifts in position, for long, excruciating surgeries to happen, for skin grafts to take, for bandages to be changed, for progress, for tears, for physiotherapy. For each other. For release.

Lynne, Jo and I work in shifts as we rotate from bedside to bedside, from Kev to Mom to Curtis. I would like to say Dad is doing this, too, though that's not quite true. For him, there is no moving; his is pretty much a vigil at Kev's side. Lynne and Jo take turns bringing him cafeteria food. Matt and David take turns bringing me books and toys, stuffed animals and family photos for Kev. This is quite an undertaking, since I'm determined to cover this room in comfort—in so many reminders of the sweetness of home that his body will heal in record speed, just to get there.

Everybody here at the hospital is on board with that. No one is interested in keeping these kids here longer than they need to be; it's common knowledge that healing happens best at home. But there is so much to learn about taking care of Kev before we can get him there.

"Puff" was his first word. And pretty much his only one in his morphine-induced fog. "Where's Puff? Curtis wouldn't let me see him."

Kev floats in and out of consciousness, in and out of making sense. He's one of those people who really enjoys his vivid morphine-inspired dreams, and actually resents being awake.

On the third day after the ambulance brings Kev here, as soon as they stabilize him, they take him in for his first skin graft surgery. His burns are mostly concentrated on his upper back but his shoulders and neck are involved too. Which is really complicated, because so much surface area and so many joints are involved. It's extra excruciating dealing with burns that encompass joints, because burnt skin always wants to contract back in on itself, like spasticity coming in from the outside. I know spasticity from the inside which is hard enough, but Kev is burned, too...well, I don't want to think about it. He's sedated, especially when they change his dressings every week. Oh, the pain he's in. It hurts my own heart as if it, itself, in my chest, has been burned alive. My stomach, its own elevator, drops away even at the sight of Kev's intubation tube snaking out of his nose, and later, once he's out of ICU, I'm queasy at the sight of the NG tube that keeps him fed and provides the extra caloric intake he needs to heal the burns and fight the threat of infection.

So, the psychologist on this unit has her work cut out for her. Every family with a kid here is marinating in guilt. But when it comes to guilt, *we* are a family of Olympic athletes. How could I have left Kev alone at the barn, without knowing where that child was every minute of the day? How could I not have been there, watching him, myself? What the hell was Matt thinking? What the hell was he doing, messing with matches in a barn filled with wood and hay, containing my brother and my horse? I think if anyone had put *me* on morphine during these days, I would enjoy dreaming of wild revenge...

There is an army of doctors, nurse practitioners, nurses, nurses' aides, psychologists and child life specialists that stream through the burn unit. The child life specialist is to the kids what the unit social worker is to us adults. (Although someone craving morphine revenge dreams must, I realize, use the term adult loosely). But when I talk to said social worker, Mavis, she says I'm completely within my rights to have these feelings, 'Talking' is another term I use loosely, as most often I ramble. It's not lost on me that Mavis doesn't use the word normal around me. She's very observant and evidently quickly figures out what I think of that word.

Mavis says she's seen much worse, and I guess it must be true, with all the emergencies that find their way in here. The little girl who spilled scalding tea on herself while unsupervised, the toddler who was heading for the cookie jar and knocked a pot of boiling water, meant for spaghetti noodles, on himself while trying to use the stove to climb. All (thank God) have families, and all of them know these accidents were preventable. All are anguished. All of us will be reminded of our negligence whenever we look at the children in pain because of us.

Kev's child life specialist is wonderful. Ramon is all about helping Kev come to terms with his burns. He answers his questions about how he'll be, what he'll look like after what happened, helps him draw, tell or write stories about how he feels, what he's scared about and why. Ramon says Kev must learn to believe he is beautiful as he is after the fire. The outside world will be a hard place for a child with burn scars. He must be strong, face prejudice with courage, face stares and ignorance with the knowledge that the fire has become part of his story—one that he can tell with his head high.

"It's a story of rebirth. He must understand it that way, and cherish it. He must be around people who can teach him that as a way of life, consistently. That's the only hope he has of not getting lost in this as a tragedy."

Ramon doesn't have to tell me twice. He's singing my song.

Kelly hasn't showed up on the burn unit even once to see her own son. She keeps saying she can't take Kev's suffering—can't handle it, can't abide that any of this happened at all. She rages at us every day on the phone with sobs and screams and threatens to sue for sole custody of Kev and anything else she can take from us. But she hasn't got what it takes to care for Kev if she can't even manage to look at him and his burns, so her threats are empty. Every day, she says that if Kev had died in that fire, she would've showed up to the funeral and wept as hard as any of us. That's her way of insisting she loves Kev just as much as we do, but that does no good. What counts is what you do for people when they need you.

Mary

Curtis Walcott.

Glenore Alexander stands at the nurses' station and stares incredulously at the hospital chart in her hand, then takes off at a run, her colleagues staring after her.

"He saved my stepbrother's life," Naomi explains simply, as they both stare at Curtis in his bed.

"Well...I'll be..." Glenore exclaims softly. "Natalie would be so proud. Relieved, mostly."

Naomi jolts. "You knew Curtis' mother?"

"Not as well as I wanted to, and she didn't let me help the way I could've and should've before it was too late. But I met her when she was carrying Curtis." At this Glenore grows quiet. "Did her ultrasound. Should've done more."

Naomi shakes her head. "It wasn't your fault. Just like Curtis isn't responsible for who The Sire was."

"He pled guilty y'know. I was in the courtroom with that no-good bastard."

"Really?"

"Oh yes, honey. Stared right at the back of his sorry head the whole time. I just wish the whole mess never happened, is all."

At this, Naomi bursts into tears, her whole body shaking. "Me—oh, me too."

"You're not the only one," Glenore soothes. "You can grieve Curtis and your little one and the pain they're in, but don't grieve them like they're dead." She leans over the back of the wheelchair and wraps her arms around Naomi. "They need you strong." Her head at Naomi's shoulder, she begins to whisper that beautiful Bible verse, from the Book of Jeremiah, in the Old Testament. *For I know the plans I have for you, says the Lord, plans to prosper you and not to harm you, plans to give you hope and a future.* Naomi wonders how she can possibly explain her guilt. She had not abandoned Kev, neglected him, or willingly left him to burn. She loves him with her whole heart, and yet...She should have been there.

"There's no way this is your fault, Sugar," Glenore is saying now, as though reading her mind. "Your mom's been sick. You had to be with her."

She's taken the words right out of my mouth.

Naomi

Dad, Jo and I learn everything we can about taking care of Kev so we can take him home as soon as possible—how to change his bandages, how to massage his scars four times a day to keep the skin stretched and not shrinking. The most painful time for Kev is first thing in the morning, after his body has been curled up in sleep. We have to keep his splints on 23 hours a day so the skin doesn't shrink over his joints, and it's important that we stay positive and let him be a kid as much as we can.

My heart hurts so much over this thing that had no business happening at all. But I must be stronger than that—than the 'what if' of that day. I must put my money where my self-acceptance mouth is, and teach Kev to love himself as he is, now.

Matt tries to bring me books to read while I wait. For what purpose, I'm not at all sure—forgiveness, benediction, time reversal? Maybe all of the above. I tell him to take them away. But I don't throw Matt out. I tell him if he has the guts to stay, I won't make him go. If Kev and Curtis have to lie here in a city of unbearable pain, I decide I will sit there, too, with nothing to distract me from prayer, from song, from the ticking of the clock and the drip of morphine. It's less decision and more instinct, really, like flying south or following the North Star, because it points the way to a bright, solid, loyal place—a place of constancy and direction. Even in chaos, the North Star is orientation. Stability. Home. A tried and true light, worthy of trust.

Please, dear God, do not let Kev die. Do not let Curtis die. Do not let it end this way. Do not let anymore loss come to us for a very long, long time. I would say we cannot take it, but at the same time I know that if it comes to us, we will find it in us to make it. But please protect us. I can't imagine my life without Kev, and now not without Curtis, either. He was so brave, God, going into that raging, impossible fire, to save Kev and to rescue Lance—and he managed both. He has such a big, big heart, Lord. Thank you for making him brave. Please save him and show him what he's worth.

God, I want you to know I accept what's happening to Mom, even though the way she's dying was the hardest thing ever. We thought she was going to be at Grace Lodge for a long time. She was happy there, and it was much easier on Dad, not feeling responsible for her 24/7. I can't stand to see him so overworked and devastated. There was no way to know how difficult it would be on him to shuttle back and forth, visiting her every day, guarding her care so that he was sure she was comfortable, was safe and felt safe. It's not obvious how much care and vigilance that takes, but Dad is so drained by everything...If he's with her, he feels anxious that he's not with us. And when he's with us, the opposite is true. We can't win. He can't win. Mom can't, either. It's awful.

The worst is that the strokes have taken away her speech completely. She can't tell us she when she's in pain, that anything out of the ordinary is wrong, until it's far past too late.

"I'm going to die soon now."

I had been at Grace Lodge feeding her one afternoon. When she says that, I drop her spoon, disbelieving that those words issued forth from her mouth, or any words at all, for that matter. She hasn't said anything to anyone in months, and this is how she breaks her silence?

"Why would you say that, Mama? Does something hurt?"

She says nothing. Irene's words are gone as quickly as they had come, and she goes blank.

I wish I'd paid better attention. How I wished that, as she lay on the verge of coma, as the nursing home explained that there's been an insidious blood infection, lurking for almost a year.

"We can transport her to the hospital, but—"

"NO!" I boom. "No hospitals!"

The entire room stills at the sound of my voice. I shock even myself. "What would they be able to do for her, if you took her to the hospital now?" My voice is suddenly a drained whisper.

"Not much, at this point." At least the doctor is honest. "But the palliative care unit will keep her comfortable, with very strong I.V. antibiotics, but we'll have to see if her body is still strong enough to fight."

Now I tell her everything as she lies there. How I forgive her and I will hold her memories—the ones I know and the ones I will search out and find after she is gone, and think of her as brave. How I will take care of Dad and Jo and Kev, and how I understand now more than ever that, for better or worse, right or wrong, keeping away from me was her way of keeping her problems and hurts away. I tell her I would not have handled things the way she did, but I wouldn't change her. For all the pain involved, she managed to play her part in making me, me—and us, us.

I start begging her to fight. I tell her I'm not ready to let her go. I begin weeping.

I take both her hands in mine and squeeze. I beg her to squeeze back if she can hear me and understand. A moment later, I feel a tiny, unmistakable pulse from her fingers to mine, in response.

The tears flow afresh.

The vigil begins that night. One by one, the best of her life—Dad, Yiayia, Jo, Lynne and I converge on Mom's bedside.

Sarah McLachlan's lyrics for I Will Remember You float through Mom's room, carrying memories with them.

Somewhere in those hours, I change my tactic and tell her it's all right to let go. We all cry and sing, and face the work of releasing her.

"My girls are the most beautiful girls in the world. Do my girls know that?"

The memory is a butterfly, landing in my heart. I remember us three looking in the mirror together in one of those early good times. I remember her talking about how my eyes sparkle, how my words are kind and smart. She said Jo's smile was like rain after drought or sun after thunder. She said her daughters were her truest accomplishments.

Why did I let that memory go? I should have held it all these years with the tenacity of Lancelot's reins, but instead, I let all the hurtful things crowd it out. So I resolve now that I will begin doing what I should have done then. I will hoard the good. I will do that with and about everything and for everyone. I will bring good thoughts, good memories, prayers of thanks and peace and assurance to Kev's and Curtis' bedside.

I will.

When she passes, we are all holding her. In that last moment, the sensation of her goodnight kiss brushes my cheek, and I close my eyes to keep it with me.

I love you.

Epilogue
As We Are

Dear Mary:

This is, hands down, the best birthday ever! I can hardly believe how beautiful Prince Edward Island is. There really is red everywhere—red cliffs, red beaches, red soil and sand. The contrast of blue water and sky and little white popcorn puffs of cloud make me feel like I've stepped into Anne of Green Gables' life, or a pastel painting of it. But this is not a painting, or Anne's life. It's mine, and I love it.

You should see our footprints on the beach, Mary. You would be so proud. My shoe tracks are firm and sure, and you can see my careful lean reflected in the sandy print of my shoed feet. My tracks are bracketed by Lynne's and Jo's footprints. Lynne's feet are quick and unwavering. She's done the supportive pillar thing so often with me, there is no doubt in the way she moves in relation to me. Jo's prints are more tentative and arched toward me. She's learning fast, but there are missing years in our march. Maybe it's not so much that, though. Maybe her lean isn't about doubt. It's more, I think, a tête-à-tête—a picture of what we know

369

now, my lost-and-found sister and I. That sometimes, you do lose the ones you love the most. And sometimes, they come back to you. It doesn't work that way often, so when it does, you hang on and lean in close. When it does, I've learned it's important to remember to breathe. When it does, it's the coolest thing. I'm so in love with second chances. But then, I'm partial to sisters...the ones we're born to, the ones we choose, the ones we lose and rediscover.

When I think of all the time Jo and I lost, sometimes all I want to do is curl up and cry. All the things Jo faced with me at arm's length, all the pain I should have supported her through. I didn't know everything, but I knew what Mom was like, I knew their lives couldn't have been easy. I knew enough. I could have done more. I should have.

But I also could do that every day for the rest of my life—coulda, shoulda...And then I would turn around and find that I've missed the time we have now. Stupid, no?

There's no one else quite like Lynne or Jo in my life, Mary—no one with their particular brand of loyalty, trust, honour. Not even you, because I never knew you. You haven't had a chance to show me who you would really be. Jo's not you—she's not my twin, but she's my flesh and blood, the only sister I have, on my official family tree, at least. She's priceless, and it's priceless, the way we've come back together. It's like we lost no time at all, but it's not like we're unchanged. I've changed because I lost her, and Mom. Jo's changed because she lost Mom, and, for so long, me and Dad. And we'll never be the same again. How could we be? But we've come together changed as we are, understanding that we're different now. Different from what we would have been, different from the images of each other we've built up in our heads, different, too, from what we would be without each other. And there's how we're different because of Matt and Curtis, different because of what the world does, and doesn't do, with difference. Different because now, we only have time and space for the truth.

Different because of the fire. Oh, God, the fire.

Curtis is refusing to forgive himself for Kev's burns. According to him, somehow he was automatically supposed to know that Kev was in the loft. Somehow he was supposed to check Kev's hiding spot because he knew where it might be. And in his irrational, guilt-stricken mind, Curtis was supposed to go to someone he hadn't known was in the barn, rather than to two horses he did know were there. Never mind that he was the one who heard Kev and figured out who it was, where he was and how to get to him in a barn that was burning down around them. It's ridiculous that to Curtis, even that amazing, intuitive rescue is not good enough.

But Curtis won't hear logic right now. He will someday, because I won't stop telling him he's not to blame. Charlotte blames herself, too, for Curtis and Kev's injuries. Charlotte has said more than once "If only I had kept Kevin with me when he came into the kitchen..." 'If only' is useless. Inevitable sometimes, but useless. So Charlotte is sad, but she's here on this trip to heal, too, so that's something. She'll be all right.

Lancelot is all right too. He is in a stall right by the door at a stable near Charlotte's place until the barn is rebuilt.

The stable manager there has been warned about Orion and his forays into flower beds, no matter the circumstances.

I wish I could tell you Dad is okay, but that would be a lie.

Losing Mom, and watching Kev and Curtis suffer has really done him in. He's not here, although this place in all its splendour is exactly what he would need. But Dad is stubborn, like me. I couldn't convince him to stop getting stuck on how upset he thinks he would be, watching us make this work. How much he misses! But I do love him so.

Yiayia is in Greece for another trip. She left just as we did. She had to go, to heal after Mom died and after Kevin got hurt. She went with thia Sophia, and that's no coincidence, as Sophia is the aunt whose face was burned in that kitchen fire when she was younger and almost married. If anyone can teach my grandmother the strength to be at peace about her grandson's injury, it's her youngest sister Sophia.

In other news…Surprise! I've decided to major in creative writing. Don't worry, I'll make you proud. There will be no 'inspirational' autobiographies from me. But I'm a good writer, and I can use my degree to teach, and use words to raise awareness about my politics, tell the truth the way people need to hear it. I'll take my writing and my politics and make a career out of it. I know I'll need to have a really awesome career, because I do want to adopt a kid one of these days, and that will be an odyssey. But I can do it. One day at a time. I don't have all the answers, and that's okay.

Something else I'm not sure of is how to find peace about Matt's role in the fire. He wanted to come on this trip, you know, but I wouldn't let him. I don't know how he could have even asked that. I won't allow him anywhere near Curtis.

We'll never get back together, but I want to forgive him, so I don't have to go around carrying anger. It's heavy, and I can't very well teach Kev to be free of it if it's a weight on my own back.

The fire was an accident, and almost purely so. Matt left the box smouldering not realizing there was heat left in the fibres of the stuffed penguin. He didn't plant it and leave it to burn, and as I've learned so many times already in this life, intention is everything. He told the police the whole truth about what he did to Curtis' box, told them he didn't set the fire on purpose. Matt had wanted to hurt Curtis. (The coward was afraid to tell me that for the longest time, but that's the thing about truth: it always comes out on top in the end.) But he didn't mean to destroy the barn and get Kev burned. Matt's reason for setting Curtis' possessions on fire, his arrogance, the pure foolishness of his assumptions and actions...I'm having trouble forgiving all of that. It's not fair. None of this needed to happen, but for Matt's ridiculous, irrational thinking. It makes me furious. At the same time, I just refuse to obsess over it. It's so much simpler to know that here, where the sea just does its thing, its ebb and flow, whether I'm hyper-focused or not. It's not indifferent, it's relaxing.

Whatever happens, I know I can't be afraid of change. I used to be so sure that if I took a trip like this, it would be with Matt. I used to think, too, that I would help Eva, she would sober up, and we would always be friends. Not so much. I'm not Superwoman, I'm just me. I'm not God, and I can't control her choices. God can, and He gave us free will, because he wants to steer us with love, not make us robots. So if He gave us free will and didn't have to, that's quite a lesson, isn't it? Eva will be Eva. If she punches me, knocks my lights out because her path has taken her to drowning, what good would I be? I can't do that rescue. Other people need me. Boy, that was a long lesson to learn!

That said, if Eva ever does really figure out that she wants clean and sober more than high and drunk, I'll be there again, as long as she's finally real about it. At first, after the scene she made getting drunk in Mom's ward, I was tired and angry enough to never want to see her again. But now that I've calmed down, I know I'll never turn her away if she's willing to fight for herself and stop hiding. I'm not gonna chase her again, ever. But if the mountain comes to Mohammed, well...that'll be a different story. Hope springs eternal.

Did you know, Mary, that birds have no fear of heights or open spaces, no vertigo at all? They're kind of fearless. In a way that's obvious, but isn't it so cool? They just launch themselves. That's all. Just a split second decision to fly, and there they are, in free space—with every risk and adventure that implies.

I want to be like that. I used to think I admired birds for flying south, and coming back—always coming home. I still admire them, but for different reasons now, too. For coming home, yes, but also for knowing when it's right to move, face the unknown, fly not just despite the fact that anything could happen, but because anything could.

I've changed a lot, haven't I?

Kev is shrieking with delight, as Jo's Sam—our Sam now—carries him close to the water, lifting him up as an offering the waves can't have. Kev is still bandaged, puckering scars are a procession along his body. He has to be achingly careful getting wet, careful about pretty much everything. He's still in pain, but he's been crying less ever since he was cleared to take this trip. Just in this moment, he looks, with the sun in his face and glinting off the water, like he doesn't remember pain at all. It was worth the logistical puzzle it took to get here, just to witness that—to see him giggle and beam. Now the boys are floating paper boats. Sam is acting as Kev's hands, paying close attention to Kev's every instruction. I can only hear wisps of words over the wind and water, but I love what I see.

I wish someone had explained to me, when physio was being reduced to transfers and dressing and socks and underwear as my entire height of purpose—'life skills,' my eye—that I could work toward seeing the sea, climbing Peggy's Cove, rolling through the Bay of Fundy, strolling through the woods in L.M. Montgomery's exquisite estate...I could have loved working for that...And those are the gems I'll make sure Kev has, to love.

We three—Jo, Lynne and I—are watching as Sam sits, holding his little brother-in-law, on the sand. He's amazing with Kev—gentle but full of just enough boyishness to keep rip-roaring fun in the mix.

As angry as I am with Matt, I can't escape the conviction that there's purpose in everything that went wrong. Maybe this time, as I'm helping Kev learn to love his life and his body, I can get through to Dad, too. You never know. And there's another thing, and it's huge. If he had not been burned, Curtis would never have proven to himself that he has a huge, amazing heart, and had a selfless, daring rescue in him. Curtis is wonderful. I wish I were in love with him, I really do. I'm still not, but that can change, as we keep bonding. We're friends for life, that's a given. Something else is for sure, too: Curtis is not The Sire and will never turn into him. He knows that now, because of the fire. And if he hadn't been burned, he never would have found Glenore.

So he's here, too, with Glenore, who's taking care of him. When we get back Curtis will move in with her, and she can be the spinal column of his family, which she should have been from the beginning. Glenore will never be his mother, and we three will never be the sisters he lost, but we are new ones. A fresh start. Proof that fire is so much more than a destroyer—it can purify, and teach us to begin again, by making it impossible to go backwards.

A lot like faith.

Jo and Lynne are going to have to make a blanket burrito out of me tonight in our huge rented cottage. We're such a strange motley crew on this trip. If you look on this beach, you'll see a metaphor for all of us in the zigzagging, supported steps of Lynne, Jo and me, my wheelchair, Kev's wheelchair, Glenore acting as both Curtis and Kev's nurse. People looking on might see the picture of this trip and what it takes and think "What a shame! Look at the circus it takes for them to be here!" Dad was oddly sad as we were planning this. He said he didn't want us to be a 'procession of the injured', he called it. We're not, though, we're us, and we've come as we are. No apologies. Nothing to apologize for, just the right and the freedom to be. Shaped by all the parts that need to be embraced, not resented.

I couldn't convince Dad of that. I still haven't, and maybe I never will. That's okay. Besides, if he doesn't let me work on him about that, he might let Glenore. They've got a tiny bit of a thing going on, Mary. They're really quiet about it, but it's there, and it's growing. I can see it in the way they smile at each other, or watch each other when they think no one can see. I even saw them hold hands once, but I didn't let on at all. I thought for sure Glenore would get him to come with us, but I don't think she wanted to push it. I see her point. Dad gets to be who he is, too. Like a tree growing in an unconventional spot and shape, he has to find his own trajectory toward sky and light.

That—just that—is the point. The entire point.

This is us, as we are, and we have exactly what we need to be here. That's the best, really, the miracle. The truth.

Did I tell you, Mary, that after Mom died, I found a chest of knitted baby clothes that she had made and left for my child or children? Jo has one, too. And oh, the baby clothes, Mary! Tiny dresses and jumpers, a small jacket, a few soft, handmade stuffed animals. And in the bottom, money put aside for my wedding dress. I wept for her then, with fresh tears. She died not knowing if I would be married or have children, and knowing that if I did, my journey would be quite something, as it always is. But she conceived of it as possible. And I know now that in her heart she really did consider me to be Jo's equal. Yours, too. I don't need to tell you how much that means to me. I love her for that, and so much more besides.

I have to turn off my laptop—I'm almost out of power and I'll have to recharge because there will most certainly be more to write after we go for lobster. The sun is setting now, and the wind is cold. But it's so beautiful, Mary. So beautiful. Just as I always will, I wish you were here.

So I will describe the scene for you. The sun is a flaming red head sinking on the horizon's pillow. It's so bright, it looks for all the world like Kev and Sam's boats are burning, engulfed in golden flame because we've decided to stay.

That, my dearest, my love, my heart, is all you need to know now. Happy birthday to you! I'll write more tomorrow...

Naomi

Acknowledgments

From the moment I woke up on a June morning in 2009 with a whole new idea for a second novel, I knew I had the beginning of a game changer in the works. The story of getting from there to here is a novel in itself. Writing the story miraculously gifted to your mind is a daunting task. It takes more than education and career savvy, more than even talent or skill—even though you do need heaping helpings of all of those. It requires people—those willing to take the time to fill gaps in a writer's knowledge with their own expertise, those ready and willing to support a writer through thick and thin, along the twists and turns and winding roads of required research, tough, complex decisions, crises of confidence, piles and piles of drafts and revisions. I am amazed at how the very best people have converged around me during this project. I am wholeheartedly grateful.

Thank you to the Ontario Arts Council for your financial support of this project, and for all you do for writers and writing.

My sincere gratitude to the wonderful team at Friesen Press, all of whom have competently and efficiently brought this novel to publication, all the while trusting and respecting my vision for this work.

My heartfelt thanks go to Nancy LaFever, my wonderful editor who shepherded the final draft of this novel. Nancy, you were indispensable in sculpting and refining this book. There's nobody better at straightforward, honest, insightful, productive critique. Naomi would not be ready for the big wide world without you.

I (almost) have no words for my gratitude for Rie Yamagishi and Tina Bauer. Your expert and detail-oriented help in the very last days of work on this book have made this book as glitch-free a read as humanly possible. Thank you for your support, grace and patience under pressure. Naomi and I will always love you. Any errors left are completely my own oversight.

Thank you to Margie Wolfe and Kathryn Cole for your support, advice and thoughtful feedback.

Heartfelt gratitude also goes to Marie-Lynne Hammond, who read a first draft of this novel and declared it a project worth fighting for and thinking big. Thank you also to Sarah Sheard and the Humber College Creative Writing Program, for a productive mentorship. Love and thanks also to Frances Stocker for her friendship, good advice and sharp proofreading skills.

Thank you to Ed O'Meara, John Tomlinson and Sheryl Freeman, the three best English teachers ever to cross my path. Also, much gratitude to Nancy Arbuckle for your memorable teaching in my childhood. I have thought of you all often during the writing of this book, as well as my previous novel. My gratitude goes to Dr. Joanne Harris

Burgess, one of the most compassionate people I've met, a superb mentor and supporter of my work and writing, and the most insightful professor of Canadian History I could ever have hoped would teach me.

Gratitude always for the long-time friendship and mentorship of Dr. Cyril Greenland, who always believed in me, my dreams and potential since the day we met, when I was nine years old. I will always miss you, and I know you would have loved and been so proud of this book. I am also so very grateful for Dr. Aharon Galil's faith in me, from childhood until the present moment, and, I am sure, well into the future.

My sincere gratitude goes to the amazing ladies who were part of the 'patterning team' involved in supporting my early years. You were all so hardworking and committed to bringing essential learning, laughter and fun to my childhood during a complex time that changed my entire trajectory for the better. My family and I couldn't have handled it all without you. Special thanks and love to Rebecca Mailliarelis, Diane Anger, Eileen Kennedy, Mary Cross and Penny King, for enriching those challenging days and bringing the world to my door.

Love to Rebecca and Alex Mailliarelis for covering me, my family and this book in prayer. Thank you for all your caring and your incredible example of faith over all these years.

Gratitude, love, respect and blessings to my friends in the writing and publishing industry, who gave me priceless support, answered phone calls and emails with crucial advice, brought me news and plenty of encouragement, shared my woes, made me laugh and closed ranks around me whenever needed during the writing of this novel. Kathy Kacer, Sharon MacKay, Beverley Brenna, Allan Stratton, Melanie Florence Hannah, Dr. Janine Darragh, Erin Bow, Sharon Jennings, Teresa Toten, Gillian O'Reilly, Brenda Halliday, Ken Setterington, Kathleen Bailey, Hilary Dawson and Theo Heras—all of you made sure this wild ride was full of friends who understand the bumps and bruises. Your faith in me makes all the difference.

So much love and so many thank yous to my beloved East Coast Crew for the trip and the bonding experience of a lifetime, which inspired the epilogue of this novel: Sharon MacKay, Tina Bauer, Bonnie Mathisen, Rie Yamagishi, Juan Manuel Aldana and Claudia Crouse, you are friends of and for a lifetime.

Many thanks to the staff and volunteers at the Canadian Association of Riding for the Disabled (CARD), who gave me the experience of riding and riding instruction that I needed for this book, and for giving me Merlin, who inspired Lancelot. Many thanks also to Jennifer Day at Horses Of Course for allowing me to learn so much about the workings of a horse barn. Gratitude and love also to Fran Elliot Streeter for your friendship and the example of your passion for horses and riding.

Thank you to the research librarians at Toronto's North York Central Library for great reading recommendations when it came to researching alcoholism, foster care, Obsessive Compulsive Disorder and the bond of twinship. Thank you for letting me hide behind stacks of books, 'nesting' for whole days at a time, for answering my questions knowledgeably and thoroughly and always finding what resources I needed.

Thank you to my open-minded thoughtful friend, Robert Besunder, for so many encouragements and much good advice and loyal support.

Love and many thanks to Susan Amanatides for your support of me and this project, and your connections, which enabled an essential part of my research to go smoothly. Thank you over and over to Charis Kelly and all the other amazing nurses, doctors and child life specialists at the Burn Program at Toronto's SickKids. I'm so grateful that you took the time away from your immensely important work to answer so many questions and tell me much I didn't realize that I didn't know. Your input has contributed greatly to the authenticity of this book. Thank you for all you do with such skill and compassion.

Much gratitude to my long-time friend, Keka DasGupta, for all your warmth, support, and wise marketing and publicity expertise. Thank you also to my friend Frances Karulas, for your help in keeping my website working reliably while I was so busy writing.

Immense gratitude to Dr. Tanya Titchkosky for your friendship and unwavering support, and all of your profound teaching in Social Justice Education and Disability Studies. Your captivating teaching, and you, changed my life and my work and gave me such purpose and energy, both in completing my graduate studies and writing this book. Special thanks to the warm, caring, strong and vivacious Gorett Reis for your support and thought-provoking coaching when I was struggling. Thanks and love always to the rest of the amazing SESE gang: Samantha Walsh, Carrie Anne, Dr. Katie Aubrecht, Dr. Eliza Chandler, Dr. Patty Douglas and Isaac Stein, for making life-changing thinking and learning such a joy.

Special thanks to Samantha and Desiree Walsh, for sharing your wonderful insight into the twin relationship with such honesty and humour.

My sincere gratitude and every blessing to Dr. Grace Feuerverger for your transformative, passionate teaching in Peace Education, and your rejuvenating, restorative approach to teaching and writing when I needed it most.

Love and thanks to Dr. Susan Mahipaul, for living and teaching disability differently, with passion and grace, and without compromise. I've tried to write Naomi a little like me and a lot like you. If this worked, she'll be all right now that she's going to be out in the world. Thank you for being a pillar of strength, honesty, insight and support. I am so proud of you.

Thank you to Tina Bauer, although thank you is not enough, for supporting me on this bumpy road through thick and thin, without reservation. Thank you for being loyally 'in my corner' throughout everything. Thank you for your humour and encouragement, for reminding me that I am worth it and this will be worth it, and for really believing that a book can change the world. Thank you for making bad days better and good days the best. Huge thanks also to Tina's wonderful family: John and Ann Bauer, Elizabeth and James Watt, Heather and Peter Watt, and Claudia Crouse. Love to you for all the laughter and fun when I need it the most, for welcoming and including me in your circle, giving me a home away from home. Thank you for believing in me, this novel, and all my work and goals.

So many thank yous and love always to Bonnie Mathisen for long talks, long drives and great books. Thank you for reading drafts of this book in progress, and related documents, and always telling me the truth. Most of all I have so much gratitude for the gifts of your integrity, your steadfast supportive friendship, your gentle, caring listening ear and your trust. Thank you for sharing your strength when I need it and trusting mine when you do. Thank you being there for the mundane and difficult just as much as the profound and happy—my all-weather, no matter-what friend.

Gratitude and love always to Tara Geraghty-Ellis, for years of wonderful friendship, for the gift of your tenacity, your example of bold business-building and for knowing just the perfect things to say in giving me the courage to push this book 'out of the nest.' Much love to Nisha Batra, who always knows how to be there with such a genuine heart. You could write your own book on true friendship, and I'm very grateful. Love and much gratitude to Michelle Benincasa, whose strong friendship has taught me so much over the last twenty years, and whose example of life with an anxiety disorder is a study of boldness, dignity and staying power.

So much gratitude to the rest of my priceless pick-up-from-where-we-left-off, tell-me-everything, I-trust-you-with-my-life friends. You are the family I choose, from near and far, and from every stage of my life and growth. I couldn't imagine my life or the years it took to write this novel without you: Tara and Todd Ellis; Heather, Mike,

Matthew and Nathan Cameron; Monique Hodge; Kevin Williams; Jillian Dempsey, Tabitha and Clint McTague; Sukanti, Samir, Lana and Suniya Husain; Vanessa and David Holden; Anthony Styga; Steph, Andrew, Robin and Elly Dafoe; and Ruthann, Raul, Silvia, John and Lucy Garcia. I love you all.

So many thanks and blessings to the wonderful, irreplaceable Wafaa Wabha, for your stellar counsel, your compassion, your razor-sharp yet gentle truth-telling and guidance. I could not have 'let go and let God' without you.

Love and blessings to my genuine, profound, caring and Christ-filled friend, Hilary Price, for your amazing Biblical teaching, warm friendship, prayers and reminders to lean on God, write from His light and trust His love.

Gratitude and love always to Susan Miller, Bernice Alexander, Helen Bluku, Helen Tzogas and Lucia Moraga, for your friendship, reliability, and humour. God bless you all. A big thank you and many rich blessings to Annette and Albert Koene, who help me juggle everything and make it look easy.

A special thank you to Bernice Alexander for your amazing photographic skill in capturing my wonderful author photo.

Many thank yous and much respect to my healthcare team: Dr. Sonja Kustka, Dr. Joseph Kahn and his wonderful clinic staff, Tamara Der-Ohanian, Michael Vertolli and Tom MacFarlan, for working to keep me healthy during demanding times.

To my family: My mother, for supporting me and this project in every way, and teaching me the power of self-discipline, love and commitment. Thank you for being my first teacher. I love you very much. Loving gratitude to my sister Nicole and my brother-in-law Keith, who are always so proud and supportive of me. To my nephew William and my niece Abigail, I love you so very much and I am so proud of you. Much love and so many thank yous to my aunt Elsa, for being there for me and our family for as long as I can remember.

To my beautiful beloved, gone-too-soon niece Charlotte, I love you every day. The memory of you is in my heart always.

I thank my beloved father, gone too soon, for his gentle, constant love and humour. How I miss the twinkle in your eye! I thank you, Dad, for giving me a soft, safe place to fall, for always putting family first and honouring your commitments. If today I am 'unsinkable', it is in no small way thanks to you. I love you and miss you so very much.

Love and gratitude to my wonderful cousins, Fay Rizoulis and Georgia Rizoulis, for your love and support as I worked long and hard on this project, struggled with times of indecision and managed long stretches of waiting. Thank you for always being there for me and waiting so patiently for this book. Much love to Stavroula and Alkisti Krissilas, and Matthew Caruso, who are also so proud and excited about this novel, and are growing into wonderful people. My love and thanks also to my Uncle Paul Vlahos, for faithfully checking on me, caring and offering advice, and respecting my decisions.

My final thank you is for God, who created me right and doesn't make mistakes. Thank you for planning my path from start to finish, for being there for me at every moment, both big and small. Thank you that you are the author of grace, mercy, and equality. Thank you that you are not the author of injustice, but instead you are the author of our quest and desire to rectify it.

Dear Reader

It has been said that all the problems in the world begin when some lives are deemed less valuable than others. As a social justice educator, I have kept this wisdom with me during the writing of this book, and it has informed my motivations as I worked to tell a story of not only grief and abandonment, but also one of hope and belonging. You've read of the repercussions of being, or feeling, deeply unwanted when you've read about Curtis and Eva in this novel. You've read about the consequences of exclusion and prejudice in Naomi's life as well. On the surface, there is abandonment, discrimination and stigma in this book, but dig a little deeper and you'll find, along with that, a journey toward peace and acceptance. This is not achieved after the struggle—'after the fire' if you will—but in the midst of it. *Burning the Boats* is a story about choosing commitment when that choice is most difficult and yet most important.

At one of the turning points in the novel, Naomi states the following: "Nothing is ever really only one thing: all sorrow, no joy, all catastrophe, with no healing, all tragedy and robbery, no blessing." This wisdom is key to the novel, which works to get at some of the complexities of life, some of the nuance of reality, the experience of which always resists being limited or boxed in by categories. The good, the bad, the ugly, the complex, the bittersweet, all combine to pull us together. It is my hope that you have loved these characters, who work and strive, grow and change, and have so much beauty. I love that they are flawed and not always right, but also certainly not always wrong. Even—or especially—when you expect them to be.

Although I am a physically disabled woman, Naomi's story is not directly mine. In the writing of this book, I did do a lot of research into life experiences that are not directly my own: twin relationships, foster care, Obsessive Compulsive Disorder and mental health issues, alcoholism and fires, for instance. I see this novel as more than literature featuring disability and predictable related themes, portrayed in predictable, life-as-usual ways. This would only lead to the pigeon-holing of this book as 'for disabled readers.' Ask yourself the following: Is *Anne of Green Gables* meant to be only for orphans? Definitely not. Disability is part of the wider world and wider life. It is a rich life experience, and needs to be written in realistic and life-affirming ways. Anything other than that leads to disabled lives being misunderstood as less than worthy or valuable, and the consequences of such a misconception are real, far-reaching and potentially devastating.

This novel *is* autobiographical fiction, based on many of my own poignant experiences as a disabled woman. It feels very much like the book I was 'born to write', and at this time of debates and discussions of the importance of the portrayal of diversity in literature, I know that Naomi's story is important and authentic.

Naomi is truly unique in literature featuring disability. She is a young disabled woman who is comfortable in her own skin and never wishes to be 'normal' or 'just like everyone else.' She has lots of problems, and there are lots of twists and turns that move her story along, but a lack of self-confidence is not an issue for her. It is groundbreaking that Naomi finds not one but two teen boys interested in her, instead of the usual stereotype that surrounds the portrayal of dating and disability—featuring the disabled person either as asexual or forever struggling with unrequited love. In this day and age it truly should not be, but it is also groundbreaking that Naomi has several friends, a paid job and a full busy life with many responsibilities, including the care and co-raising of a child. She has agency and she acts decisively, instead of only being acted on by others and being restricted by the biases, limits and oppressions of a strictly medicalized view of disability. She not only has needs but is needed, instead of being portrayed as a disabled protagonist who is passive, and whose primary role is to inspire compassion and kindness in the able-bodied world.

The complexity and nuance of Naomi's close but often tense relationship with her father is also a crucial aspect of her story. Teens have a huge struggle with asserting independence in general from nervous parents, and those issues, struggles and resentments are even more complex for disabled teens in an ableist world. The themes common to teen life are highly amplified for teens facing various kinds of discrimination and misconceptions.

When I wrote my first novel (*Zoe's Extraordinary Holiday Adventures*, Second Story Press, 2007) I told a story for young readers that I wish had been written when I was a child – a unique book featuring disability squarely in the midst of vibrant family, school and neighbourhood life, portrayed along with themes of multiculturalism and the immigrant experience. In writing *Burning the Boats*, I have written the book I would have loved and needed to read while finding and sculpting my own voice and identity. It is also the book I know others needed, and need, to read— featuring a journey into family, reconciliation, sisterhood and friendship, growth, love and forgiveness.

The striking strength of the women in *Burning the Boats* is not meant to overshadow the important role of the boys and men in this book. Curtis and Matt, for example, are both 'good guys' who bring good intentions to the table along with misconceptions and mistakes. Curtis brings the wounds of his past with him, and Matt is a young teen grappling with the complexities and choices which come in any dating situation, but which are even more layered when a disabled partner is in the mix—on either one or both sides. Remember, we live in a society where the struggles and joys of that experience are largely unimagined, unexplored, and little discussed. Notice that even the events leading to the barn fire began with Matt's misguided, misinformed, irrational attempt to protect Naomi. It is my hope that no one is either idolized or villainized in this story. Like Eva, all the characters in this book are "…half covered in shadow, the other in light."

I hope this book has entertained you with a story you find compelling and thought-provoking. If Naomi and the people of her world leave you thinking and re-thinking, and talking with others about your thoughts, for some time after you reach the end of the last page, I've done my job.

Go well always,

Christina Minaki, M.A. (Ed.), M.I.St.
Toronto, Ontario
November 2017

Lightning Source UK Ltd.
Milton Keynes UK
UKHW03f1336160318
319572UK00001B/31/P